About the Author

PHILLIPA ASHLEY writes warm .... fiction for a variety .... famous ....

After studying English at Oxford, she worked as a copywriter and journalist. Her first novel, *Decent Exposure*, won the RNA New Writers Award and was made into a TV movie called *12 Men of Christmas* starring Kristin Chenoweth and Josh Hopkins. As Pippa Croft, she also wrote the Oxford Blue series – *The First Time We Met*, *The Second Time I Saw You* and *Third Time Lucky*.

Phillipa lives in a Staffordshire village and has an engineer husband and scientist daughter who indulge her arty whims. She runs a holiday-let business in the Lake District, but a big part of her heart belongs to Cornwall. She visits the county several times a year for 'research purposes', an arduous task that involves sampling cream teas, swimming in wild Cornish coves and following actors around film shoots in a camper van. Her hobbies include watching *Poldark*, Earl Grey tea, Prosecco-tasting and falling off surf boards in front of RNLI lifeguards.

🐦 @PhillipaAshley

Also by Phillipa Ashley

Summer at the Cornish Cafe
Christmas at the Cornish Cafe
Confetti at the Cornish Cafe

Christmas on the Little Cornish Isles

The Driftwood Inn

Phillipa Ashley

avon.

This novel is entirely a work of fiction.
The names, characters and incidents portrayed in it are
the work of the author's imagination. Any resemblance to
actual persons, living or dead, events or localities is
entirely coincidental.

Avon an imprint of
HarperCollins*Publishers*
The News Building
1 London Bridge Street
London SE1 9GF

www.harpercollins.co.uk

This paperback edition 2017

1

First published in Great Britain in ebook format by
HarperCollins*Publishers* 2017

A catalogue record for this book
is available from the British Library

ISBN: 9780008259792

Set

Printed a   4YY

All
repr
in
phot   r

For my wonderful mum and dad

Prologue

Maisie Samson was the only living soul on Gull Island. At least, that's how it felt as she padded over the sand towards the silver-smooth waters of the Petroc channel that morning. Behind her, the Driftwood Inn basked in the first rays of autumn sunlight at the top of the beach. The rising sun brought out the pink in the granite walls of the pub that Maisie had returned home to eight months previously.

A cormorant dried its wings on a sandbar in the middle of the narrow channel that separated Gull Island from its neighbour, Petroc Island. Rubbing her arms to warm herself, Maisie picked her way between the bleached sticks of driftwood that gave the inn its name. In the damp sand, tiny shells glimmered in the sunlight, uncovered by the retreating tide.

Letting the chilly wavelets nibble at her toes, she turned back to look at the inn. The curtains were still drawn in the windows of the flat over the pub. Last night, the bar was rocking with a folk band, and Ray and Hazel Samson were having a well-earned lie-in.

Despite falling into her bed at half-past midnight, Maisie had woken early and decided to go for a swim while she had the beach to herself. Hers were the only footprints leading down the beach and probably the first ones to be made on any beach on the whole of Gull Island today. That was something, wasn't it? To be alone for a few minutes in a busy overcrowded world? No matter what had happened over the past year, she wouldn't swap places with anyone this morning.

She poked a toe into the water, took a deep breath and waded in, huffing and cursing. The sea might look like the Caribbean, but this was still the Atlantic. Ignoring the chilly bite of water at her waist, Maisie took a deep breath, splashed water over herself. Bloody hell ...

One. Two. *Three*.

Argh. She couldn't feel her fingers or toes. Oh God, why did she do this? And why was it always so much colder than she expected?

As the initial shock subsided, Maisie switched from a frantic doggy paddle to a steady breaststroke. She didn't bother with goggles; she was no Rebecca Adlington, and goggles would have defeated the object of her swim, which was to take in her surroundings. To have a few precious moments of peace before a frantic Saturday running the Driftwood.

It was hard to believe that Christmas was only two months away. How different this one would be: the first in eight years that she'd spend with her family. Relatively relaxed compared to being rushed off her feet running the big chain pub near St Austell where she'd been manager until the start of the year. Not that she'd minded working hard. In fact, she'd always loved her job, but last Christmas Day had been the worst she'd ever known.

Which made Maisie even more determined to enjoy Christmas Day with her own family. Unlike the mainland pub, the Driftwood would be closed on the 25th. Hazel Samson was dying to share the traditional full-on turkey dinner with all the trimmings, and Ray was itching to drag the tree and decorations out of his shed at the back of the pub.

Her parents were treating the coming festive season as if Maisie was fourteen, not coming up for forty, but Maisie didn't mind. She knew they were eager to give her a proper Samson Christmas after spending nearly a decade with just a snatched phone or Skype call while Maisie lay exhausted in her flat after making everyone else's day special.

The raw pain of her last Christmas Day had faded a little, but it reared up at unexpected times. She tried to focus on her swim and the good things in her life now ... friends and family, the Driftwood and the beautiful place she lived in.

As Maisie swam up and down parallel to the shore, she spotted a young black Labrador romping out of the grassy dunes and onto the sand on the opposite side of the Petroc channel. Even from a hundred metres away, she could tell the excitable hound was Hugo Scorrier's dog, Basil. Seconds later, Hugo himself appeared, in his trademark green wellies and a waxed jacket. He threw a large stick for the dog and Maisie caught a snatch of him shouting, 'Fetch, Basil!' above the gentle swoosh of the waves.

Basil scampered around, obviously having no intention of getting his paws wet. He shot off along the shoreline towards

Petroc Island's tiny harbour where Hugo's gleaming motor yacht, the *Kraken*, was berthed alongside the quay. The Samsons kept a motorboat too, an old sixteen-footer that kept them from relying completely on the ferries between the islands. However, the *Puffin* was nothing like the smart vessels moored off Petroc's quayside. The quay was lined with chic pastel fishermen's 'cottages' that no real fishermen had lived in for decades. Petroc Island was now a resort run by the Scorrier family and the cottages had long been converted into plush holiday villas, galleries and eateries.

Maisie turned back towards the shore, feeling a current of slightly warmer water pushing against her and the breeze quickening against her face. The Driftwood was opposite her again, with its terrace still in deep shadow. Throughout the spring and summer, gig boat racers, yachties, tourists and locals alike flocked to the isles and the Driftwood itself. Even now, in late October, Gull Island was still buzzing with day-trippers, holidaymakers and bird watchers hoping to catch a glimpse of the rare birds that were often blown off course to Scilly on their way to Africa.

Soon the sun would rise higher and the terrace would be filled with people in shirt-sleeves enjoying their last taste of late-autumn sun before heading back to the mainland and all its pre-Christmas mayhem.

Maisie was still far enough out to see around the small rocky headland to the east of the pub, towards the Gull Island jetty. The sturdy quay had been there for a century and was recently refurbished thanks to a generous donation from Hugo, damn him. Without the two jetties – one near the Driftwood and the other on the far side of the island – the tripper boats and Gull Island ferries wouldn't be able to land, and as they brought vital customers and supplies to the residents, perhaps she should thank Hugo for that.

The swell lifted her gently and snatches of Basil's joyful barks reached her ears as she turned again and swam parallel with the shore. A clock chimed from the tiny church on the north side of Gull. Eight-thirty. Maisie was suddenly aware of how cold she was. She'd been out for twenty minutes, which was surely enough for anyone in these chilly waters, even Rebecca Adlington.

She lingered for a moment and trod water, taking one last glance at Petroc and at Basil chasing into the waves to retrieve Hugo's stick before dropping it at his master's feet. At least someone loved Hugo ...

Basil shook himself and Hugo leapt back as he got a soaking. Maisie smiled to herself. The day had started well and who knew what it had in store. Maybe a tall, dark, handsome stranger might walk into the pub and sweep her off her feet. The trouble was, a tall, dark – or any other type of – handsome stranger was the last person she wanted to walk into her life again.

Chapter 1

'Another day in paradise, eh? You are *so* lucky to live here.' It was almost lunchtime and Maisie's customer-friendly smile was firmly in place as she handed a large G&T to the customer waiting at the bar. Maisie guessed the woman was in her early fifties, but her designer skinny jeans, Converses and butter-soft leather jacket made her look ten years younger. With her carefully downplayed cut-glass accent and expensive 'off-duty' outfit, Maisie could guess where she was staying.

'Tell me about it,' she said, pulling a pint of bitter for the woman's partner, who, she assumed, was enjoying the midday warmth on the Driftwood's terrace.

The woman let out a sigh of pleasure. 'Look at that amazing sky, and the colours in the sea are just to die for. Harry and I were only just saying how much Scilly reminds us of Sardinia or Antigua. Honestly, you could absolutely be in the Grenadines and who would possibly *believe* it was only eight weeks to Christmas?'

'It is hard to believe,' said Maisie, stopping the tap at just the right moment when the glass was full and topped with a thin layer of froth.

'Although I expect it can get *terribly* claustrophobic if you have to live here full-time.' The woman lowered her voice. 'I expect you all know each other's business.'

Maisie placed the beer on the drip mat next to the G&T and adopted the same conspiratorial tone. 'That's *so* true. There are no secrets on Gull Island, no matter how much we'd like to keep them.' The posh woman was right: nothing and no one escaped notice in such a small and tight-knit community. People tended to know if you went to the loo before you'd even locked the bathroom door, but Maisie had had this conversation a hundred times before.

With a knowing smile, the woman nodded as if she'd been let in on a secret too and tapped the side of her nose. Maisie deposited notes in the till and handed over some change.

'Oh, no, keep that,' the customer protested, waving her G&T airily.

'Thank you. I'll add it to the staff tips box. How are you enjoying your break on Petroc?' Maisie asked.

'*How* clever of you to guess we're on Petroc. Yes, we are enjoying it. It's half term and we've rented the sweetest cottage for our daughter and the grandchildren. Well, I say it's a cottage but there are five bedrooms.' She laughed. 'Hubby and I are on babysitting duty tonight while Phoebe and her husband have dinner in the pub.' The woman laughed. 'Not that the Rose and Crab is *just* a pub these days of course, now it's been awarded its Michelin star. My husband and I tried it last night. Gosh, it was a-mazing. The turbot was incredible and don't get me started on that brill. Of course, I don't mind sharing cheesy pasta with the little ones tonight.

7

It's just so lovely to spend some quality time together with Saffron and baby Tom. They live so far away.'

Maisie mustered all her patience, aware that a small queue was forming behind the woman. 'I hope you all have a lovely time,' she said. 'You'll stay for lunch with us hopefully?'

The woman's eyes widened. 'You do lunch here?'

'Yes. We can't match up to the gourmet food at the Rose and Crab, of course, but we have local lobster salad on special today and we can rustle up some fresh crab sandwiches. You could eat them in the upstairs bistro or outside if it stays warm.'

'Yum. Local seafood, you say? How lovely. We'll check out the menu.' With a happy smile on her face, the holidaymaker picked up the drinks and turned away. Through the open front door, the sunlight danced on the turquoise water of the channel and the white sand flats. The woman sighed dreamily. 'Gosh, this view is just divine.'

With a polite smile, Maisie turned to her next punter as the woman carried the drinks out to the terrace. He was a bearded sixty-something in a cycling helmet and eye-wateringly tight Lycra shorts. 'And what can I get you, sir?' she asked, trying not to laugh, very glad that the counter hid the lower half of his body.

For the next half an hour, Maisie handed over glasses of wine and foamy pints of the local brew, relieved to see the inn so busy this late in the year. She'd taken over the Driftwood in February when her parents had decided to semi-retire. Hazel and Ray Samson could still be found behind the bar sometimes, or helping in the upstairs bistro, but Maisie was now in charge. She made the decisions and did the hiring and firing – mostly hiring, thank God. She set the prices, broke up the arguments (also rare) and presided over the Driftwood with a smile on her face, even when her feet were killing her and her heart was breaking. Always a smile. No one wanted a gloomy hostess; the customers were there to enjoy themselves and enjoy the glorious view, whether they were tourists or locals.

Fewer than a hundred people lived on the island year round and most of them at some time popped into the pub. Some had been born and bred on Scilly, while a few were 'incomers' who'd moved to this isolated corner of Britain in search of a more peaceful life.

While she helped to clear glasses and serve drinks, Maisie chatted to Will Godrevy from the Flower Farm on St Saviour's island who had popped in for a half a Guinness while he was visiting Javid, who ran the Gull Island campsite. Will's sister, Jess, was Maisie's best mate, but Jess was busy today, helping her team send out the first crop of narcissi to customers on the mainland. Maisie expected to see Javid at some point when he came to collect his sandwich or pasty from the bistro.

Maisie had already had a quick word with Una and Phyllis Barton, the sisters who owned the aptly named Hell Cove Cottages on the rugged western coast of Gull Island, which was open to the full brunt of the Atlantic storms. They'd sat on the terrace with a coffee while they waited for the island ferry to St Mary's. Every Saturday morning, come hell or high water, they did their shopping in Hugh Town after they'd finished the breakfast service at Hell Cove.

Then there was Archie Pendower, an elderly artist from St Piran's island to the north of Gull. If the weather was as good as it was today, and Archie was feeling inspired, he might sail across to the Driftwood. Thinking of the growing gallery of paintings that adorned the first floor bistro, Maisie smiled to herself. Sooner or later, Archie might settle his bill – but not in cash. The Driftwood already had a dozen of his paintings and Maisie reckoned they were worth a lot more, financially and creatively, than a few quid. Such bartering would never have been allowed in the big pub where she used to work, which was another reason why Maisie loved the Driftwood, even if its lax and quirky ways would never make her family rich.

Time flew by while Maisie made her 'figure of eight' between the bistro, bar, kitchen and terrace, checking that everything was running smoothly and helping out where needed. With only a handful of seasonal staff compared to the big pub she had managed, she was used to mucking in on any task and loved it despite the long hours.

She was halfway through serving pints to some kayakers when a new customer blocked the doorway, obviously deciding whether he could be bothered to queue up. He shone out from among the khaki-clad twitchers like an exotic toucan among a group of sparrows. Dark-blond hair brushed the collar of his faded blue-and-yellow hooped polo shirt. His navy cargo shorts showed off a pair of muscular calves the colour of tea and he wore olive Goretex hiking boots. The frame of his red rucksack brushed the door lintel and blocked out the view of the terrace and sea completely.

He ducked under the wooden door beam and stepped into the shade of the bar. Maisie's breath caught in her throat. For a few seconds she couldn't quite believe her eyes.

Now she was certain.

It was him.

So what was he doing on Gull Island?

Chapter 2

With most people she'd met before, Maisie might have called out a 'hello' or waved a greeting. The problem was she didn't know this man's name nor did she want to draw attention to herself – she was still flustered and shocked at his appearance in her pub.

She might not know the exotic guy's name but she could never forget how amazing his lips had felt on hers when they'd shared a passionate kiss outside the Galleon Inn on St Mary's the previous week. She'd nicknamed him 'The Blond' in her mind and tried to forget about him, knowing she'd been tipsy and that she'd never see him again.

Her hands fumbled with the change she'd just taken off the previous customer, but she shut the till drawer and tried to concentrate on serving the person in the queue in front of him.

Who had she been kidding? She hadn't forgotten about him. How could she? They'd bumped into each other at a food festival being held at the pub. She'd gone along on her own, really to check out how the event was going with a view to running one at the Driftwood. She'd meant to stay for a couple of drinks, make mental notes and then leave, but the Blond had struck up a conversation with her.

Or maybe she'd spoken to him? Her memory of how it had all started was fuzzy, especially as a couple of drinks had turned into more. Somehow, they'd ended up walking away from the pub up the beach. She didn't remembering exchanging names – bloody hell, she must have been tiddly – but she did know that names hadn't seemed to matter as they'd wandered away from the pub towards the headland at Porthmellon.

Apart from a brief word about him travelling around the UK on holiday and her working in a bar, neither of them had seemed to care about pasts or futures. They'd sat for a while on the rocks by the headland, watching the sun sinking and making the odd comment about the festival before the conversation had trailed off.

He'd taken her hand and it had happened. She didn't know who'd instigated the kiss. She only knew that their lips had come together and that it had been amazing.

Too amazing. The feelings it had aroused had scared her. She'd backed away, laughing and mumbling about having had too much to drink. Without a goodbye, she'd almost run back up the beach and joined the tourists in the streets of Hugh Town.

She'd bought a black coffee from the deli-café and found a quiet corner in which to drink it, dreading he'd walk in and find her. She'd sobered up fast. If she'd been herself – watchful and on guard – she'd never have kissed a stranger whose name she didn't even know ... and never have let herself respond so rashly, holding on to his waist, pressing against him, drinking in that kiss.

'Thanks.'

Smile fixed in place, Maisie watched the customer turn away, pint in hand, and the Blond approach the bar. He shrugged off his backpack, and dug out his phone. Perhaps he hadn't recognised her. He was next in line after a kayaker who ordered several pints of beer.

Maisie tried to focus on pulling the pints. There was too much head on the last one and the foamy beer overflowed onto the drip tray.

She gave an apologetic grimace at the kayaker. 'Sorry.'

He sipped the excess froth. 'No problem.'

She gave him his change and he joined his mates outside.

The Blond was next.

Maisie flashed her customer smile. 'Good afternoon, sir. What can I get you?'

He smiled back. 'Coke, please.'

'Pint or half. Diet or full-fat?'

'I don't do diet anything and a pint will do nicely. I'm dry as a drover's dog.'

That accent. It struck her again, as it had the day at the food festival. He was every bit as sexy as she remembered: and she'd tried *very* hard to forget him over the past few days.

'Ice?' she asked.

'What do you think?' His blue eyes, not far off the colour of the deepest part of the Petroc channel, sparkled with amusement and mischief. Maisie could have done with some ice herself to cool her down.

Maisie scooped the cubes into a pint glass. 'Where's the accent from? Sydney?' she teased.

He pulled a face. 'You have to be joking. Wouldn't be seen dead within a hundred miles of the place.' His eyes twinkled. 'Try again.'

'Adelaide?' said Maisie, testing him to see how much of their conversation he remembered. She'd joked that her knowledge of Aussie cities was confined to having to listen to endless hours of *Test Match Special* droning out from her dad's radio.

He winced. 'Too hot for me and I'm not impressed by the wine. I'm from Melbourne. Sunshine, penguins and tennis.'

'And Fosters,' Maisie shot back.

'Hey, there has to be a downside to every dream location.'

Maisie rested his glass on the drip mat but he didn't pick it up. Their eyes met over the top of the bar. The look was at his instigation so she felt duty bound, as the hostess, to return it, even if gazing into those roguish blue eyes had the same effect on her as it had the first time. 'I bet no one gets the better of you, Maisie Samson,' he said so quietly that even she could barely hear.

She snapped out of her momentary trance. 'How do you know my name? Has the Gull Island grapevine been at it again?' she said, wondering if he'd made enquiries about her after she'd hurried away from him. She knew now why she'd run away. Having him here in the flesh in front of her brought all those emotions flooding back: desire, lust, longing. Those feelings had overwhelmed her. It was too soon to feel so strongly attracted to a man again ... Too soon after losing Keegan. Too soon after losing everything.

The Blond was cool as a cucumber. He grinned and flipped his thumb over his shoulder. 'No grapevine. It's over the door.'

'That could have been my mum's name.' In fact, her father's name had hung there until she'd taken over the new licence earlier in the year.

'What's your mum's name?'

'Hazel.'

'Nah. You're no Hazel.'

'What do you mean, "I'm no Hazel"?' said Maisie, fascinated despite the fact that a couple of the regulars had started to pay attention to her conversation with the Blond.

Almost as if he sensed they were being watched, he lowered his voice but still made no move to pick up his drink. 'There's nothing wrong with Hazel. Sure it's a very nice name and your mother is a lovely woman, but *Maisie* ... hints at mischief. Trouble.'

Maisie rolled her eyes while her heart thumped. 'Trouble for you if you keep on with the cheesy lines.'

'Cheesy?' He laughed out loud. 'I'm the customer here. Aren't I always right?'

'You're forgetting the other sign.'

'And what sign would that be?'

She pointed to a small plaque hanging off a nail on the brickwork next to her. 'The landlady's never wrong.'

The smile made his eyes crinkle at the corners. Close up, she could see a few more lines on his face, around the eyes and on his forehead. She reckoned he was about her own age, or a couple of years younger.

Maisie heard the nerves in her laugh, and inwardly cursed

16

herself. What the hell had got into her, flirting with him again and reacting like a schoolgirl? He'd probably be gone in five minutes, five seconds, in fact, when he took the Coke outside onto the terrace. She didn't dare assume he'd sought her out and she didn't want him to have come looking for her. She wasn't interested in a man and definitely not one charming enough to tempt her into a passionate kiss on half an hour's acquaintance. She felt suddenly embarrassed for appearing to fall for his blarney, so she told him the price of the drink and nodded at the door. 'I expect you'll want to take it outside, sir, and enjoy the last of the sunshine while you can.'

She glanced over his shoulder as if she'd seen more customers enter, signalling politely but firmly she wasn't interested in anything beyond the cash for his Coke – saving herself from rejection, even of the smallest kind, because she'd had it up to here with types like the Blond. She'd met plenty of men like him before, and that included her ex, Keegan.

She didn't even want to know this one's name.

The Blond handed over some coins and took his drink. 'Keep the change,' he said cheerfully, obviously fine at being passed over for an imaginary customer.

'Thanks. Enjoy your day, *sir*.'

Maisie popped the coins in the RNLI tin in full view of him and turned her back to polish some glasses that didn't need it. The buzz of chatter rose as more customers walked through the front door. She turned back ready to greet them, joking about the late 'heat wave' that had hit Scilly.

When she finally made it out onto the terrace again to take a break, the Blond had gone.

The disappointment was like being plunged into cold water on a sweltering day but Maisie told herself to get a grip. She should be relieved he'd walked away this time and that she wouldn't have to see him again. She wasn't sure she would be so strong the next time he came across her path.

Fortunately she was kept busy as the pre-ferry rush started. Maisie's parents and her seasonal barman joined her behind the bar and they served up a constant stream of cold drinks, coffees and teas. Restaurant customers from the bistro ordered after-lunch liqueurs and took them onto the terrace. Maisie was pinned behind the bar, the flood of people never letting up until finally she heard the warning toot of the ferry as it moored at the jetty.

Five minutes later, the Driftwood was as deserted as the *Mary Celeste*.

Chapter 3

Abandoned glasses, bottles, packets of crisps and dirty plates littered the tables in the bar area. Maisie wiped her forehead. Her feet throbbed and her arms ached. It had been non-stop pretty much all day apart from the few minutes she'd spent sparring with the Blond.

'I need a breath of air,' she told Debbie, the Kiwi bistro manager who was setting off on her long journey home later that week now that the season was almost over. Maisie was already wondering how she was going to manage once the staff had all left. It might be the quiet season but there was still a ton of essential maintenance work to get through on top of opening the pub over the weekends and for special events – not to mention Christmas. She'd already resigned herself to being just as busy in the off-season unless she could get some of the locals to lend a hand with the repair work and some shifts behind the bar.

Grabbing a bottle of spring water, she slipped out of the side door for a breather after the rush, and to give herself time to think after her encounter with the Blond. The terrace still held a few people, the odd local and a party of students from the campsite finishing pints and eating their own picnics. A couple of middle-aged yachties and a few clients from a local holiday home lingered over their G&Ts. She recognised some of them and nodded.

She considered having a sneaky fag, as she had every day at around this time since she'd given up ten years before. Then decided, again, that she could manage without one today and walked across the narrow road to the beach in front of the inn. She'd quit long ago but had lapsed back for a few weeks after Keegan had left. She'd got a grip on it again now, fingers crossed.

As the afternoon drew to a close, the sun sank lower over the sea. Rocks glistening with bright green seaweed cast long shadows over the shell-pink sand. Maisie selected a dry perch on her favourite rock, which was tucked away out of sight of the inn but had a great view of the Petroc channel. She kicked off her Skechers and buried her toes in the cool sand. Yachts glided past, or bobbed at anchor over sandbars. On a spring tide, you could wade right across to Petroc Island, where people stood on the battlements of a ruined fort, looking down at the Driftwood.

Petroc had been owned by the Scorrier family for centuries and all of its original buildings had been converted to luxury holiday homes, unlike Gull Island, where most of the buildings were still largely owned by the families who lived there. Most people on Gull just about made enough to get them through the winter, but that was the price of living in paradise, she reminded herself, and the Driftwood provided a living for her and her family, and jobs for a few seasonal staff.

Maisie rested her gaze on the fortified tower across the channel, telling herself to get a grip. She'd accepted that with her fortieth birthday coming up on New Year's Eve, some things probably weren't going to happen for her and she should be content with the life she had. She should have known better than to fall for a good-looking smoothie who'd promised her the moon but legged it faster than Usain Bolt just when she needed him.

Her, Maisie Samson, of all people. Streetwise, on-the-ball Maisie who had an answer for everyone and everything. How had she let herself need someone – something – so very badly? How had she been left with a heart that resembled a smashed bag of crisps?

The memories were still painful, even now she'd physically recovered.

On Christmas Day the previous year she'd had everything to look forward to. She was happy living with Keegan, her boyfriend and boss at the brewery, and she was looking forward to the birth of her baby – Little Scrap – in the summer. She'd been thinking about what colour to paint the nursery while she worked in the pub that Christmas Day, and how she could combine her job with looking after the baby once she'd returned from maternity leave. She'd even thought she'd felt him or her kick, though it was too early according to the textbooks.

Within the hour, she was on her way to hospital and, sadly, there had been nothing that could be done to save her baby.

As it was Christmas, her parents hadn't been able to get a flight over until it was all over. Maisie had told them not to come, and that she'd be fine. Keegan would look after her, she'd told them, thinking that although the pain of grief was agonising, her partner was by her side to comfort her.

A couple of weeks later, Keegan had told her he wanted to end their relationship.

Her parents had been horrified. Her mum had flown in to care for her and her father had immediately asked her to take over at the Driftwood, if she wanted to. They said they would stay on as part-owners and help out when required but Maisie would manage the place and have full responsibility and control of the pub.

Maisie didn't hesitate to say 'yes'. She wanted a new start and to leave the unhappy associations behind her, but they hadn't all been so easy to shake off.

Maybe that was why she'd been so reckless in taking a chance with the Blond on the beach: she'd wanted a moment of escape – a moment of abandon – even if it wasn't like her.

Who knew?

She stayed a few minutes longer, finishing her water, when she spotted something guaranteed to make her smile. A small and elderly yacht had dropped anchor off shore and a man with a long grey beard was rowing a small RIB towards the shore. Maisie grinned. She'd recognised the yacht as it had sailed into the channel.

She slipped off the rock and hurried forward as the old man reached the shore and jumped into the shallows with a splash. Archie Pendower was as much a part of the landscape of the isles as any rock or tree. He was well over eighty and his work had won a reputation that spread beyond the isles, although you wouldn't know it to look at the sorry state of the Starfish Studio these days. Like many islanders and many artists, even he found making a living tough. Not that Archie cared about money.

Water soaked the ragged hems of his denim dungarees as Maisie paddled into the water to help him haul out the RIB. He wore a salt-encrusted fisherman's cap and a chunky jersey with patches on the elbows. Funnily enough, Maisie couldn't recall ever seeing him wearing any other clothes, although he smelled fresh enough apart from a faint tang of cigars.

'Hi, Archie. I wasn't expecting you today,' she said as they hauled the RIB onto the sand.

Archie grinned. 'I wasn't expecting to be here either, but the light is so beautiful. I haven't painted Petroc from Gull for years and I'm expecting a cracking sunset.'

'Fen decided to stay at home today?' Maisie asked, enquiring after Archie's neighbour and, according to some, 'lady friend', although no one had any idea exactly what their relationship was before, during or after Archie's wife had passed away a decade ago.

'She'd be bored watching me paint all day and she has a work of her own to complete. She's giving the bathroom a lick of paint,' he said with a grin.

'And have you heard from Jake lately?'

Archie pulled a face. 'He Skyped me last week from some far-flung place in the south seas. I can't recall exactly where. Fen's the one who uses the computer. She came round and set the call up for me.'

'Do you think he'll make it home for Christmas?'

'Who knows? My son and daughter-in-law have asked me to go to them, but I'd rather stay here. Jake wasn't too sure. He's not too keen on the isles since that terrible business with his fiancée.'

'I can understand that,' said Maisie, reminded of the dreadful day when Jake Pendower – Archie's grandson – had lost his fiancée in a boating accident off St Piran's treacherous coast.

'Awful thing. He's never got over it, even though it's been a good few years now. I don't think he ever will. I'd hoped he'd take over the Starfish Studio from me one day but I don't hold out much hope of that.'

Archie reached into the boat to lift out his easel and workbox.

'Will you be setting up on the beach?' she asked, holding the easel while Archie shrugged a khaki duffel bag onto his lean shoulders.

'Yes. If I'm not disturbing you.'

'Oh no. I'd love to stay and watch you paint, but I ought to scoot back to work. Can I get you the usual?'

Archie rubbed his hands together. 'You know me too well, Maisie. Always oils the creative juices.'

'I'll send someone out with a pint.'

'Put it on my tab,' said Archie.

Maisie gave a wry smile. Archie's tab was as old as the hills but he wasn't such a frequent visitor to the pub these days so she didn't mind.

'Are you busy?' he asked as he set up his easel on a dry patch of sand facing the Petroc channel.

24

'For today, yes, but things will be a little quieter after the weekend. I doubt I'll be able to savour this sunset. I'll be too busy running the inn and making sure everything's not going to cock in the restaurant.'

'You work too hard.'

'Not as hard as I used to on the mainland. It's different being your own boss.'

The reminder of the mass exodus of her small but hard-working team made Maisie's heart sink again. She'd sorely miss Debbie's energy and enthusiasm. The pot washer, chef and barman were going too, leaving Maisie and her parents plus a couple of locals who might be able to spare the time to help out occasionally over the quiet season. She didn't need and couldn't afford to keep all the staff on over the winter.

'They never stay here these days, the young people,' said Archie. 'I was surprised when your mum said you were coming home. Still, some of us old-timers need to stick it out and keep the place limping on, eh?'

'Yeah. Some of us,' said Maisie, half amused and half horrified that Archie counted her as an 'old-timer'. She hadn't thought of limping on anywhere when she came back to Gull Island; she'd thought of making improvements and securing the future of the Driftwood and helping out her neighbours too, if she could. Archie meant well but he'd added to her wistful mood. Or was it the prospect of winter and dark nights that dampened her spirits? She didn't like to think it was the tick tick tick of time and her biological clock. Thirty-nine was still young-ish, whatever Archie thought.

She was only human and perhaps a fling with a stranger

was exactly what she did need. The lean, rangy figure of the Blond loomed in her mind again, with his tousled hair and laid-back charm. Maisie laughed at herself. He was very likely chatting up some other woman in the pubs of Hugh Town now. Well, good luck to him – and her.

Chapter 4

Who turned off the sun? Patrick McKinnon opened his eyes onto darkness and wondered where he was. Still in his flat in Melbourne? Had he woken up after another bender? Was he in bed with Tania? He reached out for her warm body.

'Jesus!'

A drop of cold water hit him smack on the nose.

Ah, *now* he remembered. It was Sunday morning.

The roof of the tent glistened with condensation and another drop fell onto his face. The heavens had opened in the night and wind had started blowing in off the sea. Patrick had thought he'd wake up in three feet of water so he considered himself lucky that the tent, his sleeping bag and all his stuff was only damp, not soaked. He'd have to find somewhere to dry his clothes before he packed away and left Scilly or everything would be rank in no time.

Patrick rubbed the rain off his nose with the back of his hand and unzipped the sleeping bag. Condensation had formed on the inside of the tent and there was a musty scent that made his nose twitch. Urgh. Was that him? It was no surprise he didn't smell too great following a day spent playing rugby on the beach with a load of students from the Gull Island campsite, and a night spent under canvas in a one-man tent. That was his agenda for the next hour: a shower, probably a cold one, and then cook a fry-up with his newfound mates. They were fifteen years younger than him and although he'd played Aussie Rules and Rugby Union as a young man, last night's game and a cramped night under damp canvas had left him stiff in all the wrong places.

After he'd finished his drink outside the Driftwood the day before, he'd lingered for a while, reading a guidebook and hoping Maisie Samson would come out onto the terrace. He wasn't quite sure what he'd say to her if she did. He was as surprised at seeing her behind the bar of the Driftwood as she was at seeing him. He'd recalled that she said she worked in a pub but he hadn't deliberately sought her out, even though he'd wanted to after she'd run away from him on the beach on St Mary's.

He'd thought she was better off without him. He didn't need any romantic entanglements while he was here.

He guessed she hadn't planned to kiss him; he certainly hadn't expected it to happen. They were having a good time and she'd probably let her guard down because of the drinks she'd had. She certainly wasn't anywhere near drunk though or he'd never have walked away with her that evening ... He hadn't expected that walk to lead to anything so when he'd taken her hand and she'd led him away for the kiss, everything had seemed completely natural.

Patrick was reminded of how natural right now. His body

responded to the memory of Maisie's body pressed to his. It wasn't only her body that had kept her at the forefront of his thoughts over the past few days. He'd liked her warmth, her sense of humour, the way she'd made him laugh and the way her eyes lit up when he'd made her laugh.

He'd tried and failed to clear her from his mind ever since his last sighting of her at the pub the previous afternoon. She'd been balancing an unlikely amount of glass and crockery in her arms as she picked her way across the terrace with a smile and a bit of banter for the customers. She was five foot one at the most, and built like a pixie, her wavy red hair caught up on top of her head in a messy up-do of the kind that he longed to *undo* and make a hell of a lot messier.

There was a woman with a mission, he'd thought. A woman who knew what she wanted. A woman who hid what she needed. And, he must admit, a woman with a bloody amazing arse, curves in all the right places and hair that smelled like a country garden. It was probably only some potion or other, but he'd always been a sucker for a woman with a lovely scent. Tania, his ex, had wafted around in clouds of potent fragrance, but Patrick preferred a subtler perfume.

When she showed no sign of appearing, he'd come to his senses and headed back to the campsite. Gull Island obviously wasn't the place for him. He'd have to come up with a Plan B. Maybe he shouldn't have even come to Scilly at all … maybe he should just put up, shut up and head back to Melbourne. He would wash his hands of this whole business if he hadn't made a promise.

Granted, he'd broken promises before and Greg Warner

would never know he'd reneged on their deal because Greg was six feet under. But breaking a promise to a mate was different. As for breaking a promise made to the dying mate who'd practically saved his own life? Patrick would rather have thrown himself off a bridge, so that's why he was here in Scilly, with no idea of what he was going to do with the rest of his time.

Towel wrapped around his shoulders, Patrick queued outside the shower block. He wondered if there would be any hot water left by the time it was his turn. It didn't matter, he'd had plenty of cold showers over the years, at boarding school and in other institutions. He wasn't afraid of hard work or hard conditions, but he was afraid of what lay ahead, which was one of the reasons he'd flown out of Melbourne a few weeks ago and headed for the UK.

'Bet that's perked you up, mate?'

One of the rugby-playing students – Sam, if Patrick remembered rightly – grinned at Patrick as he emerged from the shower, rubbing his damp locks vigorously and shivering in the sharp morning air. It was still misty and the dew clung to the grass of the camping field.

'I needed it. You blokes too by the looks of some of you.' Patrick flipped a thumb at the group of tents where the students were staying. A couple of them were only just crawling outside, rubbing their eyes. 'Why aren't you hard at it studying, anyway?' he teased.

'Bunked off for a long weekend. We're all studying at Falmouth, in Cornwall.' Sam grinned then winced and rubbed his temple. 'Don't think I could even think about looking at a book or a screen this morning. We hit the beers hard last night. Now an old guy like you can feel smug for not boozing.'

'Not smug. And not so much of the old. I'm not decrepit yet.' Patrick knew anyone over thirty-five would be a pensioner in their books and while he wasn't that far past that number, there was no point arguing. He'd enjoyed his night pretending to be twenty-one again, even without alcohol and notwithstanding the aches and pains this morning. Patrick pulled the towel off his shoulders.

'Um. I was wondering if you fancied a fry-up?' Sam asked.

Patrick shook his head. 'You mean you can handle a full English after last night?'

'Why wouldn't we?' Sam looked puzzled. That was another thing about being young, Patrick thought, you could neck a skinful and still devour a plate of bacon and eggs a few hours later.

'If you're asking if I'll cook the brekkie if you provide the bacon and eggs, then you're on,' he said.

Sam rubbed his hands together. 'I'd hoped you'd say that.'

'I'll be over as soon as I've got dressed. Get the stove and a brew on and I might even rustle up some tomatoes and mushrooms to go with it.'

Patrick pulled on a hoodie, shorts and flip-flops. No boxers or T-shirt but he wasn't planning on stripping naked, so who'd know? He needed to do some laundry. He took his chance to pile his damp stuff into the washing machine, bought up the tiny camp shop's stock of mushrooms and tinned tomatoes and headed for the students' tents.

More of them were surfacing now, one or two resembling

31

extras from the *Living Dead* but he guessed they'd cope once they smelled the bacon. With all that hard work on the water and the impromptu rugby, Patrick had soon discovered they were always ravenous. Sam had set up the camp kitchen outside the tents and the sun was rising in the sky as Patrick cracked the eggs and slapped the rashers in the pan. The sizzle of bacon hitting a hot pan made him smile, as did the faces around him. They were like dogs waiting for their bowls to be filled.

'That smells awesome.'

A lanky ginger youth scratched his boxers and hovered by the pan. You might want to wash your hands first, thought Patrick, but handed over a plastic plate of bacon and eggs anyway. Around a dozen students lined up for their breakfast while Sam piled slices of crusty bread onto the lid of a tin and placed it in the middle of the grass. Finally everyone was served and Patrick made himself a bacon and fried egg sandwich.

He sat cross-legged on the drying grass, washing his breakfast down with a mug of steaming tea. The sun was rising, as yellow as the yolk oozing between the crusts. It wasn't as fine a day as yesterday but he supposed it was fair for England. At home, it would have been considered pretty dull and cool. Melbourne had its moments and you could get four seasons in one day almost any time of year, but when the sun shone, man it shone. That had been the hardest thing to take about England: the dull autumn skies. Coming to Scilly had given him a glimpse of the full glory of this strange northern land. It was as if someone upstairs had decided to open the blinds and let the poor sods below have a taste of summer.

'What you doing today?' 'Ginger' asked him. 'Are you up for some kayaking? We're paddling round the Eastern Isles to see the seals.'

'Thanks for the offer but I might go over to St Mary's.'

'For the nightlife?'

'No. I might stay over there and ship out on tomorrow's ferry.'

'I thought you were staying until the end of the week,' Sam butted in.

'I thought I was but something's come up back home,' Patrick fibbed. 'Bloody pain in the arse but I suppose I ought to go back.'

'That'll cost you to change your air ticket.'

Patrick grimaced. 'Can't be helped.'

Until that moment, Patrick hadn't known he was going home. He had no idea where the impulse had come from but Sam's question had tripped a switch inside his brain. What was he doing here? Why had he thought this was a good idea? Greg was dead, and Patrick had done his duty. He'd been to England and he'd fulfilled his promise: he no longer owed anyone a thing, alive or dead.

He looked around him at the students, fifteen years younger than him, and wanted to laugh at himself. He pushed the plate away with a quarter of the sandwich still uneaten. The yolk had soaked through the bread and the bacon fat had congealed on the plate. The sight and smell of it made him queasy.

Sam pointed his fork at the leftovers. 'Don't tell me you're leaving that after cooking for us.'

'Yeah. Cooking it ruins your appetite. You have it, mate.'

'If you're sure,' said Sam.

Patrick handed the plate over. 'Get it down you. If you're heading out on a voyage, you'll need it.'

Feeling no obligation to wash up, and wanting to be on his own, Patrick padded back to his tent. He crawled inside intending to pack up, but half an hour later he was still lying on the sleeping bag, staring at the canvas roof. Outside, excited voices chattered away as the students set off on their adventure. Patrick was cold and stiff. He'd never felt so lost in his life. He felt as if he'd been cut adrift in the ocean. Was this loneliness? Or just lack of sleep and perhaps, his rational mind whispered, delayed grief?

He'd loved Greg, though the two men had never admitted it to each other. You just didn't say those things, but he *had* loved him, as a father or an older brother, neither of which he'd ever really known. He even missed Tania, even though she'd left him for her hairdresser shortly after he'd heard that Greg's illness was terminal. She'd be out to dinner on a yacht in Darling Harbour now, or maybe sipping champagne in some cocktail bar.

Good luck to her. He was no longer bitter.

The zip of the tent flap rasped. Sam's head poked through the flap.

'We're going. Probably won't see you again so just wanted to say nice to meet you and have a good journey.'

Patrick propped himself up on his elbows, hoping to Christ that his eyes weren't wet. 'Have a good trip. Watch out for Great Whites,' he said.

34

Sam grinned awkwardly. 'We will. Er ... we wanted you to have this as a thank-you for cooking the breakfast. We know you're on the wagon and this was all we could find that was alcohol-free but ... enjoy, old man.'

Patrick sat up. Sam thrust a bottle of Vimto at him. It was almost full.

'Thanks.'

'Pleasure. Don't drink it all at once.' Sam saluted and was gone.

A few minutes later, Patrick crawled out of his tent. The campsite was empty of humans. Only the tents stood, gently flapping in the breeze. On three sides, the sea spread out like an inky cloth, speckled with whitecaps. People crawled over the tower of an old fort that looked like it was part of Gull but was actually on the coast of the island opposite. Crows cawed and small birds twittered and darted in and out of the bushes. It was autumn here – spring was on its way in Melbourne. The weather would probably be even worse than here, but on sunny days the skies would be a full-on honest sapphire, not this half-hearted couldn't-make-its-mind-up blue.

He took a deep breath and started to pack up his tent.

Chapter 5

'Bloody hell. He's keen.'

Hazel Samson peered through the slatted blinds of the front bar window as Maisie stocked the chiller cabinets with bottled drinks ready for a busy Sunday. It was only ten o'clock and the first ferry from St Mary's or the off-islands didn't arrive until eleven, though walkers and guests from the campsite and Gull Island's handful of holiday cottages would soon be up and about and in need of coffee or something stronger.

'Who is it?' Maisie asked.

'Some young bloke with a bag.'

Hmm. Maisie was puzzled. The Blond had had a rucksack not a bag, but her mum couldn't see too well and might have been confused. 'What does he look like?' she asked, slotting bottles of 'posh' juice into the soft drinks chiller.

'I don't know. He's got his back to me. Youngish. Fair hair. Funny, he seems vaguely familiar although I haven't got my specs on. He looks a bit like that singer you like. Tom O' Donnell?'

'Tom Odell,' said Maisie, straightening up and peering over

the counter. She picked up a cloth and started to wipe down the bistro menu covers.

'What's he doing?'

'Just hanging about, I think ... oh, wait, he's going now. Running towards the jetty ... no idea why.'

'Right,' said Maisie, feeling guilty for losing interest in her mother's mystery man. She hadn't slept well, and her insomnia had nothing to do with the Blond. She'd heard her father up and about several times and muted voices coming from her parents' room down the hallway from hers. It wasn't easy living in such close proximity, for her or them, but in general, they all got along pretty well. However, living in the same premises had brought home to her that all wasn't rosy with his health. Maisie was convinced that the stress of running the pub was a contributor to his problems. She needed to find someone reliable to help out, if only part-time.

She stacked the menus neatly at the end of the bar. Hazel was still peering through the blinds.

'What's up?' Maisie asked.

'He just ran along the beach the other way. I've no idea what he's doing.'

'Well, if he wants to come in here, we don't open until half-past so he can wait. Mum, would you mind checking we've enough vegetables for the Sunday lunches? I can get Dad to dig up some more if not, and I want to make sure we're stocked up before Helmut comes in to do the prep.' Helmut was the chef. He and the seasonal barman lived in the tiny staff studios behind the pub. Debbie, the bistro manager, had been lodging in a caravan at the campsite. They would all be gone on the ferry to the mainland the next morning.

Hazel closed the slats. 'No problem.'

Hazel went into the kitchen while Maisie gave the bar another wipe down and checked the float in the till. Could they manage without any help at all over the winter? she wondered. It would be a lot more cost-effective but it meant having no time off. She could handle that, somehow, by closing an extra day, but it would also mean relying more and more on her parents. They were in their late sixties and they'd had enough. Her dad wasn't too well, though he tried to hide the fact and claimed he was just tired. Maisie could see he struggled to get his breath sometimes and he was pale under his year-round tan.

Maisie heard a scuffle outside on the terrace and angry shouts. She risked a discreet glance through the bottle-glass pane in the pub door. There was a figure out there, but it was so distorted, it could have been anyone. She glanced at the big clock above the bar. It was twenty past ten.

Sharp raps on the door made her jump.

Winter was coming and she needed every penny of revenue, didn't she? She could open ten minutes early. She drew the bolts on the top and bottom as carefully as she could, then turned the key and lifted the latch.

'Jesus Christ!'

'Sorry to startle you.' A handsome man about her own age, with blond, almost white hair, stood in the porch. He must have been waiting right in front of the door and Maisie had almost knocked him flying.

'Hugo? What do you want?'

Hugo Scorrier held his laptop bag protectively in front of his privates. 'Apologies for the early visit but I wanted a quick word before the inn opened. Basil! Bad dog! Stop that!'

At Hugo's shout, Basil pulled his snout out of a patch of weeds topped by the remains of a rotting seagull. The Labrador's coat glistened like wet coal and there was a green strand of weed stuck to his tail.

Hugo flashed an apologetic smile at Maisie. 'Sorry, he may whiff a bit. He goes his own way, never listens to a word I tell him. I've been chasing the devil up and down the beach for ages.'

Clever Basil, thought Maisie, but answered Hugo as civilly as she could. 'We open in ten minutes and I'm afraid I'm rather busy.'

'I would have been here at ten,' he said as Basil sniffed around the tables on the terrace, 'if Basil hadn't had other ideas involving seagulls and going AWOL.'

'You should have phoned me to make an appointment.'

'Well, I hadn't planned on calling *as such*,' said Hugo. 'Not on you specifically, but I've been to the morning service at the chapel and had a coffee with a few of your neighbours afterwards. I thought I'd drop in on my way back to my boat.'

Maisie shivered in the cool morning air. Hugo wore olive cords, a waxed jacket and shiny brogues on his feet. He was like an apparition from another era. A very unwelcome one at that.

'Can you spare five minutes?' he asked.

'Who's that, love?' Hazel shouted from the bar.

'It's Hugo Scorrier, Mum. We're just having a very quick chat.'

'Oh, shit.'

Worried that Hugo had heard her mum's curse, Maisie cringed and quickly pulled the door to behind her. 'I can spare a few minutes.' She ushered Hugo to a table near the beach. People were already wandering along the path, eyeing up the inn. Basil ran off to investigate some old lobster pots.

Hugo perched on the edge of a bench, looking for a spot without any seagull poo. 'I know you're a busy woman so I'll get to the point. Have you thought any more about our offer to take the Driftwood off your hands?'

'"Take it off my hands"? Hugo, I think I've made it quite clear that I don't want to sell the Driftwood at this time. Or any time. I've only recently taken over here.'

Hugo placed his bag on the table. 'Yes, I know. You came from a very senior role with a successful pub chain. I'm sure that your experience has thrown the – um – limitations of the Driftwood into stark reality.'

'Yes, it has, and my experience has also shown me how it could be more profitable and successful. I hope you're not suggesting that my parents haven't worked incredibly hard to keep the place viable. We turn a reasonable profit, enough to give us all a basic living and allow us to stay here on Gull.'

'I wasn't suggesting anything like that. Your parents are troupers. They've stuck it out far longer than anyone could have expected them to. All I'm saying is that, if you accepted our offer, which is a generous one, you could still live and work at the Driftwood without the worries of living hand to mouth. Let's face it, the Driftwood could do with a make-over.'

Maisie sat her on hands, resisting the urge to throw Hugo off the terrace. She'd tried hard to put herself in his shoes when she'd first come home and she did feel sorry about his father's illness. It must be tough having to run the business while seeing his dad suffering from Alzheimer's at such a young age. Hugo was a year younger than her and his father, Graydon Scorrier, had had to hand over the reins to his son five years previously. He was now in a nursing home on St Mary's. Hugo's parents had split up when Hugo was still a teenager and his mother now lived in London and as far as Maisie knew, had never come back to visit her ex.

'Firstly, we don't live hand to mouth,' she said. 'And secondly, why would we want to be tenants here when we can be owners?' She hated Hugo in that moment, not because what he was saying was wrong or insulting but because actually his offer did make some sense. The Driftwood was only just holding together and probably did need a lot of work doing. It could do with a repaint over the winter, and the window frames needed varnishing and the roof needed repairing at the very least. The cost of re-slating it was unthinkable. Then there were the toilets: they could do with a total refit. In fact, in her dreams, it would be a lot smarter than it looked now and she'd love to expand the bistro and terrace too. They were pipe dreams, however: the basics needed tackling first.

Hugo opened his mouth to speak. He had a beige moustache of sorts clinging for dear life to his upper lip. Maisie cut him off before he could get any words out. 'Before you say any more, I have seriously considered your offer and yes, there are advantages ...'

Hugo broke into a smile. 'I thought you'd see it that way.'

'But on balance, I – and my parents – have decided that we're going to decline it.' There, thought Maisie, I'll use the type of business language he can understand. She was really rather proud of herself.

Hugo was silent for a few seconds then sighed. 'I'm sorry to hear that and very disappointed, naturally. The Driftwood would have made a wonderful addition to our portfolio on Gull. We'd be able to make a significant investment in it and extend it.'

'You mean turn it into a clone of the Rose and Crab on Petroc?'

'Not a clone. Gull would be given its own distinct identity. We've had a top London agency draw up the branding. In fact' – he sniffed – 'I have the designs in my bag here. I've just come back from showing them to some of the other islanders who attended the service and coffee morning. There was a good turnout. I'd say about half the islanders were there.'

Maisie rolled her eyes. 'That's because the coffee and bacon rolls were free.'

'Probably.' Hugo grinned. He had lovely white teeth and wasn't unattractive in a Hooray Henry kind of way, Maisie was forced to admit. He reminded her of a less hunky and fairer version of the vicar in *Grantchester*, one of her mum's favourite shows.

42

Hugo smirked. 'I can see there's no point trying to bullshit you.'

'You're not wrong there.' Maisie got up. 'I *really* have to start serving. We've customers already waiting as you can see and the morning tripper boat will be here soon.' She nodded at the half a dozen punters hovering expectantly on the terrace. Basil seemed to have sensed Hugo's time was up too and lolloped over. He nudged Hugo in the crotch.

'Basil. For God's sake,' said Hugo, pushing the dog away and wrinkling his nose at the damp patch on his trousers. 'As you're obviously busy, I'll leave you with a copy of my plans.'

He unzipped his bag and pulled out an A4 folder. 'There's no harm in taking a look, is there? You know where to reach me if you change your mind.'

'Thanks,' Maisie ground out. She didn't touch the file he'd placed in front of her. Hugo pushed his floppy lock of hair off his face. 'I'll be off then.'

Maisie wiggled her fingers. 'Byeee. Have a safe journey back over the water!'

'Thanks.' Hugo turned away, but he'd only got a few steps when he doubled back, just as Maisie had picked up the file. 'By the way, I think you should know that two more of your neighbours are seriously considering selling to us – Hell Cove Cottages and the Fudge Pantry. I think that makes five businesses on Gull who have sold or agreed to sell to us now. There's not much left, is there?'

Then, leaving Maisie too stunned to reply, Hugo sauntered down the path and along the beach towards the jetty and his boat, calling Basil to heel and being ignored. Maisie sat back down on the bench, staring at the folder. She should be in the pub now, ready to serve the first rush of customers but she couldn't move.

Una and Phyllis at the Hell Cove Cottages had agreed to sell up to Hugo? Pete and Davina at The Fudge Pantry in the middle of the island too? Both families had been on Gull for generations. They'd once told Maisie they'd sell to the Scorriers over their dead bodies. Was Hugo winding her up, or bluffing? If he was right, it left only a handful of significant businesses on Gull Island that were still independently owned, along with the land around them. Hugo would be free to apply to develop them as he chose. Despite what people said, if offered enough money, it wouldn't take much for the rest of the families to fall like a pack of dominoes. And who could blame them when it took such commitment and energy to eke out a half-decent living on Gull?

Maisie glanced over to Petroc with its chichi cottages and businesses clustered around the harbour. Was she the one who was wrong, trying to make sure Gull kept its slightly shabby but fiercely independent character?

It wasn't only the Petroc channel that had separated her and Hugo. He'd been despatched to boarding schools in Cornwall from the age of seven and had only returned for the holidays. Maisie and the island kids had hung out with him occasionally when their paths crossed, swimming and playing cricket on the beach. Hugo had been hopeless at football, Maisie recalled – they only played rugger at his boarding school. More often than not, however, Hugo had friends to stay and then he and his chums had kept in their own little clique.

It was hard to judge after all these years, but Maisie had felt that when Hugo was with his school friends, they'd turned up their noses at Maisie and her mates. He'd been far less sure of himself when he was on his own, but maybe that was natural. Kids were quick to realise when an 'outsider' wanted to join in and at times Hugo hadn't met with the friendliest of welcomes. When she was older, in her late teens, she used to think he fancied her and that had made her even more distant with him. Now she was older still she suspected he'd probably just been lonely.

However, none of this was an excuse for Hugo being a total prat now he was a grown man.

Ray Samson appeared in the doorway of the pub, waving frantically. 'Maisie!' he called.

'Coming!'

Maisie hurried into the Driftwood, smiling at punters and apologising for the late opening. She slid behind the counter and after a moment's hesitation, stepped on the pedal of the bin and dropped Hugo Scorrier's plans inside. Then, with a heart as heavy as stone, she turned back to the room with a huge grin.

'Right, you lovely thirsty, hungry people. Welcome to the Driftwood. What can I get you?'

Chapter 6

After packing up on Monday morning, Patrick had shoul-
dered his rucksack and strolled out of the campsite. His
plan had been to spend the night on St Mary's before he
caught the flight back to Cornwall at lunchtime, but in the
end he'd decided that it was easier to camp on Gull one last
time and get the early ferry to St Mary's.

He'd spent his final day walking around the rugged
northern side of Gull before heading back to the campsite.
The students were surprised to see him but very happy when
he rustled up a homemade chilli for them. Patrick listened to
Javid bemoaning the months of dark evenings that lay ahead
and the fact the *Islander* ferry would stop its daily visits altogether at the end of the week, leaving the air service as the
only way off the isles – if the planes were able to fly and
weren't grounded by fog or storms as he'd been warned they
could be. Then it was an early night, a quick breakfast and
off towards the jetty near the Driftwood. His pack was full
to bursting but it felt good to have it on his back. It was solid
and the weight of it reminded him that he had, actually, made
his decision to go back to Melbourne.

Once he reached Penzance, his plan was to hop on an overnight train to London and get the first plane out of Heathrow to Oz. His lawyers in Sydney would be delighted that he'd stopped messing them around. He knew someone else who'd also be delighted that Patrick had finally made his decision. The prospect of their glee made his heart sink but he'd have to get over it.

As he walked down the road – just a single tarmacked track – that led down the slope to the Driftwood and the jetty, Patrick could see two people working in the allotment behind the pub. A woman was crouched down, weeding a patch of vegetables. A man had a ladder rested against an outhouse attached to the side of building, which must be the Driftwood's toilet block. He was hammering some slates onto the roof and cursing. Presumably these were Hazel and Ray Samson, who Javid, the campsite owner, had told him about.

Patrick bent down to tie the laces on his boots and allow himself a last look at the inn. There was no doubt that the Driftwood occupied a knockout spot and its location was probably the equal, in its own way, of any bar he'd ever been to. Even the slightly shabby end-of-world feel to the old building held its own charms.

On the other hand, judging from the way Ray Samson was puffing and wiping his brow as he tackled the lichen-spotted slates, Patrick guessed the inn wasn't quite so charming to live in. He wasn't sure the guy should be up the ladder at his age, although it wasn't any of Patrick's business. In fact, he reminded himself, nothing that went on at the Driftwood was his business.

He had half an hour to spare before his ferry to St Mary's arrived so he walked down the track and onto the beach. The tide was slowly filling the channel between Petroc and Gull Island and the remaining islets of sand glittered in the morning sun. Soon they'd shrink to nothing, presenting one smooth and silvery expanse of water between Gull and Petroc.

Leaving his pack by a rock on the powdery sand, Patrick sauntered down to the sea. He picked up a small stone and cast it over the water. It skipped a couple of times then sank. The water was so shallow, he imagined he could see it resting on the bottom. He tried again with a larger flatter stone. Feeling confident, he snapped back his wrist but fluffed his aim and managed only one bounce.

'Here. Let me try.'

Maisie Samson's voice was unmistakeable; her soft local accent was tinged with dry amusement. He didn't think she was laughing at him, and even if she was he wouldn't have blamed her. He found himself ridiculous most of the time. He turned around to see her standing a few feet behind him, her arms folded. How long she'd been watching him, he didn't know, but he felt as if he'd been caught smoking a fag at school by the matron. She wore skinny jeans and an old Arran fisherman's sweater that hung off her slight frame. It had obviously been her dad's at one time – or a boyfriend's. It could still belong to a boyfriend now, he supposed. He shoved one hand in his pocket.

'Good morning,' she said.

'Morning,' he said, jiggling the stones in his pocket nervously.

'I thought you'd left already.'

'I'm waiting for the ferry. I decided to stay one more night. How did you know I was going home?'

She shrugged. 'I assumed. Everyone left yesterday.'

'The kayaking students are still around,' he said.

'Apart from them. Javid told me the rest of the site was empty and I don't think there are any other tourists in any of the B&Bs or holiday cottages on the island at the moment.'

'Do you and Javid monitor everyone's comings and goings?'

'Pretty much. Like I said, everyone knows everything on Gull. Sooner or later.'

How *much* later, he thought. How long would it take for the islanders to know his comings and goings – and secrets?

Maisie shrugged and rubbed the sand with her sneaker. Patrick had the feeling she was embarrassed about her comments when they'd been flirting again the previous day, and she'd certainly been eager to get rid of him after their banter was over. Unable to meet his eye, she scraped the shingle with the toe of her Converse, but if she were so keen to avoid him, why was she hanging around now?

He considered collecting his pack and leaving her alone but she suddenly peered at the shingle and picked up a stone. She crouched low at the water's edge and, without a word, set the stone free with one deft flick of the wrist. It skipped over the water once, twice ... seven times in all until it finally disappeared.

'You should have been in *The Dambusters*,' said Patrick.

She laughed out loud. '*The Dambusters*? That's an old one. You're surely too young to have seen that?'

'Ditto,' said Patrick.

'Mum and I have been force fed that film by Dad, every bank holiday without fail. Now he has it on DVD so we're made to watch it regularly as an example of our glory days.' She shook her head and a smile, a heartfelt one, tilted the corners of her mouth. 'How could we not watch it? My great-great-uncle Horace was a mechanic on those planes in the war,' she said. 'Horace knew Guy Gibson, the man who led them. My dad remembers Uncle Horace from when he was a boy.'

Patrick whistled. 'I'm impressed.'

'Me too. Sort of. Can't imagine being in a war, but Horace is still a terrible name ... Why don't you have another go with your stones?'

'You only want to show me up when I fail spectacularly.'

'Of course I do and I hope you're not going to disappoint me.'

In two minds as to whether Maisie wanted him to disappoint her or not, Patrick tried his very best over the course of the next five minutes. He found stones every bit as good as Maisie's yet she beat him each time by at least two bounces.

'Damn it!' he said in exasperation as another stone sank just feet from the shore.

Maisie stood by with her hands on her hips, watching him critically. 'Your technique needs honing,' she said.

While Patrick selected another pebble, round the headland, out of sight, a whistle tooted.

Maisie nodded in the direction of the jetty. 'That's your ride to St Mary's,' she said.

His ride out of there and his escape plan, thought Patrick. His last chance to do the right thing and leave Gull forever. His fingers curled tighter around the stone in his palm. Ignoring the whistle, he bent low and flung his stone.

Three skips.

Still crap.

He wandered down to the water and fished another promising-looking stone from the wavelets. The water ran down the cuff of his sweatshirt.

The ferry whistle tooted again, twice and more urgently.

'If you don't leave now, you'll miss the ferry and that means you'll miss the Islander ferry to Penzance and have to stay another night, unless you're prepared to fork out for a plane ride.' Maisie's voice reached his ears from behind.

'This is true,' said Patrick, enjoying the weight of the stone in his hand and the cold water trickling down his arm. He'd soon found out that the ocean was as cold here as at home, where it pounded the coast, chilled by the Antarctic. People – tourists – thought it would be like a warm bath and were shocked and disappointed when it froze your nuts off, same as their own seas. Same here, he guessed ... but he wasn't disappointed by Gull Island yet. He might be, given time. He'd always been disappointed and always messed things up ...

What about this time? Judy had asked him to give the place at least a chance. Greg and Judy had given him a chance before, many many chances ... so maybe he owed it to them both to stay a bit longer now.

It would be no hardship to spend a little longer in Maisie Samson's company, that was for sure.

He flung the stone away, not expecting anything. It glanced off the water, again and again. Five, six, seven times and maybe more until it slipped under the surface.

'Wow.'

Patrick turned. Maisie was silhouetted against the morning sun, miming applause while her auburn hair blew across her face in the breeze. She reminded him of a girl in a Shakespeare play he'd been forced to study at school.

Though she be but little, she is fierce. He smiled at himself. If Maisie knew what he was thinking, she'd probably walk straight off.

Toot. Toot. *Toooooot.*

'That's your last chance. You'll have to run,' she said.

'My pack's too heavy to rush.'

Maisie grabbed the top of it. 'I'll help you if you want.'

She's daring me to go, he thought. Or daring herself. Or am I kidding myself?

He stayed where he was. 'One more stone first.'

She let go of his pack. Patrick doubted she'd have got far with it anyway. 'OK but it's your funeral.'

He thought about throwing another stone but something kept him rooted to the beach, looking at her looking at him.

Patrick thought back to the notice pinned on the corkboard in the laundry room and to his chat with Javid last night. Maisie wasn't the only one who had her spies. He glanced at the fort on Petroc opposite and in the distance he heard the putter of a boat engine. The ferry nosed its way beyond the headland and headed back to St Mary's.

The breeze freshened. Maisie pulled her hair off her face

and held it out of her eyes as she joined him at the shoreline. Water lapped at her shoes but she didn't seem to mind. 'You're too late. You missed your chance to escape from Gull,' she said. 'You'll have to make other arrangements now.'

Maybe not, thought Patrick as madness seized him. He turned to her and the words came tumbling out. 'I could be wrong, but I hear you're looking for a barman.'

Chapter 7

If Maisie had been sitting on her favourite rock when she heard the Blond's announcement, she was sure she'd have fallen off it. All her smart replies flew out of her mind in favour of a strangled: '*Sorry?*'

'Sorry? As in sorry, the vacancy's been filled? Sorry, if it was a choice between Hitler and me, you'd hand the job to Adolf?'

Maisie spluttered. 'Don't be so daft. You'd be perfect. I mean, you'd make a perfect – a very good and competent – barman. I'm sure.'

'But?'

'Five minutes ago, you were leaving. Your bags are packed. Look.' She picked up the rucksack again, which was about as tall as she was, and almost toppled over.

'Careful, Maisie Samson. Don't want you doing yourself an injury.'

'I'm worried I might do an injury to more than myself if I take you on at the Driftwood.'

Patrick folded his arms and raised an eyebrow. 'So you're not up for the challenge?'

Maisie bit back a reply. Her heart was beating faster than

she liked and she was on very dangerous ground. She wanted him to work for her and dreaded it in equal measure, for entirely opposing reasons.

'There was a notice advertising the job in the campsite reception ... that wasn't a figment of my imagination, now was it?' he said.

'No. It was a real notice and there is a vacancy.'

'And you just said, if my hearing didn't deceive me, that I'd be perfect.'

'That was wrong of me. You don't have any experience ...'

'I thought I'd make a very competent barman?'

'I only meant you've the gift of the gab. You seem to like talking, anyway.'

'Miaow,' said the Blond. Maisie could have cheerfully hit him with his rucksack, if she could have got it off the ground.

'I need someone who can hit the ground running. I can't carry passengers.'

'Two transport metaphors in one sentence. She's smart.'

'And you're fired,' said Maisie, thinking of lobbing a stone at him and hoping it bounced off his head. 'I don't even know your name.'

'What? You mean the Gull Island grapevine hasn't worked this time?'

'Don't flatter yourself. You're not that famous yet, but it would probably be a good idea to introduce yourself if you're interested in applying for the job.'

The Blond stepped forward and stuck out his hand. 'It's Patrick. Patrick McKinnon. I don't think we've been formally introduced.'

Heat rose to Maisie's cheeks. That kiss they'd shared in St Mary's had been anything but formal but at least she had a name at last.

Patrick McKinnon. It was a nice, normal name that suited him well. She shook his hand briefly but firmly then stepped back to maintain her distance. Her heart was beating much faster than she wanted it to.

'I appreciate it's an unconventional way of going about things and if you don't like the look of me or can't stand my cheek, then fair enough, but I do have plenty of experience. I've worked in half a dozen pubs and bars in my time, including one in Melbourne for the past five years as bar manager. I can even turn my hand to some cooking if it's basic. I can get references that'll prove I'm not about to run off with the takings or the customers.'

'OK. I'll admit that sounds tempt ... I mean satisfactory, but how do I know you have the right to work here?' Maisie said, recovering her composure a little. 'Gull Island may be the back of beyond and, yes, rules are broken, but I can't afford to be in trouble with the powers-that-be.'

Patrick smiled. 'I have the right to work here, rest assured, and I can prove it.'

'It can get lonely here in the winter,' she said. 'Lonely and monotonous. Seeing the same old faces day after day, being stuck on the isles – on Gull Island – for days at a time when the weather closes in. This island can send people nuts, believe me.'

'All the more reason to have a fresh face around the place, eh?'

For me, thought Maisie, but maybe not for you.

'That flyer had been up so long the sun had almost faded the words away. You need someone urgently and from what I hear, staff are in short supply on Gull Island. I can help you in the pub and kitchen but I can also help you in other ways.'

His eyes twinkled. Maisie went all shivery. 'Such as?' she said, as prim as a maiden aunt.

Undeterred, Patrick pointed at the pub. 'I could help your dad re-slate that roof and paint the woodwork that's peeling off. The place will need a new coat of render before spring by the look of it and that terrace furniture needs re-varnishing. Your dad's not been too well, I hear, so perhaps he could do with a hand.'

The Driftwood Inn sign creaked in the wind. The seagull picture was so weathered it might have been a penguin and the lettering was starting to dissolve. Maisie pursed her lips but her stomach did a flip. She'd winced when she'd seen her dad struggling with the roof earlier and she knew her mum was worried sick. Everything Patrick said made sense. Too much sense, so why was she hesitating? She desperately tried to get a grip and think rationally about the situation.

'OK. I accept you have experience and we do need some practical help around the place as well as in the Inn but I don't know anything about you. I only learned your name five minutes ago. If I'm to take you on, it's only fair that I interview you properly and check all the paperwork's in order.'

'Fine. Is now a good time?'

'As good as any as you're not going anywhere in a hurry.'

57

Patrick held out his hand to let her walk ahead of him across the terrace. 'Bring it on, then.'

Maisie gave him six weeks tops. Less if the weather was particularly crappy over the autumn. He'd definitely be gone before her mum had made the Christmas cake. She led the way into the pub and suggested he take a seat in the far corner while she collected some paperwork and her tablet.

What have I done? What the chuffing heck have I *done*? she thought, her inner voice nagging at her like a stroppy toddler. He'd make a great barman but he'd also have the female population of the island falling at his feet, not to mention some of the guys. And while he'd doubtless be very handy to have around, he might also prove an unwanted distraction to *her* while she was trying to run the place and get ready for Christmas and get a hundred-and-one jobs done over the off-season.

She had to remind herself that she hadn't actually given him the position yet. She was in control, she had to remember that, whatever the outcome of the next half-hour.

Patrick dumped his pack on the floor while Maisie went through to the tiny back room next to the kitchen that served as an office-cum-staffroom. She could just make out her dad wheeling a barrow through the archway at the rear of the garden that led to another allotment where there was a glasshouse and her mum's flock of chickens. It was just as well that her parents were safely out of the way for a little while at least. She didn't want an audience while she interviewed Patrick, and she wanted to make up her own mind about him.

The advantages of taking on Patrick McKinnon were

obvious: he'd draw in what scant custom there was and, she was sure, he'd work hard and long hours. He was the answer to her dreams, in so many ways, and that's what bothered her most. Setting aside the fact that she fancied the faded jeans off him, it was too good to be true that an attractive, person-able and experienced Australian barman had rocked up at the arse end of nowhere just when she needed a personable and experienced barperson.

Maisie found her tablet, a notebook and pen and tried to focus on the questions she'd usually ask her potential staff for the Driftwood. Patrick, she reminded herself, was no different and deserved no special treatment. If he didn't tick all her boxes, he could be on his way back to St Mary's or wherever. This was business now.

'OK,' said Maisie, returning to the table and putting her iPad and notebook down. 'Before we go any further, I have to ask you this. Why do you want to lock yourself away for six months here when you could be enjoying the sun in Australia? I hate to ask it, but why are you here at all?'

Patrick smiled. 'Now, that,' he said, 'is the question I've been asking myself for the past ten minutes.'

'I'm not going to answer it for you,' she said with a smile.

'You don't have to. Until half an hour ago, I was going back to Melbourne. Although that's not strictly true. I've had a mind to stay on here ever since I set foot on the isles. I came over to London a week ago with the intention of having a working holiday.'

'Funny time to come here, the end of October.'

'A mate told me there would be a lot of seasonal bar work

going, with the festive season coming up. I believe it starts at Easter over here.' He grinned.

'It's crazy,' said Maisie. 'Christmas cards in the shops in August ...' She realised she was agreeing with him too readily. No matter what had gone on between them before, this was meant to be an interview. 'I can see why you'd want some work in London, where there are tons of jobs at Christmas, and I can even possibly understand why you'd want to be here when the weather's crap, but why would you want to stay on Gull Island itself?'

He sighed. 'I'll be honest with you. I could have got a job in London just like that.' He snapped his fingers. 'And earned a lot more money, but it'll be a nice change to get out of the city, even a city like Melbourne.'

'Why did you leave your last bar in Melbourne?' she asked, still unconvinced. 'Did they let you go?'

He smiled. 'They didn't let me go as in sack me. I'm on a sabbatical as you'll find out if you take up my references.'

'*When*,' she said. 'I will be taking them up, I can promise you. If I take you on. How many busy city bars can afford to let their managers have a sabbatical?'

He nodded. 'It does sound fishy, I agree. I can see I'm going to have to be straight with you.'

Maisie's hackles rose at his flippant reference to telling the truth. 'I won't stand for an ounce of bullshit, let's get that straight from the start.'

'Well, it's a long and boring story ...'

Maisie folded her arms and firmed up her tone. 'Why don't you try me?'

Patrick held her gaze, but she refused to flinch. He could try it on all he liked but she had to show him who was boss from the start and she wouldn't be fazed by any diversion tactics, however much they might make long-dead feelings stir, deliciously, low in her belly.

'There was this bloke ... let's call him a special mate ...'

Chapter 8

The penny dropped in Maisie's brain with a loud 'kerching'. Damn it, how had she not realised before? A bloke, a 'special mate'. Patrick was gay and running away to Gull from a wrecked relationship, just like herself. That relationship just happened to be with a man.

Argh. Maisie kicked herself for her naivety in assuming that he was straight and fancied her. She smiled encouragingly at him, rueing her presumption.

'I see,' she said.

Patrick frowned as if he couldn't see why or what Maisie 'saw' at all. 'Do you?'

'Yes, I mean, no. Sorry to interrupt you. Please carry on.'

'This bloke, Greg is – was – a good friend of mine. A *very* good friend, you could say ...'

Maisie arranged her face into sympathetic-good-listener mode. She felt sorry for him, having to explain himself, and perhaps she should tell him now that his personal life was none of her business unless it related directly to his work.

'Greg was like a father to me,' said Patrick.

'Father?' Her voice was almost a squeak. Maisie had to

make a physical effort to wipe the grin of relief from her face. Not gay then. But ... what other surprises were coming from left field? Plenty, if her hunches about Patrick McKinnon were right.

'Yes, or a father figure, though he would have laughed at me for saying anything so schmaltzy. He thought of himself more as a good mate, which he was. Sorry, I'm not making much sense, am I?'

'Greg was also my boss at my last place of work in Melbourne. The Fingle Bar, which of course you'll know all about when you google it and email or phone to talk to them.'

'Will Greg vouch for you?' she said, noting his name on the pad.

'I'm sure he would if he could ...'

Maisie glanced up.

'He's been dead for six months.'

'Oh God. I'm so sorry.'

'So am I. Sorrier than I can tell you, but there's nothing he or I can do about it. Greg had cancer, and he was only fifty-one. He'd taken me on at the Fingle as a pot washer and by the time he passed away, I was managing the place. It's a big bar overlooking the Yarra River in the heart of the city. You'd like it.'

He hesitated. She smiled encouragingly. 'Sounds great. Go on.'

'Cutting a long story short, Greg was my mentor and friend. He helped me out at a time in my life when I was going way off the rails. Without him I'd have ended up in a bad place – I already had, to be honest – and finding out that he was sick made me and him rethink a few things. Greg told me his cancer was terminal late last year and that I should use his bad luck as a wake-up call for my own life.'

'I can understand that,' said Maisie, surprised but pleased by his honesty. Losing Keegan – and losing their unborn baby at the same time – had turned her own world upside-down. For the first few weeks after her miscarriage and Keegan walking out on her, she'd felt like someone had picked her up, shaken her until she didn't know night from day, or anything at all. When she'd slowly emerged from a cocoon of grief and loss, the world had looked completely different.

'Maisie?'

'Sorry. You were saying? Greg's illness made you re-evaluate your priorities.'

He smiled at her. It wasn't like her to use language like that but she'd been reminded of what she'd written in her resignation letter to her line manager at the pub. She'd used cold and formal words then to describe the raw pain and anger she'd been feeling over her double loss.

'Greg asked me if I was really happy running the Fingle; he told me to get out and see the world while I was young and fit. He told me he regretted staying so long in one place and now it was too late for him. He wished he'd taken his wife and kids to live in and experience other places when he'd been younger. I stayed on to help Judy but now I've decided to take a break and made my plans to see the world.'

'So you came to Britain first?'

'Yes.'

'Any particular reason?'

He ran his fingertip over the table top, a smile creeping over his lips. 'Ah, that's simple. I *am* British.'

OK. He was full of surprises.

'My parents emigrated from London when I was a baby so I think of myself as Aussie. I have dual citizenship and two passports, so there shouldn't be any problem with my right to work. Crazy, really, when I'd never set foot in the motherland before last week.'

'OK, but why Scilly? Why not Stratford, or Scotland or Yorkshire? Cornwall even?'

'Because Greg's great-grandparents on his mum's side used to live on Scilly way back in the day. He was always going on about their heritage and vowing he'd come over and see it but he never made it. He made me promise I'd include it on my trip, so here I am.'

'Wow. What were their names? Do you know? Many Scilly families have lived here for generations so some of their descendants are sure to have known Greg's ancestors.'

His brow furrowed. 'God. I can't think. He never said, or if he did I wasn't listening hard enough. The granddad's first name might have been Rex ... or Robert. Or was it Harry? Sorry, Greg just referred to him as "the old boy". I didn't take too much notice of the details and, to be honest, most of what he told me was while he was in a bad way at the end. He was confused and on a truckload of meds for the pain, but he made me promise I'd come over and see the UK and his roots.'

'Doesn't matter. Does Greg have family? They'll be interested in what you've found here and that you've decided to stay.'

'He has a wife – that's Judy – and a couple of grown-up kids … Have you decided I should stay then, Maisie Samson?'

She hesitated just long enough to give him doubt. 'I'm still making up my mind. Here, fill in this form while I make us a coffee. I'll be back shortly.'

Leaving Patrick with a job application and a pen, Maisie escaped to the kitchen. She didn't want a drink but she did want time to think about her decision. His story about Greg was plausible and actually very touching. She could check out the Fingle in seconds on the Internet and chat with Judy Warner and any other referees Patrick supplied. Again, Google would be her friend when cross-checking that the bars really were owned by Greg and Judy. She was used to hiring and firing and as long as Patrick's story checked out, she should feel confident in taking him on. Except, he was different to any other employee. Or was that simply because she fancied him? If so, that was her own lookout. Eventually, she took two mugs of coffee back to the bistro. Patrick had finished writing and handed her the form.

While he sipped the coffee, Maisie scanned through it quickly.

'It all looks OK. You haven't murdered anyone, have you? You didn't list any criminal convictions.'

He laughed. 'I haven't murdered anyone, but …'

The hairs on the back of Maisie's neck stood on end. '*But?*'

'I have been in prison.'

Maisie's heart plunged. Here we go, she thought. Here we go.

'In Australia?'

'Yeah. I spent six months in a young offender's place. I got drunk and vandalised a kids' park in one of the suburbs. It wasn't my first offence and I did a lot of damage. I was with some mates – at least I thought they were mates at the time – and the judge said I was the ringleader.'

'And were you?' she asked him, amazed her voice was so calm. Of course she'd interviewed applicants with a criminal record before, and taken on some over her years as a pub manager. She'd only regretted it once when one had taken advantage of her trust and stolen some cash from the till: the other ex-offenders had tended to work twice as hard once they'd been given the chance of a job.

'Oh yes. I was the ringleader. I was angry at the whole world back then. I thought I owed nothing to anyone.'

'Was there a reason for that?'

'I've spent too long with social workers and shrinks to answer that quickly. I don't know. They say it was because I lost my parents "at a vulnerable stage in my formative years". I want to be honest with you from the start. I went off the rails when I was young. I went a bit wild, quit school, bummed around, got into all kinds of minor trouble, smoked some weed, tried some stronger stuff ...'

'I'm sorry. Your parents must have been young themselves.'

He shrugged. 'Youngish, yeah ... I don't want to bore you with my family history. I got back on the straight and narrow, thanks to Greg and Judy's help.'

'They sound like good people. I'm sorry about your parents. I can't imagine losing one of mine, let alone both at once ...' She was curious about what had happened but didn't want to ask him directly. 'What a terrible thing to deal with when you must have still been very young too,' was all she dared to say, but Patrick seemed to want to carry on in the same open manner.

'I was at boarding school when it happened. It was a light aircraft crash ... they were travelling between the Outback and Adelaide where we were living at the time,' he said, evenly, as if he was so used to saying it that by now it was like relating a story about someone else.

'Who looked after you?' said Maisie, deciding that as Patrick had already revealed some of the details himself he wouldn't mind her asking.

'I stayed at school in term time and in the holidays I went to a distant older cousin's, although she packed me off to summer camps and the like, which suited us both. Soon as I was seventeen, I left and picked up a load of odd jobs and lived off the small trust fund Mum and Dad left when they died.'

'What about your other relatives? Grandparents, aunties and uncles in Britain?'

'At the time, one elderly grandfather in a nursing home. An auntie on Mum's side who had four kids and had just remarried a man with twins. An uncle who has his own family and definitely wasn't interested in me. And even if they had wanted me, I would have jumped in a shark-infested ocean before I'd have left Oz. I didn't want to come here: all I heard of it was shit weather and whingeing moaners who were always complaining about the shit weather.

'The thing is, I met Greg while I was at low point. One of

the regulars at the Fingle was a volunteer at one of the youth centres where I'd rocked up – forced to by my probation officer. He saw something in me, God knows what, and he told Greg about me. Greg and Judy took me on as a pot washer in the bar. They gave me a chance.' He smiled. 'Many, many chances until I finally realised how bloody lucky I was and got my act together and decided to live a pure and sin-free life henceforth.'

'Pure and sin-free? That sounds boring,' Maisie joked.

Patrick laughed. 'Not as boring as staring at four walls for twenty hours a day, or waking up in a pool of your own vomit.'

She winced, then it clicked. 'Ah. The Coke. You're teetotal, aren't you?'

'I am. Does that put you off taking me on as bar staff?'

'On the contrary, I consider it an asset.'

Maisie blew out a breath, trying to take in the story she'd heard. Patrick was so blasé about his terrible childhood and youth. Breezing through a tragic tale as if he were talking about an exciting rugby match. Maisie was certain that there was a lot more to discover about Patrick McKinnon, but how much did she want to know? His smiling eyes hid so much, she thought. As did her gobby, sassy façade. 'Interesting way of trying to impress your new boss,' she said. '"Shitty weather and whingeing moaners", eh?'

Patrick gave a wry smile. 'With some exceptions, of course. Gull Island's not too shabby, when the sun's out ...'

He left the sentence hanging, tantalisingly. Left her waiting for the line about the Driftwood and its owner: her.

But nothing.

'You made a reference to "my new boss",' he added instead of a compliment to Maisie. She wasn't sure if she was disappointed or relieved he hadn't tried to flatter her. She really had no idea how she felt about taking on Patrick McKinnon. 'So, does that mean you're not put off by my history?'

'Well, there's been nothing I need to know about since your spell in prison, has there?'

'So I'm hired?'

She had a feeling she might be making the biggest mistake of her life ... Maisie smiled and held out her hand. Patrick grasped it firmly but without trying to prove some point by mashing her bones. 'Subject to your references checking out, yes. Congratulations and welcome to the Driftwood. Now, let me show you the staff accommodation.'

Patrick raised an eyebrow. 'You have staff accommodation?'

'Yes. Where were you expecting to stay?'

'I wasn't,' said Patrick. 'This was a spur of the moment decision ... I hadn't even thought about where I might live.'

Maisie shook her head. 'You really do like to live in the moment, don't you?'

'Don't you?' he said. The glint in his eyes left her in no doubt he was hinting at their kiss on the beach the previous week.

Ignoring the question because she didn't know how to answer, Maisie got up. Her cheeks were burning. 'It's this way but I hope you're not expecting too much,' she said briskly.

She led the way through the catering kitchen and the staff-room at the rear of the pub to the garden. 'It's not the

Melbourne Ritz.' She was acutely aware of Patrick's presence behind her. Something about knowing he was so close and in her private territory made her skin tingle. She wasn't scared of him; she was scared of no man, and the feeling of being followed was more thrilling than scary. Yet his presence seemed to do something to the air. Goosebumps popped up on the back of her neck and her arms under her sweatshirt.

'Through here,' she said, and crossed the small paved area behind the kitchen to a low granite building at right angles to the inn itself. An assortment of garden furniture stood on the patio area, discarded cast-iron and plastic pieces that had seen far better days. The good stuff was all reserved for the customer terrace at the front. Maisie was aware of the fag ends on the flagstones where the staff had been enjoying a sneaky ciggie despite her disapproval. The grassy area outside the granite outbuilding was still green and lush and the tubs had bright red geraniums blooming in them even though it was late October.

'Unless you can find accommodation elsewhere on Gull Island, the Piggery is your best option, I'm afraid.'

'The Piggery?'

'Staff quarters. These buildings once housed pigs and a couple of cows. Nothing posh, but there's a bedsit, kitchenettes and shower room.'

Maisie opened the door of the Piggery and immediately muttered a rude word under her breath. The young barman had only vacated the place the previous day, and hadn't been keen on housework, judging by the unsavoury tang and the empty cans rolling around the floor. The bed looked like it had come straight from a Tracey Emin exhibit.

She barred the door, leaving Patrick right behind her. 'I haven't had the chance to clear it out yet. I'm sorry.'

'It'll be fine.'

She hesitated before walking in and letting him follow her. Maisie cringed. It was even worse than it had appeared on first glance – and sniff.

'It's great,' he said, sitting on the single bed. The mattress sagged under his weight and he bounced on it a couple of times. 'Seen some action, though.'

She wanted to melt through the floor. Actually, the floor was as minging as the bed. 'It's not fine. You can't stay here.'

Patrick stood up. 'I can clear it out. Give me a few bin bags, some bleach and scrubbing brush and it'll be shipshape by opening time tonight. I've slept in places that would make your hair curl.'

'Just because you've been in jail, doesn't mean you have to sleep in a stinking pit. God knows what that boy has been doing.'

'You could be right. From what I recall, jail was a lot cleaner than this.'

'Thanks!' She had to smile at his nerve. He definitely might brighten up a long, dark winter on Gull.

He joined her in the kitchenette. 'That was a joke, though well disguised. My sense of humour doesn't always translate.'

She lifted her trainer off the sticky vinyl floor and put out her tongue. 'Maybe not but this place is the pits. You can't stay in it until I've had it fumigated.'

'Give me the cleaning kit and I'll do it. You didn't know I was going to rock up so soon.'

She ignored him. She was deeply ashamed, not of the mess, which was par for the course with some of the young staff, but of not checking the room first. She wouldn't have dreamt of showing a new staff member such a hovel, let alone expect them to sleep in it. She ran a tight ship at her last pub. She should have kept a better eye on the staff quarters, but she'd been flat out at the end of the season.

'Wait here, please.' Leaving him, she walked back outside, pushed open the door of the neighbouring studio and swore. The place reeked of unwashed clothes and lager. Maisie didn't even want to cross the threshold. She was surprised her parents hadn't realised, although it didn't take long for a place to get rank if left. Both rooms needed a deep clean and she'd be the one rolling up her sleeves later.

'Any better?'

She almost bumped slap bang into Patrick's chest. Which wouldn't have been unpleasant. In fact, it would have been pretty awesome. In contrast to the rooms, up close, he smelled of some kind of woody body spray.

'I thought I told you to stay put?' she said, half joking.

'I thought the air was fresher out here.'

'You're enjoying this, aren't you, Mr McKinnon?'

He held out his hands. 'Enjoying watching you getting worked up over nothing? Not really. Either of these places is fine if you'll only let me help you sort them out. Or I can find somewhere else to kip. I've still got my tent. I can camp out here or Javid might let me stay on site and use his facilities.'

'No! I'll be the laughing stock.'

He frowned. 'Why?'

'People will say I can't look after my own staff. Just because you can clean the place up doesn't mean you ought to. I'll get a cleaner in later and until then ...' Maisie was floundering. She wasn't even sure herself why it had become so important to her to sort out a decent place for Patrick to stay. Maybe it was because she was trying so hard to prove to both of them that she was determined to be professional in their working relationship. She knew what people would say when they heard she'd taken on an attractive single Aussie who she knew next to nothing about.

She knew what her parents would think, let alone her neighbours. She could see and hear them now. Archie Pendower, Phyllis and Una and Jess Godrevy ... oh shit, Jess, her best mate, was going to put two and two together and make at least a hundred and four. Maisie felt her cheeks growing warm and hated herself. The only way this arrangement was going to work was if it was kept strictly professional despite any previous encounters.

She closed the door to the second studio then opened it again. 'It needs to air, before it has a proper clean,' she said, and before Patrick could give her any backchat, she bulldozed on. 'Look, I need to draw up a contract and check out the references you gave me. Obviously, with the time difference I don't expect to hear from Judy or the other referees you mentioned until morning. However, if you wanted to help out in the bar tomorrow night, to see how we roll here, then that might be a good idea.'

Patrick beamed. 'Great idea.'

'Until then, can you keep yourself out of trouble? You're welcome to make use of the pub kitchen to make some lunch and you can have some peace and quiet in the bistro upstairs. You can bed down up there overnight if I don't get a chance to clean the cottages.'

Patrick saluted. 'Yes, ma'am.'

Maisie pretended not to be amused. 'Just "boss" will be fine. Come on inside, and I'll break the er ... good news to Mum and Dad.'

Chapter 9

You've really gone and done it now, Paddy boy.

Later that afternoon, Patrick closed his laptop in the upstairs bistro and gave himself time to reflect on the crazy, impulsive decision that had led to him signing up for six months at the Driftwood Inn. He'd emailed Judy at the Fingle and the owner of the restaurant where he'd worked previously to warn them he would be staying in the UK over the winter and to expect his new employer to take up references.

He crossed to the window and took in the magnificent view over the channel towards Petroc. With its white sand, flowers and low-lying islands set in a turquoise sea, it could easily be Port Fairy in western Victoria. He'd not expected to find a place in England that so reminded him of home; but then again, the beauty of the place was the least surprising thing about the situation. He'd only been in the country a few days and here he was, staying for half a year.

If he made it that far, of course. If Maisie didn't throw him out first, or he quit in sheer frustration.

Hazel and Ray Samson had been – how could you put it – 'taken aback' when Maisie had delivered the news and introduced him. Ray had shaken his hand warmly and seemed relieved that there would be an extra pair of hands around the place. The guy wasn't well, his face was pale and drawn and he'd been breathless and sweating while he was up on that roof. Hazel was trickier to read. She'd recovered from the initial shock quickly and joked that Maisie hadn't wasted any time in taking on new staff, yet there was something about the way she'd watched him, when she thought he wasn't looking, that made his hackles rise. She didn't trust him: and he didn't blame her. If Hazel had been thinking that Maisie could do with a man, for practical and other purposes, he definitely wasn't the right one in Hazel's eyes. Patrick suspected that they might be bothered about his criminal record.

He could understand their concerns and was prepared to live with Hazel's distrust but there was an even bigger hurdle to get over. Even as she was introducing him to her parents, he suspected Maisie was already kicking herself for giving him the job. Her discomfort radiated from every pore and showed in her tight smile as she introduced him; in the way she stood with her arms wrapped around her chest while her dad shook his hand and her mum made jokes about kangaroos and boomerangs. He had a feeling Maisie Samson was regretting letting him into her home, her business and her life and he didn't think that was entirely down to his chequered past.

So why had she agreed to take him on?

And what bloody stupid idea had made him ask?

Six months he'd signed up for. Half a year at this tiny pub with this determined woman who already occupied his thoughts far too much. He'd never seriously thought she'd say yes to his offer to work for her. He'd been amazed when she'd agreed, even after he'd told her the worst of him: the jail, the drink, the drugs.

And yet a voice nagged at him. Gnawed at him. He still hadn't told her the *very* worst about him, had he? He'd kept back the part that would freak her out. It would have got him thrown out of the pub, and off the island too, if she knew.

'Penny for your thoughts?'

Patrick glanced up to find Hazel Samson standing a few feet away. She'd walked into the bistro from the upstairs flat and was carrying a plastic bucket with cloths and cleaning products.

'They're not worth as much as a penny.'

She gave Patrick a hard stare. Her red hair was greying at the temples and her face was weathered from long years working in the sun, but she still had her daughter's slight frame and sharp green eyes that missed nothing. 'I bet they are,' she said.

He pointed at the laptop, aware the screen was dimmed from lack of recent use. 'I've been letting a few people know I'm staying on.'

Hazel's eyebrows lifted. 'Maisie says you don't have any family?'

Wow. Straight to the point. Maisie had shared at least some of his 'colourful' history with her parents, then. He supposed he shouldn't be surprised as the Samsons were going to have to work and live very closely with him. He didn't mind.

'A cousin I've lost touch with, some distant relatives in the

UK who have probably forgotten I exist. I do have a few mates, though, who might be interested to know I haven't been kidnapped by an irate Brit who took exception to me taking a bar job ... the current climate towards foreigners being what it is.'

Hazel's smile was about as sincere as a croc's. 'I don't think you're in any danger from the locals here on Gull.'

You could have fooled me, thought Patrick, freezing his rocks off under Hazel's sub-zero glare. Winning her trust was going to be harder than he'd thought. 'I wondered if there was no wife or girlfriend in Oz that you had to break the news to. She won't be very happy you've decided to extend your stay here, will she? Don't tell me there's no woman waiting back home? You're still young and not exactly the Hunchback of Notre Dame, now are you?'

'What makes you think it's a woman?'

She smiled for about a nanosecond. 'Call it a wild guess.'

Well, thought Patrick, he had to admire Hazel's directness. Now he knew who Maisie had inherited her feistiness from and perhaps it was better to be honest with each other than enduring months of suspicious looks.

'You don't have to answer if I'm being too nosy, but I look out for our Maisie. She's had enough heartbreak lately,' she added, although Patrick didn't think she gave two hoots whether she was being nosy or not.

'You're right: there's no partner on the scene at the moment,' he said mildly. 'Of either sex.'

'Hmm. I suppose that makes sense, or you wouldn't have come halfway round the world and left her for six months.

Unless you *had* to leave Australia of course, and I doubt that's the case.' Hazel paused. 'As for partners, you said "at the moment". Am I right in thinking there *was* someone special?'

Maisie would cringe at this line of questioning but Patrick couldn't blame Hazel. It was obvious she saw him as a threat to the equilibrium of the household. She might be right about that too, he thought, but perhaps not in the way she suspected.

'You're right. There was a woman, but that was a while ago now.' The image of Tania walking out of the door slid into his mind. He waited for the slice of pain low to the gut but he felt as if he was watching that movie now, not living it. But still, an enigmatic smile was all he was prepared to give Hazel.

She nodded slowly. 'Fine. I should mind my own business, though you'll appreciate I like to know a little about the people who've come to live in our house and share our lives.'

'I don't blame you, though I've already discussed my reasons for wanting the job with Maisie. Your daughter gave me a thorough grilling when she interviewed me,' said Patrick, still wondering exactly which details Maisie had shared with her parents.

'I know she did. I wanted to hear it direct. Oh well, you never know who you might meet while you're here on Gull Island,' she said and flashed him a smile that told him Maisie was off the menu – or else. 'Do you want another coffee or a soft drink?' she asked, nodding at his empty cup.

'Thanks for the offer, but no. I've got some more emails to send before I get ready to learn the ropes in the bar tomorrow night.'

'OK, I'll be getting on with my jobs, then.'

Hazel picked up the bucket and headed downstairs. Patrick waited a moment until the footsteps quietened before padding down to the bar himself. He heard the door to the staffroom open, crept forward and peered around the edge of it. He could see Hazel walking across the patio to the staff studios where Maisie was outside the first cottage with her sleeves rolled up and a pair of Marigolds on. Hazel handed over the bucket and the two women exchanged some words. They had their backs to him so Patrick ventured further into the staffroom. The window was open a crack but he couldn't hear their conversation. He suspected from Hazel's grim expression that it might have been about him.

He almost jumped out of his skin as the phone out in the office next to the staffroom rang out.

Maisie and Hazel immediately turned and Patrick just had time to duck out of sight. Maisie pulled off her rubber gloves before she marched towards the office. Patrick made a hasty exit back into the bar, listening around the door as Maisie answered the phone in a breathless voice. His own heart thumped. That would teach him to eavesdrop, but this was his only chance. He had to hope that Hazel wasn't still in the garden or coming round the side of the pub, although even if she was, he could make up some kind of excuse for being outside.

As quietly as he could, he slipped out of the front door of the bar and made his way around the side of the building to the garden. The bucket was abandoned and Hazel had joined Ray at the top of the garden.

Patrick spotted Maisie through the office window, standing by the desk, talking into the cordless house phone. With one final glance to check the coast was clear, he picked up the cleaning bucket and Marigolds and slipped inside the open studio. The key was on the inside of the door and with a surge of triumph, he closed it behind him and locked himself in.

'Patrick McKinnon. Are you in there?'

Patrick had only cleaned down the washbasin and had just thrust the brush down the toilet, when Maisie called through the front door. Damn. He'd hoped the conversation would have gone on longer than that.

'What are you doing?'

'I was caught short while I was on the patio,' he called. 'I thought you wouldn't mind me using the loo as I'm going to be living here. I won't be long.'

Silence.

'OK. I'll come back when you've finished.'

'I may be a while,' he shouted, trying to sound embarrassed.

More silence. 'Um. Right. Sorry to disturb you. I'll be back in a bit.'

Cruel of him, thought Patrick, but he couldn't stop the broad smile as he squirted bleach down the loo and started to scrub with the brush. He decided he could get away with a jaunty whistle too, and figured he had at least half an hour before Maisie would dare to return, even if she dared at all. It would be long enough to get the shower room into non-toxic condition and most of the kitchenette. He checked his watch, took a cloth and bathroom spray from the bucket ready to wipe down the cistern and seat. Just in time, he remembered not to flush the loo.

Chapter 10

Maisie tapped her foot on the patio. She'd seen a lot while she was managing pubs but asking Patrick McKinnon why he'd spent so long in the loo was possibly one of the most excruciating moments of her career.

'Patrick. Can you please let us know you're OK? We're um … getting slightly concerned about you.'

There was no reply. Maisie was not only worried but seriously pissed off. What the hell had he been doing in the studio for over an hour? She'd tried to peer through the curtains but they'd been drawn tightly. She'd left them closed from earlier but possibly not that tightly closed. Damn, she couldn't remember. It would be getting dark soon. Oh my God, what if Patrick had come to the other side of the world to do something *stupid*? She thought back to their conversation and the one she'd just had with Judy Warner at the Fingle Bar.

She tried the handle of the door again. She'd half tried once before, stopped and decided she didn't want to barge in if Patrick had picked up a bug. Maybe he'd decided to have a shower too or had fallen asleep. Although she had no reason to think he'd done something more unusual or worse than any of those scenarios, she still felt a fluttering of anxiety as she applied more pressure to the handle. It didn't budge and was obviously locked from the inside.

'Patrick. Please open the door. We're worried about you. If you're not feeling well, we can help.'

She put her ear to the door and thought she could hear noises. Muffled thuds, the sound of a loo flushing. Maisie slumped in relief. He was alive then, and hopefully OK.

Maisie fell on top of Patrick as he pulled open the door. He caught her by the tops of the arms and she glanced up into his smiling face. His tanned, cheerful and very healthy face. Her heart raced. Relief flooded through her closely followed by a strong urge to wring his neck.

'Whoa. Be careful,' he said.

She sprang back, away from his chest. Waves of pine-scented disinfectant and furniture polish emanated from the studio.

'What the bloody hell have you been doing?'

Patrick held up a cloth and a bottle of Cif. 'Cleaning.'

'What? I told you not to. I told you I'd get it done. I thought – *we* thought – something had happened to you or you'd been taken ill.'

'Sorry, I didn't hear you after I'd used the loo. I was intent on my work. Would you like to see it?'

He held up his hands in surrender. The Marigolds waggled. 'Caught me – yellow-handed, boss.' He held out his upturned wrists. 'I'll come quietly if you promise not to punish me too harshly …'

Her skin tingled all over and her throat dried. Patrick was wearing a ripped T-shirt that had shrunk in the wash and stretched across his broad chest and flat stomach. The rubber gloves reached just above his wrists, highlighting the golden hair sprinkled over the golden forearms. She was in massive trouble here. All it would take was for her to turn the key behind her again. The curtains were already closed. Her parents had gone shopping on St Mary's and were at least two hours away. It was just her and Patrick and a single bed.

No one would know.

With great effort, she shook away the feelings of lust: she'd only known him two days. Thinking that way was ridiculous. 'I wish you'd do as you're told,' she said.

'And I wish you'd let me help you. That's why you took me on. You've enough to do with the books, and the pub and bistro and God knows what else. Your dad's not too well, you know ...'

'I know that!' She hadn't meant to snap, she was just worried about her dad. 'I know he isn't very well but he won't go to the doctor. I've seen him out of breath and sweating and he's pale and he's lost a stone since the summer. Mum's worried sick and so am I.' Maisie felt her bottom lip trembling. She hadn't cried for so long; not over Keegan leaving her or the loss of Little Scrap, but she felt perilously close now. Teetering on the edge of losing it totally in front of Patrick because of a row over cleaning the studio.

'I'm sorry. I'm just worried about Dad and it's been a long hard season here. I'd forgotten how much there was to do.'

'I'm not trying to add to your worries, but I noticed he was struggling on Saturday and he probably shouldn't have been up there fixing the roof.'

85

'You try stopping him. There's so much needs doing around here, as you pointed out. Dad's a typical male; his leg would have to fall off before he'd go to the doctor and it's not as if he can toddle down the road to the surgery. Mum and I have tried to persuade him. I worry so much about him.'

'He's probably afraid of what he'll find out if he goes, but it could be something that's easy to sort. Either way he needs to make sure.'

Maisie's stomach clenched. 'Tell me about it.'

'Come in and sit down,' he said gently. For a split second, Maisie was reminded of Keegan, in the early days, when she'd first thought he was a rock of a man, not a flaky sandcastle who crumbled with the first rough tide. But Patrick McKinnon wasn't a rock either, she reminded herself: just a drifter with a cleaning fetish.

'I don't need a shoulder to cry on,' she said.

'I'm not offering one.' He smiled. 'You wouldn't want to get too close anyway, I've been hard at work and I need a shower.'

'Not in that health hazard of a bathroom,' she said, sniffing the air: a bit of a chemical factory but definitely clean.

'You could eat your dinner off the floor now,' he said. 'Let me wash my hands and I'll make you a cup of tea.'

Maisie glanced at the kitchen. The units, cooker and fridge were basic and old but clean. The stainless steel sink sparkled and the work surfaces gleamed. She hated showing weakness but she was too weary. Hugo had phoned her again and asked her if she'd had time to think over his plans. It had been all she could do to give him a civil answer. He'd said that more residents were 'seriously thinking' of selling and although he might be bullshitting her, Maisie wasn't sure. She'd felt like telling him to stuff his offer but for a few seconds she'd also felt like caving in and saying, 'Have the bloody place.' If her dad was ill and needed urgent health care, or decided to leave the island, circumstances could look very different.

'It'll have to be black coffee or hot chocolate,' he said, holding up a jar of Nescafé and a tub of Cadbury's Highlights. 'I've inspected the contents for weevils and they look OK, even if the previous occupant was a Neanderthal.'

Maisie laughed. What harm could it do to have a drink with him? And she was really, very relieved that he'd cleaned the place up himself. One less job on her list.

'I'll risk the hot choc, please.'

'Wise choice.' He filled the white plastic kettle and switched it on. Maisie sat down on a rattan chair in front of the single bed. The place had been dusted and had had the Henry Hoover round it, by the looks of the tracks on the carpet. It was *very* basic, but at least it was clean. The cost of getting new furniture – new anything – out to the island meant that things couldn't be thrown away unless absolutely necessary.

As the kettle boiled, Maisie tried to compose herself and let her heightened feelings calm down. Patrick opened the kitchen window and the top light in the bedsitting area to let some fresh air in. He'd also left the door open a crack so there was a route for escape if necessary. If she wanted it.

Patrick handed her a mug of hot chocolate and lifted his own, chipped mug from the rattan table next to her.

'Cheers,' he said, clinking her mug with his. 'Here's to our working relationship.'

Maisie smiled. 'Back at you, and here's to you doing as you're told from now on.'

'Good luck with that.'

His eyes gleamed with mischief. Maisie caught the open door through the corner of her eye. Anything could happen: whether she wanted it to or not. She'd brought this stranger into her family's home and she knew almost nothing of him. Apart from, that is, the word of a woman who was eleven thousand miles away. Except … Judy Warner had seemed genuine. She was obviously a blunt, kind woman who thought the world of Patrick McKinnon and spoke of him like he was her own son.

'I spoke to a friend of yours while you were playing Mrs Mopp,' she said.

Patrick's cup stopped half to his lips. 'Who might that be?'

'Judy at the Fingle.'

'You spoke to Judy while I was in here? It's the early hours in Melbourne.'

'She was just closing up after a late shift when the email came through so she called me.'

'And?'

Maisie enjoyed teasing him.

'She told me on no account to let you cross the threshold and to call the island bobby immediately.'

'Well, I am armed and dangerous.' He nodded at the Marigolds and bucket of cleaning stuff. 'Did I pass muster?'

'She said you hadn't had your hands in the till, or started any brawls – in fact, you were quite handy at stopping them, and, in short, she said, "as long as you keep an eye on him, he'll probably do".' Maisie tried an impression of Judy's accent.

'Keep an eye on me? Judy would never say that, and by the way, you should be shot for that accent. She's not Dame Edna Everage.'

Maisie tried hard not to smile, delighted to have wound him up and shifted the focus back onto him. She wished she hadn't shared her concerns about her dad: that was the problem with this claustrophobic life. It was hard to find anyone to share your troubles with who didn't already know every intimate detail of your life.

Maisie laughed. 'Be warned, I'm going to drop you in at the deep end because we've a very busy evening tomorrow. If you hadn't noticed the posters in the pub already, it's our Hallowe'en Karaoke Party. We should have lots of people from the off-islands – that's the smaller ones like Gull – and you can get to know loads of locals all in one go. They can give me their verdict on your performance.'

'Great,' said Patrick. 'Trial by jury.'

'That won't be a problem, will it?' said Maisie, slapping her mug back on the table. 'After all, it's not as if it's your first time.'

He made a little bow. 'Touché.'

Maisie stood up. 'Oh, and by the way, you'll need a costume and everyone's expected to join in, so I hope you can sing.'

Chapter 11

31 October

On the morning of Hallowe'en, Maisie was waiting at Gull Island's lower jetty when her friend Jess Godrevy puttered in to the stone quay. The tides dictated which of the two jetties were used, but the lower was also the most convenient for Jess who had brought her little motor dinghy from St Saviour's for the day and evening. From this side of the island, you couldn't see Petroc but you did have a magnificent vista over most of the other islands: the four larger inhabited ones and the scores of abandoned isles, tiny islets and rocky skerries that only appeared when the tide was out.

Clouds hung low on the horizon and the sky was a muted blue, as if someone had turned the dimmer switch down on it. However, the waters were as dazzling in their myriad turquoise and azure hues, and the sandbars gleamed silver as the clouds scudded overhead. While most of the UK was savouring its first frost of the autumn, Gull Island was basking in clear skies and double figure temperatures. OK, it wasn't tropical, but it was better than shivering at some bus stop or scraping the ice off your car window.

Maisie stayed on the jetty to help Jess tie up her boat. A couple of islanders chatted as they waited for the Gull Island service boat to arrive with morning deliveries or to take them to the main island for shopping, visits or appointments. Adam Pengelly, the off-island postman, arrived just as Maisie and Jess had secured the boat. He backed his Royal Mail van with its open metal trailer, to the bottom of the slipway and climbed out of the cab. He was wearing a navy fleece gilet over his red polo shirt and regulation shorts that showed off a strong pair of tanned calves. Maisie didn't think she'd ever seen him in trousers.

When he caught sight of them both his face lit up. Maisie didn't have to be a rocket scientist to know why he was smiling.

'Hello, Maisie. Hi, Jess,' said Adam, walking the few yards to the steps and gazing down at them. His smile had faded and they couldn't see his eyes because of his shades.

'Hi, Adam.' Jess flashed him a brief smile. Her greeting was pleasant enough but Maisie wasn't too sure how happy she was to see him. They had recent history but Maisie suspected she only knew part of the story. Adam was a relative newcomer to Scilly and had moved into a rented flat on St Saviour's island a couple of years before.

As one of the only island postmen, inevitably Adam had got to know Jess and her brother, Will, on his rounds, and he'd joined Will's rugby team and rowed for the St Saviour's gig crew. After circling round each other for a while, Adam had finally asked Jess out. They'd dated for a couple of months but by late August, things had fizzled out. Maisie still hadn't got to the bottom of why yet, but as Jess had been moping around ever since, Maisie could only assume Adam had ended things. Until (and unless) Jess enlightened her, she couldn't blame Adam outright, but her loyalty lay firmly with her friend either way. They climbed up the steps and joined Adam on the stone jetty where there was a brief but very awkward silence before Adam spoke.

'Need a hand with the mail?' Maisie asked him, just for something to say.

Adam pushed a pair of dark Ray-Bans off his face and shook his head. 'Thanks, but I can manage today.' He seemed relieved that Maisie had broken the ice.

'Are you sure?' she teased.

'Well, I am feeling a bit weak.' He deliberated for a few seconds. 'But I'll try to cope. There's nothing too heavy today, hopefully.'

This was an in joke with Maisie. Adam was six foot four, spent his days lugging parcels and his spare time playing rugby, rowing or training for the island's part-time fire service. Maisie was five foot one in her boots but whenever they met, they'd share the same banter about Adam being a wimp. The Gull Island supply boat, the *Merlin*, could just be seen making its way from St Mary's towards them, bearing any heavy deliveries and the mail. Adam left them and unhooked the trailer from the van and pushed it onto the damp sand. The *Merlin* crew would help him unload the mail and parcels into his trailer, but it was up to Adam to haul it up the sand to the van. It was hard work. No wonder Adam had muscles like an Olympic rower. If the Royal Mail did a firemen-style calendar, Adam would definitely make Mr January, thought Maisie. And possibly every other month too.

All the more reason not to get involved with an islander, thought Maisie, although that meant either moving away or not getting involved with anyone at all.

Adam was busy loading mail into his van. Jess showed no sign of wanting to leave the quayside so Maisie waited with her, watching the supply boat crew offloading goods into the back of one of the other islander's battered pick-up truck.

Jess and Will ran the Flower Farm on St Saviour's, one of the other off-islands, growing scented yellow narcissi through the winter and spring and pretty pinks for the summer. They were slowly taking over the business from their mother, who, like Maisie's parents, was looking to retire. Maisie, Jess and Will had been to school together on St Mary's and, like all the off-island children, had had to board during the week because the boat journey between the islands was too unreliable and too disruptive to their education. Five years younger than Maisie, Jess had been horribly homesick for the first term but Maisie had taken her under her wing and acted as a big sister.

At the time, Jess and Will's parents had been going through a rocky time in their marriage and although they'd patched things up for a bit, they were now divorced. It was hard to go through rough times in the cauldron of a tiny community. Mr Godrevy had had an affair with a local nurse and people had taken sides, causing broken friendships that persisted to this day.

'I'm really glad you could come over. I fancy a chat,' said Maisie, wondering what Jess's reaction would be when she met Patrick.

'We're so busy harvesting the early narcissi, but Will can manage without me for a day. We've only just started picking the crop and I already need a holiday. Sometimes I wonder why I do it at all.'

'You'd go nuts without the Flower Farm keeping you busy.'

'True. I must admit I can't imagine doing anything else. I'm not so sure about Will though. I think it gets him down. He was all set to go to university before Dad buggered off and left us in charge.'

'That was tough, hun.'

Jess smiled. 'But I love running the farm really, even though it hasn't been all plain sailing. It's relentless at this time of year, or any time. No wonder I don't have time for a love life,' she said. It was such a pointed remark that Maisie didn't know what to reply, even though Jess was a close friend.

Adam closed the doors of the van with a clang. Maisie wasn't sure if he'd overheard them chatting or not. He hovered by the van and finally came back over.

'How's things?' he said in their general direction, but Maisie was sure he was talking to Jess.

She shrugged. 'The same as usual. Busy time at the farm, as you know, Adam.'

Adam nodded. 'You work hard ... you and Will.'

Jess pursed her lips. Maisie wanted the stone to open up and swallow her. She felt like she shouldn't be there but she also wanted to support her mate.

'Shall we get going?' Jess said.

'Sure. Bye, Adam,' Maisie said cheerfully.

'Bye. Goodbye, Jess.'

Jess muttered a 'bye' and started to walk off along the path that led over the field to the pub. It was obvious to Maisie that she didn't want to even share the same road with him. Maisie caught up with her, keeping an eye on Adam's van as it drove off on the road that led to the Post Office.

As they walked along the road back to the Driftwood, Jess seemed to have brightened up, or at least was determined not to discuss or dwell on the awkward encounter with Adam. She shared the latest gossip from St Saviour's – which didn't take long – and news of a new gig, which one of the island teams had managed to get hold of. She and Jess had moved on to plans for Christmas celebrations in the various island communities by the time they reached the hillock above the pub. It was a time of year when many of the islanders who lived away from Scilly came home to see their families. Most people celebrated in their own quiet way with low-key events, and there was a popular nativity parade through the main street of St Mary's.

There would be some visitors too, of course, staying throughout the islands and in the chic apartments and holiday homes on Petroc. They would be booked by families getting away from it all and seeking a little winter warmth. Maisie didn't begrudge Hugo his festive bonanza: God knows his guests spent their money in the Driftwood Inn and bistro and helped keep the islands' economy ticking over.

'I had a visit from Hugo the other day,' Maisie said, knowing Jess would be intrigued.

'How nice for you. Not a social call, was it?'

'No, although you never know with Hugo. He tried to persuade me to sell the Driftwood again.'

'Oh God. He never stops trying, does he? What did he offer this time?'

'The opportunity' – Maisie bracketed her fingers around the word while sticking out her tongue – 'to be a tenant and manage the place.''

'No way! Don't give in, Maisie.'

'Don't worry. Hell will freeze over first. I just wish so much of what he says didn't make sense. We're getting by – just – but Dad's not well and Mum's obviously not up to the long hours and stress that she used to take in her stride. Which is another reason why I came home, aside from the obvious one. With the summer staff leaving and with winter to face, I sometimes wonder why we all do it.'

Jess gave her a sympathetic smile. 'I know. We've been through some tough times at the Flower Farm. Remember those years of frost when we were at school and then the wholesale flower market collapsed? That period almost finished Mum and Dad. They were so close to losing everything and having to leave St Piran's. I don't think Will and I realised how bad things were, but we do now we run the business ... but who could ever leave here to work in a city? You tried it.'

Maisie smiled. 'St Austell's hardly a city, but I worked in London briefly after I'd finished college. It was great for a few months but I couldn't go back now. Mind you, not everyone feels that way. Hugo says that the Fudge Pantry and Una and Phyllis have also agreed to sell to Petroc Holdings.'

Jess grabbed Maisie's arm. She looked horrified. 'You're joking? Una and Phyllis? The Jenkins? I'm gobsmacked.'

'Business hasn't been too great after the summer we had last year and I guess Mr Jenkins wants to try life on the mainland since their kids moved to Truro. There won't be many of us left to resist at this rate. Hugo already owns a couple of properties on Gull and I suppose he could buy the businesses piecemeal, but what he really wants is to make us all lose hope and buy the whole of Gull Island, complete, so he can turn it into a mini Petroc.'

'He's a megalomaniac,' Jess said, curling her lip. 'I'm so glad he's not interested in St Saviour's too.'

'If it was over the water from Petroc, he might be. Gull is just too close to Petroc for comfort. I wouldn't put it past him to try and build a bridge between the two islands if he can get his hands on most of the land.'

'If there's anything Will and I can do, shout up. Help you rally the islanders, dump a pile of manure in Hugo's gardens … anything at all, you know we're here.'

'Thanks, hun,' said Maisie, feeling the thrill of resistance flood her veins. 'Nothing and no one – and definitely not Hugo Scorrier – will hound me out of the Driftwood or off Gull Island.'

They reached the top of the gentle rise as the clouds parted and a weak but very welcome sun shone through. The sun shone bravely. The thermometer hadn't budged between nine p.m. last night and this morning. It was still T-shirt weather outside – if you were active, that is.

Maisie wasn't superstitious but it felt like a good omen,

and Jess's support had renewed her determination to fight the Scorriers. She would visit the Fudge Pantry and Hell Cove House and organise a meeting, but for now, she had more pressing concerns.

The garden behind the pub was clearly visible, as were the people working in it. Jess grabbed Maisie's arm. 'Oh my God. Who is *that*?'

She sounded as if she'd seen a leprechaun working in the garden of the Driftwood, not a fully grown Australian. Patrick and Ray were repairing the wall that separated the vegetable garden at the rear of the pub from the rough farmland behind it.

'Looks like my dad, if I'm not mistaken.'

Jess sighed in exasperation and pointed a finger. 'Not your dad, *him*.'

Both men had their backs to Maisie, standing in the field next to a wheelbarrow and a pile of grey granite. Patrick was bending down to lift a rock from the ground. He placed it in a gap in the wall and repositioned it as Ray looked on. Ray bent down next to him. The contrast was both funny and disturbing. Maisie had no desire to see the waistband of her dad's ancient briefs but Patrick was a different story. His faded jeans had slipped down, revealing half an arse's worth of dark-blue boxers stretched taut over his muscly cheeks. The tan line between his lower back and his bottom was clearly visible.

'Well, you don't see that every day. Who is it? A guest? Friend of your dad's?'

'Neither. That's our new barman.'

Maisie shaded her eyes. Her dad stood aside as Patrick

picked up a heavy rock and dropped it in the barrow with a clunk. Ray wiped his brow with his handkerchief, but made no attempt to help Patrick with the next, even bigger rock. Fair enough, Ray was sixty-seven and Patrick was a full thirty years younger, but there was a time when her father would never have let another man outdo him in the work stakes, even if his back had been breaking.

Jess let out an audible gasp. 'Bloody hell. You're joking. He looks like a Greek god.'

'I wouldn't know. I've never met a Greek god. He's an Aussie, actually.'

'You mean as in a genuine Bondi Beach-type surf dude Aussie?'

'He's from Melbourne. I've no idea if he surfs, but he's experienced.'

Jess squeaked in delight. 'I bet he is!'

'What are you like? He's experienced as a *barman* and his references checked out.'

Jess was grinning so hard Maisie thought her face might actually crack. 'I'm sure they did,' she said, still giggling.

Maisie sighed. If this was Jess's reaction to Patrick from a distance, what would she be like when she experienced the full force of his charms close up? And why did Maisie feel faintly annoyed that Jess had homed in on her new barman so quickly?

Jess broke into her thoughts. 'Your dad must like having him around.'

'Hmm. Yes. He seems to, but he's only here until Easter,' she said.

99

They started walking again, talking while keeping an eye on the progress of the wall. 'If he has your dad's seal of approval, he must be OK. What about your mum?'

'She's reserving judgement,' said Maisie.

Jess sighed. 'What a bum.'

Maisie too found it impossible to tear her eyes away from the flex of Patrick's glutes in his worn Levi's. 'Mmm ...' she said wistfully, before giving herself a mental slap and leading Jess the back way into the pub. It was mild enough to sit outside so Maisie left Jess in the garden admiring the wall-building while she made tea and tried to remind herself that Patrick was here to work. After emerging with two steaming mugs, she and Jess sat there enjoying the view of the garden – and the gardeners.

'And he's leaving in the spring?' Jess said in a low voice.

'Yes. Six-month contract then he goes back home.'

'Pity,' Jess whispered, and sipped her tea delicately.

Maisie allowed her gaze to rest on Patrick, now standing up, facing away from her, while Ray inspected his work. Patrick tilted his head from side to side and then lifted his arms over his head and stretched his back. The muscles shifted under his cotton T-shirt. Maisie shifted in her seat. This was agony, and he'd only been here three days. She hadn't slept much last night, partly worrying about the business but also thinking about Patrick, sleeping a few yards away in his single bed, in his navy boxers, or possibly in no boxers at all ...

'Actually, it will be a relief when he goes,' she murmured.

Jess met Maisie's gaze head on. 'You're not saying that you've already ... he's only been here five minutes, though I can't say I blame you and it's none of my business.'

Patrick looked up. He spotted them and saluted. She had a feeling he knew they were watching him and talking about him.

'Shh!' Maisie groaned. She hadn't told a soul about her passionate beach kiss with Patrick.

'Well, I wouldn't blame you,' Jess repeated, slightly less loudly than a foghorn. 'Where's he staying?'

Maisie paused because she knew what would happen as soon as she shared the information about their household arrangements with Jess. 'In one of the staff studios.'

'On site?'

'Yup. Just like most of the seasonal staff, as you well know.' She despaired at Jess's raised eyebrows and look of sheer disbelief. 'There is nothing going on between us. Nothing beyond employer and employee, Jess. Read my lips. Patrick McKinnon is my – our – barman and I have no intention of getting involved with him in any way. I'm done forever with men like him who fancy themselves as charmers, and besides, I don't want to do anything that might cause an experienced barman and general dogsbody to leave.'

Jess sniggered and sipped her tea significantly.

'Don't you think I can share a house with a colleague without it turning into *Fifty Shades of Grey*?'

'So as you're not interested in Patrick at all, you'd have no problem with me getting to know him better?'

'Why would I?'

Jess snorted and tea sprayed out of her mouth. 'I'm s-so sorry b-but ...'

Maisie was seriously pissed off now. Tea dripped down her

101

jeans. 'You are disgusting, Jess Godrevy. In all kinds of ways; for snorting tea over me and imagining all kinds of filth between me and my new employee. I wish I'd never rescued you from those bullies at school. I wish you weren't my friend.'

Jess wiped her face with a tissue and gave a series of little coughs interspersed with giggles.

'Have you finished or will you continue to be a serious health hazard to this hostelry?' said Maisie.

Jess rearranged her face into something resembling a human and not a hysterical clown. 'Oh, hun. I didn't mean to upset you. God knows you deserve to be happy after Keegan and everything. And I'll admit I'm envious.'

'Of what?'

Jess touched Maisie's arm. 'Of the sexier, older brother of Chris Hemsworth living and working alongside you. Of the way you can't take your eyes off him and the way you keep trying to pretend you're not looking at him. Oh, *hello* ...'

Abandoning further pretence, they both watched the men stand back from the wall to admire their handiwork. Ray lifted his hand and made a tea-drinking sign. Patrick wiped his forehead and grinned. He knew better than to ask for a cuppa. Patrick knew better than to ask her for anything Maisie wasn't prepared to give. She was in the driving seat and anything that happened was her decision. For all his flirty charm on their first meetings, and the fact he'd asked for the job, things between them had been strictly professional since.

'Coming up,' Maisie mouthed and gave her dad the thumbs up.

'Typical men. They do a bit of work and they want a reward,' said Maisie, although she didn't really mean it. She was pleased to see her father enjoying his garden again and he definitely needed the help.

'Like a dog hoping for a chew?' said Jess.

Maisie laughed and hoped the colour in her cheeks hadn't betrayed her. 'Just like that.'

After a brief chat with Patrick and Maisie's parents over their tea, Maisie introduced Jess to Patrick ahead of the party that evening. Maisie waved Jess off when she left to pop in on Katya at the campsite, and Maisie and her mum decorated the pub ready for the Hallowe'en party. Patrick and her father were still in the garden, although Ray spent more time leaning on the wall watching Patrick than helping.

Having adorned the bar with spray-on cobwebs, cardboard pumpkins and bats, Maisie sang along to 'Monster Mash' on Radio Scilly while she made sandwiches and baked some frozen sausage rolls to serve later in the buffet. She found it hard to keep her mind on the job because Jess's mention of Keegan had disturbed her.

'You deserve to be happy after Keegan and everything,' Jess had told her.

Keegan and everything.

Maisie turned the words over in her head. When she'd emerged from the initial stage of grief, she'd consigned Keegan to the bin marked 'life's too short for toxic men', but the 'everything' to which Jess had referred couldn't be dismissed so easily, if ever. The 'everything' was the loss of her unborn baby. She'd thought of him as her little scrap of life and even called him that. Her Little Scrap who'd gone far too soon ...

but it was after the twelve-week scan, and it was a terrible shock.

Bread knife in her hand, Maisie paused and took a deep breath. It was 'just one of those awful things', the doctor had said. There was no reason that they could find. 'Don't blame yourself, my love,' the kind midwife had told her when it was all over.

But the questions and doubts ate away at her and never left. Had she been working too hard? Had she eaten something she shouldn't have? Let herself become too stressed about her job? Stepped on a crack in the pavement? No matter what the medics told her, she *did* blame herself, and a few days after she'd come home and was recovering, Keegan had told her he was leaving. Not because she'd lost his baby, but apparently because he didn't want her to have it in the first place. He'd tried for her sake to pretend he was happy at the prospect of becoming a father but the 'whole trauma' of the past few days and the fact that he no longer owed any real obligations had given him the chance to 'reassess his priorities'.

Just like he did with work when he decided to close down a failing pub, thought Maisie.

She concentrated on slicing a fresh loaf from the Gull Bakery, trying to focus on getting the slices perfectly even, but she couldn't banish her gloomier thoughts from her mind. Hearing voices outside the kitchen window, she glanced up to see Patrick wheeling a barrow full of rubble down the path towards the house. Chips of stone slid off the pile, pinging on the path. Ray was close behind, issuing orders on where to take the rubble and telling Patrick to be careful not to tip the heavy barrow up.

Maisie smiled. Her dad had a little more colour than earlier and obviously loved having someone to boss around and let do the heavy work.

'And I'm not *that* old ...' Maisie said to herself, laughing at her pessimism. Lots of people suffered miscarriages and went on to have healthy babies. One of the customers had three beautiful daughters, all grown up now, after four miscarriages.

It could happen to her ... even though the chances were growing slimmer by the day.

Maisie stared out of the window. Having deposited the rubble, Patrick was pulling off his builder's gloves and had caught her eye. He smiled and raised his hand in a tea-drinking gesture.

'You cheeky—' Her voice was drowned out by the screeching of the smoke alarm. The smell of burning filled her nose. *Oh my God, the sausage rolls!*

Chapter 12

Patrick was used to noisy bars packed with people, but not a tiny pub that was the hub of the community where he was the star attraction. Within half an hour of the Hallowe'en party kicking off, he already felt like a newborn panda at a city zoo.

Michael Jackson's 'Thriller' was belting out over the speakers so that people had to shout above the noise. Patrick would have turned the sound system down but the music was in Ray's hands and he didn't want to interfere.

There was standing room only in the bar. A corner had been cordoned off to create a makeshift stage with a speaker and a microphone, and was festooned with fake cobwebs with rubber bats hanging from the beams. He knew that this was his debut at the Driftwood, and that he was probably as much a part of the entertainment for the evening as any of the 'acts'. He'd braced himself for the fact that being a newcomer in this tiny community would make him an object of interest, but he hadn't quite been prepared for so much attention all in one go.

Ray was dressed as Dracula with Hazel as his bride. Maisie

flitted about the bar in a slinky red 'devil' outfit and black pointy boots, which Patrick was finding a major distraction. She had a red plastic pitchfork behind the bar that she used to prod people at regular intervals.

In desperation, Patrick had decided on a makeshift Zombie outfit, ripping up an old T-shirt and, with the help of some of Hazel's make-up and a YouTube video, had managed a passable impression of a rotting corpse. He wasn't a natural costume-party person but had long become used to joining in themed events at the Fingle. Besides, the outfit gave him a literal and metaphorical mask to hide behind during his baptism of fire behind the bar at the Driftwood.

'Nice costume,' said Maisie briskly, when he'd arrived for work.

'You too,' he replied, trying not to make the comment sound pervy in any way, even though she looked edible in the slinky scarlet Lycra. 'Nice ... um ... horns.'

'Thanks, and may I say, being one of the living dead really suits you,' she'd fired back in return.

They'd barely had a chance to speak since people had started arriving as soon as the doors opened at seven o'clock. Patrick had been surprised at the amount of people willing to venture out across the seas on an October night. However, he'd soon learned that most of the islanders were skilled boatmen and women, used to navigating their way around the seas of Scilly even in the dark and less than ideal conditions. Really bad conditions did keep some of the smaller vessels in port at times, that was inevitable, but fortunately it was a calm evening and no one was going to miss the

Hallowe'en party night – not to mention the added attraction of an exotic new face, even if that face did look like he'd risen fresh from the grave.

Vampires, werewolves, Frankenstein's monsters, witches, ghosts and ghouls piled into the bar. The costumes were largely homemade, some more convincing than others. In minutes, the questions and banter flew at him and he tried to give as good as he got, all the while serving drinks under Maisie's watchful eye. You're on trial, Patrick, mate, he told himself as she shot a sideways glance at him when she was collecting glasses. You always will be with this woman.

He turned his attention to the locals at the bar.

'So are there crocodiles in Melbourne?'

'Nah, mate. That's up in the top end.'

'Snakes and spiders?'

'Both, and most of 'em will kill you.'

'Bet you're not used to this kind of weather, mate.'

'It's balmy here. Melbourne gets four seasons in one day and Sydney has more rain than London.'

'Nice costume. I'd have thought you'd come as a kangaroo.'

'What are you doing on Gull Island?' He'd heard that one a dozen times.

'I got fed up of the crocodiles,' he replied.

He did his best to remember all the names and, despite the costumes, even recognised a few who he'd encountered already on the island.

There was Maisie's friend Jess who was friendly enough but couldn't seem to decide if she wanted to flirt with him or not. She was made up as Morticia Addams but still looked very pretty. A bloke dressed as Frankenstein's monster seemed to have his eagle eye on her. Patrick had learned that he was 'Adam' and was a postman. The monster disguise suited him: he was as big and fit as a Marlee bull and kept staring at Jess and shooting less than friendly looks at Patrick for some reason.

As well as Jess and her bolt-necked admirer, Patrick recognised the middle-aged couple that ran the Fudge Pantry and the white-haired, leathery-skinned Archie Pendower who had an artist's studio on St Piran's. His lady friend was with him, a sharp-eyed pensioner in a long shabby velvet coat. Everyone called her 'Fen' and she reminded Patrick of something out of *Harry Potter*. Archie hadn't bothered with a costume and Patrick wasn't sure if Fen had or not.

Javid the campsite owner, aka Grim Reaper, wandered in before the Open Mic sessions, accompanied by Katya, who was back from a temporary teaching post abroad and planned on staying on Gull over the winter.

The entertainment started. There were singers of both sexes and all abilities, plus a very well-fed skeleton doing impressions of politicians and celebrities – not that badly either. Archie sang a sea shanty in a quavery baritone that made the hairs on the back of Patrick's neck stand on end.

In the interval, Jess's brother, Will, arrived with their mother. Even given Will's werewolf costume and make-up, the family resemblance was obvious and they handed a large bunch of yellow narcissi to Hazel Samson who greeted them with a warm embrace before taking the flowers up to the flat.

Halfway through the night, a striking forty-something

woman in a dog collar, cowboy boots and flashing devil's horns walked in to the bar, carrying a pug. A man got up, said, 'How lovely to see you, vicar,' and greeted her like an old friend. The pug yapped when anyone approached, so the vicar, who Patrick discovered was known as Rev Bev and recently posted to Scilly, soothed it with dog treats and kisses.

As he served an endless stream of people, Patrick added the names of unfamiliar customers to his mental list, trying to remember faces, names and jobs. There were boatmen, airport workers, ferry operators, shopkeepers, nature wardens, hoteliers, waiters, farmers, fishermen and smallholders from Gull and the other isles. Some of them had two or three jobs, which added to his confusion. Those who hadn't introduced themselves might be holidaymakers, although he doubted it. Anyone who was in the pub either lived on Gull or had their own boat, or a mate with a boat, because there were no ferries in the dark evenings.

Maisie and Jess produced sandwiches, a new batch of unburned sausage rolls and pickles and the customers fell on them like gulls round a herring boat. Glasses were refilled and the second half began. Somebody produced a banjo and Adam the postman, Will Godrevy and a few of their mates belted out some local folk tunes. By the end of their set, everyone joined in.

A chorus of voices, few of them in tune but all of them enthusiastic, shook the Driftwood Inn to the rafters. Patrick's arms ached from building walls and pulling pints and his jaw ached from smiling. Over the past few weeks while he'd been travelling from Australia via the Far East to London and down to Scilly, he'd forgotten how hard bar work was, and how much he loved it. Doing a real job, losing himself in the crowd, serving other people helped him to avoid having time to think and dwell on other things.

Jess's admirer, Adam, was watching him like a hawk as he served another glass of wine to her. She'd relaxed a little now and stayed next to the bar, asking Patrick about his life in Australia while he worked. Turned out she'd done some grape picking in Victoria after she'd left university and seemed happy to have someone to share her reminiscences with. Patrick had no problem spending time with her but was all too aware of Adam and the other locals keeping an eye on him. He was also aware she was Maisie's friend, and that he was very new in town and on trial in more ways than one. There was being sociable to your boss's attractive best friend and then there was flirting and Patrick wanted to stay the right side of the line.

'Will you be doing a turn later?' Jess asked as a zombie juggler received a warm round of applause. Will began to set up the backing track for 'Someone Like You' by Adele ready for a woman who worked in the tourist info centre.

'Only if I'm forced,' said Patrick. 'We don't want any broken windows.'

'Oh come on, you can't be that bad.'

'Wait and see ... what can I get you, officer?'

Patrick took a J2O from the chiller for the island policeman who was still in semi-uniform, though not on official business apparently. While he opened the bottle he caught Jess glancing at Adam with a wistful look on her face. Adam returned the glance briefly and then pointedly turned his back. Jesus, what was wrong with the guy?

Jess bit her lip. 'I'm going into the back to help Hazel and Maisie with the buffet,' she said. Her eyes looked suspiciously bright to Patrick but he wasn't going to go there. He had enough trouble keeping his own love life – or lack of it – from becoming complicated and he was sure to hear the gossip about Adam and Jess sooner or later, whether he wanted to or not. In fact, he'd learned long ago that see no evil, hear no evil and definitely speak no evil was often the best policy for a barman, as long as no laws were being broken, or only minor ones, and as long as no one was being physically harmed.

A man, about Patrick's own age, strolled up to the bar. He wore a waxed jacket, cords and brogues like he'd stepped out of a country estate and his blond hair was damp with rain and sea spray. A black Labrador trotted in after him and stood next to him, gazing up at Patrick through soulful eyes. Faces turned towards man and dog and a few people nodded but most immediately turned back to their own conversations.

He appeared to have forgotten it was Hallowe'en.

'Pint of the usual,' he barked while scrolling through his phone.

'The usual?' Patrick echoed. 'I'm afraid you'll have to help me out, mate. I'm new here.'

'I know that but I thought Maisie might have briefed you on the regulars' tastes.'

'Not all of them,' Patrick replied pleasantly.

'I'm a Rat & Ferret man,' said the man. 'I'm Hugo Scorrier by the way.'

'Pleased to meet you,' said Patrick, feeling anything but.

'Basil. Come on.'

The dog looked at Hugo briefly, wagged his tail then ran off to sniff Archie Pendower's trousers. Archie patted him but Hugo shot his hound an angry look.

'Don't let him bother you,' he said.

'He isn't,' said Archie.

Patrick went outside to the storage shed behind the pub to restock with more bottled lagers and soft drinks because even the cellar had run dry. He wedged open the door and picked up a crate but stopped short of stepping outside when he heard Maisie and Hugo Scorrier talking on the patio. They weren't arguing but Maisie sounded agitated while Hugo's tone was as smooth as butter. Patrick put down the crate carefully, feeling guilty for lurking in the shadows but needing to hear what was said.

'I'm not here to spy or act like the villain,' Hugo said.

'I wish I believed you.' Maisie sounded exasperated and he didn't blame her.

'Now, that's not fair. You've known me since we were children,' Hugo replied in a hurt tone.

Patrick peered round the door where Hugo and Maisie were highlighted by the lights spilling out from the pub kitchen. Hugo was smoking and the tip of his cigarette glowed in the dark.

Hugo put his hand on her arm. Maisie moved away. Patrick tensed.

'Let's not discuss this now. I'm here to enjoy a relaxed evening off.'

'And I'm working,' said Maisie. 'I have to go inside.'

Patrick told himself he shouldn't be listening and that the

exchange wasn't any business of his. Maisie didn't need a knight in shining armour, and she wouldn't thank him for interfering, *but* if Hugo Scorrier touched her again, and didn't take the hint, Patrick would step in, no matter how pissed off Maisie might be.

Maisie hurried back into the kitchen. Patrick waited, watching Hugo inhale and blow out a long plume of smoke. Patrick could smell it from the outhouse. He picked up the crate, put it on the path outside and locked the door behind him, making as much noise as he could before marching past Hugo with the bottles.

'Busy night,' said Hugo, blowing smoke just as Patrick walked past.

'It is,' said Patrick, trying not to cough as the acrid smell filled his nose.

'Just as well. This place needs all the help it can get, no matter what Maisie might have led you to believe.'

Patrick rattled his bottles and pretended not to hear. 'Sorry, mate? Didn't catch that.'

Patrick and Hugo were face to face, under the light from the back door. Smoke curled up between them. Hugo did a double take, as if Patrick had suddenly sprouted a comedy wart on the tip of his nose. The hairs on the back of Patrick's neck stood on end but he smiled, as the heavy crate strained his arm and shoulder muscles. He felt Hugo's contempt for him with every breath the bloke took.

Hugo smiled. 'I'd better let you get back to your duties.' He dropped the fag end on the patio in front of Patrick and crushed it under his boot. '*Mate*.'

114

Chapter 13

For some reason, Maisie had expected Patrick to be able to belt out a tune as good as any of the locals but *ouch*. He really was terrible. So awful, it was actually funny.

An embarrassed silence settled over the pub as he warbled out the first few bars of the song, and regulars exchanged grimaces over their pints. Maisie cringed as Patrick soldiered on. He was out of tune, off key and had to keep humming when he forgot the words but boy, he was giving it his all, and acting as if he was Frank Sinatra which made his performance all the more hilarious.

'Myyyyyy wayyyyyyeee!' he howled.

People started to laugh and egg him on. Will wolf-whistled and Patrick threw out his arms and waved a glass cloth like Pavarotti.

The inn descended into uproar. Maisie stopped wincing and started smiling. Patrick was obviously enjoying himself and the regulars were wiping tears from their eyes. She raised her glass of water at him in tribute as he bellowed out the chorus at the top of his voice.

'My wayyyyy!'

Tears ran down her face and she knew her mascara would be a mess. Although his singing was laughable, she also admired him for having a go. Finally, the song finished and the customers burst into applause. Will whooped and whistled and even Adam Pengelly gave him the slow handclap.

'Sounded like a cat was being strangled,' muttered Archie as the hubbub subsided.

'Well it is a full moon,' said Will.

The police officer shook his head. 'I think I may have to arrest you for crimes against popular music.'

Patrick gave a deep bow. 'I'm here all winter, folks, apart from the O2 next weekend. It's sold out, but if anyone wants tickets, I can get you a back-stage pass.'

'Only if you're paying us, mate,' Will roared. He slapped Patrick on the back. 'Little piece of advice: don't give up the day job.'

Maisie shook her head, relieved that Patrick had survived his baptism of fire and secretly a little bit proud of him. Jess leaned over the bar, a sly smirk on her face. 'Well, he won't win the *X Factor*, although I have to say I've heard *almost* as bad on there. But he's definitely a big hit with the customers.'

'So it seems.'

'He'll bring more people into the Driftwood,' said Jess. 'Of both sexes.'

'Good. We need the money,' said Maisie, refusing to rise to the bait as Patrick made his way back to his post behind the bar through a barrage of banter and good-natured insults.

'It's not only the money, though, is it? You like having him around. You were worried when he started to sing – sorry – howl.'

'Worried? Why would I be worried?'

'In case he was upset by the reaction. I saw your face. You were holding your breath.'

'The only thing that bothered me is that he might empty the place in ten seconds flat. There's a buffet going to waste.'

Jess smirked. 'You're in denial about the hunky Patrick and you refuse to admit it.'

'Just like you and Adam Pengelly, then?'

Jess pursed her lips. 'That's below the belt, *best* friend.'

Maisie touched her arm. 'I know. Sorry to put my oar in there. I don't know what's going on between the two of you but I don't like seeing you unhappy about it. Or Postman Pat, either.'

Jess rolled her eyes. 'Let's just forget it for tonight. I'm here to enjoy myself and I don't want to talk about Adam. He obviously thinks I've done something wrong, and if he wants to act like a hurt schoolboy, that's his problem. He's always been moody and I can't handle that kind of drama right now. We've enough on our plate managing the business since Dad left. I'm not sure Mum's ever really got over him running off with "that young floozy", as she calls her, though she tries to pretend she's OK.'

Maisie gave Jess a quick hug. Roger Godrevy had caused shockwaves when he'd left the Flower Farm to live with a woman younger than Jess after a twenty-four-year marriage to her mother, Anna. Will and Jess had had to take over the business much sooner than they'd anticipated.

'I agree. The last thing you need in your life right now is more drama. You really don't know what's wrong with Adam?'

'No ... I haven't a clue,' said Jess. 'Look, Patrick's even a hit with Will.'

Jess inclined her head towards Patrick who was pulling a pint for Will who was leaning on the bar, laughing at some joke.

'Hmm, they seem to be getting on. I don't mind. Anything that makes Will laugh. He always acts like he's the life and soul of the party but I know him better. There's something not right with him and it's not just the stress of the business. Anyone would think he and Patrick had known each other for years.'

'Yes, they would,' said Maisie, struck by the sight of Patrick at ease behind her bar and Will and his mates exchanging banter. It could be just a blokey thing. She thought women took longer to let their guard down with new people; she did, anyway. Then again, Patrick did already seem like part of the furniture. That was a good thing, wasn't it? She'd needed someone who could slot into the Driftwood seamlessly. However, it was slightly disturbing just *how* perfectly he'd fitted in, almost as if he'd been born on the isles. It was only when he opened his mouth and you heard his accent that you were reminded that Patrick McKinnon was a very exotic cuckoo in the nest.

Chapter 14

Now that his karaoke ordeal was over and he'd survived his baptism of fire with the locals, Patrick relaxed and threw himself wholeheartedly into his new job. Although the environment, prices and drinks were very different, the skill of serving drinks swiftly and accurately, while keeping up a cheery stream of banter, had come back to him sooner than he'd expected.

The entertainment had ended but a dozen or so punters lingered in the bar, getting in their last rounds before closing time. Patrick went to change the keg of lager in the cellar and as he was about to climb up the steep steps, he heard a shriek from the kitchen.

He took the steps two at a time and found Hazel in the kitchen doorway. Her face was as white as a sheet and she grabbed him by the arm.

'Patrick. It's Ray. He's collapsed!'

'Collapsed? My God.'

Patrick hurried after her into the kitchen, and his stomach lurched when she saw Ray flat out on the tiles. His deathly pallor had nothing to do with the white make-up that was running down his face as sweat poured out of him. Patrick's first thought was that he looked like Greg had at the end, and his second thought was for Maisie.

'D-don't f-fuss,' Ray ground out. The effort of speaking made him fight even harder for breath.

Her tattered veil hanging down her neck, Hazel knelt next to Ray, clutching his hand tightly. 'Shut up, you silly old bugger, and let us take care of you.'

Patrick crouched down beside her. 'Do as you're told for once, mate,' he said, patting Ray's hand.

'I'll get Maisie, but I'll call an ambulance first,' said Patrick, digging his mobile from his pocket. 'Jesus, what happens here when you need an ambulance?'

'There's a medical boat. Hand me the phone and I'll call the ambulance. You find Maisie and see if any of the first responders are in the bar. Javid was here earlier.'

'OK.' Patrick leapt up, ready to rush into the bar.

'Patrick!'

Hazel clutched his hand. It was bizarre to see her face plastered in white make-up and her lips outlined in blood-red lipstick. Her voice quavered. 'Try not to worry our Maisie too much.'

Wondering how he could possibly not worry Maisie when her beloved dad was gasping on the floor, Patrick walked quickly into the bar, trying to keep a cool head for everyone's sake. He'd seen plenty of emergencies in his time as a barman and called out the paramedics numerous times, but this was different. Ray looked bloody awful and Patrick suspected he was having a heart attack. How was anyone going to help him out here? It was way more isolated than the middle of Melbourne where sophisticated medical care was minutes away. They might need a helicopter for Ray, *if* it could even land in the dark, and by the time it got here and got him to the island hospital or mainland it could be too late.

Patrick scanned the faces for Maisie. By now, people had realised something was amiss but Patrick focused on finding her, just saying to people that Ray had been taken ill.

Adam grabbed his arm as he passed. 'She went upstairs with Jess. What's up with Ray?'

'Don't know, but he needs medical care and fast.'

Adam's green painted face fell. 'Shit. Can I do anything?'

'Hazel said there might some of the first responders in here? Can you send them to Ray?'

'I'm on it.'

'Thanks.'

Leaving Adam to find the first responders, Patrick ran upstairs and found Jess and Maisie walking out of Maisie's bedsit. Patrick spoke to them as calmly as he could.

'Maisie. Don't panic, but can you come downstairs now? Your dad's not too well.'

Maisie frowned. 'Not well? What do you mean?'

'He's conscious but he's collapsed on the kitchen floor. Your mum is with him.'

Maisie's hands flew to her mouth. 'Collapsed? Oh my God. I knew something like this would happen.'

'It's OK,' Patrick said as soothingly as he could. 'Help's on its way. The island first responders are coming and a call's already being logged on the mainland.' He felt he was floundering and saying the first thing that came into his head, but he had to try and keep Maisie calm somehow.

Jess slipped her arm round Maisie as she seemed to stagger a little.

'Oh Jesus, I knew he was worse than he was letting on. I bet he's had a heart attack.'

'We don't know that. He's breathing and talking. Your mum said try not to worry,' said Patrick.

'How can I do that?'

Maisie dashed for the stairs, her horns falling off.

'Be careful, hun!' Jess held up her long skirt and hobbled after her with Patrick bringing up the rear. Christ, he'd only been here a few days and he'd jinxed the bar owner. He'd no wish to see another good bloke die in front of him. As he followed Maisie and Jess through the packed bar and a sea of anxious faces, he forced himself to calm down. The Samsons needed him to stay calm now and there was no point him caving in.

Hazel was trying to care for Ray as best she could, keeping him calm while Jess looked after Maisie whose face was grey with anxiety. Ray kept mumbling about 'not making a fuss' while being told in return to shut up and lie quietly. Patrick returned to the bar to try and soothe the locals before waiting outside for the first responders, who arrived in a Land Rover ten minutes later.

They were already kitted out in green paramedic uniforms and carrying equipment. They looked familiar and turned out to be Javid and the vicar, who had only been gone an hour. Jesus, thought Patrick, I hope Ray doesn't think she's come to give him the last rites.

'Where is he?' Javid asked as they entered the bar through a gaggle of locals who'd already gathered outside to allow the responders a clear path.

'Kitchen floor,' said Patrick and showed them through, rapidly revising his concerns about there being no emergency cover on the island. He was amazed by how professional the responders were. Javid and the vicar checked Ray's pulse and blood pressure and after talking to their colleagues on St Mary's decided to strap him into a chair. The upshot was they didn't think he'd had a heart attack but he obviously needed medical help and fast.

'What happens next?' he asked Jess quietly as Maisie and Hazel tried to reassure Ray, who was looking slightly brighter and breathing more easily.

'They'll take him to the ambulance boat and he'll be assessed in the hospital on St Mary's or airlifted to the mainland if necessary. Poor Maisie and Hazel, what a worry.'

'He's not looked well for days.'

'He's not been well for weeks,' said Jess. 'It's a good job you've been doing the heavy work tonight or it could have been even worse. Whatever's wrong with him, he won't go to the GP.'

'I don't blame the bloke. I hate the docs too.'

'I still say Ray's a silly old sod,' said Jess, shaking her head but looking almost as worried as Maisie did.

'Maybe he's afraid he's got something they can't do anything about,' said Patrick. 'I can understand that.' He thought of Greg.

'Don't say that to Maisie,' Jess murmured as Ray was made comfortable.

'I wouldn't dream of it.'

'Looks like you'll have to hold the fort tonight, with the Samsons all off to the hospital,' she said.

'Fine by me.'

Ray was carried through the pub and the hushed customers, who cleared a path for him. Jess hugged Maisie and said she'd stay the night in the pub, if Maisie wanted.

'Thanks, hun, but you can't do anything. Patrick – I'm sorry but you'll have to take over here. I'll phone as soon as I can.'

'I'll be fine. I've nowhere to run if I do go off with the takings,' he joked.

She flashed him a weak smile. If she was worried about just such a thing, she had no choice but to trust him. 'Thanks.'

'Take care. I hope your dad's better soon.'

He wasn't sure if Maisie heard him as she climbed into the front of the Land Rover while Hazel sat with Ray. Patrick and Jess waited outside with some of the customers until the bright yellow ambulance boat rounded the headland in front of the pub, its lights gleaming on the dark sea. It was a short journey to St Mary's and the hospital but Patrick was still very concerned about the Samsons. Although she'd been putting on a brave face in front of her parents, Maisie must be out of her mind with worry.

Patrick shivered in the damp night air. Even though it wasn't raining, the atmosphere was heavy with moisture.

Nothing we can do now.

Poor old Ray.

Poor Maisie and Hazel.

'He's in good hands.'

The voices rang in his ears when he walked back across the terrace and into the inn. The pub was still busy, but the evening festivities were naturally well and truly over. Most people were shrugging on coats and preparing to go back to their cottages, St Mary's or the other off-islands on their boats. Despite his protests, Jess and Will went into the kitchen to help put away the food and load the dishwasher. Patrick followed them to offer a hand but they seemed to know what they were doing so he left them to it and went back to the bar to clear the tables and lock up.

The bar area was empty except for Hugo Scorrier.

'Hello again. We haven't been introduced properly yet. Patrick McKinnon, isn't it?' he said, holding out his hand. Patrick was nonplussed. It was hardly a time for formalities but he shook Hugo's hand briefly.

Hugo was more polite than he had been when ordering his drink. 'Good job you're here to help out the family right when they need it,' he said.

'Sheer luck, mate,' said Patrick. 'I'll do what I can.' Patrick started collecting glasses. To his amazement, Hugo picked up a tray and started doing the same.

'No need for that,' Patrick said cheerfully, wishing Hugo would leave. He wanted to get on, not make chit-chat, and take a few moments to collect his thoughts after he'd locked up. Ray's collapse had shaken him more than he'd expected and he hoped to God the guy would pull through and that it wasn't anything too serious.

'Ray looked in a bad way,' said Hugo helpfully.

With his back to Hugo, Patrick cursed and carried a tray to the counter. He knew Ray took medication as he'd seen the pills in the kitchen, but a lot of people his age did. Perhaps his collapse was due to something unpleasant but not life threatening, something like indigestion.

Hugo put a tray of glasses and dirty plates on the bar counter. 'Let's hope it's nothing life threatening.'

'Thanks,' said Patrick.

Hugo smiled. 'Anything to help.'

Patrick restrained himself from telling Hugo that if he really wanted to help the Samsons, he'd stop harassing them to sell.

Patrick turned away to gather more glasses but Hugo obviously wasn't going to take the hint and go home.

'I must admit I was surprised when I heard Maisie had taken on a new member of staff for the winter,' he said.

'Why's that then?' replied Patrick.

Hugo clutched pint jugs with the dregs sloshing about in the bottom. 'I wouldn't have thought there was enough work to keep a full-time member of staff employed over the quiet season. Tonight's about as busy as this place gets. Place is closed three days a week, apart from Christmas and New Year.'

'Maisie wouldn't have taken me on unless it was worth her while,' said Patrick. Suddenly, the penny dropped and he guessed exactly what the bloke was up to, and it was about more than just the Driftwood. So Hugo had designs on Maisie and thought Patrick was a rival for her affections? Patrick smiled to himself. From what he could see, Maisie didn't do 'affectionate'. 'And besides,' he added with a sly grin, 'she's keeping me busy in other ways.'

Hugo smirked. 'I'm sure she is. Formidable woman is Maisie.'

'She is that. I wouldn't want to get on the wrong side of her.'

'No ... although then again, that could be rather interesting.'

Jesus, thought Patrick. If Maisie heard them talking like that about her ... Patrick decided the conversation had to come to an end. It was disrespectful to Maisie and descending into dodgy areas. He was about to tell Hugo he wanted to lock up when Hugo piped up again.

'You're from Melbourne, then?' he said, handing a couple of wine glasses to Patrick.

Patrick took them off him with a forced smile. 'You'd be right there.'

'Wonderful city. I know it a little. I have business associates there.'

'Really?' said Patrick, thinking how much Hugo reminded him of the persistent flies that sometimes plagued the bush in the hotter months.

'Hmm. Vibrant place. I've only been once but I'd love to go back and explore the place in more depth. Perhaps I'll go this winter and get away from Scilly. It's a small community and it can become very claustrophobic, as you've probably already realised. Nothing stays a secret for long here.'

'Just as well I don't have any secrets then,' said Patrick, depositing the last of the dirty glasses on the bar.

Hugo retrieved a stray pewter tankard from the window ledge and handed it to Patrick. 'Everyone has secrets.'

'Not me. I'm the most boring bloke on the planet. What

you see is what you get. Anyway, thanks for your help, mate. I appreciate it, but if you don't mind, I'd like to lock up now and phone Maisie to see how Ray is.'

Hugo smiled. 'Of course. If there's anything I can do to help in the meantime, don't hesitate to ask. I'll text Maisie myself in the morning when we'll hopefully have more news.' Hugo looked around the pub with a shake of the head and a sigh. 'Whatever the outcome, judging by the state that Ray's in, *if* he recovers of course, the Samsons are going to need your help more than ever to keep this place going.'

'Then let's hope Ray does get better,' said Patrick, disliking Hugo more by the second. 'And I'm not going anywhere soon.'

'They're lucky to have you. Goodnight. Tell Maisie I'll be in touch and send my good wishes to Ray. It'd be a tragedy if the Driftwood lost him now.'

Patrick let Hugo out and locked the door behind him, thinking what a tosser the bloke was: creeping round Maisie, hassling the Samsons and barely concealing his delight that more pressure had been heaped on the family.

He checked his phone but there was no message from Maisie. He didn't expect it yet: the ambulance had probably only just reached the hospital on St Mary's or maybe the paramedics had already decided Ray would need to be airlifted to the mainland. Patrick hoped not. His stomach turned over with concern but worrying would help no one. He joined Jess and Will and told them to head home over the hum of the dishwasher and glass washer.

He saw them off via the rear door and went back into the pub. It was bizarre to think he'd only been here a few days and already had been left in sole charge of the place. God forbid there was a fire this evening, he thought, looking around the sturdy old building. It would be just his luck if something disastrous happened on his watch.

Then he told himself not to be so stupid and set about washing up the remaining crockery and glasses that he hadn't been able to slot inside the dishwasher. Steam rose into the air and suds soaked his arms as he stood at the sink, trying and failing to banish the image of Maisie's drawn and anxious face as she'd knelt by her dad's side. Ray's Dracula cloak, used as a temporary pillow, lay crumpled on the chair nearby. Patrick scrubbed at a plate, trying to scrub away the memories of Greg lying in bed when he'd been ill.

He'd tried for much of his early life not to become emotionally attached to anyone. After his parents died, he'd spent his life constructing a shell around himself. He'd been reluctantly taken in by his cousin, who'd made it clear she was merely going through the motions out of duty and had no real emotional connection to him at all. At boarding school and later on the streets and in prison, that hard outer-shell had protected him. Or he thought it had, until finally the years of pretending not to give a toss about anyone or anything had caught up with him.

After he'd been introduced to Greg, and started work as a pot washer, he'd tried it on a few times, coming in late – and drunk – and giving Greg and Judy backchat constantly. Time and again, they'd given him another chance until one day Patrick had had a blazing row with Greg. Instead of chucking him out, as Greg should have done – as Patrick himself would have done these days if he'd been managing a layabout member of staff – Greg had taken him aside and said, 'What's making you hurt so badly, son?'

And Patrick had been stopped dead in his tracks. He remembered the moment clearly when instead of a string of expletives and curses, a great big girly sob had erupted. That was the lowest point, or rather the start of the upward turn of his life. Things hadn't run smoothly but slowly and steadily he'd pulled his act together, got himself sober and knuckled down. To become a model citizen ... well, not quite, thought Patrick with a smile as he finished the glasses. Eventually Judy and Greg had helped him find a decent place to live, promoted him to barman, and become his surrogate parents. Inch by inch, day by day, he'd grown to care for them and love them as he might have done his own mother and father if they'd survived. So it had hit him hard when he'd found out Greg was terminally ill. He felt as if he'd lost his father twice over and the pain had been sharp.

Patrick looked down. The water was barely lukewarm and his fingers were wrinkled. He thought of Maisie pacing up and down a hospital corridor waiting for news. Jesus, he didn't want her to go through that. But like everyone else on Gull, all he could do now was wait.

Chapter 15

1 November

It was all Maisie could do to drag herself out of the cabin of the Gull Island supply boat and onto the jetty late the next morning. Most unusually, she accepted a hand from boat to quayside from the boatman, but she didn't care. She was absolutely exhausted and she didn't mind who knew. One of the nurses at the hospital had lent her a coat, which she'd buttoned up over her costume.

How weird, she thought, to be dressed as a she-devil at ten in the morning. Not that she cared about that either. All that mattered was her father. Hazel had stayed with Ray in St Mary's hospital. Thankfully he hadn't suffered a heart attack. They were running more tests but the doctors had told her it was likely he could have pernicious anaemia.

She was surprised to find Patrick waiting for her at the jetty. He wore a new IOS sweatshirt that he must have purchased in the Isles of Scilly shop on St Mary's, jeans and his flip-flops, which he insisted on calling thongs. Even in her fraught state, the sight of him made her pulse beat a little faster. He stirred up physical feelings as powerful as any in the early days with Keegan.

She threw him a weary but grateful smile. As she drew closer she had the feeling he was going to put his arm around her or hug her but at the last moment he shoved his hands in his jeans pockets.

'How's Ray doing?' he asked the moment she reached him.

'A lot better for being in professional hands. They think it's pernicious anaemia.'

'Sounds nasty. What's that?'

'It's when your body can't absorb enough B12. It can make you feel very tired and even cause chest pains. Apparently his uncle also had it and family history can make you more prone. Poor Dad must have been suffering in silence for quite a while but at least they can treat it with injections and he'll be well looked after from now on.'

Patrick let out a sigh of relief. 'That's something to be thankful for.'

'Yes. It is.' Maisie was so tired, she could manage only a few syllables.

She walked beside Patrick along the track to the pub.

'You look like you were run over by a bus,' he said.

Secretly, Maisie was glad he hadn't offered sympathy because in her wrung-out, exhausted state she might have done something stupid like burst into tears. She was fragile enough as it was. Her stomach rumbled loudly and she was in dire need of a change of clothes and a shower, but she was too tired and hungry to bother.

'Bacon and eggs do?' said Patrick, following her down the path at the side of the inn.

Her stomach gurgled again. 'Sorry. Is it that obvious I'm ravenous? I've lived on machine coffee and packets of Cheddars since yesterday teatime.'

Patrick quickened his step. 'I'll join you, I'm hungry myself and I haven't slept much either.'

'Thanks for holding the fort.'

'It's what you hired me for.' He opened the back door and ushered her into the kitchen. 'Now sit down. I'll put the kettle on and get a fry-up going.'

Maisie sank into the carver chair at the kitchen table and looked around her in wonder while Patrick started breakfast. Her gritty eyes took in the gleaming stainless worktops, and the pots, pans and equipment all neatly stowed in their correct places. The table had been scrubbed and it looked as if the windows had had a much needed polish too. Maybe he really did have a cleaning fetish.

The aroma of frying bacon and the sizzle of eggs hitting the pan made her mouth water. Patrick sliced up thick hunks of granary bread and popped them under the grill alongside some tomatoes. He placed a fresh block of creamy butter on the table and a steaming mug of tea.

'I've put sugar in it. It'll do you good.'

Maisie sipped it. It was too hot, but boy it tasted better than the finest champagne.

'This must be what having a fairy godmother is like,' Maisie couldn't help commenting as Patrick slid fried eggs onto two plates next to some bacon rashers.

133

'You're no Cinders though.'

'And you're no Prince Charming.'

'Thanks for the breakfast, Patrick,' he said sarcastically, but she knew he wasn't really offended. He pointed his fork at her plate. 'Dig in before it goes cold and the clock strikes midnight.'

'Why? Do you turn into a rat?' she said, cutting up her bacon. Her appetite was back now as the tension and worry of the night had eased a little. It was nice to come home and find someone waiting and ready to wait on her. She didn't need a man but it was good to have a smiling face, however cheeky, and one that didn't seem to mind cooking a fry-up either.

His mouth quirked in a smile. 'Something like that.'

He rescued the toast and tomatoes from the grill and added them to a large plate in the centre of the table. While they tucked in, Maisie told Patrick more about her father's possible diagnosis and what was likely to happen next.

'They think the anaemia may be related to the medication he's been taking for long-term digestive problems. His stomach upsets were caused by the stress of running this place, which is one of the reasons I decided to come home earlier this year,' she said. 'But the doctors want to rule out other causes too.' Maisie felt her own stomach tighten again but she forced herself to calm down. 'Anyway, let's hope it's nothing more sinister and once it's confirmed, the GP can treat him with injections and monitor him.'

'He's going to have to take things easy for a while though,' said Patrick.

'Yes ...' Maisie tried to think positive. At least her father had been well taken care of and was in the best hands now. If he'd been taken ill while up on the roof of the pub, or out walking on his own, she didn't want to think about what might have happened.

Patrick topped up their mugs of tea from the family teapot.

'How did you get on after we left last night?' she asked. 'I was worried whether you'd be OK with having to chuck everyone out and lock up on your own.'

'No problems. Apart from having to break up the mass brawl that is and tidy up after the fight with the bar stools ...'

'What! Who was fighting? Adam Pengelly, I bet. My God, Jess never mentioned that ...' Her voice tailed off. Patrick's broad shoulders were shaking and he was spluttering. He turned round, wiping the tears from his eyes.

'You total git,' she cried. 'Winding me up like that after the night I've had.'

'I'm sorry. I couldn't resist it. I just wanted to bring a smile to your face.' He turned back to the table but Maisie batted him on the arm. 'Ow, that hurt.'

'You deserve it,' she said. 'You asked for it.'

'Sorry.' He was trying and failing to rearrange his face into a sombre expression. 'I like to see you laugh.'

Maisie opened her mouth to throw back a riposte but the smart reply died on her lips. Patrick was looking at her seriously again, only this time, his expression was genuine. His eyes were full of something she'd only imagined before, but now it was unmistakeable: desire.

He was barely a foot away. She heard him breathing deeply; and felt her heart pound.

135

'Maisie ...' he murmured. 'I—'

She jumped on him. God knows what got into her but she was in his arms, her hands around his waist, bunching his T-shirt in her fingers, digging her fingers into his back. She was kissing him too, pushing against him before she even realised that he wasn't pushing back and that his hands were at her waist but lightly, carefully. She'd gone for him like a tigress on heat, he was holding her like a fragile bird.

She pulled away, sick with shame. 'Oh God, what was I thinking. I'm sorry. I must be out of my mind.'

'No. You're not. You're wrung out, worried, you've had no sleep.'

'That's no excuse for going for you like that. I'm sorry, forget it.'

He lifted his hand to her cheek. She snatched it away like it was a hot coal. 'I was out of order. You work for me. My God, you've only worked here a few days. Please forget this happened.'

'It's not that I don't find you attractive. You know I bloody do, but now isn't ...'

Maisie forced a laugh to hide her embarrassment. 'Thanks for the compliment but you're right. I'm not myself. I can't be to have ... done that.' She rubbed her hands over her eyes exaggeratedly as if to wipe sleep away but in reality tears were burning for release. 'I need some sleep. Thanks for the breakfast. I need to get to bed.'

She hurried to the door but Patrick called after her.

'Maisie. Don't go off like this.'

Though burning to get away, she turned round. 'I'm grateful

for your help. We all are, Mum and Dad too, but please, can you just get on with your job now? We need to open tonight. I'll be down later as long as Dad's OK.'

Maisie half sprinted out of the kitchen and up the stairs. Tears ran down her face as she opened the door of her room and slammed it behind her, locking the door.

How could she have been so stupid as to misread the signals from Patrick?

She'd thought he wanted her when he'd only been concerned. She was furious with herself for letting her guard down, being vulnerable, and technically she'd sexually harassed an employee. It had never happened before. She'd always come down strongly on any staff who bullied or harassed their fellow workers. Just because Patrick was a man didn't mean that the normal rules didn't apply.

And yet she'd thought he wanted her. The way he'd looked at her. That was desire, wasn't it?

It's not that I don't find you attractive. You know I bloody do, but now isn't the time … His words made her cringe. She pulled the pillow over her face and let out a muffled howl of shame and indignation. Was she that desperate and lonely that she'd imagined the first decent bloke who walked into her life had designs on her? She thought about how Patrick had behaved the night before. He flirted with everyone, male and female, in his own way. With Jess a little bit, with the locals and customers. She wasn't special, but she was his employer.

It was never going to be the right time for her and Patrick and she could never let anything like that happen again.

She could never let anyone get as close as Keegan had, especially not a man who'd actually signed in writing that he was leaving in April. From now on, she and Patrick McKinnon would be colleagues and nothing more.

Maisie's phone buzzed from the bedside table. She threw the pillow on the floor and her pulse rocketed. It was probably her mother from the hospital.

She grabbed at her phone. Oh no. Hugo Scorrier. She should ignore it, she really should, but she couldn't help herself. She opened the text.

'Heard your father's having tests.'

How had Hugo found out about the tests? Bloody island grapevine.

'Chin up.'

Chin up? What was this? 1943?

'He's in good hands. If there's anything I can do, you know where I am. I'm on your side, Maisie. H.'

So. Her dad was in hospital, she'd made a pass at Patrick and been rejected and Hugo was on her side. And just think, eight weeks from today, it would be New Year's Eve and her fortieth birthday and then things would really start to go downhill.

Chapter 16

Later that day, Maisie carried a large box of sweet treats from the Fudge Pantry into the kitchen. She put it with other gifts from the locals including several golden bunches of narcissi and garden flowers that had been delivered by hand or by boat since she'd woken up. A homemade sponge in a tin was next to a bottle of homemade damson gin from Una and Phyllis. It was comforting to know that their friends and neighbours were thinking about them and the sight of the gifts gathered together brought a tear to her eye again.

Despite her churning state of mind, exhaustion had eventually taken its toll after breakfast and she'd fallen asleep on the bed in her clothes. By the time she'd woken and had a quick shower, it was early afternoon. She found Patrick tidying away the tools after he'd been working in the garden. Still embarrassed after her pass at him earlier, she gave him the briefest of instructions about the evening opening schedule and scooted off as fast as she could. If he'd wanted to discuss her lunge at him, she hadn't even given him the chance and had almost run out of the garden, saying that Jess Godrevy was waiting for her at the jetty to give her a lift to St Mary's.

Thank heaven for Jess who tried to reassure her about her dad and distract her with gossip about Will and his latest 'fan', one of the seasonal workers who'd come to help with the pre-Christmas harvest.

'Of course, Will's not interested because this woman works for us and he doesn't want to put everyone in an awkward spot,' Jess said, shouting above the noise of the engine and the slap of the waves on the hull. The wind had got up as they bounced over the waves on the lagoon between Gull and St Mary's. Maisie and Jess huddled in the shelter of the wheel-house cabin. The wipers flapped frantically, clearing the salty spray from the motorboat's windscreen.

Maisie tried to focus on her friend's chat but she was torn between how she'd find her father and her blunder with Patrick, and then she was annoyed with herself for not thinking about her father solely.

'Does Will fancy her?'

'I don't know. She's very pretty and in her late twenties and doing a gap year after her PhD. She's quite posh, really, and she's definitely crazy about Will but I don't think he's inter-ested. We're both thirty-five in February and there's still no sign of either of us "settling down". Mum despairs of us, to be honest.'

Maisie didn't know why Jess and Will weren't happily settled down either. The twins were both very attractive, with dark, thick unruly hair and green eyes. Their breezy personalities too had gone a long way to making the Flower Farm a success and hiding their worries at having to take over the business so young.

Will had also started at the island school on the same day as his sister, but he hadn't suffered with homesickness like Jess, at least as far as Maisie could remember. It was a long time ago although she seemed to recall that Will had seemed glad to get away from the Flower Farm. When you were twelve, even St Mary's used to seem big after life on a tiny off-island and Maisie knew that the atmosphere at home had affected both of the twins in different ways.

They reached the harbour at St Mary's and puttered onto the shore in the boat's tiny RIB. Maisie had managed to calm down ready to present a cheerful face to her parents. Jess went to buy some food while Maisie headed for the hospital.

With the help of some injections, her father was looking much brighter, his colour was returning and he was joking with the nurses. They were hoping to discharge him the next morning, with luck, and he could see his GP for the results of the tests.

After reassurance from her parents, Maisie had felt able to return to the Driftwood by late afternoon on the Gull Island ferry. It was already dark by the time she walked through the back door of the pub. Patrick asked after Ray, and Maisie replied as politely and pleasantly as she could, hoping they could both pretend the earlier incident hadn't happened. She needn't have worried. He was as friendly and cheerful as ever, but obviously as keen to forget the whole thing as her.

Now she was back doing what she did best: her job. If there was anything positive to be taken from her horrible past twenty-four hours, it was that the Driftwood was busier than it had ever been on a damp November evening. Almost every

141

Gull Islander had turned up since opening time, even Naomi Savage from the tiny cottage next to the church who, as far as Maisie knew, hadn't been in the Inn since Maisie had left to work on the mainland so many years before.

Maisie was almost hoarse from telling the tale, answering concerned enquiries and thanking people for offers of help. People hadn't only flocked to the Driftwood for the latest news on Ray, they'd come to support the Samsons in their hour of need, and she was grateful.

'Busy again tonight,' said Patrick as they met briefly in the passageway between kitchen and cellar.

'Everyone wants to see how we're getting on. This is one of the biggest things that's happened on Gull for months.'

He rolled his eyes. 'I know how it is in a small community.'

'I wouldn't have thought Melbourne was a small community. I heard it was bigger than Birmingham now.'

'It is, but I've lived and worked in tight-knit places too, and then there was boarding school. And prison of course.' He gave a wry smile. 'Still. Can't stand here gossiping, I'll get that bar restocked, shall I, boss?'

Ignoring the 'boss' comment, Maisie nodded. She desperately wanted things to return to normal between them, although she'd barely had time to discover what normal was with Patrick. Perhaps there would never be a 'normal' while he was here. Perhaps she should never have agreed that he could work there in the first place and in fact, she still wasn't entirely convinced by his reasons for ending up on their tiny patch of earth in the middle of the Atlantic. She'd love to know more about him but was worried any attempts at personal probing would look like she was trying to chat him up.

Gradually the bar quietened down as people went back to their homes, satisfied to have heard first-hand how Ray was and to have shown their support.

Maisie started to collect glasses but was waylaid by Archie Pendower, sitting in his favourite corner chair, nursing a pint.

'Now you've got a moment, I want to show you something,' he said, tapping a large canvas bag by his side. The square shape was a dead giveaway.

'Oh, you didn't need to do that, Archie.'

'I don't *need* to do anything, my dear, but I wanted you and your mum and dad to have this.' Archie pulled the canvas from the bag. It wasn't that large, about twelve inches square, but the subject was instantly recognisable. It was the view from the top of the little hill behind the pub, looking down on the Driftwood, with its gardens behind and the Petroc channel in front.

'Wow, that's beautiful. I've never seen a painting of the pub from that angle before. Are you sure it's for us? Let me pay you for it.'

'Now, don't insult me, madam,' Archie chided. 'It's a get-well gift for Ray.'

The old man propped the edge of the canvas on the table as Maisie leaned down for a closer look. Behind her she could hear approving noises as customers also admired the picture.

The colours were perfect: the Driftwood on a balmy autumn afternoon in mellow light. Cornflower blue sky, shades of green and turquoise in the sea and the off-white walls of the pub basking under the slowly sinking sun. And the detail ... just enough to give the picture life and soul without overcrowding it.

'Recognise anyone?' Archie said, proudly.

Maisie peered closer at the figures. There were two in the garden behind the pub. Although small, one was obviously her dad with his iron-grey hair and bottle-green overalls, digging the potato patch. Hazel Samson was by his side, in her favourite mustard sweater, holding a watering can.

'That's Mum and Dad.'

Archie winked. 'Of course.'

Maisie turned her attention to the bustling scene on the terrace where Archie had painted people lolling in shirtsleeves in the sun, drinking pints.

'Wow, is that me?' she said, spotting the small figure with a tray of drinks, chatting to a group of kayakers by the entrance to the terrace.

'Yes,' said Archie as customers crowded around the picture for a better look. Some murmured as they thought they'd spotted themselves.

'And Will and Jess ...' She pointed to two figures carrying armfuls of narcissi at the edge of the picture. 'And Adam ...' Maisie looked harder, recognising the island regulars Archie had captured with a few deft strokes and choice features. It reminded her of how much she loved her parents – and friends – and how awful it would be to lose any of them.

'The painting's not meant to be a photograph of one moment in time. It's my impression of the Driftwood and how I feel about it ... Why? Don't you like it, love?'

'Of course I like it. It's wonderful. I love it.' Maisie smacked a kiss on his papery cheek, acutely conscious that a dozen faces were focused on her and the painting. 'I can't wait to show it to Mum and Dad when they're back. You're so lovely to let us have it.'

'It's only one of my daubs, love. It's not the *Mona Lisa*. It won't be worth anything.'

Maisie laughed at the typical Archie bluntness. 'It's priceless to me, and I know Mum and Dad will feel the same. Thanks.'

Archie rubbed his hands together. 'Good. Now we've got that over with, you can get Crocodile Dundee to pull me a nice pint of Guinness if he can manage it.'

'Is someone taking my name in vain?'

Patrick became visible at the rear of the group as people went back to their seats and pints.

'It's a very fine picture,' he said. 'If an Aussie can be allowed to have an opinion.'

Archie's eyes twinkled mischievously. 'Of course you can. I'm not one of those Brits who think the only difference between yoghurt and an Australian is that the yoghurt has some culture.'

Maisie rolled her eyes but Patrick laughed.

'I'll take it up to the flat ready for when Mum and Dad get home,' she said.

'Maybe Crocodile Dundee here can help you hang it,' he suggested.

'I might be too busy wrangling crocs,' Patrick said good-humouredly as Maisie allowed herself a little smirk at Archie's nickname for him. It was sure to stick with the other regulars and Patrick would never hear the last of it.

'Thanks again,' she said. 'Mum and Dad will be touched and hopefully they can thank you themselves soon.'

Maisie took the painting upstairs, grateful to have an excuse for a few moments to herself. She propped it up against the back of the sofa in her parents' sitting room so that it would be almost the first thing that greeted them when they walked through the door. She sat on the chair opposite and took the chance to check her phone again, to make sure there was no news, good or bad. There was a text from her mum, telling her that she was staying over with a friend on St Mary's while her father had another night's rest and waited for some more test results. If all was well in the morning, they'd probably be home for lunch.

Maisie took a few deep breaths of relief, rested her head on the back of the sofa and closed her eyes. Pernicious anaemia wasn't a good thing to have, obviously, but her father could be treated for it and at least any underlying problems – and his general health – were now being taken care of.

She woke – God knows how much later – but the first thing that struck her was that someone had covered her in a coat and that the flat, and the whole building, was almost silent. Almost silent apart from someone speaking. She could only catch snatches of conversation, and from one side, naturally, but it was obvious that it was Patrick talking to someone. The clock showed it was past one a.m. and her pulse fluttered momentarily as she wondered if something was wrong with her father and the hospital had called the landline. Then she realised that Patrick was laughing and that while everyone was tucked up in their beds on Scilly, it was a busy sunny morning on the other side of the world.

Maisie pulled off the coat and stretched her stiff neck and limbs. Patrick must have covered her up. Damn, she hadn't meant to doze off and let him clear away and lock up ... She got up and went onto the landing. His voice was clearer to her now and she stopped to listen, kidding herself she didn't want to interrupt his conversation but feeling a guilty fascination at this illicit peek into his other life.

'I'm fine. No, they haven't driven me nuts yet. They're not a bad bunch ... for Poms, naturally.'

'She's OK. A fair boss, from what I can see so far. Not sure what she thinks of me but you'd like her.'

'What? Shit. Why are they writing to me at the Fingle? I told them I needed time. I haven't made my mind up yet. No. Don't forward it ... why can't they email? Jesus. Why not? It's the twenty-first century.'

By the sound of his footsteps on the flagstones, he was pacing up and down.

'I'll email and phone them when I can. Don't worry, Judy, you've enough on your plate without dealing with this. I'll sort it. Right. It's past my bedtime here so I'd better get some shut-eye.' A pause then he laughed again. 'No. It's my day off soon. She won't be cracking the whip over me then. I might hit the bright lights of the big island ... What? Er, no, it's not quite like the Gold Coast. Speak soon ... love you too.'

There was a brief moment of quiet then footsteps, the chink of glasses and the sound of the dishwasher firing up. Finally Maisie heard the back door shut and the house was left in silence.

Maisie went back to the sitting room to turn off the lights before she went to bed properly, wondering if she could sleep.

She picked the coat off the carpet and uncovered a white A4 envelope that must have slid off the coffee table or arm of the chair when she got up to listen to Patrick.

It was addressed to her and had been delivered by hand. She'd open it in the morning although from the stiff card inside, it looked like an invitation ... Changing her mind, she slid her finger under the flap and pulled out a piece of paper folded in two.

And wished she hadn't bothered. It was from Hugo.

Dear Maisie,

You are invited to Scorrier House to view Scorrier Holdings' exciting new plans to make The Petroc Resort & Estate a global destination. Join us for a sumptuous champagne afternoon tea and a tour of the grounds while discovering how our latest development opportunities can benefit you and your business ...

Nada, nada, nada.

Maisie's name was scrawled in by hand – by Hugo, Maisie thought – and at the bottom he'd added:

Hope you can come. NO pressure. Do bring your parents if they're up to it – I didn't want to include them in the current circs. H x ☺

H? x? A smiley?

Maisie dropped the invite onto the sofa in horror. Hugo doing a smiley and a kiss. Was it a tactic or did he actually fancy her?

Groaning, Maisie covered her face with her hands. She was deluding herself. First assuming Patrick fancied her and now Hugo, when in reality neither of them saw her as anything more than a soon-to-be-middle-aged pub landlady who needed careful handling. And her mum and dad would definitely freak out at the prospect of afternoon tea and soft soap from Hugo.

Maisie picked up the invite again and took it with her into her bedroom. She didn't want her parents coming home to a shock like that. It might be enough to finish her dad off.

Not really, she thought, as she brushed her teeth viciously – trying to brush Hugo away – but she'd let them settle in at home again before she mentioned it. And she wouldn't show them Hugo's note at all.

Chapter 17

Maisie made it to well over a week before she found her resolve to not fancy Patrick weakening. It had wavered on several occasions over the past ten days but this morning it was seriously crumbling.

No matter how hard she tried, she couldn't help admiring his rear view as he set a match to the bundle of firelighters and wood in the hearth. It was the second week in November and the nights and days were growing chilly so Patrick had volunteered to light the fire. The flames crackled as they licked the wood. Patrick had fetched it from the woodstore earlier that day and then chopped some more to replenish it. The pops and hisses and the sweet tang of wood smoke reminded Maisie of her childhood at the Driftwood and she knew the fire would cheer her dad up. Ray had been home from hospital for a week now and was looking and feeling much better, although being driven mad at having to rest.

If lusting over Patrick in a pair of faded Levi's was a crime, then she was going down for a long time, but things were looking up. Her dad was doing well and it looked as if she'd hired a popular barman just at the time the Driftwood needed it most. Now, if she could avoid making a fool of herself again with Patrick, they might all get through the winter in one piece.

Patrick straightened up, rubbing his palms on his jeans. Maisie shot back to tidying menus, a little too late. He caught her eye and smiled.

'That should cheer the place up a bit. It's so dark.' He grimaced.

'Missing Melbourne?'

'The sunny skies, yes, but there are other attractions here.'

Maisie was unsure if he was flirting with her nor not. Considering he'd pushed her away after she'd got back from the hospital, she couldn't see why he would encourage her now. 'I'll be cracking the whip over you extra hard now that Dad can't lend a hand,' she said briskly.

Patrick arched an eyebrow. 'And that's meant to be a threat, is it?'

A glow touched Maisie's cheeks that had nothing to do with the fire he'd just laid. She hadn't meant her remark to be an innuendo.

Ray walked into the bar. 'I love a good blaze.' He bent down in front of it and prodded it with the poker. 'Hmm. Not how I'd have done it but it's alight I suppose. That's the most important thing.'

Maisie winced at her dad's bluntness but was secretly relieved that he'd interrupted her and Patrick. What was going on with Patrick? Warning her off one minute and flirting the next?

'It's no trouble,' said Patrick mildly.

Ray dropped another stick of wood on the fire and poked it again.

'You're supposed to be taking it easy, Dad.'

He eased himself off his knees. 'I'm not an invalid, love. I'm being well looked after by the docs and I feel a hundred times better. You're as bad as your mother. She'd have me tucked under a blanket and wheeled round the island in a bath chair if she had her way.'

As Ray stood back to admire his handiwork, Maisie and Patrick exchanged glances. She rolled her eyes and Patrick nodded, his mouth curving upwards in amusement. Despite her gentle warning to her father, Maisie was finally starting to relax a little and worry about him a little less. His tests had shown nothing sinister and his treatment was making a big difference. He'd been sent home with a warning to take plenty of gentle exercise but to avoid heavy work in the garden, so no wall building or roof-tile mending.

He and Hazel had also been back to the GP and the hospital, journeys that required more planning than simply jumping in a car or popping down the road to the health centre. So Maisie had been on her own more often. At least for practical purposes, she was glad she'd taken Patrick on. She actually had to smile when she remembered his words to Judy on the phone. She *did* crack the whip ... which reminded her again of Patrick's joke.

In danger of betraying herself with another blush, she gave her dad a peck on the cheek. 'Fancy a cuppa, Dad? Patrick can carry on getting ready to open up, *if* he doesn't mind,' she added.

'No problem,' said Patrick evenly.

She looped her arm through her father's and could see he was taken aback by this unexpected display of affection. 'Come on then, Dad. Come into the kitchen. I want to talk to you about some of the Christmas events.'

'Sounds good. None of that herbal or decaff rubbish that your mum wants me to try though. Tastes like the shavings off my shed floor.'

'I'll make you a builder's brew and I can even find you some chocolate digestives,' said Maisie. 'But don't tell Mum.'

That evening's curry night was quiet due to heavy seas and high winds keeping anyone from the off-islands in port, but a dozen locals turned up and stayed on, mainly wanting to talk to Ray now that he was on the mend. Hazel whipped up a lamb balti and a veggie korma in the kitchen and people ate it in the bar area, soaking it up with hunks of naan bread.

Ray joined the regulars for a couple of hours before heading up to the flat for a 'cocoa and an early night'. Maisie could see he was tired and glad to get to bed, even though he'd put on a good show. He was still unwell, she reminded herself, and it was early days in his treatment, no matter how much of a brave face he put on.

The next morning, Maisie was up early, sitting in the bistro with her laptop. With its airy views over the Petroc channel, she preferred it to the office. She'd been surfing the web to see what the other Scilly pubs and eateries were planning for the festive season. Hugo's invitation was nagging at the back of her mind but she'd decided to accept it, if only to see what

153

her 'enemy' had in mind and who else might attend the meeting. Outside, the mist had rolled in and it was a dark and gloomy morning, but the thought of seeing the Christmas lights in Hugh Town and decorating the inn had lifted her mood no end.

She and her parents had already decided they wouldn't open on Christmas Day but the pub would be holding some Christmas lunches and a 'turkey and tinsel' night if there was demand in the run-up to the big day. Ray had come up with the idea for a festive quiz, and then there was New Year's Eve, of course.

Ah. New Year's Eve. The biggest event in the whole Gull calendar and her 'special birthday'. Yippee. Jess had asked her if she'd like to go out for lunch at her favourite restaurant on St Mary's in the daytime before the Driftwood New Year's Eve party. She had to admit, being taken out for a lunch would be a lovely change. At least she'd be working that evening so the latter half of the day would just be another normal day for her, only even busier, with the Driftwood the centre of the celebrations. She decided to ask her father to choose and order in some fireworks. It was a job he'd always done and could carry out without doing himself any harm.

Would Patrick want to go home to see Judy and her family? He must have originally planned to be in Melbourne for the holiday. Maisie wasn't sure if she wanted him to leave or not. She'd started to rely on his help and support more than she'd care to admit.

Anyway, back to the task in hand. She scrolled through half a dozen island websites, looking for ideas for Christmas events at the pub. There were fancy-dress parties, festive menus, Christmas craft fairs ... they all sound great *but* ... outside of the tourist season, the Driftwood's catchment was always going to be limited. She'd really have loved to come up with an original idea for a seasonal event that could stretch from day into the evening. That way they could tempt other off-islanders and even a few day-trippers to the pub. There were still a few people who flew to Scilly for birding, storm watching and a break from the festive craziness of the mainland.

Footsteps on the stairs from the bar below startled her, then Patrick appeared, in jeans and a chunky jumper.

'Morning,' he said. Maisie was surprised to see him around because it was officially his day off. He was sporting a couple of days' stubble and his dark honey hair was damp and tousled. Maisie's fingers clenched under the table at the sight of him.

'Hello. What are you doing up so early on your day off?'

'I needed some more cleaning stuff for the Piggery. Your mum keeps it up here so I thought I'd help myself, if that's OK?'

'Sure ... Patrick, forgive me if this is a personal remark, but do you have some kind of cleaning fetish?' She couldn't resist it.

He feigned a hurt expression. 'Of course I have a cleaning fetish. I like to dance around the Piggery naked wearing only a pair of Marigolds when I'm on my own.'

The image of Patrick jigging around without any clothes on was burned into her brain. She tried to scroll through the page in front of her but the cursor whizzed all over the screen under her shaky fingers.

Instead of collecting his cleaning supplies from the storeroom at the back of the bistro, Patrick joined her at the laptop. 'You're working early too. I'd have thought you'd want a lie-in after the curry night.'

'I'm trying to come up with some ideas for a Christmas event that's a bit different to the usual. At the St Austell pub, Christmas started in October, and I never had time to enjoy any of it, but strangely I feel full of enthusiasm here.' He smelled of citrusy shower gel or body spray. Nothing posh, but the scent was doing potent things to Maisie's senses.

'Melbourne's almost as bad as the UK. It's a huge commercial opportunity and everyone cashes in, especially with the cricket season falling at the same time. I couldn't wait for it to be over, to be honest.'

'I never got home to Gull until the second week of January and I felt that the moment had passed by then. It wasn't the same. Don't get me wrong, I loved the customers at the big pub, the regulars and the tourists – mostly. That's how I was promoted to manager. Because I seemed to be good at dealing with the difficult people. Maybe I gave too much to that job. I think I loved it too much.'

Patrick took a seat opposite her. 'What do you mean, you loved your job too much?'

'I sometimes wish I hadn't worked so hard. You know what it's like running the bar. You get promoted, take on more shifts, end up covering for people and before you know it, it's your life.'

'This is your life too. Running this place really is a labour of love,' he said, waving a hand at the bistro.

'Yes, but it's my place. I'm not slaving away for someone else, wasting my time and killing myself for their profits.'

'Was the workload why you decided to come home?'

'Partly. It was also partly to help Mum and Dad out. And as you've seen, I made the right decision.' She hesitated.

She wasn't ready to tell Patrick about Keegan and the baby yet, if ever. It was one of the few secrets she had left. While some of the other islanders knew she'd split from her partner, only her parents and Jess and Will knew about the baby. Of course, it was a small world and the staff and a few customers at her previous pub knew what had happened. People did travel to and from the mainland all the time so news might have travelled with them, but Maisie didn't think so. Losing Little Scrap had been a private thing. Maisie hadn't wanted to talk about it with anyone but her closest family and friends.

She realised Patrick was waiting patiently for her continue and perhaps reveal more. She felt a compulsion to be honest with him and tell him everything or maybe like most good bar staff, he was just a good listener. 'You might as well know there was a man involved. We split up. He also happened to be my boss.'

Patrick winced. 'Ouch. When was this?'

'New Year – can't believe it was so many months ago ... it's flown by.'

'Any regrets?'

'No. Not about leaving him.' She blew out a breath, already feeling she'd revealed too much and picked at an old wound that had almost healed. 'Let's talk about now and all your bright ideas for Christmas at the Driftwood.'

'*My* bright ideas? How has the Christmas schedule suddenly become my problem?'

'Because I have absolutely no clue what I'm going to do. I'm already behind with the planning. Some of the bars have had their events up on their websites for months.'

'Good for them. I don't like planning too far ahead. Decisions made off the cuff can be the best ones.' There was a twinkle in Patrick's eye as he said the words that left Maisie in no doubt that he was referring to him taking the job at the inn – or possibly their kiss on the beach.

'There's only so much we can organise in a small community. Only so many people to join in, but on the other hand, any gathering of islanders is a welcome relief in these long, dark nights. All ideas welcome.'

Patrick scratched his chin. 'Hmm. This is an idea I've had for a few days but you might think it's way off the mark. I suppose we could have an Australian evening.'

'Australian? What do you mean?'

'The usual stuff we'd have at the Fingle. A barbie with kangaroo steaks followed by a cricket tournament and a good punch-up afterwards.'

Maisie rolled her eyes. 'Ha bloody ha. Mind you the kangaroo steaks and barbecue sound promising.'

Patrick wrinkled his nose. 'Not keen on 'roo personally, but we *could* have a barbecue if it's not blowing a gale and an Aussie Rules tournament might go down well with the rugby crew.'

'You know, that's not a half-bad idea. I could get in some decent Aussie wines from the wholesaler. If there is such a thing as a decent Aussie wine, of course.'

Patrick smirked. 'You'll be lucky. We only send the crap over here.'

'Don't be such a snob,' said Maisie, and a wicked mood came over her. 'Christmas Down Under: the more I think about it, the more inspired an idea it is. Gull will never have seen anything like it. In fact, Scilly won't have seen anything like it.'

'Now wait a minute. I wasn't offering to organise the whole thing ...'

Maisie flashed him a grin. 'Too late. I'd like the details by the end of tomorrow, if you don't mind, and I'll leave you in sole charge of sorting it. Thanks, Patrick. That'll be sure to have the Driftwood rocking. I'll put up some posters round the island and get it on the websites and local media.'

'I guess I've dropped myself in it. I'll mention it to Will and the guys when I see them later.'

'You're meeting Will?'

'Yes. He's asked me to try out for the rugby team. I played Aussie Rules at boarding school and a bit of rugby union, but that was a few years back. I'm very rusty.'

'Even if you had a wooden leg, an eye patch and a parrot, they'd still take you. In fact, they'd even take me on if I'd do it. They're desperate.'

Patrick laughed. 'They must be to invite me. Will says they have to play eleven a side sometimes. Adam Pengelly's team have the same problem, but since the league has only the two teams, they have a gentleman's agreement depending on who each team can muster.'

Maisie raised an eyebrow. 'Gentlemen? Are you sure we're talking about the Pirates and Corsairs here?'

He smiled. 'Practice starts at four and there's a curry night at the Harbour Inn afterwards, so I'll be late home. Javid's giving me a lift in his boat.'

'Try not to get arrested.'

'Don't worry, I've been there and done that.'

Maisie smiled and then had another idea.

'I'll see you later then ...' said Patrick as if he'd seen her hesitate and thought she wanted him gone.

'Yes, but ... wait a minute. I'd like to ask you something.'

He frowned. 'Sounds serious.'

'It is ... sort of ... or it may turn into a farce. Would you like to come with me to Hugo's meeting? It's about his plans for expanding his resort but in reality I think it's an opportunity to show us how wonderful and powerful Scorrier Holdings is, and that resistance is futile.'

Patrick hesitated. Maisie guessed she'd made a mistake. Why had she asked him? Because she wanted a bit of moral support and she didn't want to bother her parents ... but he looked as happy as if he'd been invited to a wake.

'You really want me there?' he said.

'No. Yes. No, it was a terrible idea. It's none of your business, I mean it would be boring for you ...'

'I can come if you like,' he said. 'If you think I'd be any use.'

'I just wanted ...' She decided to be honest: 'I wanted someone else with me who's got no axe to grind. I'd like to know what you think about his proposals, give me an impartial opinion and also you might stop me from shouting at Hugo or causing a scene.'

'I don't think you'd do that and I hardly know the bloke, but I agree, he does get people's backs up. What about Ray and Hazel? Won't they want to go.'

'I don't think they've got wind of it yet, though it won't be long and I know Dad has a doctor's appointment on the Main Island that day. I'll speak to Mum on the quiet. It might be better if Dad doesn't go because it will only send his blood pressure rocketing.'

'OK. I'm happy to join you if you want a minder.'

'A minder?' She laughed. 'I can handle Hugo myself, but I'll introduce you as that, cause a bit of gossip.'

'I'm sure me turning up will cause gossip, whatever you introduce me as. I'm happy to do that.'

'Thanks.'

'A pleasure. See you later.'

Patrick collected his bleach and loo rolls and left her, and although it pained to admit it, he also left an emptiness behind him. She didn't begrudge him his day off but she couldn't help thinking how good it would have been to spend the day with him herself. Maybe going for a walk, or a swim in her favourite haunts and afterwards ...

She glanced at the screen again but realised she had no interest in the Christmas festivities any more. All she could think of was Patrick joining the rugby team, being invited on a boys' curry night and scrounging lifts on islanders' boats. He had settled in very well, very quickly.

Maisie got up and stared out of the window. A short while later, Patrick, now wearing a waterproof jacket, strolled down the side of the pub and along the road towards the jetty. He was whistling a tune that Maisie recognised but couldn't place. She caught herself smiling. He could whistle a hundred times better than he could sing, that was for sure, and she felt pleased that he would be by her side at the meeting. It was comforting to know that she had at least one ally when she faced the might of Scorrier Holdings.

Chapter 18

By the time Ray heard about Hugo's meeting, it was too late for him to change his doctor's appointment. It was a miracle he hadn't found out about it already. Ray wasn't as upset as Maisie had thought about missing it, which could be a sign that he still wasn't feeling as feisty as he once had been. He agreed that Maisie should go with Patrick, and report back.

Maisie piloted the *Puffin* the short hop to Petroc Island and they tied up at the jetty. It was a few minutes' walk from there to Scorrier House, where Hugo lived alone apart from Basil, a housekeeper and a team of gardeners who kept the extensive grounds in tip-top condition.

Maisie already knew the way to Scorrier House – you could hardly miss its Gothic tower rising above a stand of trees in the centre of the island – but just in case, neat signs pinned to posts along the track guided the way to 'Scorrier Holdings VIP Event'. Maisie wondered what Patrick's reaction would be when he saw the mansion house and the rest of the estate. She also wondered how Hugo must feel, living there on his own since his father had been moved to the nursing home. It would surely do him good to have a partner, Maisie thought, if he could find someone to put up with him. It was even possible that the right woman – because as far as she knew Hugo was straight – might make him a much happier person and less of a pompous twit.

Maisie exchanged a glance with Patrick who pointed at the VIP sign.

'I've never been a VIP before,' she said.

'Nor me. I'm still not sure you should have brought me. The invitation was for your parents. Hugo won't be impressed.'

'All the more reason to ask you then,' said Maisie, feeling up for a fight, although also aware that Hugo might assume that there might be something going on between her and Patrick beyond a professional relationship.

'A cynical person might think you're using me to score points off Hugo, boss,' said Patrick.

Maisie let out a gasp. 'How could you possibly think such a thing?'

They approached the entrance to Scorrier House along a gravelled drive that led under the arch of an imposing gate-house. Maisie had been inside a dozen times for various charitable events and functions, and knew what to expect but it was fascinating to see Patrick's reaction.

Looked at through the eyes of a newcomer, the contrast between Gull and Petroc was stark and Patrick seemed awestruck. Maisie had never noticed him so quiet and his eyes missed nothing. Petroc's tracks and lanes were free of potholes and the neat pastel cottages were surrounded by manicured gardens filled with sub-tropical plants. A guy trundled past on a sit-on mower because the grass needed cutting, even in November, and was still lush and emerald green. Another was on his hands and knees ruthlessly culling any tiny weeds that had dared to poke their heads through a flower border.

'It seems as if there are still people on holiday,' said Patrick as they saw uniformed staff removing piles of towels and sheets from one of the cottages.

'There are a few,' said Maisie. 'This way to the house. The meeting's being held in the ballroom.'

Patrick lifted an eyebrow. 'Ballrooom?'

Maisie grinned. 'Don't worry. I think they'll let you in.'

Scorrier House was mid Victorian at its core but had been extended over the decades and was a grand but rambling Gothic place, by far the biggest and most imposing building across the whole of the isles. To the rear, the former stables and outbuildings had been converted to offices, housing a team of staff who ran Hugo's lucrative resort.

They paused on the driveway leading up to the elaborate façade with its gargoyles, battlements and a tower topped from where the Scilly flag was fluttering in the breeze.

Patrick held up his hands. 'Bloody hell. It's Hogwarts.'

Maisie giggled. She was glad she'd brought him along, if only for light relief.

Inside, Patrick gawped at the tiled floors, heavy oak furnishings and tapestries, which Maisie whispered were 'only Victorian copies' not original medieval ones. Two waiters met them at the door and handed over fizz or juice as they walked in. Hugo was chatting to a couple of faces Maisie recognised from St Piran's and some people nodded as she and Patrick made their way inside. There were also a dozen or more faces she didn't know whom she presumed were business associates. The ballroom was exactly as Maisie remembered it from her last visit, a few years previously: ornate plaster ceilings, walls with paintings of seascapes, shipwrecks and the odd Scorrier ancestor.

'Oh my. Hugo's had himself immortalised in oils. Look,' she whispered, ushering Patrick as close as she dared to a huge new picture in a prominent position. It showed him in his garden, in his country squire outfit with Basil by his side looking adoringly up at his master.

'Bet that's the first time Basil's ever behaved for more than a minute,' Maisie whispered.

'I expect he was painted in afterwards,' said Patrick, still transfixed by the painting. 'Where is he?'

'One of Hugo's "people" is probably taking care of him.'

'Why do you think Hugo has been so successful?' Patrick whispered.

'He and his father have managed to attract a very well-heeled clientele over the years, willing to fork out massive amounts for the privilege of staying on a private island. They've invested in luxury accommodation and posh facilities and so it all keeps rolling in. You have to hand it to them; they're good businesspeople. Oh, here we go. Hugo's about to do his thing.'

Hugo was joined on a low plinth at the end of the ballroom by one of his staff members, a woman whom Maisie recognised as his resort manager. He welcomed everyone to the meeting, including islanders, neighbours and newcomers, and then his manager, India, took over. Maisie had to admit the presentation about Petroc and its expansion plans was very slick. She waited with bated breath for mention of his designs on Gull, but that part of the plan for world domination was left out of today's event. Maisie kept glancing at Patrick to see if he was bored but he seemed glued to every word and PowerPoint slide. He was like a kid watching his favourite cartoon, although he wasn't exactly laughing out loud.

The presentation ended to a polite round of applause.

'If anyone has any questions, India or myself will be happy to answer them. Afternoon tea is available on the buffet table so please help yourselves.'

'So what did you think?' Maisie asked Patrick while they helped themselves to scones with clotted cream.

Patrick waited until he'd swallowed a mouthful of scone before replying. 'It's all very smooth ... to be honest, I hadn't expected the meeting to be so well organised or this place to be so grand. You have to hand it to Hugo, he knows how to make money.'

'Well, I'm surprised that Greg didn't tell you more about the place. His ancestors must have known about Scorrier House and they might even have been here. Petroc Island wasn't a resort then; it was an island for fishermen and farmers.'

'Like I said, Greg only mentioned his great-grandparents a few times and that was near the end of his life when he was urging me to come back to Britain to see my own birth-place.'

'And where was that exactly?' asked Maisie, selecting a violet macaron filled with passionfruit crème from a silver platter. 'I don't think you've told me yet.'

'Somewhere in London ... I'm not sure exactly where. I was a babe in arms when they emigrated to Australia. Obviously, I don't remember a thing about it. Being in nappies, that is.'

He helped himself to another scone. Maisie knew she'd been warned off and while she longed to ask him more about his parents, she guessed that he still found it very painful to talk about them. Losing both when he was only thirteen and then being passed between institutions and distant relatives who didn't want him was too horrible to contemplate. No wonder he'd been traumatised and gone off the rails. The truly amazing thing was how he'd turned his life around with the help of Judy and Greg.

While polishing off a slice of Victoria sponge, Patrick gazed around the room, seeming awestruck by its grandeur.

Then he turned round and groaned. 'Uh huh. Hugo's spotted us. He's coming over. Time for me to visit the little boy's room, I think.'

'Don't abandon me now,' Maisie protested.

'Sorry. Needs must. I'm sure you can handle him and I'll be back in an hour or so judging by the size of the place. If I get lost, send out a search party.'

Maisie arranged her face into a polite smile as Hugo homed in on her as enthusiastically as Basil going after a rotting seagull.

'Maisie. So glad you could come. Are you enjoying the tea?'

'Yes. Lovely. Delicious scones.'

'Good. And how about what you've heard about my plans? Are those to your taste too?'

God, Hugo was trying to joke again. Maisie wished he wouldn't but as he was obviously on a charm offensive, she was determined to respond in kind. 'It was all fascinating.'

'And does your barman find it fascinating too? I was surprised to find you'd brought him along instead of your parents. I'm sure they'd have been very interested in what I had to say.'

'They've gone to the hospital,' said Maisie.

Hugo's smile melted away and he adopted a sympathetic tone. 'I'm sorry to hear that.'

'No worries. It was a scheduled appointment but I'm sure you can understand that they didn't want to miss it, even for an important presentation like this.'

'Of course,' said Hugo. 'Where is Patrick, by the way?'

'He needed the bathroom.'

Hugo smirked. 'I see.' He paused. 'You'll notice I didn't mention my proposal to bring some of the Gull properties into the Scorrier Estate,' he said.

'I had noticed, yes. Why is that?'

'Well, those plans are at an early stage and as you know yourself, negotiations are delicate. It's very easy to upset people in a tiny and close-knit community so I'm treading very carefully. For heaven's sake, I'm not some kind of Bond villain. I'd never force you out of the Driftwood against your will. Not if you – and your parents – didn't want to. They are the legal owners after all, aren't they?'

'They are,' said Maisie, thinking how glad she was that Ray

wasn't around to hear Hugo's thinly veiled threats. 'And I'm glad to hear you would never put any undue pressure on us, especially now that Dad's recovery is still quite fragile,' said Maisie, turning the tables on Hugo.

Hugo lowered his voice and winked. 'Softly softly, that's my approach … and I have your best interests at heart. I always have had a soft spot for you. More than you know.'

Maisie's reply caught in her throat. Was it possible that Hugo really was *flirting*? Or was he simply trying a different tactic? Either way it was seriously creepy.

Over Hugo's shoulder, she spotted Patrick watching them intently. He wasn't smiling but he was staring. Was he jealous? Or was she fantasising again?

'That's kind of you, Hugo, and your plans make sense in many ways apart from the fact that we're all totally happy with things the way they are. We're not going to sell, not for a very long time, if ever, but thanks for inviting us to the house.'

Maisie noticed that people had started to drift away from the ballroom. In fact, she and Patrick were the only guests left.

'Why don't you stay for a proper tour of the place? You haven't been here for years, have you? I've made a lot of improvements to the house as well as the resort, all in keeping with the building's heritage status, naturally.'

Maisie floundered. She absolutely didn't want to stay on any longer and looked across to Patrick who was coming towards them.

'We were ready to leave …' she said in a loud voice that finally caught Patrick's attention. He walked over with a smile.

'What have I missed?' he asked.

'Actually, I'd just invited Maisie to have a tour of the house,' Hugo cut in smoothly. 'You're welcome to stay too, of course.' Hugo looked dismayed at the prospect of Patrick joining them, and Maisie waited for Patrick to jump in with a refusal.

But Patrick virtually rubbed his hands together. 'Sounds great. If you're sure I won't be playing gooseberry.'

Hugo smirked but Maisie could have killed Patrick. 'Not at all,' he said, then addressed himself to Maisie. 'If it's OK with your boss?'

'If Patrick wants to see the house, we'll stay, but it will have to be quick, I'm afraid, as we must get back to the Driftwood.'

Hugo beamed. 'Shall we go outside first while it's fine? The gardens aren't at their best at this time of year but there's still plenty of interest.'

Maisie had no idea why Patrick wanted to look around Scorrier House. Curiosity, she guessed, or the opportunity to wind Hugo up. She could understand both of those, but she would still much rather have been on her way to the jetty now.

Hugo led the way outside after collecting Basil from one of the offices where he'd been looked after by one of the gardeners.

An excited Basil shot off, sniffing bushes and sticking his muzzle into anything and everything. Hugo pointed out some of the plants and trees, although Maisie's mind was still on his cryptic – and slightly skin-crawling – remarks about having a soft spot for her.

Patrick lingered by a jacaranda. Even Maisie knew that in

171

spring, the tree would be in its full glory with bright mauve flowers. Unlike Maisie, her mum did visit the gardens from time to time and raved about the jacaranda and showed her photographs. Maisie joined him and Hugo.

'Feeling homesick?' Hugo asked.

'Once in awhile, yeah,' said Patrick.

'As I said the other day, the Scorrier Estate has business interests in Australia but I haven't been to Melbourne for a few years. I hear you worked in a bar there. Would I know it?'

'I doubt it, mate. I wouldn't have thought it was your kind of thing.'

'You'd be surprised what my kind of thing is. I have eclectic tastes.'

'The Fingle's a down-to-earth place. Like the Driftwood.'

'You'll have to come and see the Rose and Crab,' said Hugo.

Maisie saw Patrick's lips twitch in a smile at the pub's name and Hugo obviously noticed it too. 'I know ... It's a quirky name. I cringed when our ad agency came up with it but the guests seem to love it.'

A flash of red and a rustling above them caught Maisie's eye and suddenly she was yards from a red squirrel sitting on the rim of a fountain, eating a nut. It was so sweet, smaller than the greys on the mainland and with red tufts on its ears.

'Shhh ...' Hearing Hugo and Patrick behind her she held up her hand. The squirrel froze and looked up at them, before going back to his nut.

'Woof!'

Basil tore out of a clump of shrubs and headed straight for the squirrel. His barks echoed over the glade.

'Basil! Stop this instant!'

Hugo might as well have not existed. Basil raced for the squirrel but it leapt across to a low branch and scurried up the tree out of sight and reach.

Basil stood at the bottom, barking non-stop.

'Basil. Shut up!' Hugo ran over and grabbed Basil's collar. Basil growled.

'You bad dog. Do as you're told. Miscreant!'

Maisie exchanged a glance with Patrick. His shoulders were shaking as he tried not to laugh.

'Miscreant?' he mouthed.

Maisie shrugged as Hugo tried to drag Basil away from the tree. The dog dug his claws in and barked even louder.

'I think we'd better be going,' said Maisie loudly. 'We need to open up this evening and I don't want to leave Mum and Dad on their own too long.'

'Wait a moment. I've something to say to you,' Hugo called above Basil's protests.

'Basil doesn't want to leave. He wants to play with the squirrel,' said Patrick.

Hugo's face was like thunder. 'It's not funny!' said Hugo, turning round.

Basil stopped barking and wandered off over the grass.

Hugo sighed. 'That animal is a law unto himself. I must take him to classes.'

Once Basil had calmed down, Hugo marched back to Maisie, his mouth set in a grim line. 'I'll be in touch,' he said, addressing himself to her alone. 'I've a proposition to put to you.'

173

'If it's relating to the papers you gave me, I don't see much point,' said Maisie, wishing she could tear off after a squirrel too. Patrick had picked up a small branch and was waving it at Basil.

Hugo lowered his voice. 'It's something different. I think you might find it very interesting.'

'Can't you tell me now? We're *so* busy, especially while Dad's recuperating. Or phone me?'

Hugo looked at Patrick. He and Basil were playing tug-of-war with the stick.

'It's a private matter,' said Hugo. 'That I'd prefer to discuss face to face, just the two of us.'

Maisie's heart sank. She couldn't imagine what Hugo had to say that he hadn't already told her or couldn't share now.

'Please. I'm serious, Maisie. This is important. Can you get away in the next few days? I can come over to Gull if it helps, or we can meet on neutral territory?'

Maisie had never seen Hugo so solemn. She had no choice but to hear him out but she was also more determined than ever to rally the troops to her way of thinking. However, it was always better to 'know thine enemy'.

With an inner sigh, she nodded. 'OK. I'll call you.'

Finally, Maisie ended the visit, pleading the state of the tides and darkness falling. She was a reasonably confident helmswoman and could have found her way home in the dark if she had to but the tides waited for no one.

'How can you name a pub the Rose and Crab?' Patrick said as Maisie steered the *Puffin* away from the quay and out into the channel.

Maisie giggled. 'How can you name a pub the Fingle? What does it mean?'

Patrick shrugged. 'I don't really know. Some joke of Greg's.'

'I wonder what Hugo's got in mind for the Driftwood? The Seal and Primrose?' said Maisie as the boat dipped and rose over the waves. She and Patrick huddled in the little cabin but they were still spattered with spray.

'How about the Agapanthus and Lobster?' Patrick suggested. Maisie giggled and got a mouthful of salt spray. 'Don't mention that to him. It's far too close for comfort. He might actually use it if he gets his hands on the place.'

'But he won't, will he?' said Patrick. 'You won't sell?'

'No ... of course not ...' She sighed. 'I just wish a lot of what he says didn't make sense. His offer for the place isn't *that* bad and Mum and Dad have had a lot on their plate. Sometimes I hear them talking to my Auntie Rose in Truro and she keeps trying to persuade them to go and live on the mainland and buy a new bungalow that's easy to maintain.'

'Maisie Samson. What's Hugo put in your tea?'

'It isn't only me, Patrick. How can I persuade people who are living hand to mouth and struggling to hold out against Scorrier when it might actually be better if they sold? I can't dictate their lives to them.'

The sea had grown rougher and the sky was dark grey over the Hell Cove end of Gull Island. She opened the throttle and gave all her concentration to navigating her course back to Gull. It wouldn't do to run aground on a sandbank with dusk falling.

Chapter 19

A couple of days later Maisie and Jess walked over the hill to the northern side of the island. The pub was closed and Jess had wangled a couple of hours off from boxing up narcissi at the Flower Farm to meet Maisie for a coffee. The wind was blowing hard and Maisie was glad that Jess had made it safely across from St Saviour's over the rough seas. Jess wanted to talk about Adam, and Maisie wanted to talk to her about Hugo – and Patrick – so they'd wrapped up against the wind and headed out of the pub with a flask of hot chocolate. They stopped on top of the hill by some of the ancient prehistoric ruins that could be found throughout the isles.

'How was Hugo's event?' Jess asked, giving Maisie a hand down a rocky outcrop that led to the road again.

'The scones were nice.'

Jess laughed. 'But full of bull?'

'Yes.' Maisie decided not to tell Jess that Hugo had invited her to call to see him again. She still hadn't decided absolutely whether to meet him after all. He probably wanted to get her on her own to persuade her to sell the Driftwood. Divide and conquer etc. – which actually had given her an idea of her own.

'You know I'd been thinking about calling a meeting of everyone from Gull myself but I wonder if it would be better to visit people individually. No one likes to say what they're really feeling in a public meeting so I might drop in on them casually over the next couple of weeks. I can find out why the waverers want to sell and see if we can all come up with a strategy together.'

'That's brave, but also a good idea. If anyone can do it, you can.'

'You have too much confidence in me. But while the pub's relatively quiet, I could give it a try. At least I'll have done my best.'

Jess patted her back. 'Good luck. If we can help in any way let us know.'

'I will. Don't tell Mum and Dad or anyone, though. I don't want to worry them or alert Hugo. I want it all kept under wraps.'

'What about Patrick? He's on your side, isn't he?'

'Yes. I think so. Well, he doesn't have any stake in the place, does he? I'm sure he wishes us well and he works for us, so he's bound to agree with what we want, but this isn't his livelihood or birthright, and he's leaving in the spring, so he can't afford to care, even if he wanted to. I don't want to drag him in so I think we should leave my conversations between us for the time being.'

'OK, but word's bound to get round once you start chatting up the neighbours.'

'That's a risk I'll have to take. It's their decision to sell or stay, at the end of the day. I can only do my best.'

And I have a sneaking feeling it won't be enough, thought Maisie. Hugo couldn't force her to sell the Driftwood but if he owned and developed the rest of the island, its character would disappear and all the cottages would be occupied by time-share tourists or holiday guests. The look and feel – the very essence – of Gull would vanish forever. The Driftwood would be a shabby island of its own, holding out. Hugo had said there would be more money for it, and selling would ensure its survival. Maybe financially, but as for its soul – Maisie and her parents and future generations of Samsons would lose the building and land, meaning Hugo could kick them out at any time. Even if they held out, he could convert other buildings to posh cafés and taverns like on Petroc and destroy them that way.

Maisie genuinely believed there was no need for that if everyone worked together. Somehow. She really didn't want to speak to Hugo again if she could help it. He could only want one thing: to persuade her in some way to cave in and get her parents to sell the Driftwood. In fact, she was surprised he hadn't called her himself by now to try and arrange a meeting.

'Where's Patrick?' Jess asked, giving Maisie the chance to move on to an altogether more appealing topic than Hugo.

'He's gone to see Rev Bev,' Maisie said sarcastically.

'What? I didn't know he was religious.'

'He's not. He's gone to tea at the vicarage.'

Instead of gasping in astonishment as Maisie had expected,

Jess nodded. 'Well, she is a very attractive woman ... what is she? Forty-three? Forty-five?'

'Forty-nine according to Archie. He fancies her.'

Jess laughed. 'She has some fabulous boots. I asked her about the zebra-print ones – the Louboutins with the red soles – and she said she bought them in an online auction in aid of a refugee crisis centre.'

'How very charitable,' said Maisie, amazed at Jess's reaction.

'She does her own hair colour, you know,' Jess said admiringly. 'I thought she must have it done professionally but she trained as a hairdresser and beautician before she became a priest, so she knows what she's doing.'

Maisie thought of the salt-and-pepper roots appearing in her own tangled mop and how she needed to make an appointment. 'According to Patrick, she likes to get to know newcomers to the isles, and was wondering if he was missing his family as the festive season grows near,' she said.

Jess let out a low whistle. 'Well, that's a new chat-up line.'

'So you think she *is* after him?' Maisie asked, barely able to keep the dismay out of her voice.

'I've only met her a few times since she got here in the spring. I wish I could say she was a snob or holier-than-thou but she seems like a nice person with a good sense of humour ...' Jess pulled her own dark hair out of her eyes. They gleamed with mischief. 'Maisie, why do you care so much if Patrick and Bev are sharing a pot of Earl Grey and a clotted cream scone, or anything else?'

Maisie shrugged and stuffed her hands in her pockets. 'I don't. Oh bugger it. I *do* care.'

Jess shook her head. 'You don't seriously think that Patrick is interested in the vicar, do you?'

'He might be. Don't be ageist,' said Maisie.

'I'm not. Bev's a hoot and an asset to the community and even Will said she was way too sexy to be a vicar.'

Maisie groaned out loud.

'*But* the reason that Patrick isn't interested in Rev Bev or any other woman is because he is so obviously interested in you, you silly mare!'

'Really? Is he really?'

'You know damn well he is but you keep pushing him away and giving him the cold shoulder. My God, if I thought he was up for grabs, I'd be down that vicarage myself and fighting off Bev with a stick or a crook or whatever she might have.'

'I thought he was at one point – oh Jesus. I came back from the hospital after Dad had been taken in and I was tired and flaky and I misread the signals from him ...'

'Go on.'

'I can hardly bear to say it out loud but I – I jumped on him. I thought he wanted to kiss me, and more, and he didn't. He told me, very politely, that now wasn't the right time so ever since then, I've kept well away from him.'

Jess didn't seem shocked. 'He was right. That probably wasn't the right time. He'd known you – what? – three days and you were in a right old state. I'd have hated him if he had taken advantage. But I'd say, from my observation of him now, that he's changed his mind and would definitely respond if you'd only lower that spike-topped drawbridge and let him within five feet of you.'

'I don't dare try it again. It was excruciating to be pushed away the first time even though I deserved it. I'm not as tough as I look.'

'Not tough, but you are strong, hun. You must be to have survived the past year, but don't confuse being strong with being hard and pushing everyone away. I'd love a fling with Patrick myself but he's not interested. He made that clear at the Hallowe'en party ... mind you, with Adam giving him the evils all night, I can hardly blame Patrick for being put off.'

Maisie had to concentrate as they scrambled down the bank that led from the old hill fort to the sea. At the bottom, they regained the main track and she and Jess stopped for a breather. 'Adam is a pain in the arse,' she said. 'Acting like the jealous lover and then ignoring you. I'd like to bang his head against a wall until he sees how great you two could be together.'

'That's never going to happen. Because Adam's leaving Scilly.'

'What?' Maisie said, shocked. 'Oh, Jess, I'm sorry, I've been so wrapped up in worrying about Dad, and saving the Driftwood and bloody Patrick that I've ignored you. Leaving Scilly? Why? How long for?'

'For good, as far as I know. He's being transferred to the mainland at his request. I don't know where to. Someone said he might even be going abroad, someone mentioned New Zealand ...'

'I'm so sorry, Jess. I haven't wanted to poke my nose into your business before, but I know you've been putting on a brave face since things went wrong, and I have to ask you:

until August, you and Adam seemed so happy. I don't know what happened but I can't stand seeing you so down now.'

'I haven't done a very good job of hiding my feelings, then?'

'You seemed OK after you told me it was over. I assumed that you'd made the decision to end it and that's why Adam's been acting cool. But is that true?'

Jess heaved a sigh. 'Yes and no, but mostly no. Everything was great until the bank holiday Adam went back to see his family in Cumbria. Something changed while he was out there but I don't know what. He refused to talk about it and not long after, he said we should take a break. That break is now permanent. He didn't even tell me he was leaving. Will did.'

'Shit. That's terrible. You must be so hurt.'

Jess shrugged. 'I'm too busy to be hurt. Adam doesn't seem to have told anyone why he wanted to split, not even Will. There's gossip about us but I won't give people the satisfaction of letting them see I'm upset. I won't let Adam see, either. If he wants to go all mean and moody on me, then he can do. I'm better off without him.'

Maisie hugged Jess again, seeing her friend fighting back tears. She was almost in tears herself. Jess was so warm and loving, she didn't deserve to be dumped without an explanation.

'Thanks for being so lovely, and I do appreciate someone to talk to. It's good to finally tell you how I really feel but let's change the subject for now.' Jess smiled. 'And even if Adam is off the scene, and I'm free and single again, I won't be challenging Bev to armed combat over Patrick because he's already taken. He's mad about you and you are about him so why the hell don't you both just accept that fact and get together. Your friends are all sick of you mooning around.'

'My friends?'

'Me. Will.'

'Is it that obvious? Mum and Dad wouldn't like it. Mum still doesn't completely trust Patrick.'

'Who wholly trusts any man? But you're not looking for wedding bells and eternal love, are you? If a winter of fun's on the table, are you up for that? Sounds like the best of both worlds to me.'

Maisie sighed. 'I don't know. I mean, yes, I can't deny that sex would be great.' She sighed. 'Really amazing ...'

'Then you know what to do. Grab your chance the next moment he shows any sign of being interested and make it clear what the terms of engagement are. I doubt he'll put up any more resistance.'

'Do you know something I don't?'

'No, but Will tried to sound him out and without actually admitting he fancied the pants off you, Patrick kind of gave off enough signals to let Will know he'd be up for it.'

'And your brother's an expert on other people's love lives, is he?'

'He's crap, actually, but I'm only passing on the message.'

'Great. I'll bear it in mind.'

They walked past the Fudge Pantry and the Gull Island Post Office, its roof spattered with orange lichen. Jess lingered by the post box as if she was thinking of Adam again before a strong gust almost knocked them over.

'I think we've had enough fresh air for one day,' said Maisie, sighting the roof of the Driftwood. She led the way down a narrow track through the gorse, her mind humming with plans.

She decided she would personally visit each business and resident who was rumoured to be considering selling up, rather than tackle everyone at a possibly hostile meeting. Then she would call a meeting to have an open discussion, without Hugo's knowledge, if possible. She'd start with Una and Phyllis and as she was on that side of the island, she might even call in on the vicar to get her on side – and see if there really was anything between her and Patrick.

Chapter 20

15 November

The next day, Maisie pulled the zip of her fleece higher as she turned on to the gravelled track that led down to the Hell Cove Guest House and Cottages. A whitewashed cottage sat just back from the cove itself, sheltered from the full brunt of the weather fronts straight from the Atlantic.

On the western side of the cove, the rocks of Hell's Teeth glistened like a sea monster's fangs as they were uncovered by the receding tide. Many ships had foundered on those on a foggy night, or been driven onto them in a gale. You could still see the bones of wrecks on a very low tide and, occasionally, gold and silver coins were washed ashore. However, Maisie's favourite treasure lay hidden within the smoother, more benign rocks behind the 'teeth'. The Mermaid's Pool was tidal and Maisie had brought her rucksack with a towel for a dip. She'd planned the swim as a treat – or therapy – after her conversation with Phyllis and Una. If she was very lucky, perhaps her bathe would turn out to be a victory swim.

On reaching the bottom of the slope, Maisie decided to

take the beach route to the cottages rather than keep to the track, and clambered down through the sea holly and gorse onto the creamy sand of Hell Cove.

Welcome to Hell – your little piece of Heaven on Earth

Maisie smiled at the fading sign, written in curling script by Archie Pendower. Hell Cove House definitely needed an upgrade, but she'd hate to see its quirky charm absorbed into a corporate brand. The gate was hanging low on its hinges so she had to give it a shove and wriggle through the gap to reach the path that led to the front door. The shutters were faded from pale green to grey and flakes of paint fluttered in the wind. Grey and gold lichen crawled over the window sills and broken slates of the holiday cottages.

They were all shuttered up and silent. There were no guests at this time of year, though there was no real reason why they should be empty. Maisie had had 'storm-watching' customers from Petroc in the pub at the weekend who'd told her that Petroc's trendy time-shares were fairly buzzing with out-of-season breaks.

Phyllis Barton hurried round the side of the house, a broad smile on her face, wiping her hands on an oily rag. She wore gardening gloves and a boilersuit that had once been bottle green but was now spattered with a variety of paint colours, oil and indefinable stains.

'Maisie. How lovely to see you.' She held up her greasy hands. 'Sorry. I've been servicing the mowing machine. Bloody grass will keep on growing, and I need to trim back the laurel if I can get the hedge cutters to work again. The garden's run rampant over the summer.'

Una Barton joined them, carrying a hoe. She was the taller of the two sisters, her greying hair falling in wild crinkly curls over her bony shoulders. Phyllis preferred to home dye and cut her mop in an ever-changing array of colours and styles. It was best described as an aubergine bob today. Both women were lean and wiry, even though they must be the same age as Maisie's parents.

'How's your dad?' Una cut in, frowning hard at her sister.

'On the mend, thanks,' said Maisie, secretly admiring Phyllis's stamina.

Phyllis clucked her tongue in sympathy. 'We heard he was back but we've been too busy trying to keep this place from falling down or we'd have called in to see him ourselves. Pernicious anaemia, isn't it? An uncle of ours had it. Uncle Gerald ... you remember, don't you, Una?'

'Oh?' said Maisie, bracing herself for a barrage of advice.

Una nodded. 'Yes. I do. Poor old Gerald. Of course, he's long gone.'

'Right ...' said Maisie.

'Not of the anaemia. He had a heart attack while he was playing bowls,' said Phyllis.

'I see.' Maisie was torn between amusement and frustration.

Phyllis pulled off her crusty gardening gloves. 'Anyway, what brings you to Hell, dear?' she said.

'Come to swim in the Mermaid Pool, have you?' said Una.

'Yes. I have. Thought I'd have a dip while the weather's still fine,' said Maisie.

Una wrinkled her button nose. She reminded Maisie of Aunt Sally from the Worzel Gummidge books. 'Bit chilly for me these days or I'd join you.'

'Wimp.' Phyllis snorted in disgust. 'I went in last week. Not for long though. It was a tad bracing so I shan't bother again until spring. Are you going straight there, dear, or did you decide to call in for a coffee?'

'I saw you in the garden from the hill and thought I'd say hello,' said Maisie, quite truthfully. 'How are you both doing? How's business?'

Una pulled off her gloves and pushed her silver curls out of her eyes. 'Mustn't grumble.'

'There's such a lot to do, even when we don't have guests,' said Phyllis. 'Not that some guests wouldn't be welcome, but who's going to come all this way when there's no boat and you can never be sure if the planes will fly? Not to mention that fog we had last week cutting us off for days. It's hard to attract people, but once they do come, they're gobsmacked.'

'Most of the time,' said Una crisply. 'You do get some who turn up and act like they've been marooned on Devil's Island. It's not for everyone here. One of them asked me where was the nearest McDonald's and could he have a pizza biked down here? I said the farm on St Agnes delivered meat and dairy and he could get a pizza at the Driftwood if he was prepared to walk.'

Maisie smiled. 'That's an idea. Pizza delivery by bike ... Gull Island can be a Marmite kind of place. Love or hate,' she said, pleased to have the topic of business brought up.

'Are you coming inside?' Una asked. 'I could do with a cuppa and I think we've a slice of lemon drizzle loaf left.'

'I shouldn't eat, I'm going swimming, but a coffee would be great. Thanks.'

Maisie sipped her coffee, perched on an old wing-backed armchair from which the stuffing was escaping. The rest of the furnishings were clean, but old and shabby. She was used to old, worn interiors. Everyone had to make do on Gull. Even if you had some spare cash, the cost of getting goods on and off the island could be prohibitive and disposing of old stuff wasn't simple, either. She'd had a few newer pieces shipped from her old flat in St Austell so her bedsit room at the Driftwood still looked relatively decent and modern.

'I expect you want to talk about Scorrier, don't you?' Una said, cutting a slice of lemon drizzle for herself.

Maisie was wrong-footed but decided not to lie. 'Is it true you've sold to him?' she asked, trying to sound casual.

Phyllis glared at her sister. 'Not yet. We said we'd think about it. There's the documents on there.' She pointed to a folder on a carved-oak sideboard. 'Una wants to sign and get it over with but I can't bring myself to do it.'

'We promised him we'd *seriously* consider his offer, Phyll. Bookings are way down. We're embarrassed to show people round, the fixtures and fittings are so dated but we can't afford to pour in thousands on refurbishing them.' Una popped a chunk of cake in her mouth.

'We've cut the prices,' said Phyllis. 'But we daren't drop any lower. This place needs a big investment and we haven't got it.'

'And we're not getting any younger,' said Una gloomily through a mouthful of cake.

'Hugo suggested we apply for a retirement bungalow on St

189

Mary's. It makes sense and yet …' Phyllis looked round the cottage and sighed. 'I'll miss my garden and the guests and this view.'

All Maisie's persuasions had vanished. She didn't have an answer, but Hugo clearly had his plan very well thought out. 'What will you do?' she asked.

Phyllis shook her head. 'I don't know.'

'I do,' said Una. 'You do too, Phyll, you just don't want to face up to it, but Hugo won't wait forever. We have to decide soon or he might change his mind, and who'd buy this place, then? No one with any sense, that's for sure.'

Maisie's heart sank further. 'It's so beautiful, though. I'd love to have it.'

'Would you, dear?' said Phyllis. 'Could you buy it? Maybe we could live in one of the cottages and keep an eye on it.' Phyllis shoved the cake plate at Maisie. 'Go on, have a little bite. Won't do you any harm.'

Maisie smiled and picked up the slice of cake that Phyllis had offered. She didn't want to offend them. The Bartons were amazing women and although she felt slightly guilty at telling them what to do with their lives, she was also determined to put up a fight against Hugo's bullying tactics.

'Sorry, I wish I had the cash and an answer for you – mmm, this is gorgeous cake, by the way – and I know exactly how you must feel about having to leave here and I'd want to stay too, but I also know that a place like this is a lot of work and needs investment. But please, don't let Hugo rush you into anything or bully you out of your home. You know what he can be like.'

'He's tried smooth talking us,' said Una curtly. 'And while

I've told him his offer makes sense, I've also told him we won't be railroaded.'

Phyllis sighed. 'I expect we will end up selling to him. I'm sorry if that's not the answer you wanted, Maisie.'

Maisie swallowed a large chunk of cake before replying. 'It's none of my business, even though I'm very sorry to see it happen.'

'Of course, if we had children to take it over, it would be different, but neither of us married and there are no nephews and nieces. Too late for that now.'

Maisie finished her coffee and cake and listened sympathetically while Una and Phyllis related a list of jobs that needed doing in the garden and to the house. Finally Maisie replaced her empty cup in the saucer. 'Look. I know it sounds like a mammoth task to maintain this place but I'm sure we can come up with some way of helping you stay here.'

'But how?' asked Una.

'I um – don't have the exact details yet but I'm working on a plan,' said Maisie, narrowly avoiding adding the word 'cunning'.

Phyllis let out a squeak. 'A *plan*? That sounds very interesting.'

Una replaced her cup in its saucer carefully. 'Can you tell us more about this plan, *dear*?'

Panicking a little, Maisie stood up. 'Not yet but I promise you, you'll be the first to know as soon as I've formed up the – er – specifics. Don't give up hope,' she said, way more confidently than she felt. 'Hugo hasn't beaten us yet, not by a long way. Now, I'd better be going but rest assured, I'll be in touch very soon.'

Una saw her to the door. 'Thank you for calling. We can't wait to see what you've come up with.'

Neither can I, thought Maisie as she walked down the path away from the house.

What plan? What specifics? What had she said that for? Damn.

She'd already been clutching at straws by imagining the sisters might have a secret source of money, or that they'd found people to buy the cottages and take them on without Hugo's help.

Now she'd given them false expectations – unless she could really come up with a cunning plan in the next couple of days.

Her phone buzzed in her backpack. Maisie dug it out and let out a groan as she saw the screen. It was a text from Hugo.

'Been away on business. Call me as agreed? Don't be a stranger. ;) H xxx'

Don't be a stranger? Three kisses and a winking smiley?

Had she given Hugo the wrong impression by even agreeing to visit him? It was too late now and she supposed it was better to keep her friends close and her enemies closer, though the prospect of being up close to Hugo made her shudder.

Deciding to put off her reply until she'd decided exactly how to respond, Maisie took a few calming breaths. A swim might clear her head. Slinging her pack over her shoulders, she headed for the pool, trying to fill her racing mind with calming and positive thoughts. It wasn't really working but the sight of the sparkling sea did boost her mood and, she reminded herself, she should make the most of the blue in the late autumn sky and the gentle breeze. Storms were forecast over the coming week and she might not be able to use the pool for weeks, or even months, if she didn't seize the moment.

She stopped for another look at Hell Cove before it finally disappeared from view as she walked around the corner to the pool. The roof of the house and cottages had several slates missing or chipped. There was a lot of work to do, no wonder the sisters found it daunting. It had taken Patrick and her father a week to repair the slates on the Driftwood and if anything Hell Cove House was in a worse state. Maybe she and Patrick could lend a hand to Una and Phyllis, at least to get the place ready for a new season ...

She picked her way over the beach towards the pool. Old crates and rope had washed up, and rubbish that had fallen from ships or been thrown into the sea. Sadly, there was no Spanish gold today that might have helped her fend off Hugo.

Then again ... An idea formed in her mind at the same time as the Mermaid Pool came into view. Maisie felt a lift of pleasure as she caught sight of the dark green waters.

Hmm. It was a long shot and would take all her powers of persuasion and organisation and but it might *just* work.

Mulling over the thought that was taking root, Maisie opened her rucksack and pulled out her towel so it would be instantly ready for when she climbed out after her swim. The breeze rippled the surface of the pool and the odd wave still broke over the lip. It was time to start using her shortie wetsuit after today, wherever she chose to swim. She was pulling off her trainers when she heard whistling from above her on the footpath and a second later, Patrick appeared.

Chapter 21

He spotted her immediately and jogged down the rough steps to join her, his boots ringing out on the rock.

'Are you going in there?' he asked. 'That's brave.'

He grimaced but his eyes glittered with amusement. Their summer sea colours took on an intensity that made Maisie's limbs feel almost liquid. A couple of days' stubble shaded his jaw and without warning, she had an image – and a feeling – of it rasping against her cheek, her neck and her breasts.

Maisie dug her nails into her palm, willing the feelings swirling in her belly to go away. 'It might be my last chance until spring so I thought I'd go for it.'

He nodded. 'Seizing the day. I get that.'

'Where are you going?' she asked.

'It's where I've been, actually.' He smiled. 'The vicar's cottage.'

So, Patrick had been round to the vicarage again. Maisie raised an eyebrow. 'Prayer meeting, was it?'

'Unlikely as I'm a fully paid-up heathen ... but I suppose I could be open to conversion. With enough persuasion.'

'Rev Bev's made quite an impression on the community,'

said Maisie. 'Vicar and first responder. I was glad she was around to help Dad.' She felt she had to say something super nice about the vicar. She'd hate Patrick to think she was in any way jealous. Which she wasn't, of course.

'Just passing, were you?' Maisie teased, hoping she didn't sound sarcastic.

'No, as a matter of fact I had an invitation.'

'Oh,' she said, picking up her trainers and putting them on a rock. She refused to give him the satisfaction of seeming interested.

'Beverley wants to see my slides,' said Patrick.

'Does she now?' Maisie rolled her eyes and sat down on a low rock ready to take off her socks, half wishing Patrick would leave but also dying to know what had gone on between him and the glamorous Bev.

'She asked me if I'd give a talk on Australian wildlife at the community hall.'

Maisie laughed out loud. 'Well, that's what passes for entertainment on Gull.'

He feigned a hurt look. 'Don't knock it. I'll probably be mobbed like Justin Bieber.'

'You'd go down better if you were Tom Jones given the average age of the parish group. Will you?'

'I don't know.' He wrinkled his nose. 'Will people really want to see a few bored 'roos and a blurry shot of an echidna?'

'They'd probably turn up to see a photo of the vicar's pug. I hate to disillusion you, Patrick, but I don't think the wildlife is the attraction.'

'What are you trying to say? That *I'm* the attraction?'

195

'No! The free tea and biscuits are. People will do anything for a free cuppa and a Hobnob.'

'And here was I thinking I was an exotic species that the locals would flock to examine.'

You are. I would. Maisie kept her thoughts buttoned away. She'd abandoned any idea of taking off her socks or anything else while Patrick was in such close proximity. Keeping up the mindless banter was her way of trying to stop her simmering desires from boiling over completely. Boy, did she need a dip in that cold pool!

'How was your meeting?' he asked.

'What meeting?'

'With Phyllis and Una? I saw you walking along the beach to the cottage on my way to the vicarage.'

'Oh. OK, I've been trying to persuade them not to accept Hugo's offer.'

He paused before responding, as if he didn't know how to answer. Maisie half wished she hadn't told him about the purpose of her visit. After all, it wasn't his problem, even though he seemed to be no big fan of Hugo.

'And how did that go?' he asked.

'They've almost made up their minds to sell to Hugo, but they're not totally sure. He's charmed them and convinced them they'd be better off in a little bungalow on St Mary's.'

'Would they really move?'

Maisie glared at him. 'I honestly don't know. There's a lot of maintenance on the cottages and they're not getting any younger and the income is dwindling so ... argh. Probably, yes, but that doesn't mean they should sell the place to Hugo.

They could find new owners willing to invest in the cottages, perhaps even expand them.'

'I'm guessing that would take a lot of time and energy on their part, not to mention luck. It's a massive decision to move somewhere as isolated as Gull.'

Maisie felt faintly annoyed with Patrick even if he was making reasonable observations. Reasonable wasn't what she wanted now: she wanted his support. 'I could help them. I know the agents from all the lettings companies and they'd do their best to find them a buyer or tenant.'

'You have a lot on your plate with the Driftwood.'

'Living here is a labour of love. It's a lifestyle choice, you can't dabble, you have to throw yourself heart and soul into making a go of life here, even when things get tough. You have to be committed to the isles. To Gull, especially, as it's so tiny.'

'And are you? Committed to it? With your heart and soul?'

'What else am I going to do with the rest of my life?' It was meant as a joke but it was true. She laughed. 'Right at this moment, I'm only committed to getting in that water.'

She pulled off her fleece, enjoying the look of disbelief on Patrick's face. There were salty tangles in his hair, which had darkened as he spent longer away from the blazing skies of his homeland.

'Are you coming in?' The invitation was out of her mouth before she could stop it.

'I'm not sure I'd do myself any credit swimming in there. Besides, I haven't brought my swimsuit.'

'That's your problem. Luckily I have.'

Patrick peered into the water and pulled a face. 'I don't know ...'

Deciding not to wait any longer, she took off her socks and fleece, and laid them on a flat rock. Trying to act casual, she unzipped her skinny jeans and pulled them down her legs, making sure her bikini bottoms didn't accidentally come with them. An undignified struggle to get her jeans over ankles followed and she almost overbalanced.

Finally, she pulled off her T-shirt. If Patrick was expecting a show, he was going to get less than he bargained for because she'd worn her tankini top under her T-shirt. Even so, he was seeing more of her than he'd seen before and she was glad that the cold air calmed down the heat that raced to her cheeks.

'Good luck,' he said, but made no move to leave.

'Thanks.' She wished he'd either go away or join her in shivering by the pool but he sat on the rock next to her clothes, and gave her a cheeky wave, as she walked down the rough steps that had been hewn into the rocks a century before. A fresh tide had refilled the pool with ocean water and waves still broke over the edge. She tried to focus on her senses, the sounds of waves crashing on the reef and the tang of wet seaweed in the air, but she was painfully aware of Patrick's eyes on her.

She stepped down into the pool, onto the last step. Normally she'd have spent a few minutes dithering, dipping her toes in the pool and sitting on the edge, splashing herself while she plucked up the courage to go in. No way was she going to show any kind of hesitation with him watching, so she held out her hands and pushed off into the water.

Oh God. Oh fffff—

She'd expected it to be cold but arghhh.

She gasped, her heart pounded but she tried to strike out in a proper crawl straight away, instead of her usual frantic dog paddle. Salt stung her eyes but she swam as fast as she could to the far edge of the pool, blowing hard and praying she'd acclimatise before she had to turn back towards Patrick and he could see her agonised face.

Eyes stinging, she reached the far side. It was too cold to stop and rest so she pushed off from the rocks and did a breaststroke back towards him.

He was watching her. Not smiling, just looking. It unnerved her.

A few feet from where he was sitting, she stopped and trod water, managed a laugh. 'Are you coming in or are you going to chicken out?'

'Nothing wrong with being chicken,' he said.

She clucked and squawked at him. It wasn't difficult to make a strangled noise like that, she was so damn cold. Then she kicked and turned and swam as hard as she could for the side of the pool again. The waves had stopped breaking over the edge as the tide retreated so the water was calmer. On her next turn, Patrick had kicked off his boots. He tugged his sweatshirt and long-sleeved T-shirt over his head in one motion and dropped them next to her own clothes.

She stopped and kicked to stay afloat.

She'd seen him shirtless before, in the garden, but here she felt exposed, even though he was the one half naked. He was fit and lean, not in any fake cover-model way, but it was obvious he did physical work. His shoulders were broad and his arms muscular and long. His torso was tanned, of course, not the deep gold of his face and forearms but tawny, in a way no islander could hope to achieve. She thought of the day he'd first walked into the Driftwood and stood out like an exotic creature.

Her breath caught in her throat again and she turned away and swam back to the far side of the pool, her heart racing. When she reached him again, Patrick was down to his navy boxers, and shivering ankle deep on the rock steps. He bared his teeth in disgust.

'Are you out of your mind? It's glacial in here.'

Laughing, she trod water and flicked a stream of water into the air, soaking him.

'Bloody hell!' His shout echoed round the pool but she giggled. She scooped up more water with her hands and he cursed her.

'Wimp!'

'Just you wait ...' He pushed off from the steps, half diving into the pool. Popped up shaking his head. 'You ... r-really are b-arking mad!'

'Hadn't you worked that out yet?' Maisie agreed. The pool, replenished twice a day by the rollers, chilled you to the bone. Her legs were numb and even swimming constantly, hypothermia was probably a real possibility. She would and should have brought her wetsuit, but she was damned if she was telling Patrick that.

Huffing with cold, he thrashed up and down while she wondered how much longer she could stand being in the pool. The water was clear, with weed and kelp swishing gently below her. There were fish, of course, and if you wore goggles you could spot them shimmering below you or weaving in and out of the seaweed. Orange crabs too, and ruby snakelock anemones. Sometimes seals popped their heads up over the edge of the pool, alarmingly close, to take a look at you, and once when she was swimming off the Driftwood one had nudged her from behind, scaring the life out of her. The only thing scaring her today was Patrick.

His hair was plastered to his head, his face ruddy as he swam towards her. 'Call me a wimp but I've had enough,' he said, his voice cracking with the cold.

'You're a wimp,' she said, secretly relieved as she'd been about to give up herself. 'Let's get out.'

She let him clamber out first and not only because it gave her a view of his muscular bottom encased in soaking-wet cotton. He brushed droplets from his torso and jogged on the spot to keep warm.

She climbed out after him. 'I've brought a towel in my backpack if you don't mind sharing,' she said.

'You first. And I've no intention of going home in dripping wet underwear so you'd better turn away or point me in the direction of a private place to change. I'll go commando on the way home.'

She tried not to look down at his boxers.

'Not that I'm in any kind of condition to shock anyone after that cold water.'

You could have fooled me, she thought. 'There's a rock outcrop just over on the other side of the pool. I use that to get changed and it's not overlooked. I'll go first and be as quick as I can.'

Clutching her clothes and backpack, Maisie jogged to the outcrop and wormed her way between the rocks into the bathroom-sized space. She knew from experience that once within its 'walls' you couldn't be seen from the pool or the path above the beach. Few folk knew the little chamber was even there. Mindful of Patrick shivering on the path, she wriggled out of her damp tankini and dried herself hastily. She was still damp and it was a challenge pulling on her dry clothes but she wanted to be as quick as possible and not soak the towel too much.

She called to Patrick even before she was fully dressed and was at the entrance in her bare feet when he jogged over. He was carrying his clothes.

Her toes curled on the gritty surface. His body was drying but water dripped from his hair in narrow rivulets over his shoulders and in tiny pathways through the tawny hair on his chest, minuscule glistening droplets. It ran down his stomach and thighs. His boxers clung to everything, not that there was much to see, as he'd joked after that immersion, but still. Maisie's whole body tensed. She curled her hand into a fist as the jolt of desire hit her. It was like being knocked over by a wave. She wanted him so much. More than she'd ever wanted any man before. Way more than Keegan. This was real, grown-up lust and it didn't matter that she was almost forty and sassy and cynical, she wanted him now.

He stopped rubbing his arms and frowned at her.

'Any chance I could borrow the towel?'

202

'Oh. Oh yes. Here you are.' She held out the damp towel. 'You look cold,' she said. He'd rejected her after she had come back from the hospital. Why should things be any different now?

He looked down at her. 'I wonder why?'

He took the towel, and disappeared into the 'changing area'. While he dressed, Maisie removed a metal flask from her backpack and unscrewed the top.

'Hot chocolate?' she asked. 'I guess it ought to be brandy, but you'd have to pass on that anyway.'

'Great idea.'

She poured the chocolate into the flask lid and offered it to Patrick first.

'Thanks.'

He sipped it and then handed it back. It was still hot and she blew steam off the top. Patrick stood by her in a chunky sweater and jeans – the most magnificent man she'd ever seen. He had that half-smile on his face and the glint in his eye that never seemed to fade, apart from on the night her father had been taken ill and once or twice at Scorrier Holdings, when she'd caught him watching Hugo with an ill-disguised contempt. She'd only known him a few weeks and her life was full of doubts – about the Driftwood and 'saving' Gull – but she knew what she wanted now, without a shadow of a doubt.

She finished the cup and refilled it, handing it back to him. He took a few sips and then put the cup down on a rock. 'Maisie?'

His smile had gone but the gleam in his eye had become

a white-hot fire. She shivered with desire and her body was like a taut glowing wire.

'Yes ...'

'You know. I'm going to take a huge gamble here and if it doesn't come off, you'll have every right to ask me to leave. We could dance around this all day. We could pretend there's no elephant in the room, but I think we both know that if we don't go to bed soon, I'm going to have to jump in that freezing cold ocean and keep on swimming until I reach Melbourne.'

Chapter 22

Maisie's legs threatened to buckle. The jolt of lust was like a lightning strike straight through her, then she was flung back to the morning she'd made a pass at him at the pub. The humiliation, the shame ...

'After I'd come back from the hospital, you weren't interested.'

'Of course I was interested. It was agony to turn you down, but you were exhausted and emotional.'

'Don't you dare tell me I was vulnerable and you did it for my own sake. I couldn't bear that.'

'Not vulnerable. You're the least vulnerable woman I've ever met.'

Patrick took a step towards her. She flinched, and wasn't sure his comment was a compliment or not. 'Really? Do I come across as that ...' She groped for a word. 'That *hard*?'

He clutched her arm. 'No. No ... please listen to me.'

Realising that he was holding her forearm, Patrick backed off, although she was desperate to hear what he meant. *The least vulnerable woman I've ever met.* His words echoed Keegan's parting excuses: *You don't need me, Maisie. You're a*

survivor. You'll get through this and be better off without me.
He was right, she had been better off without him, but only time had shown her that. In that moment, raw and lost after losing the baby, she had needed him and shown him she needed him. Unlike the Driftwood, she wasn't made of granite but the months of working hard and pretending she was fine and could just breeze on night after night in the pub, smiling, laughing, when inside sometimes she'd felt like crying and screaming, they had taken their toll.

'I'm listening,' she said softly. 'I want to hear what you have to say. I am trying to understand.'

He let out a breath of relief. 'Then understand this. That morning after your dad had been taken to hospital, I didn't know what would happen if I had ... done what you expected. What we both wanted. I had no idea if you and I ... had sex ... if you'd have regretted it and I'd be out on my ear the next morning.'

'Are you saying you refused me because you were afraid of losing your job?' she asked, in agony at having to ask yet desperate to hear the truth, however awkward. 'Please be honest with me. I don't want lies or soft soap.'

'No. I was afraid of losing a relationship that could turn into something more than a quick and regretted shag. And before you say another word, yes, it was hardly the ideal timing, was it? Admit it.'

She groaned. She hated to agree with him but he was right. 'Yes ...' she murmured.

'It's no shame to be hurt and upset. No shame to feel you need someone, Maisie,' he said. 'Is it?'

She couldn't answer him in words but her hand reached out for his. Her fingers closed round his rough ones and his eyes lit up with pleasure and desire for her.

He turned to her. 'I won't make the same bloody stupid mistake twice. I don't know how I get a bloody thing done in that bar or a wink of sleep, dreaming about you.'

He picked up her hand and did something no one had ever done before. He touched his lips to her knuckles and kissed them. It was so old-fashioned and so innocent but the touch of his warm lips on her skin stoked her need for him.

'You taste of salt,' he said.

'What did you expect? Wine and roses?'

'Come here.'

He pulled her into his arms and kissed her as the wind strengthened from the sea. Waves crashed into the pool but they were a rock buffeted by the gale. She let herself relax into his arms, and tipped back her head while he kissed her throat and then her lips again. He cupped her bottom in his hands, lifting her onto her tiptoes.

'Not out here,' she whispered.

'I'm not that daft. "The hills have eyes", remember.'

She giggled at the thought of Una and Phyllis finding them naked, making love by the pool.

'Where, then?'

'At the Driftwood. Mum and Dad are on the main island. No one will think anything of seeing us together there.'

Patrick groaned. 'I'm not sure I can wait that long. What if you change your mind on the way back?'

'You'll have to, and I won't.' Maisie got up, grabbed her

rucksack and Patrick did the same. She'd never got back to the Driftwood so fast from the pool. She longed to hold his hand and drag him back there but was terrified of being seen by someone she knew. Even now, it was possible that someone might have spotted them kissing by the pool.

By the time they reached the inn, she was almost faint with lust. She was worried there was something wrong with her, the feeling was so intense.

'My place or yours?' he asked.

'Yours. No, mine. Oh stuff it, I don't care.'

'Mine then.' He grabbed her hand and they ran into the Piggery. Patrick closed and locked the door, while Maisie drew the curtains. He was behind her before she'd even closed them properly, holding her around the waist and kissing the back of her neck. His breath was warm and each tiny kiss made her skin tingle deliciously. He put his hand on her breast. He moaned in pleasure and her nipples stiffened under his fingers.

'It's almost killed me to keep my hands off you ...' he said.

'Not as much as it's almost killed me ... oh my God ...'

She let her head rest against his sweater and closed her eyes. Could this be happening? Could she feel this amazing?

He took her hand and sat down on his single bed. She stood facing him, fitting perfectly between his open legs. He reached up and lifted the hem of her sweater. With a delicious lack of haste, he slipped her sweater and top up and over her head. She wasn't wearing a bra after the swim but she didn't feel embarrassed at his seeing her bare breasts, she felt proud and joyful. Being undressed by Patrick and naked in front of him seemed the most natural thing in the world. All her

208

doubts and troubles had evaporated as if they'd never been.

'Maisie ...'

She helped him off with his own shirt and sweater. He threw them on the floor and drew her to him again. He lowered his head and she stood on tiptoe to meet his mouth. As they kissed, she tangled her fingers in his hair, breathing the scent of him, the tang of cold clean water. His skin was warm under her hands as she explored the muscles in his back and the smooth skin stretched taut over them. She tasted the sea on his lips as he kissed her, and felt the salt thickening his hair.

Maisie flicked open the metal buttons of his jeans and pulled the fly apart. He tried to shove them down his thighs himself but overbalanced. Hobbled by his jeans, Patrick tumbled onto the bed, taking her with him. She ended up on top of him, half on and off the little bed. It was too small for him, let alone the two of them.

She giggled. 'Who'd have thought a single bed could be so much fun?'

'Right now, the middle of a field would do.'

They were a tangle of bare limbs, clothes and laughter as he tried to extricate himself. Still with his trousers round his ankles, he fumbled with her skinny jeans, cursing softly as he tried to pull down the zip.

'Bugger it. Sorry.'

She smiled. 'Here. Let me.' She tugged at the zip and it freed but she'd have cut off her jeans if she had to.

Patrick sighed in relief. 'Great. Can't wait much longer. I need you.'

She knew how he felt. She was almost bursting for him. She arched her back so he could pull the tight jeans over her bottom, dragging her knickers with them. Finally she was naked ... on Patrick's bed in the middle of the afternoon. If her parents – anyone – walked into the garden now, saw the drawn curtains and heard the heavy breathing, the moans and laughter ...

It didn't matter. She still wouldn't be able to stop. She'd still carry on and they could batter down the door. When did she ever get this wanton? When Patrick walked into the Driftwood, that's when ...

And he was above her. She bunched the quilt in her hands. There was no going back and she didn't want to go back. It would kill her to stop now. By the looks of him it would kill Patrick too. He climbed back onto the bed and lay by her side, clasping her against him on the narrow quilt. Their legs tangled, limb over limb, almost rolling off the bed at times but greedy to explore and devour each other all at once. She was as greedy as him, hungrier even, clutching at his bottom and back, entwining herself with him and wanting the grey autumn afternoon to go on forever.

Chapter 23

Too late to go back. In so many ways.

Yet how could Patrick regret the past few hours? How, with Maisie tangled in the sheets of his bed, her soft lashes against her freckled cheek, breathing softly. After his shower, Patrick slung a towel around his neck and lingered in the doorway of the shower room, drinking in the sight of her in his bed.

She was sleeping and her face was that of an angel. He smiled to himself: what they'd just done had been as far from angelic as it was possible to get but it had also been bloody wonderful.

She opened her eyes and smiled.

Not asleep then, and that smile was knockout. Pure happiness.

Relief flooded through his veins. While he'd showered, he'd had a vague sense of unease that she might have regretted sleeping with him. She sat up. She was still naked and sexy, rumpled and gorgeous. He cursed inwardly. He wanted her again, right now ... but she pushed the duvet off her and swung her legs out of bed, pouring cold water on his hopes.

She sighed but was already on her feet. 'I have to get back.'

'You could shower here.'

'I'd love to but Mum and Dad will be home soon.' She groaned. 'Sorry. That makes me sound as if I'm sixteen, not thirty-nine.'

He smiled and tossed the towel on a chair. 'We could always go public ...'

She squealed in horror. 'No!'

'OK, OK. That was mainly a joke on my part, though I'm easy on the subject.'

'I've only known you a few weeks. What would people say?'

'Do you care?' he asked.

'No ... actually that's hypocritical of me. Yes, I do care, but not because of any petty-minded opinions but because I value my privacy. We should be able to have some secrets.'

He believed her completely, but talk of secrets made him uneasy, although he decided to ignore his guilty conscience for now. 'In a place as small as Gull, it's going to be difficult to keep it under wraps anyway,' he said, struggling to cope with the fact that Maisie was still naked.

She arched an eyebrow. 'So this – us – is an "it"?'

'That depends on whether you want today to be a one-off ...' He joined her by the bed and took her hand. 'I really hope it isn't. I don't know about you, but I think I'd have to leave for my own health's sake if I thought that this afternoon, all of it, was the first and last time. Spending time with you, in every way, was way too much fun not to be repeated.'

She let go of his hand and glanced down briefly. Was he

imagining things or were her cheeks pink? He reached up to touch her face and found it soft and warm.

'Maisie, I think you're blushing.'

'No, I am not.' She rolled her eyes at herself and groaned. 'But, yes, today was fun. It was great and I want to do it again.'

He pointed at the bed. 'Right here and now?'

'No. You know I don't mean now. However much I want to spend the rest of the day with you, I *have* to go. It'll be dark soon.' She batted him on the arm and moved away but he could tell she was still smiling from her body language. He'd made her happy and that meant a lot to him. Even though, as she pointed out, they'd barely known each other a month, he cared about how she felt – and how he made her feel. His stomach knotted. *Paddy boy, you could get in a right old mess if you're not careful ... Maybe*, a voice whispered in his head, *you already are ...*

Maisie rooted around the tangle of clothes on the floor and gathered up her jeans and Patrick's sweatshirt. 'Argh. Where are my knickers?'

She pulled the duvet back off the bed and shot an enquiring glance at him. 'Patrick?'

He savoured the sight of her body a second longer before replying. 'On the sofa?'

He knew damn well they were. He'd thrown them on the couch himself. He could have found them for her minutes ago but he wanted to squeeze out every second of her scurrying around his room in the nude. Damn, he'd need another plunge in that freezing pool at this rate.

She put her pants on and wriggled into skinny jeans. 'What's so funny?'

'Nothing. Just enjoying the reverse striptease.'

She glared at him then burst out laughing. She had always been beautiful to him but this was a new, flirty, flippant Maisie. A Maisie with the weight of the world lifted from her shoulders for a couple of hours.

She put her top on. Patrick found her socks under the edge of the bed and handed them over.

'Thanks.'

'You'll need these.' He held out her trainer. 'Here.'

She gawped in amazement as he lifted her foot into his lap and slipped the trainer over her toe and heel.

'You don't have to …'

'I want to. Shh.'

She wiggled her foot inside and to his surprise, let him slip the other shoe on. A small, half-secret smile spread over her lips. He wondered what she was thinking then realised it was impossible to know what Maisie really thought about anything. As long as this hadn't been the last time, that was all he needed to know.

'When can we do this again?' he asked.

'I don't know … maybe tomorrow. Away from Gull, if we can both get away together.'

'I have rugby training tomorrow night at the community centre field on St Saviour's.'

She hesitated then smiled. 'And I'm seeing Jess. We could meet at the Flower Farm. I'll let her know. She won't tell. What about Will?'

'I haven't known him long but he doesn't seem like the gossipy type.' Patrick smiled.

'I think we can trust him, I'll tell her tomorrow evening and we'll arrange to meet later.'

He smiled as she reached to kiss him. That soft, hot mouth, the scent of her ... her skin and eyes seemed to shimmer with post-sex radiance. Jesus, he'd be climbing the walls until they were alone again tomorrow.

'See you,' she said, and unlocked the door. She peered outside to check the coast was clear and was gone.

He shoved his fingers through his damp hair. The room was quiet. It was dark now so he lit the table lamp. He sat down on the bed and sighed. The room still smelled of her – of them and of his guilt.

He lay on his bed, turning over the 'ifs' and 'buts' and bargaining with himself until he heard the voices of Ray and Hazel as they walked around the side of the pub. Ray was grumbling and telling Hazel not to fuss and that he was perfectly capable of helping out and that Maisie needed the support. The back door to the inn closed and he was on his own again.

What good would it do, he reasoned, to ruin Maisie's happiness and his own when there was no actual need to upset her? He'd be gone in a few months. Why bring the house crashing down and making everyone, including himself, miserable? Life was too short – Greg was always telling him that. And anyway, what was wrong with a few little white lies, when they hadn't – and couldn't – hurt anyone?

Chapter 24

The following day, Maisie met Jess on the quayside at St Mary's harbour. Maisie could see her scanning the boat, desperate to hear the 'big news' Maisie had promised to share once they were face to face. They'd booked a table for lunch at a café overlooking Porthcressa beach but Maisie wanted to get the main news over with while they were in the open air, rather than in a confined space.

'Jess ...' Maisie began as they strolled along the pavement towards the café. 'I've got something to tell you and I don't want it to go any further than the two of us and I want you keep calm when I tell you.'

Jess stopped dead in her tracks in front of the tour-boat ticket hut. 'Oh God, hun, that sounds serious. What's the matter?'

'Nothing bad. Far from it, but something that you might be a bit shocked by.'

'For God's sake, tell me before I burst!'

'Only if you swear not to tell anyone.'

Jess folded her arms. 'Maisie. I'm getting pissed off now. You know I'd never share any secret of yours.'

'It's me and Patrick. We're sort of ... well, an item.'

'An item? You mean you're shagging him? Oh my God, I *knew* there was something going on. I just knew it!' Jess actually punched the air in triumph exactly like Andy Murray when he'd just won Wimbledon.

Maisie had expected Jess to be pleased – and justifiably a bit smug – but not actually breaking out the party poppers and champagne. 'No, you didn't. I didn't know it myself until yesterday afternoon, so how could you?'

'I could see it. Smell it. I just *knew* you were shagging him, and why not? He's gorgeous, for a toy boy.'

'Toy boy? He's only two years younger than me.'

Jess winked and pointed a finger at Maisie. 'Gotcha!'

As they walked along the cobbles that led from the harbour to Hugh Street and over to Porthcressa, Maisie took her arm. 'Please, Jess. Keep your voice down. I wasn't shagging him. I absolutely had no intention of shagging him. Until yesterday.'

'Oh my God. How was it?'

'You can't ask me that. Argh. I wish I'd never shared this with you. I've changed my mind. I was going to ask if we could use the Flower Farm as somewhere discreet to meet up.'

'Oh, but you must. I love the idea of you using the farm as a love nest.'

'It's not a love nest.' Maisie had to say the last two words through gritted teeth. It sounded so tacky but asking Jess had seemed a good idea before she'd actually got the words out.

'A lust nest, then.'

Maisie gave up. 'What about your mum? Won't she suspect something?' she asked Jess.

Jess looked around her as if checking for spies that might be lurking behind the tourist information centre. 'Not if we're – you're – careful and discreet.'

Maisie snorted. 'Discreet? With you dancing round with a megaphone shouting: "Roll up, roll up to see Maisie and Patrick at it".'

'A megaphone? You know, that's not a bad idea. I could charge a couple of quid per person and give the money to the lifeboats.' Jess pointed at Maisie. 'Maisie, your face. Stop worrying. I can be the soul of discretion when I want to be. You know you can trust me, don't you?'

'Yes. Yes, I do.' Maisie knew Jess was referring to the business with Keegan and her miscarriage. Jess had been wonderful. Her parents had been sympathetic and loving but she didn't know what she'd have done without Jess to talk to and cry with.

'And the good news is that Mum's gone to see her sister in Camborne for a while so you'll be safe. Poor Auntie Gill's broken her ankle ... After she comes back, we'll have to formulate an alternative plan of action.'

'This isn't an SAS mission,' said Maisie, although she couldn't stop smiling at Jess's enthusiasm for being part of the intrigue and it was very useful that Mrs Godrevy was safely out of the way on the mainland, at least for a couple of weeks. Jess was an angel for being so happy for Maisie when her own love life with Adam Pengelly had taken a terminal nosedive.

'No, but you're going to have to treat it like one if you're to keep this under wraps. You definitely don't want to go public, do you?'

'Absolutely not. I don't, and Patrick has agreed. We haven't known each other long.'

'Three weeks, give or take,' said Jess.

'Thanks for keeping tally.'

Jess beamed proudly. 'You're welcome.'

'Anyway, as you've pointed out, we've only known each other a few weeks. I know what some people will say if they find out we're an item, not that I care of course.'

'Oh, of course not.'

Maisie ignored the sarcasm, aware she was convincing herself way more than Jess. 'It's no big deal. We're having a fling and Patrick's going back to Australia. End of. It's what I want and he wants and, you know, it's a bloody lovely change. No one has any silly ideas or expectations. The lines are clear from the start and so no one is going to end up disappointed or bunny boiling.'

Maisie laughed, expecting Jess to nod in agreement or make a cheeky joke but Jess's expression had changed. She was chewing her bottom lip, a sure sign she was unsure, or doubtful – or both. Maisie had seen that look at school when Jess had been homesick or when she'd been worried about her parents' break-up or Adam's moods.

Jess's uncertainty was contagious and Maisie's own stomach fluttered with unease. 'What's up now?' she asked.

In a flash, Jess threw on the Cheshire Cat beam again. 'Nothing. Nothing at all, hun. If you're happy about the arrangement, then I'm bloody ecstatic for you and I'm delighted to help out in any way I can.'

'Good. Patrick's going to have a word with Will after rugby

tonight so if it's OK and you wouldn't mind making the um ... arrangements ...' Maisie hesitated, suddenly realising what she was asking. Her cheeks heated up.

'I don't mind at all. How does the spare room sound? It's clean but it's not been aired, you won't mind that, will you? Will and I'll go down the Seven Stars for a while so you can have some privacy. Will can take you both back to Gull afterwards if you don't want to bring the *Puffin*. Subject to the tides of course, but I think we'll be OK for a little afternoon delight.'

'I'll need an excuse for coming over here.'

'Tell your mum and dad we need an extra pair of hands with the packing and that Patrick has volunteered while you help me out in the office in your spare time. After all, it's peak season for the narcissi and you've helped me for years.'

'True. Thanks so much. I know you're busy.'

'It's a genuine pleasure as long as you don't want me to pick up the pieces when he finally goes home.'

It was said light-heartedly, but Maisie felt a tremor of unease when Jess mentioned Patrick leaving. However, she pushed it away. She hugged Jess, shimmering with excitement again. Jess might be feeling down because she'd been thinking about Adam Pengelly and Maisie felt sorry for that.

She almost wanted to punch the air herself but settled for a sigh of contentment. How very grown-up, eh? A secret affair with a sexy Australian who drove her insane with lust.

'I'll text him to let him know you're fine with us meeting here for the next week. Thank you so much for this, Jess. I won't forget when it's your turn.'

Jess wrinkled her nose. 'I can't imagine when you'll ever be able to return the favour but it's a pleasure. Anything to see you happy.'

Buzzing with joy, Maisie pushed open the door to the café, ready for a very happy girly lunch. Anyone watching them, and naturally Maisie knew most of the people in the café, would have wondered what had got into the pair of them as they giggled and shared in-jokes like school girls.

It was only when Maisie got out her purse at the end of the meal and saw her phone that the lunch turned sour. There were two missed calls and a text from Hugo, demanding to know why she hadn't got back to him.

Maisie couldn't keep the dismay off her face before she shoved the phone back in her bag.

'What's up?' asked Jess. 'Not your dad, is it?'

Maisie forced a smile. 'Nothing important. Just a few issues at the pub. It'll keep.'

'It' kept longer than Maisie had planned. Every time she considered calling Hugo, she thought of an even better excuse not to: she was too busy at the pub, or her parents needed her, or she was with Patrick (and glowing with happiness at their new 'arrangement'). She'd also made some progress in rallying the troops to Operation Resist Hugo and calling her 'enemy' just didn't feel right, no matter how much she might find out by doing so.

She'd been to the Fudge Pantry and had come away feeling more hopeful than she'd expected. The owners, Davina and Pete Jenkins, were also torn over the merits of Hugo's offer, but Hugo's claim that they had already agreed to sell to him appeared to be over-optimistic at best.

Even on a damp and misty day Maisie could see exactly why he wanted the Jenkins' cottage and why they were reluctant to let it go. Positioned on a hillock in the very heart of Gull, it had three-sixty degree views of the whole island and the Scilly archipelago, and every one of Gull's beautiful pathways passed it. Hugo had hinted it would make a perfect artisan café, deli and 'farm shop', though Maisie suspected he had no intention of stocking it with local produce. After Maisie's visit, they'd agreed not to make a decision until Maisie could arrange a private meeting with everyone affected by the proposal.

Her conscience had niggled that she was being unfair to Hugo by ignoring his calls but the more she found out about his tactics, the less guilty she felt. In fact, she felt a renewed surge of optimism and instead of heading back to the Driftwood after her meeting with the Jenkinses, Maisie dropped in on the Rev Bev.

The vicar lived in a modest but solid granite house next to the church. A fresh breeze had sprung up and blown away the mist and Bev was hanging out her surplices in the emerging sunlight, next to a leopard-print fleece and a row of racy knickers. Maisie couldn't help but smile. Apart from family events and Christmas carols, she was no churchgoer, but she liked any vicar who was prepared to drink in her pub and join in with the karaoke night.

Rumour had it that the vicar had been very popular in her mainland parish, a fishing village called St Trenyan, and Maisie could see why. Bev worked hard, had a warm, welcoming personality and the sense of humour needed to look after three island churches in all weathers. She looked after the parishes on St Saviour's and St Piran's, as well as Gull, so she was forever in and out of boats.

Maisie called hello as she opened the little wicket gate that led into the garden. 'Hi there, hope I'm not interrupting anything important?'

Beverley turned round, her arms full of laundry. 'Only the vital task of hanging out my smalls. How lovely to see you. How are your mum and dad doing after their scare?'

The vicar's Brummie accent always took Maisie slightly aback. Combined with the glamorous image and the dog collar, it was slightly unnerving – but fun. 'Dad's on the mend and Mum's starting to relax a little. We're all very relieved,' said Maisie.

'I saw them both walking along Hell Cove the other day. He looked better.' Bev dropped the washing back in the basket.

'Yes. Doctor's orders: gentle exercise but nothing too strenuous.'

'Lucky you have Patrick to help then. Fortunate that he dropped onto Gull just at the time you needed him.'

'It is,' said Maisie, wondering if Bev was implying that Patrick's arrival was some kind of divine intervention.

'And such a strong and capable pair of hands.'

'I suppose he is,' said Maisie, thinking that Patrick might not have been joking about Bev fancying him. Maisie eyed the knickers flapping in the breeze as Bev pushed her long hair out of her green eyes. The attraction was probably mutual, despite the age difference.

'I meant your hands,' said Bev.

'Oh ... I see ... I don't know about that.' Maisie flapped around, trying to regain her composure. 'Um. How are you finding it here on Gull? Isn't it a bit quiet after the bright lights of St Trenyan?'

'You mean with its wild nightlife and gin joints?' She laughed. 'I always enjoy a challenge and the diocese asked me to cover for your previous priest while he has his hip op. I was happy to experience island life in such a beautiful place. It may be small here but I'm never on my own. There's always someone I need to see or who wants to call in. This is my day off, hence the domestic duties.' Bev nodded at her eclectic laundry mix flapping in the breeze.

'I'm sorry I've intruded on your day off. I'll catch you another time.'

'No, please. No time like the present.' She smiled. 'Can I do anything for you in particular?'

Maisie took a deep breath and launched into her idea for a meeting to discuss Hugo's takeover plans.

Bev listened carefully. 'Of course I'll attend,' she said, 'and I do think that it's a great idea to gather everyone together, especially if Hugo's tactic is to divide and conquer. But you need to understand that while privately I don't like Hugo's tactics any more than you do and would hate to see the soul of Gull destroyed, I have to be seen to be neutral in this business. I'm sorry.'

'No, I understand,' said Maisie, trying to hide her frustration. She did see that the vicar was in a difficult position. 'Can I help you finish hanging out the washing?'

Bev seemed surprised but nodded and Maisie started to peg out a blouse.

'It would be different, of course, if most of the islanders were fighting a hostile takeover of the island,' Bev said, hanging up a pair of jeans. 'Hugo can't do that, can he?'

'No. He already owns a few of the cottages and the gallery and shop, but he needs to buy up at least half a dozen more and get permission to develop them before he can make a significant difference to the character of Gull and turn it into an annexe of Petroc.'

'Is he likely to?'

Maisie straightened up from the basket, holding a pair of red silky pyjama bottoms in her arms. 'A couple of years ago, I'd have said never, but times have been tough for everyone. A wet summer, loss of the helicopter service – though it's supposed to be coming back – and an increase in transport costs. It all adds up and we're already quite a hard place to reach. It doesn't take much for people to decide to choose elsewhere for their holidays, no matter how beautiful it looks in the brochures. And in real life, of course.'

'Hmm. I wish there was more I could do. I'll definitely come to the meeting and I'll gently try to remind people to look at all sides of the story and not be bullied, but in the end, I suppose that this whole issue comes down to money.'

Maisie sighed. 'Yes, and that's the one thing none of us – apart from Hugo – have got. But it's also about everyone standing firm against him. I've been sounding out a few people discreetly and had the idea that we could form some sort of co-operative to pool our resources and help each other out. I don't know how it would work, but I'm going to try. The Hell Cove Cottages are in dire need of renovation.'

'Perhaps we can get some kind of working party to help Una and Phyllis?' said Bev, resuming her pegging out. 'My brother's a painter and decorator and I know a few craftspeople from the mainland as well as here. Of course, people already help their neighbours on the islands, but if we had a co-ordinated effort, a schedule of works and ideas – a proper plan – I think we could get a lot more done.'

'For free?' Maisie laughed. 'How could you do that?'

'I have my ways. I can't make any promises but I do know some business and trades people in my former parish that might have their arms twisted to help, if they get the promise of a free holiday. Some of them owe me favours too. In fact I can think of one who owes a lot of people a lot of favours.'

'That might not be seen to be neutral,' said Maisie.

Bev winked. 'I'm merely helping my flock. Leave it with me. I'll sound a couple of folk out and I'll come to the meeting. Perhaps if you present the idea as a "third way" instead of going to the dogs or going to Hugo, people might give it a try.'

'If Hugo came to you, asking you to persuade people to sell, would you tell him the same?' Maisie asked, still amazed that the vicar was willing to help out.

'I'd say it was none of my business.'

'And has he?'

Bev shook her head. 'Not yet.'

'And if he had, you wouldn't tell me?'

Bev smiled and secured a sweatshirt in place with a peg.

The washing basket was empty. 'No. But I won't say you've been here either.'

'You must know a lot of secrets,' said Maisie, liking Bev more by the minute.

'I don't go in for hearing confessions, but yes, obviously people tell me things in confidence. I'm sure they do to you too.'

'They're usually drunk when they overshare with me and then half the Driftwood can hear their confessions.'

Bev picked up the basket. 'I'm way too stingy with the communion wine for that. Let me have your mobile number and email, and I'll be in touch.'

Maisie walked home. Patrick had said he'd been round to Bev's to confess. Maisie had assumed he was joking and had only been to discuss the wildlife talk. Of course, he was joking but ... what if there had been truth in it too? Did Bev know something about Patrick that she didn't? But why would he tell the vicar? He wasn't religious at all, he'd told her that. She laughed at herself. Reminded herself of her own words to Jess. Her fling was meant to be fun. No strings. No regrets.

Chapter 25

Maisie was brought down to earth with a bang later that week when she finally told Hazel and Ray about her plans to thwart Hugo, knowing she couldn't keep it from them any longer.

'Over my dead body will he get his hands on the Driftwood,' had been her father's first words.

'Funnily enough that prospect doesn't fill me with encouragement, Dad,' Maisie had replied and her mum had told Ray 'not to be so silly'. To Maisie's great relief, both Ray and Hazel agreed that a discreet gathering of their neighbours at the Driftwood was the best way to gauge the real depth of feeling about Hugo's plans and present Maisie's community-led renovation programme as an alternative way forward.

So on a grey Sunday morning at the tail end of November, Patrick and Ray had pushed back and stacked the tables at one end of the bistro and laid out the chairs 'like a proper meeting', according to Hazel. They could have used the community hall but that would have risked Hugo getting wind of the meeting. He might have done anyway, it was a bit of a tall order to expect everyone to keep quiet, and he'd know soon enough once work started and people told him to shove his offer. *If* they told him to shove his offer.

'I feel nervous now it's actually here,' Maisie said to her mum.

'Tell you what. Let's put the Christmas decs up, eh? It's a bit earlier than usual, but why not?' said Ray.

'It's almost December anyway and it'll help get people in a festive mood too,' Hazel added optimistically.

'Anything to get them on our side.'

So the room had been decorated with tinsel and paper streamers to make it look more festive. In the winter months the bistro acted as overspill for Christmas lunches or any bigger events, although the tree itself was down in a corner of the bar. The Samsons also had their own tree in the corner of the flat's sitting room.

Every piece of tinsel, tree decoration and Santa/snowman/robin ornament they had had been dragged out of storage and used to adorn the rooms, private and public. There was no chic co-ordinated colour scheme as there would doubtless have been at Scorrier House or in the Rose and Crab, just an eclectic mix of festive bits 'n' bobs, many of which had been handed down from her grandparents' time. They were sadly no longer alive, but Maisie thought of them fondly as she and her parents had unwrapped each item and found a place for it.

Finally, the decorations were up and the room was almost ready for the two-thirty meeting.

Patrick had been given access to the Samson family kitchen and was brewing up a large pan of mulled wine. The rich aroma of cinnamon and spices filled the whole upper floor and made Maisie's nose twitch. In the last job she'd got sick of the smell of mulled wine after she'd served up thousands of glasses of it, but she could actually grow to like it again.

Hazel added a platter of mince pies to the table while Ray filled some jugs with squash for the children. 'Do you think Hugo knows we're holding this meeting?' Hazel asked Maisie.

'I don't think so. I posted leaflets through the doors by hand and it isn't advertised anywhere, so unless someone told him, then I don't see how he would know.' Her heart had skipped a beat every time her phone buzzed over the past few days but none of the texts had been from Hugo and she hadn't had an email from him either. He'd probably given up trying to get her on her own.

People started drifting into the pub. The Jenkinses from the Fudge Pantry, Rev Bev, Javid, the postmistress and around a dozen other people who'd expressed an interest in discussing Hugo's proposal. There were a few children who settled in a corner with some of the toys she kept in the bistro. They had to wait for Phyllis and Una as they'd been milking the goats. Una's hair was carrot orange today, accessorised with a clip-on bow. Phyllis was in a clean pair of overalls so Maisie knew she was taking things seriously.

'It's a great turnout,' Hazel whispered to Maisie.

'Hmm. I'm amazed, to be honest. I think every person I asked has come along.'

Maisie was as skittish as a kitten, even though she knew everyone attending; she knew they might be a tough audience. She may have led a big team at her old pub, but here she had no sway over them as she had her staff, and no idea of the resistance she might meet. Hazel and Ray sat in the front row, while Patrick stood at the back of the room ready to serve the refreshments when the meeting was over.

'Of course, some of you may understandably think that Hugo's plans are a good idea ...' she began. There were mutterings and a few expletives from the stauncher opponents as she mentioned Hugo's plans, but she was determined to scope out the lie of the land instead of immediately dismissing his offer.

Her opening remark was met with silence, guilty looks and one 'a good idea for bloody Hugo's bank balance' from Joly Preece who ran the Gull Island Bakery and had loathed Hugo from boyhood. 'I wouldn't piss on a Scorrier if they were on fire.'

That earned him a whack on the arm from his wife and even their teenage son took his eyes off his phone for a nanosecond before shooting them back to the screen. Maisie was surprised he could hear anything with his headphones clamped over his ears.

'Joly. Mind your language.'

'Hear Maisie out. She's trying to talk some sense,' Javid pitched in.

'I can see that feelings are running high but we need to keep cool heads and look for practical solutions to our problems. I don't know about you but I don't think we should try to compete with Petroc. I respect those who feel that selling their properties to Hugo is the best idea for them,' she said through gritted teeth. 'However, those of us who are determined to stay but are

231

struggling need to take action if the island is to … er … have a sustainable future.' Jesus, thought Maisie, starting to panic, where did she get that kind of bullshit from? Oh, wait, from Hugo's presentation at the Scorrier House.

She allowed herself a little smile that eased the tension; people were listening. All except the kids of course. 'I've thought long and hard about the best way forward and I think we need to be ourselves, and make the most of our – um – rustic charm. That's what makes Gull unique, but if we could just smarten up a bit, renovate what we can, and try to look more photogenic on Instagram, I'm sure it would help bring new visitors and income.'

'Instawhatsit?' Una looked like Maisie had given her a dose of cod liver oil.

'It's a social media app.'

'I know what it is, I've seen it, but I hate this obsession with sharing rather than experiencing.'

'I agree, Una, but that's the way it works. Instagram can be our friend.'

Una mimed a fingers-down-throat sign. 'I'd rather be friends with Attila the Hun.'

'Who the hell's she?' the bored young teenager from the bakery muttered.

'It's a *he*,' said Phyllis, rising to her sister's defence. 'Ignoramus.'

'Who's he?'

Una and Phyllis shook their heads in unison.

'What we need is to win the lottery,' said the teen's mother, nudging him in the ribs.

The boy snorted like a donkey. 'Yeah, and then I'd be on the first plane out of this dump.'

Maisie restrained herself. 'That would be great, but since we're probably not going to, we'll just have to roll our sleeves up, put our heads together and get on with it,' she said firmly.

There were mutters from the floor. 'How do we do that? Who's going to organise it?'

'I've compiled a list of people who've offered to help, and drawn up a rough rota for doing the work so we know who's doing what and when. It's going to be a very moveable feast because we're all busy with other commitments. People will turn up if and when they can spare the time.'

'Anything will better than how things are today,' said Una. 'We need to complete at least some of the jobs so businesses are ready for the new season at Easter,' added Javid.

Patrick raised his hand from the back of the room. 'I know I don't come from here so I'm sorry for sticking my oar in but I think it sounds like a good solution and I'm happy to help.'

Heads turned.

Maisie flung a smile his way. 'Thanks. That would be great.'

She immediately turned her attention back to the audience, not wanting to focus on Patrick too much but secretly thrilled to have his support. Hands started flying up all over the room and there was a definite buzz of excitement.

'All and any ideas welcome. I'm so glad some of you want to give this a try.'

After much debate, only one couple was still determined to sell up and left the meeting while everyone else stayed on to work out the details. Noise levels rose so high that Maisie had to try and call people to order so they could actually make some decisions. After a show of hands, it was decided to start work on upgrading the property in most urgent need of TLC – Hell Cove House and its cottages.

The Fudge Pantry was to be next in line. It needed its kitchen area bringing up to the latest standards and a basic makeover of the tiny shop and terrace area where people sat to enjoy ice creams, cold drinks and homemade sweet treats.

When that work was complete, depending on the weather and materials and labour availability, the workers agreed to divide their resources and have two working parties on two more properties and so on, with a deadline of all the jobs to be complete by Easter. It was a tall order that they'd finish all the projects, and privately Maisie thought it would be impossible, but she didn't want to burst the bubble now so many islanders were engaged in the process. And who knew what the weather would throw at them ... On the other hand, the most urgent jobs needed to be done over the next few months in time for the new season.

'That's it. We start work as soon as possible,' said Maisie. 'Javid will be round to compile a timescale and list of volunteers, plus the materials required.'

'We've already worked out the stuff we need at Hell Cove,' said Phyllis, pulling a sheet of paper from her folder. 'I helped Dad roof it in the first place and I know every inch of it.'

'I've done a spreadsheet of the materials required and how much we think they'll cost,' said Una. 'I keep it with all the cottage bookings on the computer,' she added proudly.

'Great. If we can have a copy I'll get Javid and Patrick to look at it.'

Javid agreed to be in charge of social media and the teenage Preece was bribed and coerced to help set up and manage an Instagram account to publicise the cottages and businesses once the work was done.

After everyone had left, Maisie was loading the dishwasher in the pub kitchen while Patrick tackled the extra crockery. Ray and Hazel were upstairs, clearing away then going for a well-earned rest.

'Thanks for offering to help. I never expected so much enthusiasm. Do you mind being hired out like this?' Maisie asked.

'What else am I going to do with my time off? I want to be useful.'

'Yes, but you're not our slave.'

'I dunno. Being your slave doesn't sound too bad to me.' He winked. 'Stop worrying.'

Damn, the cheek and the Marigolds were a lethal combination. She felt optimistic, almost drunk with happiness in a way she hadn't felt in a very long time.

'You're smiling,' said Patrick. 'It suits you and I like it.' He hesitated, which wasn't like him. 'Maisie?'

'What?' she asked.

He shook his head. 'Nothing.'

'You can't say "Maisie" in *that* way and not follow it up. Come on, get it off your chest, Crocodile Dundee.' She giggled and pushed her finger into the space between his pecs. 'And it's a very nice chest at that.'

'Now, now. You'll keep me from my work.'

'I hope so ... What were you going to say?'

'Only that ...' He smiled. 'You're bubbly and happy. Smiling in a way I haven't seen you for a while.'

'So? I can be bubbly sometimes. Any complaints?'

'No. None at all. It's great ...' he said, a little wistfully Maisie thought. Perhaps she should be bubbly more often. It felt great. The banter with Patrick, his support, the sex – wow, the sex. Not only that but the comfort and joy of his warm body next to hers, making love to her. Any more dwelling on his body and she might end up taking him over the kitchen table, even with her parents upstairs. She pictured their faces if they were to walk in on her and Patrick. Him with his jeans round his ankles and her on the kitchen table, gasping. They'd managed a couple of passionate moments while Ray and Hazel were safely on the main island, in addition to their trysts at the Flower Farm, but there were never enough opportunities for Maisie's liking.

'If only we were alone now,' Patrick murmured, holding up his soapy Marigolds. The bubbles glistened in the kitchen lighting and he smelled faintly of lemon washing-up liquid.

'Mmm. I know ...'

She barely had time to breathe before his arms were around her back and his hands were on her bottom. His warm soapy wet hands. Warm water from the gloves soaked through her jeans and made her bum damp. She held his back, glorying in the flex of muscle through his shirt and sweater. He broke the kiss. She caught a snatch of her mother talking from upstairs. It was amazing her parents hadn't come down to the kitchen.

236

'While we're on our own, I've got something to ask you,' said Maisie.

He raised an eyebrow. 'That sounds serious.'

'Not really ... although you might not want to do this. It's fine if you don't, or you've other plans, but I was wondering if you'd join us for Christmas Day. You're staying here, I presume?'

He smiled but also looked a little puzzled. 'Yes. I'm staying on Gull. It's too far to go home for a short time and you need me over the holiday and on New Year's Eve, don't you?'

Maisie hadn't realised how nervous she was about asking him to join their family party. He might think it was a step too far: too much pressure or too much of a 'happy family' thing that might make him feel she was trying to tie him down.

'Yes, but ...' she said, wondering if he was trying to wriggle out of joining them.

'I don't want to muscle in on your family party,' he said. 'What does your mum have to say about me joining in?'

'Actually, she mentioned it before I even brought the subject up.'

'As in, "I'll never speak to you again if you ask that bloody layabout to share our Christmas dinner, Maisie"?'

Maisie shook her head and tried not to smile too much. 'No, her exact words were: "We'll need a bigger bird if Patrick's having Christmas lunch with us. He eats like a horse".'

Patrick laughed. 'Well, it's a kind thought but Will's mum has already asked me to join him and Jess at the Flower Farm.'

'Oh.' Maisie tried to hide her disappointment. 'In that case—'

'And Archie Pendower invited me to share a nut roast. Fen's

237

a vegetarian, as you know, and his grandson Jacob can't make it home to St Piran's for Christmas as he's on assignment in Papua New Guinea.'

'Archie and Fen asked you? Awww. That's sweet of them. You should accept.'

'The thing is that Javid also said I could join him and Katya. And Rev Bev invited me to the rectory for a roast goose with her "special friend" who's a curate from St Trenyan, "if I was desperate", she said.'

'My God, this is turning into *The Vicar of Dibley*. How many Christmas dinners do you plan on eating?'

Patrick grinned. 'Depends how many sprouts I can fit in. Of course, as an Aussie, I'd rather be having a barbie on the beach.'

'Do you really have a barbecue on the beach on Christmas Day?'

'No, because I was always working. We used to have our proper dinner a few days later after we'd raked in the cash from the partygoers and all the cricket fans at the Boxing Day test at the MCG, of course. Made most of our money over the festive season.' He quirked an eyebrow. 'Much as I'd love to crawl round Gull eating myself stupid, I'd far rather be at your table, as long as your parents really don't mind.'

'Mum would never have asked if she did.'

'Are you sure you wouldn't prefer to farm me off on the other good souls who've offered to take a hungry stranger in?' He gave her a puppy-dog look.

She suppressed a giggle. 'Stop it, McKinnon. You're getting a proper Samson family Christmas and I'll make sure you get more than your fair share of sprouts for your cheek.'

'I suppose I've no choice. Let me know if I can help out.'

'No. This is one dinner that Mum – and Dad – like to be in charge of. Don't deprive them of that.'

'I won't. I'll behave impeccably.'

He drew his finger lightly over her cheek. Maisie's skin tingled and her body thrummed with desire. She glanced around her. 'Be careful.'

'I always am careful.'

'I don't want anyone knowing. I want this to be between us: our private secret. No one else's.'

'Apart from Jess and Will?' Patrick said, with a smile.

'Apart from them.'

Patrick stopped any more words with a hot, lingering kiss that made Maisie feel as if she'd lifted into the air. Her whole body felt alive. How would she ever get through a Christmas dinner with him sitting next to her? Knowing what they'd done together and pretending to be friends and colleagues? She wanted him to share her Christmas so much and was quietly ecstatic when her mother had unexpectedly suggested it without Maisie having to hint. But would Patrick being part of their intimate family occasion be too much for them both to cope with, without her parents realising they were – well, something more than boss and barman? An item? A couple?

Maisie shivered as Patrick rested his big hands on her waist and deepened the kiss. She couldn't name what she and Patrick 'were' or think of it ending when he returned to the other side of the world. She pushed that fact to the back of the dark locked cupboard where she kept her other painful and uncomfortable truths.

Chapter 26

1 December

Once the decision had been made, no time was wasted, and a few days later, the first day of December, Hell Cove Cottages was a hive of activity, or as much of a hive as anywhere on Gull could be at dawn on a grey morning. The first of the working party had arrived at dawn. With the sun setting by late afternoon, they needed to get as much done as possible. Hazel and Ray were visiting friends on St Mary's, and had offered to get the bar ready for evening opening while Maisie helped at Hell Cove.

Both the Barton sisters were in their overalls ready to muck in. Jess was already there, along with Archie and Fen, Javid and his girlfriend, Katya, plus Pete and Davina Jenkins from the Fudge Pantry. Pete had been a builder before he'd had a change of lifestyle and had planned out a schedule of works, the first of which was to make sure the roofs of Hell Cove House and the cottages were in a good state of repair. This was easier said than done as the materials had to be found locally or shipped from the Main Island or even further afield.

Items had been scrounged or bought for a low price in return for 'favours', such as agreements to muck in with work on other island projects. Joly had apparently offered to bake a wedding cake in return for a job lot of paint, while Javid had swapped a couple of weeks in one of his caravans for some plumbing supplies. Maisie also suspected that several people had dug into precious savings to fund the project, which made her feel very guilty. She wondered how long people's energy, enthusiasm and generosity would last, but she set aside her worries for now and threw herself into the work.

Jess hurried over to Maisie, her cheeks tinged pink by the cool morning air. 'Bev says she'll be along later and some of the students from St Piran's are back home for the holidays so they offered to come too.' Maisie looked around for Patrick but didn't see him. He hadn't been in the Piggery either so she'd no idea where he was.

'I'm amazed to see so many people here.'

'Apparently Adam's going to drop in after his rounds,' she said, and wrinkled her nose. 'Probably wants to avoid me but he needn't worry, I'll be back on the farm by then.'

'He hasn't left yet, then?'

'Not until after Christmas. Then he's definitely going to work in the Lake District, according to Will.'

'The Lakes?' Maisie blew out a breath. 'Still, that's better than New Zealand I suppose.'

'It might as well be, for all he wants to do with me. It's over with Adam, not that it ever really started,' said Jess gloomily. Maisie had never heard her sound so down and in fact she seemed close to tears, which just wasn't like her bubbly friend.

Maisie vowed to have another heart to heart with Jess as soon as she could get her in private. 'I am so sorry, my lovely. Have you no idea why?'

Jess heaved a big sigh then forced a smile. 'Not really. I did try to talk to Adam when he popped in here to help out a few days ago. I asked him if there was anything I could do to help ... if there was anything worrying him, but he just muttered about "family business" and said he was truly sorry for hurting me ...'

Jess looked close to tears. 'I asked him to tell me why he'd broken up but he said to forget him.'

'You must be in bits, my lovely.' Maisie wanted to cry too.

'Nothing to be done. Plenty of fish etc. and what with the Flower Farm and helping out here, I've more than enough to distract me. Will says he'd be able to spare a couple of hours tomorrow too.'

'You're both amazing. What you've done for us and for everyone on Gull is fantastic.'

It was inevitable that people would dip in and out of the site as and when they could. Privately Maisie thought they'd be lucky to get Hell Cove House and Cottages into a reasonable condition by spring, let along starting on the Fudge Pantry. It could be years before everyone had been helped, but she couldn't think of any other way to preserve the way of life of those who wanted to stay.

'Have you seen Patrick?' she asked Jess.

'He's down at the quay waiting for a delivery of materials.'

'More?'

'A boat load, apparently.'

A short time later, Patrick and Javid trundled down the hill with an old pick-up dangerously overloaded with building materials.

They backed up the stony track next to the cottages and everyone rushed over to help unload the bounty. Maisie was hot and sweaty by the time she'd helped remove the slates, timber and several tubs of render from the back of the truck.

She rubbed her sleeve over her brow. 'Wow. Where did these come from?' she asked.

Patrick tapped his nose. 'That'd be telling.'

'This stuff is worth a lot of money, not to mention the expense of shipping it over.'

'The slates were recycled from an old hut on St Piran's. Archie tipped me off and it turned out the hut belonged to the prop forward from the Scilly Corsairs. He said we could have them free if we could get them brought over so I negotiated a good rate with the Gull supply boat and Una and Phyllis agreed.'

'Well done. That's brilliant; those would have cost a fortune if they'd had to buy them from new. What about the timbers?'

'Ah. They were washed up on the skerries on the far side of Petroc. One of the fisherman from the Pirates retrieved them and heard of our need. I scrounged the render from an anonymous benefactor.'

'You really do have the gift of the gab.'

Patrick gave a little bow. 'I aim to please.'

He sure did, thought Maisie, wishing they were alone right now. Such thoughts had to go on hold because Phyllis walked out of the back door holding a tray laden with steaming mugs, followed by Una with a cake tin.

'Here you go. Hot cocoa, Christmas cake and mince pies,' Una called.

Soon a small crowd had gathered around the rusting garden table and the working party were helping themselves to the drinks, sugar-dusted pies and slices of dark fruit cake topped with marzipan and snowy icing. The sisters watched in satisfaction as their building crew tucked in with sighs of approval.

'Delicious,' Jess mumbled through a mouthful of cake.

'Best I've ever had,' said Patrick, reaching for a second mince pie.

Phyllis glowed with pride and lowered her voice. 'I made the mince pies. Una's so heavy handed with pastry, her pies are always dry, but don't let her know.'

Maisie slid a glance at Una who was chatting to Javid. Cocoa break over, the air was filled with the sound of hammering and banging as everyone set to work again. However, Una waylaid Maisie as she pushed a wheelbarrow of slates over to the cottages.

'I'm afraid that Hugo knows about our little plan,' she said.

'What?' Maisie blew out a breath. Hugo might have stopped trying to get her alone but he obviously hadn't given up on his plans, not that she ever expected him to. 'We weren't going to keep it a secret for long, I guess,' she said.

'I don't know how he found out, but he said something sarcastic about our "construction plans" to Phyllis in the Co-op on St Mary's.'

'Hugo was in the Co-op?' Maisie asked, knowing Hugo's team usually took care of his grocery deliveries.

'Oh yes. Basil was tied up outside. Hugo was buying a packet of fags.'

'I didn't know he smoked,' said Maisie.

Una pursed her lips. 'Oh, he does. He was almost expelled from that posh boarding school on the mainland for smoking weed too. He doesn't think anyone knows, but we do. His father told us before poor old Graydon lost it, bless him. If he knew what Hugo is trying to do to Gull, he'd be terribly upset.'

It's hardly a crime to have a sneaky fag, thought Maisie, thinking of her own former habit, and so what if Hugo had been a bit wayward at his boarding school? She was actually glad he'd got some skeletons in the cupboard, even if they were very minor ones. Maisie wasn't so sure about Graydon Scorrier either. He'd been a hard-nosed businessman before the poor man succumbed to dementia. Maisie did feel terribly sorry for Hugo and Graydon but her pity for Hugo wouldn't help the islanders. Though she'd often thought he must have been under a lot of pressure since he took over the business.

'What did he say to you?' said Maisie.

Phyllis joined them. 'Hugo offered to give us a lift back to Gull with our shopping.'

'That was ... kind of him.'

'We didn't say no because it looked like the weather was closing in, but we wished he hadn't offered in one way, don't we, Una?'

Una snorted. 'Gobby little git.'

245

'Una!'

'I don't care. He's an arrogant bugger even if he has made us a good offer for the cottages. He said he'd found out we were trying to "keep the place afloat, but did we realise it was like trying to hold back the tide".'

'And he was concerned for our health, "It can't be good for you at your age, trying to do all the heavy work," he said.' Phyllis narrowed her eyes.

'He might as well have said, "Resistance is futile". Well, he can shove his offer and with this help we'll be able to manage for years. I want to end my days here if I can,' said Una.

'Not yet, I hope!' Maisie was horrified.

'Nor me. Ignore Una. She loves winding people up as much as Hugo does.'

Any sympathy Maisie had for Hugo evaporated. 'The cheeky sod.'

'Exactly,' said Una. 'I tell you what. I'd like to see that delicate flower up on a roof mending slates, or building a wall. I bet Hugo couldn't punch his way out of a wet paper bag.'

Maisie had dissolved into laughter even while she was mad at Hugo for pressurising the Bartons. They looked over to the men and women getting stuck in to the renovations. The plan had started well and while their efforts might not save everyone from Hugo's takeover plans, at least the Bartons would be able to stay on longer and run their business for a while yet.

'I wonder who told Hugo,' Una said, hands on hips, casting an eye over the work party.

'He probably heard on the grapevine,' said Maisie.

'Hmm ...' Una fixed her eyes on the figure of Patrick, pushing a barrow of slates a few yards away. 'He's the only outsider.'

Maisie fired up with indignation. 'No chance. That would make him less likely to tell Hugo, and anyway, Patrick doesn't like Hugo any more than the rest of us.'

Una turned to her and raised an eyebrow. 'You seem very confident of that, my dear, on so short an acquaintance. If you don't mind me saying.'

'I don't, and even though I haven't known him long, he'd never shop us to Hugo. It could have been anyone on the islands, Gull or otherwise; you can't make a fuss like this without someone – everyone – finding out. It was only a matter of time.'

'I don't know. We all have our skeletons. Whether they're our neighbours or from the other side of the world.' Una fixed Maisie with a meaningful look. 'I must get on with the roof. Those slates won't fasten themselves, now will they?'

Maisie gasped. 'You are joking?'

Una sighed. 'Sadly, my knees won't let me these days but I'd have loved to. I'm off to help Phyllis paint some woodwork inside the house.'

Maisie turned to Patrick who was standing over a wheel-barrow of cement bags, talking on his phone. Who to, she had no idea, but it was none of her business.

At first glance, any 'foreigner' would never have known that Patrick was an outsider. Apart from his deeper tan he could pass for one of the islanders; although in her biased eyes, no man that lush had ever sprung from Scilly stock. Jess might have to disagree with her there as regards hunky Adam, and she supposed Will Godrevy and Jake Pendower weren't too shabby, although she looked on them more as mates or surrogate brothers.

So while he might appear to be part of the landscape in Maisie's eyes, to anyone who knew Scilly well, Patrick stuck out like a sore thumb.

To Una too, by the sound of things.

But he *wouldn't* have betrayed them to Hugo, would he? Maisie gave a little snort of derision. It was the daftest thing she'd heard all day.

Chapter 27

Maisie knew it was all going too well. Four days into December, the roof repairs on the Hell Cove Cottages had just been completed when a storm blew in and battered the entire archipelago. A mass of seaweed was hurled from the shorelines across the isles and covered the beach at Hell Cove like a brown blanket. When she wandered down to the beach to see if it was safe for a quick dip, she found weed littering the sands in front of the Driftwood.

After the storm had faded away, it was followed by two days of sea fog when she couldn't see more than a few yards ahead of her. There was nothing to be done but hunker down in the pub with her parents and Patrick, doing her admin and indoor jobs. The only upside came when Ray and Hazel decided to visit Phyllis and Una, giving Maisie and Patrick the guarantee of a snatched hour together in the Piggery.

The fog lingered well into Thursday and was still about as far from barbecue weather as you could get. Maisie stared out at the window, willing it to lift, but it refused to budge, almost as if it knew how much she wanted Patrick's Aussie Christmas event that weekend to be a success and had decided to spoil the party. If no one could even reach the island, she would have to think about postponing it or even calling it off. Maisie found it difficult to believe that under that cloak of mist was a stunning landscape of jewel-bright colours. The only bright spot at the moment was Patrick's 'slide show' scheduled for that evening at the community hall. Whether anyone would go to it apart from Maisie, her parents and the vicar was another matter.

Patrick set off early to meet Rev Bev and set up the laptop and projector, while Hazel went with him to help with the refreshments. Ray was feeling tired so he'd gone for a lie-down. He offered to walk with Maisie but she firmly told him to get some rest, joking that she could find her way to any spot on Gull, blindfolded. Even though she knew the route to the community hall like the back of her hand, she still took a torch. It was a filthy night, pitch dark and damp, with clinging mist that soaked everything, so she was muffled in a scarf, her hood zipped up tightly.

She passed the campsite and spotted the lights in the windows of Javid and Katya's house. They'd said they'd probably go to the talk and Maisie was happy when she saw Javid waiting for her by the stone gate to the campsite. He lifted a hand in recognition and she quickened her step, using the torch beam to guide her.

'Hiya,' she called. 'Horrible night for it, isn't it?'

But it was Hugo, not Javid, who stepped onto the road and lifted his torch. The beam blinded her momentarily and she blinked hard.

'Jesus, Hugo!'

He was a couple of feet away, his face white inside the hood of his coat. 'I'm sorry. Did I startle you?'

'Yes. I mean, I wasn't expecting you to come.'

'I wouldn't miss it. Actually I was just looking for Basil. He ran off towards the campsite. Bas-il!' Hugo called into the darkness.

Maisie stood silently as Hugo peered into the gloom, but there was no answering bark.

'Basil! You stupid animal!' Hugo tried to sound authoritative but there was an edge of anxiety to his tone. He turned to Maisie. 'That dog has always gone his own way, no matter what I do with him.'

Maisie would have smiled, but she too was concerned about Basil. The fog was thick and there was no way anyone would venture off the path to search for him. 'Shit.' Hugo muttered under his breath, but then there was a rustling from the bushes on the opposite side of the campsite entrance. Two eyes glowed in the darkness and a furry black shape emerged.

'Thank God for that,' said Hugo as Basil licked his hands enthusiastically. 'You ridiculous hound.' Hugo clipped the lead to Basil's collar and ruffled his ears. He really did love his dog, who was probably his only real companion on Petroc apart from paid staff. Maisie felt briefly but genuinely sorry for him.

'I'm surprised you made it over in this weather. You can't even see Petroc tonight.'

'I could find my way over that channel in worse than this, you know that. And I've been to sign a contract with one of the islanders earlier. You'll forgive me if I don't say who.' Hugo had recovered his composure fast.

Maisie's heart sank but she was determined not to rise to the bait. 'It's none of my business,' said Maisie as her sympathy ebbed away.

'Come on, you're dying to know. We're both fighting for the soul of Gull in our own ways, aren't we? Only you think you're on the side of the angels while I'm some evil monster who wants to destroy the place.'

Maisie laughed. 'Don't be ridiculous. I only want to help people keep their independence.'

'Are you sure you're organising this renovation venture for their sake, not yours? Are you sure there's nothing personal in it?'

'Personal?'

'Against me? You never did me the courtesy of returning my calls, did you?' he said, then smiled. 'I expect you have so many other distractions to occupy you at the moment.'

Maisie was annoyed by his tone but tried to keep things civil. 'I can assure you there's nothing "personal" except me wanting to help my neighbours, and I'm sorry that I haven't found time to arrange a face-to-face meeting with you. I've been very busy with the pub and other things and er ... I heard you were away on business,' said Maisie, clutching at straws. The mist seemed thicker than ever and she was growing cold chatting to Hugo outside.

'Well, we're here alone together now,' he said. 'And we may not have another chance.'

She lifted her wrist as if to check her watch. 'We'll miss Patrick's talk if we don't get a move on.'

'Ah yes, Nature Boy ... I'm looking forward to that too.'

'You're interested in wildlife, then?' said Maisie innocently.

'I'm more interested in Mr McKinnon. You didn't know a lot about him before you took him on, did you?'

She fired up. 'He had excellent references and I was more than satisfied by his reasons for taking the job and his previous experience. That's all I need to know and might I say, Hugo, that whatever an employee tells me relating to work or his personal life is no one else's business.'

'I didn't mean to pry; I'm merely concerned about you.'

Maisie ignored him. 'We're going to be late, so if you really want to hear this talk, you'd better get a move on.'

Maisie marched off, her torch beam wavering as she hurried the short distance up to the hall. Basil barked behind her as if trying to call her back, but she kept on moving.

Hugo trotted up to her. 'If you'd bothered to accept my invitation for a private meeting, you'd have realised that I care for you genuinely.'

'I've no idea what you mean and I don't want to know. I'm going to this talk and you can do what you like,' said Maisie.

'He's not what you think, you know.'

'What do you mean?'

'Patrick McKinnon.'

Maisie stopped. 'What do you know that I don't?'

'Nothing ... nothing definite. Yet. But why would a bloke like him turn up on Gull in the winter? It doesn't make sense.'

'If you must know, Patrick made a promise to his dying friend and, before you ask, those reasons are personal. In fact, he put his own life on hold to come here. If you can't understand that kind of loyalty, it's not my problem.'

'A promise to a dying friend? How noble. What a golden boy he's turning out to be.'

'This isn't doing you any favours, Hugo. You can't handle that Patrick is happy here and that some people might like and respect a stranger more than you.' The moment the words were out of her mouth, Maisie could have bitten them back, but Hugo had tipped her over the edge. 'Shit. It's none of your business what Patrick does or what I do. Now, I *am* going to this talk.'

A warm wet tongue licked her hand. Basil wanted to stay, but Hugo had other ideas.

'Actually, I think I'll give it a miss after all. It's obvious I'm not wanted on Gull these days, and if you can't see beyond Mr McKinnon's dubious charms, there's nothing more I can do. If he turns out not to be what you think, don't say I didn't warn you. Come on, Basil, we've outstayed our welcome.'

And he left without another word.

Maisie pulled the curtains open the next morning. Damn it. She still couldn't make out the beach from the windows of the flat. Everyone, most of all her, would be disappointed, but unless the murk cleared soon, she would have to call off the barbecue.

After her encounter with Hugo, she'd spent most of Patrick's talk fuming about Hugo's insinuations. He could only be envious of Patrick's popularity and suspicious that he and Maisie were having an affair, which they were, of course.

Well, it was none of Hugo's bloody business and Maisie was determined not to share his ridiculous accusations with anyone, least of all Patrick. She'd simmered down a bit by the end of the evening, laughing at Patrick's funny slides of wallabies, koalas and various exotic creatures. The hot and sunny land he'd shown in the slides seemed impossibly far away, and even though the audience had been small, Maisie could tell they'd enjoyed some light relief from the gloom outside.

She joined her parents for breakfast, debating with them whether to post a notice on the Driftwood website announcing the following day's barbecue was cancelled, when she heard a boat engine. She ran outside to see the *Kraken* puttering past the pub, transporting Hugo to the main island. She may not have been pleased to see Hugo, but she was delighted to see that the weather seemed to have suddenly cleared up for Patrick's party. As if he was glad to be free of the fog too, Basil barked joyously from the stern of the boat, but Hugo was inside the cabin and, much to her relief, didn't even glance at the pub from what Maisie could tell.

The wind was blowing again and above her invisible hands were tearing apart the veil of fog to reveal pale blue patches. Maisie felt as if she'd landed in the Technicolor land of Oz after two days in monochrome Kansas.

Patrick walked onto the terrace. 'Game on again?' he asked hopefully.

'Abso-bloody-lutely,' said Maisie.

He rested his arm around her back and squeezed her shoulder. 'I'd love to celebrate properly. It's driven me nuts being stuck round here with you so close but not being able to do anything.'

'Your Australian slides went down well while we were all stranded during the fog.'

'With ten people, three of whom were me, Bev and you.'

'Una and Phyllis enjoyed your cute wallaby shots.'

'I'll let you in to a secret. Those wallabies were in a wildlife park.'

'Oh, you cheat!'

'What they don't know won't hurt them. Anyway, let's get cracking. We have an Aussie barbecue to organise and I'm expecting a delivery from the supply boat now that the fog's lifted.'

To Maisie's relief, there were no more gales or mists on the morning of the barbecue. In fact, the skies were as clear and blue as midsummer: a perfect December Saturday. Maisie wondered if any other place in the UK could possibly hold an Australian barbecue under such clear skies. They were wrapped up in fleeces and coats of course but Patrick still declared that he might have been back in Melbourne.

Humming along to a Christmas mix on Maisie's iPod, Maisie and Hazel were busy preparing food in the kitchen all morning. The Aussie Party was a chance to bond further with the neighbours and talk about their plans in a relaxed atmosphere. Maisie was proud of how people had rallied to the idea and was eager to show her appreciation with the party. Ray had decided to go fishing after helping Patrick start to set up the barbecue. When Maisie finally got outside to the terrace, her jaw dropped.

Two gazebos were pitched, both with green and gold tinsel entwined up the poles. The pub BBQ stood next to a half oil drum affair. Aussie-flag bunting had been strung between the pub and gazebos and flapped defiantly in the wind. Crowded House's 'Take the Weather with You' screeched out from speakers set up on one of the patio tables.

Patrick was stationed behind an oil drum barbecue, his hands black with charcoal. He was wearing a leather stockman's hat and an elf apron and was singing – Maisie used the term loosely – along to the song.

He hadn't noticed her yet so she savoured the sight for a few seconds longer, hoping her eardrums wouldn't be perforated in the meantime. Never mind, that hat was *very* cool and the elf apron was kind of cute too.

'*Take the weather with youuuuu!*'

Maisie winced. Mercifully, Patrick started to whistle the chorus. Thank God for that. His whistling was in tune.

The Crowded House track finished and a new one started. Maisie recognised it from the first few bars and rolled her eyes. Men at Work ... 'Down Under'.

Patrick had thrown himself headlong into the spirit of things. What next? 'My Boomerang Won't Come Back'?

She hurried towards him, trying to keep the grin off her face. 'You really have gone for it, haven't you?'

Spotting her, Patrick grimaced. 'Just you wait. We've got Slade next, then Mariah Carey and Wizzard.'

Maisie stuck out her tongue in disgust. 'I had to listen to blinking "I Wish It Could be Christmas Every Day" a hundred times a week from mid November in the King's Head. I think I might chuck myself off Hell Cove cliff if I hear it one more time.'

Patrick wagged a charcoal-blackened finger at her. 'Now now, that's not the spirit. Give the customers what they want, although my Oz-Pom Christmas mix is on a one-hour loop. Everyone might be ready to jump off a cliff by the end of the day.'

'If you plan on singing along, they'll be queuing up to leap.'

Patrick feigned a hurt look, which Maisie found annoyingly sexy. 'Thanks for the vote of confidence, boss, but secretly you're impressed by my grotto. Why don't you come and sit on Santa's knee and tell me what you really want for Christmas?' His eyes sparkled wickedly.

Resisting the urge to drag him into her room, Maisie cleared her throat. 'Where did you get all this bunting from?'

'Had it shipped in from Melbourne specially.'

'No. How much did that cost?'

'Oh, loads … Actually, it was lying around under the stage in the sports clubhouse in Hugh Town. The cricket club had an Ashes victory party a few years back and forgot about it, but Will came across it when he was hauling out the spare tables for an OAP's Christmas lunch. Took me bloody ages to untangle it and hang it up. Do you like it?' He planted his grubby hands on his hips and stood back to admire his handiwork.

'I'm … speechless.'

'That would make a change.'

'You cheeky sod.'

Without warning, Patrick scooped her into his arms. 'Yeah, but you like me.'

Momentarily breathless by being swept into his embrace,

Maisie was filled with delighted horror at the pressure of his charcoally hands on her bottom, but still made no effort to push him away. 'Your hands are filthy,' she croaked.

'They're not the only thing ... If you could see what I'm thinking right now ...' He dived in for a long, hot kiss that set every nerve tingling deliciously.

Eventually he ended the kiss but still kept hold of her.

'Watch it. Someone might see us.' Her protest was decidedly wimpy.

'No chance. I thought you said your mum had popped to the Post Office and your dad's still wrestling with Jaws by the look of it.'

'Yeah, but the hills still have eyes. I want to be careful.'

'OK.' Patrick dropped her like a hot potato and reached for the matches. 'You're right. There's no time for bed, we've got a cheesy Christmas party to organise.'

'Woo hoo!'

They both snapped to attention at the sound of a woman's voice. Maisie recognised it instantly. 'Phew. It's only Jess.'

Patrick waved his BBQ tongs in greeting to Jess who was laden with carrier bags, a cool bag and a rucksack. 'Wish I hadn't let you go now. Jess knows all our secrets,' he said to Maisie.

'Too many. God, she looks like a packhorse. Look at all those bags.'

'Yes. That'll be your 'roo steaks,' said Patrick.

'Wait there! I'm coming to help,' Maisie called and ran to intercept Jess before she toppled over.

Maisie helped unpack the meat and load it into the meat

fridge at the pub kitchen. She was relieved to find they weren't actually 'roo steaks, but beef and lamb steaks, burgers and sausages from the farm on St Saviour's. Jess had insisted on bringing them herself.

'There you go. Extra burgers, sausages, and steaks. Should be enough to go round with your other supplies,' she said.

Having washed his hands, Patrick joined them.

'Great. Thanks for doing this. I already have the prawns on ice. Scilly Seafood delivered them yesterday,' said Patrick.

'Are you sure we'll need all this stuff?' said Maisie, delighted to see the food but also worried that there would be waste.

'I didn't want to run out and we can freeze the rest for other events,' said Patrick. 'Now it's stashed away, I need to get some prep done for the veggies.'

As lunchtime approached, it was all hands to the pump. Ray was back from his fishing trip with Javid, bearing half a dozen sea bass, which he and Javid were busy gutting in the kitchen. Hazel was chopping lemons and limes and restocking the ice bucket. Patrick had been busy whipping up his 'secret' Fingle BBQ sauce, and was now presiding over the barbecue, keeping everyone else away like a faithful dog guarding its master. Maisie and Jess had helped with salads and were just finishing stacking Christmas paper plates, cutlery, baps and hot dog rolls on the table next to the barbecue. Hazel was in charge of serving up the wine, none of it crap, despite Patrick's jokes. He'd used a merchant on the mainland and had had it shipped over.

The barbecue was soon dying down to the embers ready

for the meat to go on. 'What's that noise?' Maisie asked, hearing singing from the direction of the jetty.

Patrick listened and shook his head. 'I have an idea. Bloody hell ...'

'*Waltzing Matilda! Waltzing Matilda ...*'

The singing swelled in volume and Patrick and Maisie ran to the path. Around the corner from the jetty, a party of guys marched along.

Patrick groaned. 'You have got to be kidding me.'

He shot a glance at Jess who was convulsed in giggles. Maisie held out her hands in amazement just as a band of rag-taggle men from eighteen to sixty marched around the corner. They were all wearing hats with corks attached, most of them homemade – an assortment of trilbies, cowboy hats and even a pink straw boater. Will was at the head of them followed by most of the Scilly Pirates and Corsairs.

'You blokes are seriously in need of help,' Patrick shouted.

The guys sang louder. Maisie started laughing. Patrick was shaking his head. Will was grinning from ear to ear.

'No one wears a cork hat, mate. Like *no one* but a dork of a tourist. And we don't sing "Waltzing Matilda" at Christmas. Or ever, if we can help it.'

'*Who'll come a-waltzing Matilda with me!*'

Will grabbed Patrick and danced him round to roars of laughter and whoops of encouragement.

Despite his groans of embarrassment, Patrick let Will steer him about the terrace for a few seconds more before escaping behind the BBQ.

'We had to look the part. Make you feel at home.'

Patrick shook his head and laughed.

Patrick was popular. Will liked him, the guys liked him. Maisie could tell. He was one of the boys, that was for sure. Will wouldn't have organised such a jokey entrance if he hadn't approved of Patrick.

Will rubbed his hands. 'That smells good. Where's this food? We're starving.'

Maisie weaved her way in and out of the bar and terrace. There must have been forty people inside and out and many more had come and gone or were arriving. It was a great turnout for a tiny place like Gull. The food was disappearing as fast as Patrick could slap it onto the coals. Ray had joined him. Maisie's dad seemed well enough and he was certainly in his element, clad in a Santa apron, wielding the tongs.

Maisie saw the vicar headed for her, burger in hand.

'Hello. How are you?' Rev Bev said. 'This was a great idea. Congratulations.'

'Thanks, but it's Patrick's baby really.'

Bev smiled. 'I thought he might have some hand in it, but you've all made it happen. The slide evening was fun too, even if there was only a small crowd.'

'He's turning out to be a regular pillar of the community,' Maisie joked as Patrick handed out hot dogs to a queue of eager punters.

'He is. And to donate all those slates to the Bartons was beyond the call of duty.'

Maisie did a tiny double take. 'Patrick *donated* the slates?'

'Hasn't he confessed yet ...' Bev winced. 'Oh dear. Sugar. I didn't realise you didn't know that he paid for them.'

Maisie turned her slack jaw into a broad smile. 'Oh, he did. I'd just forgotten.'

Bev sighed with relief. 'Phew. I was worried I'd put my foot in it there. It was very generous of him, wasn't it?'

'Very. Um ... You'll have to excuse me, Bev. I can see Dad signalling. I think we need more burgers.'

With her mind working overtime on Bev's revelations about Patrick paying for the roof, Maisie fetched the remaining stock of meat from the fridge and took it to the barbecue before seeking out Will.

He'd just bitten into a large hot dog when Maisie beckoned him to the side of the pub.

'Will. Did Patrick pay for the slates at Hell Cove?'

'Whad?' Will mumbled through a mouthful of sausage.

'He said that a guy from the rugby club was giving them away?'

Will chewed furiously. 'It was a guy from the rugby club,' he said eventually.

'So he gave them to us free of charge?' asked Maisie.

'Um ... it's complicated.'

'So this "guy from the rugby club"? It wouldn't happen to have been Patrick, would it?' she asked. She knew she was putting Will on the spot but she didn't care. She also knew that hangdog expression too well. It was the same look he'd had when he'd been caught doing something he shouldn't have at school.

'You'll have to ask Patrick. It's nothing to do with me. Anyway, does it really matter if he paid or not?'

'No. No, I suppose not.' Maisie decided not to make an

even bigger deal of the situation with Will. She didn't want him thinking she cared *that* much, or telling Patrick she was annoyed. Then she thought of the paint that had arrived at Hell Cove, and the brand new timbers showing no sign of having been battered on any rocks ... all, apparently, scrounged from here and there or donations from various 'mates' around the islands. In total there were thousands of pounds worth of stuff.

'The members of the rugby club seem to have been very generous.'

'We're a charitable lot.'

'Very.'

Will winked but Maisie's antennae were twitching like crazy. Will Godrevy was definitely being economical with the truth and itching to get away from her too. He drained his pint and smacked his lips.

'Right. I think I'll ask Aussie Boy if I can have another of those burgers if there's any left. See you later,' Will said, then added, 'Are you coming to the Nativity Parade on St Mary's next week?'

'Of course. I can't wait,' said Maisie.

'Great. See you there. Jess's organising a gang of us to go.' Delighted to have changed the subject, Will was already striding over to the BBQ, obviously hoping to vanish into the cloud of smoke.

Maisie started to tidy up while trying to process what she'd heard over the past ten minutes. If Will knew that Patrick had bought the slates and possibly other materials, maybe Jess was in on the subterfuge too? Nah, thought Maisie, collecting paper plates and dropping them into the bin bag. He'd never tell his sister, knowing she'd share it with Maisie.

Anyway, what did it matter if Patrick has used his own cash to help out and decided to keep it to himself – and half the rugby club? It was a small thing. It didn't matter, but ... Maisie slid a glance at the BBQ. Patrick's hat, not to mention the swirling smoke, obscured his face. He kept disappearing and reappearing through the clouds. Maisie tried to tell herself she was worrying about nothing but she couldn't help dwelling on the fact. How had he paid for it, with his humble background? And if he'd fibbed about buying building materials and didn't want her specifically to know, what else was he hiding from her?

Chapter 28

A few days later, Patrick stared into his untouched pint of Coke as if the answers to the questions swirling round his brain could be found in its sweet and fizzy depths. It was mid-afternoon and he'd decided to call in to the Galleon in Hugh Town before meeting Maisie and the rest of the gang at the Nativity Parade.

Since the barbecue, he'd found it hard to stay in the party mood, even though it seemed to be a big hit with everyone else. On the surface he'd had a good time and truly felt as if this community had taken him into their hearts in a very short space of time. The fact that he'd come up with a load of stuff for the renovation project had added to his popularity, although he didn't think that was the only reason. They were a friendly bunch, willing to give a newcomer a chance. As long as he didn't start taking himself too seriously and mucked in, he could have a good time here.

But what about Maisie?

Did he detect a subtle cooling in her attitude towards him since the BBQ? Was she a tiny bit warier around him, for some reason?

Patrick contemplated the bottom of his glass again.

If Maisie had been doubting him, Patrick had been doubting himself far more. It was precisely because he'd had such a great time at the barbecue and working on the renovations that he found himself now hunkered down in a booth in a corner furthest away from the bar at the Galleon.

The four-hundred-year-old pub's granite walls clung to the quayside above the harbour and in the summer, according to Will, was jammed with day-trippers and tourists on their way to and from the ferry. Its smoke-blackened beams, low ceilings and tiny windows barely let in any light on a sunny day, but on a gloomy December afternoon like this one the place was cave-like despite all the lamps being on.

It was on days like this that he longed for the dazzling waterfront at St Kilda's beach or to feel the sun beating down as festive revellers enjoyed a cocktail overlooking the Yarra at the Fingle Bar. And it was at times like this that he really missed a pint – or a Scotch – or a double vodka. Anything, in fact, to dull the nagging pangs of shame and guilt that had tugged at him since the barbecue.

Oh, Maisie, Maisie, Maisie. What had he done to her? He hated lying to her, but it was too late. Since he'd decided to stay on Gull, and walked into the Driftwood, his little white lies had stacked up like a pile of guano, but they were nothing compared to the great big lie that underpinned the whole shit heap.

He'd promised to meet Maisie, Will, Jess and the rugby boys after the Nativity Parade. He'd told Maisie he was going to do his Christmas shopping first, which had elicited a snort of disbelief, followed by a reference to not being able to carry home all her presents, then an embarrassed jokiness about how he wasn't to expect anything in his stocking. Patrick knew her too well.

She was worried in case she'd implied that he was going shopping to get a gift for her and trying to cover her foot-in-mouth moment with a sarcastic joke.

Well, he *had* intended to buy her a present, but having scoured the gift and clothing shops for an hour, he'd given up and found himself a dark corner in the pub. It was still early in the afternoon, the lunchtime rush was over and people hadn't started arriving for the Nativity Parade yet, so the bar was relatively quiet.

Now he knew how those unfortunates who were tied to horses and sent off in different directions felt. He'd never been so torn. Greg must have known that sending him to Gull Island would cause a load of trouble. Greg must have known it would be complicated for Patrick to open up wounds by returning home ... to his *real* home.

Greg. The cunning bugger. Judy had known, too, what might happen. Patrick came close to hating them both for a second ... but how could either of them have known about Maisie? In his phone calls to Judy he hadn't mentioned her or any woman, beyond the fact she was his boss. Judy didn't even know if Maisie was sixty-nine or thirty-nine and he'd been careful not to betray any hint of his relationship with her.

But he couldn't blame Greg or Judy for his present dilemma. It had been his own decision to offer his services at the

Driftwood and his own fault to put his hand so close to the fire and to hold it inside. Now it looked like he might get burned, and badly too.

'Shit,' he muttered and took a sip of his 'pint'. It tasted like rusty oil. He'd love a beer, he needed a beer ...

'Mind if I join you?'

Patrick forced a brief grimace of welcome to his face. Hugo Scorrier was the last person he wanted to keep him company, not that he wanted company at all. He heard scuffling on the floorboards and something heavy and furry settled on his boots.

'Suit yourself, mate, though I'm not the best company,' he said as Basil made himself comfortable.

'Why's that? Something on your mind?'

'Just knackered. Busy at the pub and I'm too old for this game.'

'What game would that be?' asked Hugo.

'Life.'

'Ah. I can understand what you mean. I sometimes feel the same myself.'

Patrick wrinkled his nose as a rank rotting cabbage smell wafted up from beneath the table. He glanced down and two dark brown eyes gazed up at him.

Hugo sat down on the chair opposite and pursed his lips. 'Sorry about Basil. I'm afraid he snaffled some old biddy's plate at the community Christmas lunch. She and her friends had piled all their leftover sprouts onto it and the effects have been making themselves known ever since. Bloody nightmare with him in a confined space, I can tell you. Not looking forward to cosying up to him in the cabin of the boat on the way home.'

Basil gazed innocently from between Patrick's legs and quietly emitted another cloud of sprout-scented fragrance. Closing his nostrils, Patrick patted Basil on the head. He'd rather have a flatulent Labrador any day than a Hugo smelling of roses.

Patrick ruffled Basil's ears while Hugo sank the rest of his pint. 'Good dog, Basil,' he whispered.

Any satisfaction Patrick drew from Basil gassing Hugo on the way back to Petroc evaporated way faster than Basil's farts. Talking of hot air, Hugo was speaking again.

'I hear you're being very community minded,' he said.

Patrick's hackles rose but that was exactly what Hugo wanted: to rile him. The guy was obviously keen on Maisie, whether that was for her, the pub or both.

'Really?'

'Yes, you've been helping out the islanders with their plan to stop me from buying Gull.'

Wow. Hugo didn't mince his words today: he'd gone straight for Patrick's jugular. 'I've been lending a hand with some renovations at Hell Cove,' he said calmly.

'Popular chap, aren't you? Funding the renovations, bastion of the rugby club, and now you're obviously indispensable at the Driftwood. You really have got your feet under the table.'

Hugo was starting to really piss him off. 'Look, mate. I know you want to take over Gull but you're pushing your luck with comments like that.'

'Apologies. I didn't mean to offend.' The pressure lifted on

270

Patrick's feet and Basil appeared by Hugo's side, tail thumping the chair. Hugo pulled a face. 'Oh, for God's sake, Basil. Can you please put a plug in it?'

Even though he could hardly breathe, Patrick could have hugged the dog.

'But you did pay for the slates, didn't you? I heard they were shipped over from a yard on the mainland, not from a mate at the rugby club. Ditto enough render to repaint the whole place and several timber joists that were initially rumoured to have been "found" washed up by a local fisherman?'

'I couldn't possibly comment,' said Patrick with a smile that almost hurt his jaw.

'No ... I'm sure you can't, but don't you think you're being rather ... disingenuous with the Samsons and the rest of the community by not coming clean about the source of this stuff?'

'Disingenuous. Wow. That's a very big word, mate.' Patrick raised an eyebrow while trying to avoid the noxious fumes emanating from Basil who wagged his tail and seemed particularly proud of his latest emission.

'It's a better word than deceitful, don't you think?'

'I wouldn't know. I'm just a simple bloke, me.'

'Hmm.' Hugo winced and wafted his hand in front of his face. 'Not as simple as you'd like us to believe, but that's your affair. I'm only concerned about Maisie and the Samsons.'

Patrick took refuge in a swig of his Coke before replying, partly to gain a few seconds respite from the fumes but also to try and calm the ripples of panic stirring in his belly. He replaced his glass carefully on the table, focusing on the condensation cooling his sweaty palms. 'Now why would that be?' he asked.

'I care about Maisie. *Deeply* care, and what's more, I've known her a *very* long time. She's had a rough few years and the pressure of running the pub is taking its toll, in my opinion. I can see that you may think you're helping the islanders by joining in this community renovation scheme but I'm worried you're only prolonging the agony by giving them hope.'

'Community renovation scheme? That's a grand description for a few mates getting together to help out their neighbours.'

'Oh come on. I know it's an organised plan. You don't think that this sort of thing would have gone unnoticed, did you? Ordering building materials, transporting them around the isles ... word travels swiftly round here.'

'Even if there is a plan, and forgive me for being frank, Hugo,' said Patrick smoothly while wanting to shove Hugo's sprouts where the sun didn't shine, 'it's actually none of your business. *Mate.*'

'I can see I'm wasting my time. My interference was kindly meant.' Hugo drained the last of his pint and stood up. 'Basil, come on.'

Basil glanced up at his master with huge soulful eyes, and then promptly ran off towards the bar, trailing a cloud of sprouty odour in his wake.

'Basil!' Hugo ordered, but the dog was now sniffing the trouser legs of drinkers at the bar.

'Bloody hell. What's that stink?'

'Was that you, Barry?'

'Those who smelt it, dealt it, mate.'

'Fuck,' Hugo snapped. 'That bloody dog never does anything he's told.'

Patrick found it as hard to keep his laughter in as Basil did his wind.

Hugo wasn't amused. His voice was butter smooth, but his eyes flashed fury. 'You think this is all a bit of a laugh, don't you? Flying in here, dabbling in our lives, playing the hero? And I know you think I'm only interested in Maisie so I can take control of the pub. You're wrong. *Very* wrong. Maisie means a lot to me and I'll tell you this. She – and the rest of the islanders – may think you're a decent bloke, good for a laugh, here for the craic and ready to lend a hand where you can, but I know differently.'

Patrick kept his voice on an even keel but the fingers gripping his glass were not as steady and his pulse was thumping as fast as Basil's tail.

'And just what do you "know", Hugo?' he said, trying to sound bored.

'I know you're a liar and that you're hiding something. I think you've told a pile of porkies to all of us and especially to Maisie. I think it's to do with something – or *someone* – you've left behind in Melbourne. I think you'd do anything if you thought it would impress Maisie. Maybe you're not as young, free and single as you make out,' said Hugo.

Patrick smiled. 'Wow. That's a hell of a deduction, Sherlock.'

'You may be sarcastic, you may laugh at me, but I promise you that if I *do* find out you're lying to Maisie and intend to hurt her in *any* way, I will do something about it and you won't like it one little bit.'

Bloody hell, Hugo had gone into full Liam Neeson mode. Patrick didn't want to get into a fight but he wasn't going to take this lying down.

'Now, wait a minute, Hugo ...' he began.

Hugo's voice descended to a whisper, which was obviously supposed to sound menacing. 'And I don't know exactly how long you really plan on staying, but I'll be watching you very closely every single second that you remain on these islands.' He leaned down close to Patrick's face. '*Very* closely indeed.'

Patrick could smell his breath. Real ale, turkey dinner and toxic frustration. He wanted to shout back at Hugo, tell him how wrong he was ... but Hugo had touched a raw nerve and come so close to the truth, in some ways – yet was so far away in others.

'Oi! Hugo!'

Hugo turned his head towards the front of the bar where the landlord stood, grasping Basil's collar and flapping his hand around like bunting in the wind. 'Can you do something about your flipping dog? He's going to clear out my entire pub at this rate.'

'Coming,' Hugo called. 'I mean it,' he shot back at Patrick before striding over to the landlord and grabbing Basil.

Hugo finally lugged Basil out of the door. From the street, the strains of carols melded with the tinkly Christmas pop tunes before the door closed behind Hugo and his sprouty hound.

Patrick returned to the bar. The landlord had opened the

doors onto the terrace despite the cutting wind. He picked up his drink and took it outside where a couple of locals were having a ciggy, presumably to distract them from the eau-de-sprout room spray pervading the bar. They smirked at him, and he rolled his eyes in return, both making unspoken comments about Hugo.

Deep down, Patrick didn't feel like laughing at Hugo. He didn't feel like laughing at all. Guilt weighed him down worse than a lorry load of slates and rubble. Jesus, he *had* to do something – say something – soon ... but that meant dragging a graveyard's worth of rattling skeletons out of the cupboard and probably destroying his relationship with Maisie. A relationship barely two months old that he'd never sought and should never have encouraged. A relationship that to his amazement and terror was now making him rethink not just the next few months, but the rest of his life.

Chapter 29

The lights of the pubs and restaurants shimmered in the dark waters of the harbour. It was high tide. Patrick listened to the slip-slop of the waves against the wall below him and the faint sound of singing growing louder in the street. He glanced at his watch. Damn. The Nativity Parade was underway already. He'd promised to meet Maisie at the start of it ten minutes ago.

'Gotcha!'

Patrick's heart almost jumped out of his chest. He turned to find Maisie right behind him, laughing. Her cheeks were pink above the green scarf pulled up over her chin. The furry pom-pom on her bobble hat waggled sexily.

'I've been looking for you. The parade's started. Are you hiding away?'

'Only from Basil. He's been overdosing on sprouts apparently. I was getting some fresh air.'

'Yes, I wondered what the smell was.' Maisie wrinkled her nose. 'Terry the landlord said you were having a bit of a barney with Hugo?'

'Not a barney. Just a joke. Basil didn't want to leave the

pub and Hugo was pissed off when he came to play with me.'

'Poor old Hugo. Basil's a law unto himself.' Maisie laughed. Her eyes were shining and there was something light-hearted about her, almost frivolous, that Patrick didn't think he'd ever seen before. Under her rosy cheeks, her freckles were just visible.

'You look ...' *Stunning, beautiful, radiant, glowing.* He grappled for the right words but all of them seemed inadequate, cheesy or both. Nothing came close to capturing the way she looked and the feelings she stirred within him, physical and emotional.

Maisie frowned as he faltered.

'You look *well*.'

'*Well?*'

'Yeah. As in, you know ... healthy, fit, shiny ... and that coat is nice. Is it new?'

Maisie glanced at her puffa coat and back at Patrick with amazement. 'Healthy? Shiny? My *coat*? You make me sound like Basil. Any minute now, you'll be throwing a stick for me and offering me a Bob Martin's.'

'Bob Martin's? I'm sorry, I ...'

Maisie shook her head at his incomprehension. 'They're vitamin tablets for dogs. They're supposed to give them a nice glossy coat. My gran used to have a spaniel and she always swore by them. For the dog, not herself.' Her tone was deadpan.

Patrick floundered. He hardly knew what she was saying, only how he was feeling. Confused. Turned on. High as a kite and in the depths of despair all at the same time. 'That too.

I do like your coat ... is it new? Shit. I'm digging a hole here, aren't I?'

Maisie shook her head but he could tell she was definitely amused. He'd made her laugh. He liked seeing her laugh, he liked making her laugh ... and making her cry out in pleasure even more.

'Channel Tunnel sized. I'd enjoy watching you reach Australia, but we're going to miss the whole Nativity Parade if we don't leave right this minute.' She glanced around her to make sure no one could hear her. Her breath was warm against his ear. 'I'd love to drag you off to bed.'

'But?' Patrick murmured, trying to regain some semblance of composure and finding it almost impossible with an offer like that whispered in his ear.

'*But* ... much as I fancy sneaking off for a quickie behind the lifeboat station, I've waited years to be back on Scilly to see the Nativity Parade and nothing and no one is going to keep me away.'

'Thanks a lot!' Patrick's protest drew a momentary glance from the smokers but they immediately went back to their fags and the view over the harbour.

'Shh, now come on before we miss the action, and don't forget, to everyone else, we're just friends. Or in your case, an underling.'

'Just friends.' Patrick shot her an exasperated grin. As soon as they stepped out into the street, he shoved his hands in his coat pockets in case he accidentally put his arm around Maisie or patted her bum. What a bum. She was wearing a skin-tight pair of faded jeans with a strategically placed rip where her cheek met the top of her thigh. Her slim calves were encased in chunky boots. Patrick was glad it was fully dark now so he could watch her without being seen too clearly. His view of her as they weaved in and out of people towards the parade was enough to make him weep in frustration.

Will and Jess soon spotted them and made their way over on the street corner. Javid and Katya were already in prime position, along with some of the rugby club regulars and their families.

Maisie was jigging up and down like an excited kid.

'We've missed the start of the parade but we'll still see most of it,' said Maisie. 'Jess says Adam's niece and nephew are taking part in the lantern parade.'

'What happens?' asked Patrick.

'They do it every year. The shepherds and angels start off from the Star Castle and they pick up other characters along the way. The three kings, Mary, Joseph and baby Jesus. He's always played by a baby who was born on the islands this year.'

'Jess. Hi!' Maisie said when the group were together.

Jess hugged Maisie. 'Sorry, we thought we were going to miss everything and I had to practically drag Will off the farm and down to the jetty. It's like Santa's grotto in that packing room at the farm, but with flowers not gifts. I feel bad enough for leaving the seasonal elves on their own but Mum's stepped in to supervise. Why does Christmas always happen at our busiest time of year?'

Maisie laughed. Patrick got a slap on the back from Will. Patrick knew how hard the Godrevy family had worked to

279

build up St Saviour's Flower Farm through two generations. On his recent visits to the farm for his liaisons with Maisie, he'd been amazed at the scale of the operation and the sight and scent of hundreds of thousands of yellow narcissi being harvested and sent off all over the UK. Judy would have loved to see it – she loved tending her own small patch on the roof terrace of the Fingle.

'Oh, there's little Todd from the jewellery workshop down the road from the farm. He looks so cute in his tea-towel headdress. And that's the new baby, Cary, from the bakery behind the Starfish Studio on St Piran's.'

'Fen and Archie will love seeing their neighbour's baby take centre stage,' Maisie said. 'I see Archie's already here with his sketchbook. Look, Jess. Here come Adam's niece and nephew, the angels with the three kings.'

Jess snorted. 'Angels, my arse. Those girls are from the market garden on St Saviour's. A serious case of miscasting there. They're *always* up to something.'

Patrick listened, quietly amused by the local gossip.

Maisie pulled out her phone and started taking photos, pointing out local characters in the parade to Patrick. She glowed as brightly as the lanterns carried by the children.

Patrick, Maisie and their friends followed the parade further down the street as a local group sang carols. They were old favourites that most people listening would recognise, even though they might be from opposite sides of the planet. 'Good King Wenceslas' and 'Away in a Manger'. Patrick could put names to some of the faces in the crowds, and recognised more. The isles' winter population was barely that of a large secondary school, although it had clearly been swollen by some hardy tourists wanting to escape the festive madness of the mainland and join in with simpler festivities.

There could not have been a greater contrast than with Melbourne, where the bars, inside and out, would be packed with office parties enjoying champagne and seafood under cloudless skies. Did he miss that big-city buzz, the heat and the long sunny days? Yes and no. He loved Melbourne, the Fingle, Judy and his mates, but there was a different kind of joy in seeing Maisie's smiling face.

He'd never seen her so happy. All her worries about Hugo's plans for the Driftwood and Gull seemed to have been temporarily set aside, and it was obvious she was thrilled to be back in her home for Christmas. He was delighted to see her in such high spirits but he also felt like a cuckoo in the nest more than ever.

The little nativity group and their adult supporters stopped to collect money for local charities. Patrick discreetly added some notes and then they moved on. It was low key but, Patrick thought, charming and touching in its simplicity. People spoke to him, made a few cracks about how he was enjoying the sunny weather, adding the usual jokes about crocodiles and beach barbecues he'd heard a hundred times before. He didn't mind the jokes, and his laughter was largely genuine. He realised that he felt happy too, but every time he caught himself feeling too content, a chill of guilt immediately replaced the glow. He'd been drawn into this community – lured onto the rocks by lights shining on the cliffs – and now he wasn't sure how he could escape without causing terrible damage to himself and all around him.

'Where do they go next?' Patrick asked.

'To the chapel for a carol service, but I assume we're going to the rugby club for a drink and a curry? For once neither of us will have to worry about being behind a bar, eh?'

Will slapped him on the back. 'Right, been there and done that. Now let's go and have a pint, shall we? Or in your case, a nice cup of Earl Grey.'

'Ha ha,' said Patrick, glad to be shaken out of his maudlin thoughts by his mate's ribbing.

A few minutes later, Patrick collected a steaming mug of tea from the urn in the clubhouse while Maisie helped herself to mulled wine.. The place smelled of spices and Deep Heat, which was strangely soothing, and Patrick would take any form of comfort, however weird, at this moment. There were a couple of dozen people milling around the room, which had been hung with homemade garlands and tinsel. A tree stood in the corner decorated with glittering paper rugby-ball 'ornaments' made by the kids of the players and friends. Someone had set up their iPad and connected it to the speakers and the usual Christmas hits were belting out so loudly that people were having to shout. Everyone was getting into the Christmas spirit and imbibing it too while they caught up with friends and family who had been away at university or working on the mainland.

Maisie sidled up to him. 'Shall we pop outside for a breath of fresh air? I want to talk to you in private,' she said with a solemn tone. 'I think you've got something to tell me, haven't you, Patrick?'

He followed her out to the car park. His heart pounded like a jackhammer. 'What would that be?'

'You *paid* for all those building materials for the Hell Cove Cottages. None of them were washed up or scrounged.'

'Who told you that?'

Maisie hesitated. 'Please don't blame him but I heard it from Will. I know they cost a fortune. You didn't need to do that.'

'It's not a crime, is it?' Patrick said the words with a cheery smile while his stomach churned like a cement mixer.

'No, but I don't want you wasting your hard-earned cash on strangers.'

'Two things. One, my cash wasn't wasted, and two, I don't see Una and Phyllis as strangers, I don't see anyone who's given their time and energy to help out with the renovations as strangers.'

She shot him a puzzled look. 'Oh … OK. That's really generous of you, but you could have told me about it from the start.'

'Well, I thought you might have stopped me if I'd told you the plan.'

'I would! You're not made of money.'

'I had a bit saved up. Greg left me a small legacy and it seemed a good use of it. What else am I going to spend my wages on round here?' So far, Patrick reminded himself, he hadn't actually told Maisie an outright lie.

He kissed her.

'Someone will see!'

'So?'

'Patrick. No.'

'I thought you didn't like us having secrets.'

'I can understand why you did it, and that it might not seem important but I'd rather you shared it with me.'

'I didn't want it to be a big deal. I don't want thanks or gratitude or people treating me any different from the way they do now.'

'They wouldn't.'

'People treat you differently if you have money,' he said. 'Look at Hugo,' he added.

'Hugo is treated differently because he's a prat, not because he's loaded, but I wouldn't know, to be honest. I've never been in a position to find out ...' She glanced at him as if she was waiting for a similar comment from him but then nodded. 'I can understand what you're getting at. My ex, Keegan, never fitted in, he wanted to be one of the boys but he was still the boss's son among the rest of us.'

'Yet he impressed you. You knew the real bloke.' Patrick seized on the switch in direction of the conversation, on any thread that led away from him or would force him into an outright lie – or a confession.

'Correction. I *thought* I knew the real bloke ... I was obviously wrong.' She let him hold her and shook her head. 'I'm sure the Bartons would be really grateful if they knew you'd forked out for those slates.'

Patrick was plunged back into agony. 'But they don't. Only Will and a couple of the lads who helped unload them from the boats do.' And Hugo now, of course ... maybe it had been naïve of Patrick to think he could keep the truth about the materials from Maisie, but it was too late for her to stop him now. 'I'd be embarrassed if anyone thanked me, especially the Bartons. I don't want anyone to think they owe me anything.'

She picked at the zip on his coat, toying with it. Then looked him full in the eye. 'And you don't want to owe anyone anything either?'

Her tone had changed. Still light but her bubble had burst. He had done that: brought her down to earth, hurt her with a thoughtless remark. He did that to women he loved, though he had always thought it was never his fault. He was beginning to realise that it was always his fault.

'I didn't mean you, Maisie. I only meant that I haven't come here looking for thanks or applause. The Bartons had a need and I could help. That's it. It was a spur of the moment decision.'

'Really?'

Patrick moved closer and took her back in his arms. She let him hold her but she looked and felt brittle. 'I only meant to help,' he said.

'Can you two just get a room or something?'

Maisie leapt out of his arms like a scalded cat.

'Bloody hell, Will. You almost gave me a heart attack.' Her face was bright pink. Patrick was relieved.

Jess appeared. 'Guilty consciences? Why don't you two go public ... oh wait, could it be because your lives will be impossible to live with for the next three months and everyone will drive you mad, ask when you're getting married and should they be ordering a hat?'

Maisie laughed. 'Something like that.'

285

Will grinned. 'If you've finished, some of the lads wondered whether you fancied a quick game before we go for a turkey curry?'

Jess tutted. 'A game? What are you like, eh? Can't you see that Patrick had other things than rugby in mind?'

'It's OK. We were finished.' Maisie laughed but avoided Patrick's eye.

Patrick was relieved, but knew his reprieve was temporary. He had to make a decision soon about everything. Bloody everything ... 'Sure. Sounds good,' he said.

Will swept him into the clubhouse. Patrick's mind raged with so many thoughts and emotions. Hugo had scared him, even though Hugo had got the wrong end of the stick – for now. How long would it be before Hugo – or someone else – got the right end?

Chapter 30

Christmas was coming up fast and since the Nativity Parade the Driftwood had been quiet apart from a handful of small scheduled functions. Although they planned to open in the week after Christmas for the sake of locals and visitors, the main event was to be New Year's Eve – Maisie's birthday – with a band, buffet and fireworks.

Maisie and Patrick spent a lot of time working on repairs, and gardening at the pub or joining in the renovations at Hell Cove. Jess and Will's mum was back from her visit to Cornwall so the Flower Farm was off the menu as a lust nest for the time being. Maisie resigned herself to a few snatched hours with Patrick while her parents were out at Christmas lunches or visiting friends.

Then, before she knew it, it was Christmas Eve itself. As if sensing that Maisie wanted some time with her parents, Patrick had accepted an invitation from Javid and Katya to join them for dinner, but he called into the flat later and shared a glass of apple juice while the Samsons enjoyed a midnight toast with something stronger. After a snatched kiss with Patrick as Maisie tidied up the kitchen, it was time for bed.

Maisie lay awake longer than she'd expected after all the physical work she'd been doing over the past few weeks. The darkness was profound: no light pollution of any kind filtered through her curtains. She thought of Patrick, hoping he'd be lying awake too and thinking of her. How much she'd love to be sharing his bed now – or that he was sharing her double.

It was ridiculous, she thought as she thumped her pillow, to carry on in this secretive way. No matter what the gossip they would have to endure, and how worried her parents would be about the future – or lack of it – of her relationship with Patrick, it was surely time to get things out in the open so they could enjoy what time they had left together properly? That prospect kept her tossing and turning until the chapel bell tolled one a.m. and she fell asleep to the sound of the waves rolling onto the beach outside the Driftwood.

For the first time in eight years, Maisie woke up on Christmas morning with no pub to open. By the time she drew the curtains, daylight – already half an hour old in London – had reached Scilly.

There was no sign of Patrick at breakfast even though he'd been invited the previous evening, he said he'd have 'too much to do'. Over bacon butties, and still in her pyjamas, Maisie opened her gifts with her parents. The contrast between her putting on her uniform and opening a massive pub ready for the most hectic day of the year couldn't have been greater, but the happiness of sharing the day with her parents was still tinged with the bitter memories of the previous year.

Worries about the renovations, finances and Patrick's

departure at some point were pushed aside, but her pleasure was laced heavily with sadness when she thought that she might have been a mum herself this year. There should have been gifts for a little one under the tree and a baby at the table.

A gentle hug from her father and a look from her mother let Maisie know that they were all too aware of her wistful thoughts. Yet it *was* Christmas and this year she was utterly determined that nothing would stop her from making the most of it and having a lovely family day. She pushed the bad times to the back of her mind and threw herself into the fun of Christmas morning. Her mum had ordered a top and jeans that Maisie had hinted she loved, plus a matching bracelet and necklace that Maisie had spotted in one of the galleries on the off-islands. Her father produced a carved French-style dressing-table mirror and stool, which he'd managed to have delivered and hidden away under sacks in his shed all without Maisie's knowledge.

Maisie had a lump in her throat as she opened the large, gift-wrapped box and saw the furnishings. These gifts had significance beyond their practicality. The main items of furniture in her rented flat in St Austell had been the landlord's, but even the smaller personal items had had to be pared down, not to mention the general 'stuff'. And she'd left the flat in a hurry so much of it was given away, or went to the charity shop. A kind friend had also held a garage sale for her while she was sorting herself out and sent the proceeds on to Maisie by PayPal but the personal items she'd been able to salvage were precious to her.

'Patrick collected them from the supply boat and hid the mirror in the store cupboard in the Piggery. We were on a safe bet that you never go in there,' her dad said proudly. 'And I know you never set foot in my shed.'

Maisie smiled weakly. She had of course been in the Piggery several times, but never to look in Patrick's store cupboard. 'They're gorgeous. Just what I would have chosen.'

Ray was quietly delighted. 'Mum saw you looking at them so we were pretty sure we were onto a winner. This is your place too. We want it to feel like your own space even if we have to share.'

Her dad hugged her. 'You're not too old for this, are you?'

'Not as it's Christmas,' she said, tears prickling at the back of her eyes. Must be because it was Christmas. It was OK to go a bit mushy then, wasn't it?

Her mother smiled warmly as her father finally let her go. 'What a relief. I wasn't sure they were the ones you wanted but your dad was convinced. Now, whose turn is it next?'

The unwrapping continued, with presents from Maisie to her parents. Clothes and a spa voucher for her mum at the luxury hotel on St Saviour's, and some new gardening tools and signed books for her dad.

Even though there were only three of them, and some of the gifts were silly stocking fillers, there still seemed a scarily large number of parcels under the tree. Many of the goodies were practical things or items that they'd put off buying for the past few months, but there were also gifts from relatives on the mainland and local friends too, of course.

Once the close family presents were opened, they started

on the gifts from the Godrevys and little treats from some of the regulars. Archie's was obvious, of course, and was left until last so that everyone could enjoy opening it together after the mayhem of family gifts.

Hazel unwrapped the shrink-wrapped frame and let out an 'ooh' of surprise.

'It's not a painting. It's a photograph. It must be one of Jake's.'

She held up the photo of the Driftwood on a winter's morning, which had been taken with some kind of exposure that made the sea look as smooth as glass and as if mist were streaking over the flattened waves.

'That's grand,' said Ray.

'There's a cutting with it.' Hazel handed a copy of an international nature magazine to Maisie. The photo had made it into a feature about island life around the world. Jake Pendower's portrait stared back from above the by-line: with his serious brown eyes at odds with the jet black hair flopping over his face and almost Mediterranean colouring. Archie had looked the same once, according to Ray who also remembered Archie's father, Bill. Some said that the Pendowers were descended from shipwrecked sailors from the Spanish Armada. Well, it was a good tale for the customers and had earned Archie many a drink and might even have a kernel of truth in it.

'Terrible thing about young Jake's fiancée. No wonder he doesn't come back home much, though I feel sorry for Archie,' said Ray.

'His parents don't see much more of him. I reckon he stays as far away from St Piran's as possible these days.'

'So sad ...' said Maisie, remembering hearing about Jake's fiancée in a call from her mum when she was working in St Austell, and feeling stunned by the news.

Ray started to gather up the wrapping paper. Maisie always felt sad that the gift exchange was over for another year. It had been such a treat to watch her parents open their presents, even though she always felt like they spent far too much of their cash on her. 'Shall I come and start the veg?' Maisie asked, eager to take part in every festive ritual, however mundane.

'That's your dad's job,' said Hazel. 'But I think he might let you help him this year.'

Ray had pulled the parsnips and carrots and picked the sprouts freshly that morning. He'd harvested and stored the potatoes in his shed some time before. Maisie had been delighted to see him back working in his garden. With Patrick to do the heavy work, he'd begun to enjoy the allotment again. 'I'll join you. I'd better go and see how the turkey's doing, anyway. Smells good.' Hazel got up from the armchair. 'What's that noise?'

The sound of the back door to the kitchen slamming attracted their attention.

'I think it may be Patrick.' Maisie propped the photo of the Driftwood upright against the tree and scrambled to her feet. Her stomach did a mini-flip. She'd got him a present and despite her jokey protests, was pretty sure he'd bought her something. She just hoped it was something she could open in front of her parents without betraying her emotions. God, please let it not be sexy underwear – or any underwear.

Maisie reached the kitchen first and squealed.

'Oh my God. What have you got on?'

Patrick stood in the middle of the kitchen with a large white cardboard box in his arms, but the box wasn't the focus of her attention. He wore board shorts, a clashing Hawaiian shirt and flip-flops.

'This is Christmas Day, isn't it? This is what I'd wear on any Christmas Day. Shorts and thongs. Now, where's the barbie?'

'But it's six degrees and blowing a gale.'

'Lightweight.' He grinned.

Maisie burst out laughing. 'You are joking?'

'Yeah. I'm joking, I'm freezing my bloody rocks off.' He deposited the box on the countertop. 'I'll be back in a sec,' he said and vanished out of the door again.

Hazel walked into the kitchen and raised her eyebrows at the box. 'Where's Patrick?'

'Gone to put his clothes on,' said Maisie.

'What?'

Maisie giggled. 'Your face. He'll be back in a minute.'

Hazel pointed to the box. 'What on earth is that?'

Maisie shrugged. 'No idea.'

Hazel went to lift up the lid but Maisie stopped her.

'No, wait. I think it's meant to be a surprise,' she said.

'Bit late for that,' said Hazel. 'What has he been up to?'

'I dunno. Shall we pretend we haven't seen the box and get on with the veg?'

While Hazel basted the turkey, Ray joined Maisie at the sink, but she hadn't got beyond peeling a parsnip when Patrick staggered back in, laden down with a rucksack and two large supermarket carriers. He'd added a Santa hat to his Bondi Beach ensemble. Ray froze midway through scrubbing the potatoes while Hazel gawped at him like aliens had invaded the kitchen.

'What the?'

'Santa's here,' Patrick declared with a grin. 'Don't look so worried.'

Ray burst out laughing and even Hazel managed a grin as Maisie helped Patrick take his presents into the sitting room.

'I'll give you yours now while we're on our own,' he said.

'You shouldn't have bought us so much,' Maisie said, looking at the gift-wrapped parcels in amazement.

'Don't get too excited. They're only stocking fillers.'

Maisie wasn't so sure.

Patrick pulled a present out of the bag. It was soft and squidgy and very light. Maisie's heart sank. It felt like clothing ...

'I hope it's not what I think it is.'

'What do you think it is?'

Maisie glanced behind her. Her dad was murdering 'White Christmas' and she could hear the clash of pots and pans. Nonetheless she lowered her voice. 'Underwear,' she half-mouthed.

Patrick's face fell. 'Oh shit.'

Maisie stared at the parcel in horror.

'Open it quick and hide it.'

She ripped the parcel open. Inside was a bright pink, Lycra and very practical ... thermal rash vest.

'You b—'

'Shhh.' Patrick put his finger on her lips. 'It's to help keep you warm on your swims. Here. I got these to go with them.'

Taking the rash vest from her, he handed over another parcel which was the same size but squidgier. Still shaking her head, she ripped open the paper and pulled out a pair of neoprene swim shorts.

She let out a little squeal of pleasure. 'Oh, just what I've always wanted.' She risked a quick peck on Patrick's cheek. 'Thanks.'

'Anyone who didn't know you would think you were being sarcastic, but I know better.'

Gleefully, Maisie tried the bright blue shorts against her for size. 'They're fantastic. I've been meaning to get a pair ever since I got back here.'

'I don't think I've ever seen a woman more excited by a surprise from me,' said Patrick with a rueful smile. 'I've got you something else too but that really will have to wait until we're on our own.'

'Ooh er missus,' said Maisie, but her pulse skittered. How was she possibly going to hide her feelings for him throughout the whole day when she already felt like a kid who'd been given the keys to the Toys R Us warehouse?

'I hope you like yours,' she said, reaching for a gift bag from under the tree.

Patrick raised his eyebrows and accepted the gift bag.

Maisie had been in agonies of indecision over what to get him: something personal yet something that could stand up to public scrutiny, something funny that wouldn't arouse suspicion as a gift from a boss to her employee. She'd taken equal care with his 'secret' gift too, but for different reasons. Nothing that might be seen as tying him to the islands. Nothing too sentimental or, God forbid, romantic.

He laughed out loud when he opened a box set of DVDs of the last Lions rugby series. 'With us thrashing Australia of course,' she said with glee.

'Thanks. Not.'

'I've saved your real present for later,' she said hurriedly before Hazel and Ray walked in.

'That's the roast spuds and parsnips in the oven and the rest of the veg ready in the pans. Oh, what on earth's that?' said Hazel.

Maisie waggled the clothes. 'A rash vest and shorts for my swims.'

'Very nice,' said Hazel, clearly amused. And, hopefully, thrown off the scent by the practical present.

'I have something for you all,' said Patrick.

He handed over bottles of wine, red and white. 'This may be coals to Newcastle but you can't get this wine in the UK. This is decent stuff.'

'Very funny ... so how did you get it here?' asked Maisie.

'One of the Fingle regulars has a small vineyard so he shipped it specially for me. I thought it would go nicely with the turkey. And this is for you, Ray.' Patrick pulled a parcel from the carrier.

Ray was taken aback. 'My God. An Aussie cricket shirt and there's writing on it.'

'It was signed by the Ashes XI and the Poms too. The year

we won, of course,' Patrick joked. 'Can you be seen wearing it, though?'

'Cheeky bugger ... it's grand but it must have cost a bit. How did you get it?'

'Some of the squad come into the bar from time to time when they're in Melbourne. One or two were big friends of Greg's and happy to do it, especially when I said it was for a Pom.' With his twinkling eyes and the tilt of the mouth hinting at trouble, Maisie didn't think she could possibly fancy him any more, even in clashing shorts and a shirt so loud she needed ear defenders.

'There was one condition, though,' he said to Ray. 'You have to have your picture taken wearing it.'

'Wear it? I'll bloody frame it,' Ray declared. He examined the signatures more closely, reading them out and shaking his head in disbelief while roundly lambasting some of the names from both sides. Despite the jokes, Maisie could see her father was thrilled and touched. She wasn't that surprised Patrick knew the cricketers, though, as the bar wasn't far from the ground, but it was still a big thing to have got the shirt and have it posted all this way.

'Sorry yours isn't quite so exciting, Hazel,' said Patrick handing her a smaller parcel.

'I'm glad to hear it. I can't stand cricket.'

'Neither can the England team, by the looks of it,' said Patrick.

Ray wagged his finger. 'Now you're pushing your luck, Crocodile Dundee ... and speaking of which ...'

More presents were exchanged. A DVD of *Crocodile Dundee*

1 and 2 for Patrick and a bottle of non-alcoholic fizz from the local vineyard. From Patrick there were purple leather gloves for Hazel, which Maisie had tipped him off about. Patrick opened a couple of gifts from Will and Jess and Javid and Katya, and a parcel that had been mailed to the pub by Judy, along with Ray's shirt. Patrick laughed out loud when he pulled out the sleeveless sport shirt with McKinnon printed on the back, explaining that it was the latest Melbourne Demons Aussie Rules kit. It was accompanied by a framed photo of Judy and the bar team and a letter which he didn't open.

'Do you miss them?' Hazel asked him.

Maisie held her breath.

'Yes. Especially today, I won't lie.'

'I bet. I'm sorry about your friend. It must be very hard for you and Judy today.'

Maisie desperately wanted to hug Patrick but she didn't dare. He nodded and said, 'Well, she has her own family around her. That might not be a bad thing.'

'And you're stuck with us, mate.' Ray slapped him on the back, and Hazel, to Maisie's amazement, gave Patrick a kiss on the cheek.

'Right. Who fancies a pre-dinner drink? Patrick, there's plenty of the soft stuff for you but if no one minds, I'm going to have a beer.'

All Patrick's offers to help in the kitchen were firmly rebuffed so Maisie found herself buzzing in and out of the kitchen as she helped with 'trimmings' and laid the table. It was quite fun, sneaking a quick kiss with Patrick while her parents were out of the way. It was like being a teenager again and reminded her of stolen snogs with the occasional bronzed young lad visiting Gull on holiday.

Hmm.

She guessed her parents might have known about some of those holiday romances but she was still confident they hadn't guessed about her relationship with Patrick. One of the downsides of moving back home had been giving up her own space, but her bedsit was OK and it just wasn't practical, economically, to rent long-term on Gull, even if she could have found a suitable year-round place. The staff cottages were needed in the season and her own little nook at the top of the main house was much cosier anyway.

Lunch was served to a round of applause from Patrick, who complimented them on the food.

'What would you be having at home?' Maisie's mum asked him as Ray carved a slice of turkey.

Patrick helped himself to cranberry sauce. 'A quick sarnie until we could finally get time for a proper sit-down dinner after the Christmas rush was over – which could be after New Year. Judy and Greg loved dishing up turkey and all the trimmings and I guess Judy will want to keep up the tradition, for her family's sake.'

'Even in that heat?' Maisie asked.

'Yup, though we sometimes have a different pudding. Something lighter.' He flashed them a grin. 'But more on that later.'

'Is that what's in the box?' Hazel asked, piling sprouts on her plate.

Patrick tapped the side of his nose. 'I know there's a Christmas pudding on the way but I've taken the liberty of making you all a surprise.'

After dinner he vanished into the kitchen and returned with a snowy-white confection, topped with pillows of whipped cream and jewel-like green and red fruits.

'Voila. A festive Pavlova.'

'Oh my word!' said Hazel.

Maisie giggled. 'It looks amazing. What's on it?'

'Kiwi fruit, red grapes, dried cranberries and pistachios,' said Patrick. 'Plus a drizzle of framboise liqueur. I think I can allow myself that.'

'It's magnificent,' said Hazel.

'Well, there goes my healthy-eating plan,' added Ray with a grin.

'We have this at the Fingle instead of a Christmas pudding,' said Patrick. 'Judy usually makes it but she coached me through the recipe so I could do one for you. Desserts aren't my forte.'

Ray rubbed his hands together. 'But eating is mine. Let's tuck in.'

Later, with everyone swearing they'd never eat a morsel of food ever again, and Ray and Hazel dozing in front of the telly, Patrick and Maisie escaped. Maisie grabbed a rug and some matches and they headed for the beach.

Chapter 31

Grey-blue clouds hung low in a peach and coral sky. The undulating outline of Petroc Island was silhouetted against the winter sun. Round the headland and just out of sight of the pub, Maisie gathered some driftwood and bone-dry seaweed and after a few false starts Patrick managed to set it alight. He kissed Maisie then put his arm around her. They sat in silence, watching the flames flickered and burned orange like the setting sun.

'Strange to think that it's Boxing Day already at home,' Patrick said.

The word 'home' wasn't lost on Maisie. 'Have you heard how Judy is without Greg? Today – yesterday – must have been tough.'

'She put a brave face on it for me. They wanted to open as usual as Greg would have wanted and her kids took a couple of weeks off to run the bar with her. They work in Sydney ... apparently the bar was rammed all day with people turning up to raise a toast to Greg. I like to think he was looking down and raising his own glass too.'

Maisie squeezed his hand. 'She sounds like an amazingly strong woman.'

'She is.'

'Doesn't she miss you being there this year?'

'Maybe. I phoned her late last night. I could hardly hear above the noise in the Fingle. I think she's OK but you're right. I do miss her and worry about her.'

Maisie thought more than ever that it was a miracle that Patrick had stayed. Could he really be here because – she dared not think it – of her?

'Oh. I have another present for you,' she said, remembering the parcel in her jacket pocket. 'Here you are.'

She'd wrapped the small gift in pale-blue tissue paper tied with a raffia bow, hoping it wasn't too twee for him, but she'd wanted to make the gift special. Now her stomach fluttered in case he hated it or thought it was naff.

Patrick turned over the packet in his large hand, laying it flat on his palm. 'It's not very big.'

Maisie rubbed her hands together in frustration. He was prolonging her agony, the devil.

With a sigh, he pulled at the raffia string and the tissue opened. 'Whoops.'

The gift fell onto the beach. Maisie looked down. It didn't look much, lying on the sand among the shells and pebbles, but Patrick reached down and scooped it up. It was a pendant. A shiny tiny starfish on a leather cord. When she'd seen it, she'd loved it immediately but agonised over whether to get it and had gone back twice before asking Archie to bring it over to the bar on Christmas Eve.

'It's from Archie's gallery,' she explained. 'The Starfish Studio, on St Piran's. He sells stuff from other makers and artists as well as his own paintings.'

Patrick held the leather cord between his fingers and the starfish glinted in the rays of the dying sun.

'It's not silver,' she continued. 'It's tin from the last working tin streamers in Cornwall. I didn't know what to get you but I wanted to give you something ... personal to remember me by, something local – or almost local.'

Patrick didn't reply, causing Maisie more moments of exquisite tension. Then he lifted it over his head and put it round his neck and smiled. 'It's grand,' he said, echoing her dad. 'In fact, it's perfect.'

Her shoulders slumped in relief. His quiet reaction seemed to say a lot more than any gushing, not that Patrick ever gushed. 'Oh, I'm so glad you like it, but you can't possibly wear it today. Mum and Dad will notice. Wait until tomorrow.'

'Why?'

'Then you can say it was from someone else. Judy maybe. Or Will.'

'Will? They really will be worried if I say he gave me a necklace.'

'Probably not as worried as if you say I did.'

Patrick leaned in and kissed her. A long, slow kiss that made the tension ebb away and a dreamy languor fill her veins like rich red wine.

'I think it's time you had your "secret" present.' He pulled a small square cardboard box from his pocket.

'I'd wondered what the bulge in your jeans was.'

'I'd have thought the shape and position of it might have worried you.'

Maisie laughed, fizzing with anticipation. So far, Christmas Day had been a weird and wonderful mix of childlike excitement and very grown-up thrills.

'Great minds think alike,' said Patrick as she eased the lid off the blue box and saw what was inside. She pulled it out and rested it on her palm, hardly daring to breathe let alone speak. She didn't know what she'd expected – a jokey present, maybe – and she'd feared and hoped for a token of affection. This was definitely not a joke. It was a small round silver disc enclosing an iridescent gemstone, the colours of which shifted constantly as Maisie turned it this way and that, flashing with an inner fire almost like the setting sun. Turquoise, mint, sky blue ... hues that were impossible to pin down, they kept changing all the time.

'It's an opal,' Patrick said. 'From Australia, of course.'

'It's amazing. Beautiful. Thanks, but ...'

'For God's sake, don't say "you shouldn't have".'

She stroked the opal, which was smooth and cool under her fingers.

'I was going to say that I'll have to say it was from Jess ...'

'I don't mind who you say it's from. As long as it's not Hugo.'

'We don't need Hugo,' said Maisie, feeling as if she could take on the whole world. 'We've shown him that Gull Islanders can pull together without the likes of him. We don't need his bribes. We can take care of our own.'

'I hope so. It's not only Judy who's an amazing woman,' said Patrick.

She put her finger on his lips. 'No. I'm not amazing at all. Just a woman. Patrick. I need to say something. These gifts cost a lot of money on top of the building stuff. I appreciate you helping us – I'm really grateful – but this isn't your battle to fight. Lending a hand at the site is one thing but using your own money, that's different. You must have used up most of your earnings here plus savings and you hardly know us ...'

'Don't I?'

'You've only been here a couple of months and I know what's happened between us changes things. I know you – we know each other – in some ways, but in others we hardly know a thing about one another.'

She felt the heat rise to her cheeks. Why was it that she was never shy or ashamed when she was in bed with him but couldn't talk about their relationship when she was in his normal company? It was like waking up with a sex hangover. She'd indulge her every passion while they were in bed but afterwards she felt awkward.

'We know the things that matter,' he said.

She'd had too much Prosecco, shiraz and Bailey's and Patrick, damn him, was still sober. But she couldn't stop herself and she didn't really think the alcohol had loosened her tongue. She had this urge to tell him, God knows where it had come from. She wanted him to know everything about her.

'I don't know ... I just ... think ... I lied about last Christmas. I wasn't working.'

He held her hands and looked into her face. 'Tell me, Maisie. Don't hold back. I guessed that things haven't been easy for you.'

'Hasn't Mum already told you what happened to me?'

'No, but I can see you're hiding some deep pain. Your mother's spoken to me but only to warn me not to hurt you.'

'Jesus. When? Today?'

'No. The day you gave me the job.'

Maisie moaned. 'Bloody hell, Mum. How could she? I'd only known you two days and she decided to assume you were after me. I'm sorry,' she said in exasperation. 'I'm not seventeen.'

'But she loves you and she was right. I am after you.'

And you will hurt me. It will hurt when you go. I can't deny that any longer. It will hurt like hell, at least as much as Keegan leaving and probably – definitely – more. Even after a few months. Why, oh, why have I done this to myself again?

Patrick broke into her thoughts. 'You said you lied about last Christmas ...'

Maisie tugged the blanket round her shoulders. It was too late to stop now, even if this was the moment where Patrick, like most other blokes, started to turn pale and run a mile at the double whammy of women's problems and emotional catastrophe. Not that he could run anywhere.

'I wasn't at work. I was at hospital. I lost my baby. My baby and Keegan's baby.'

Chapter 32

She had never shared how she felt – how she really felt – about her loss since she'd talked to Keegan in those early hours after. Not even with her mum, or father or Jess. She hadn't been able to find the words to express how she felt. The emptiness, the raw and gaping wound. Some people told her she could try again, they meant it kindly and they were right.

Patrick's arms tightened around her. His silence was more encouraging than any words.

'I was thirteen weeks pregnant and working in the pub. It was Christmas evening and we were just quietening down after serving the lunches when I felt unwell and went to the loo. I knew exactly what was happening and they called me an ambulance and contacted Keegan. He was at his parents, spending the day with them. They owned the brewery and pub chain, you see, and Keegan worked in the business. He was a director and I met him on one of his visits to the pub. I suppose you could say he was my boss although he worked at the head office, acquiring and getting rid of failing pubs.' She hesitated, knowing she was coming to the worst part.

Patrick stroked her hair and kissed her neck. He whispered: 'Go on.'

'The medics tried to help me but it was too late. I'd lost the baby. Nothing to be done, not my fault. The consultant said all those things but I have a condition that makes it hard for me to fall pregnant in the first place so it was a double blow. Everything was going right for me. In a great relationship, or so I thought, job I loved, baby on the way. I was going to take time off and maybe go back part-time after the baby arrived. I had it all planned out, but just like that, everything ended.'

'I'm sorry. Why did he leave?'

'He couldn't handle it. Not the loss or the baby. He made sympathetic noises and was kind, but a few weeks later, he told me it was over. Blamed himself for not being able to handle the responsibility: said he obviously wasn't ready for a "grown-up" relationship yet, not with a woman who wanted a family … then he confessed he didn't actually want children after all.'

'Jesus.'

'I was devastated at the time … I hated him for a while. For leaving me when I needed him most and for being a coward, or so I thought. But it was for the best. Better that I found out then than years later when we'd got married. I don't blame him now. Mum and Jess, friends from the pub, all said I was better off without him and now I agree.'

She twisted round. Patrick bit his lip. For the first time since she'd known him, he looked angry. He'd been so laid back until now but there was a fire in his expression: anger and hurt.

She didn't want Patrick to think she was asking for sympathy or wanted anything more from him than for him to simply listen.

'Why did you split up with your girlfriend?' she asked.

He blew out a breath. 'Similar sort of thing. She ran out on me when I needed her ... but nothing compared to your loss. Like you I don't blame her any more, though I admit I was cut up at the time. Tania and I wanted different things from life too.'

'Like what?'

'She wanted me to aim for more than being a humble bar bum. She said she wouldn't have minded if I'd even decided to run my own place, but I seemed content to drift along as the bar manager. I wasn't the high-flier she'd hoped. I think when we got together she thought I'd amount to more and discover some deep-rooted ambition and when it became clear I was happy to remain in the same place, she rightly told me she was off.'

'Rightly? You don't sound as if you thought she was right at the time.'

'No. Well, I wasn't thinking straight. I'd just heard that Greg's illness was terminal and Tania hit me with the news she was leaving all on the same day, not that she knew about his diagnosis at the time.'

'Ouch. That's awful. What happened after she told you?'

'I fell off the wagon big style. Went on a three-day bender and woke up on the floor of an empty flat. She'd shifted most of our stuff while I'd been hitting the bars or passed out in the flat.'

'I'm so sorry, Patrick, for your loss and Tania walking out. That must have been a bloody awful time in your life.'

'Who could blame her? I was a loser and a drunk.'

'You were an alcoholic. I doubt you were ever the loser you think you were. You're way too hard on yourself.' Maisie's heart went out to him. What a double loss to suffer.

'I haven't touched a drop since I woke up with the mother of all headaches and an empty flat. Not even after Greg died. I was on Kool-Aid at the wake, probably the only sober one in the whole place. I served behind the bar of the Fingle while everyone raised a glass to Greg.'

'You said you lost your father and mother. Was Greg a substitute?'

'Of course. He and Judy were.'

'It must be hard to be so far from her.'

'She has a wicked sense of humour but doesn't suffer fools … a bit like someone else I could mention.' His eyes twinkled and Maisie felt herself reddening. 'But she's solid gold under the no-nonsense exterior. I do miss her, but I'll be home in the spring and maybe I'll bring her back one day.'

'To see where Greg's ancestors lived?'

I'll be home in the spring. It was a throwaway line that seemed to have no impact on Patrick but delivered a sharp pang of disappointment to Maisie. He *was* going, then. Keeping to his word that this was a fling. She told herself not to be so surprised and to grow up. That was what she wanted too, wasn't it?

'Yeah. Something like that.' His voice trailed off.

She lightened the atmosphere. 'I've plenty here for you to do in the meantime.'

'I hope so.' His smile was crooked. She sensed a change in his mood. Perhaps she'd shared too much too soon. Perhaps they both had, but this had seemed the right moment, and anyway, they didn't have time. His awkwardness was momentary or could have been imagined because now he was kissing her and folding her against him, into him. Despite the size difference, she felt as if she fitted perfectly. As if his body had been made to be alongside hers. Even while he was kissing her, a soft, slow kiss that seemed to pull out her soul, she was telling herself not to get in any deeper than she had. To hold back as much of herself as she could still cling on to. As he made love to her on the sand, Patrick didn't seem to be holding back. Maybe because he didn't want to or didn't need to.

Perhaps being with her was merely a physical fling to him, though Maisie didn't think so. She thought that Patrick genuinely liked her and liked spending time with her. He must fancy her and perhaps he found solace in her arms while he worked out whatever demons and grief he was harbouring since his surrogate father had died in such cruel circumstances. Grief that had followed on from an early loss and a troubled, tough boyhood.

Maisie knew that grief didn't last forever. Although it never left you completely, and you always bore the scars, you learned to live with it eventually and you moved on.

Which was what Patrick would do, one day. One day soon.

The sex was tender and glorious, even though they were both covered in sand and their exposed flesh was chilled by the wind. After it was over, and with the greatest reluctance, Maisie started to get dressed.

'We'd better get back. Mum and Dad can't still be asleep,' said Maisie, zipping up her jeans before scrambling to her feet. Patrick stayed where he was, looking at her intently. She brushed sand off her top and then caught sight of the man watching them.

Ray must have popped out for some fresh air and was standing on the shoreline parallel with them but directly in front of the Driftwood. He was looking straight at them. Maisie didn't know how long he'd been there and even though it was dark, with the moonlight and the fire, he'd have had to be blind not to see them and to put two and two together. He might even have seen them making love. Maisie's stomach did a double back flip.

'Oh God, no. Dad's seen us.'

Patrick followed her line of sight.

'He knows,' said Maisie. 'And now Mum will too.' She tried to get up off the sand but Patrick pulled her back.

'They had guessed already,' he said softly. 'And there's no point pretending otherwise now. No point locking the stable door after the horse has bolted.'

Ray had turned away and was hurrying back to the pub. 'I know but ... oh, no, I didn't want them to find out about us like this.'

'Is it so bad that they know? We're all grown-ups.'

'You think so? That's not what my mum and dad feel, I'm sure. I'll get the third degree from Mum the first chance she gets.' Maisie threw up her hands in frustration. 'Shit and double shit.'

'Do you honestly think they'll disapprove that much?' he said, keeping hold of her hand.

'You know they will. You're right. I'm being very naïve to think they hadn't already guessed about us and I *had* thought about going public, but on our terms, when we decide, not like this.' She pulled away from him. 'I think we should go back.'

'OK. If that's what you really want, but there's no point rushing off now.'

'I know. Are you coming?'

'It might be best if you and your parents had some time on your own? You probably need to talk about this – us.'

Maisie bit her lip, then nodded, not looking forward to the conversation with her mum and dad. Why did life have to be so complicated? Why did people have to make it so complex? Or perhaps it was simple: just tell them about her and Patrick.

Wrapping her arms around herself for comfort, Maisie strode back to the pub but glanced behind as she clambered up from the sand to the road. Patrick was crouched down scooping sand over the last embers of the fire. In seconds the beach was dark and he was nothing but a half-imagined ghost somewhere on the sand.

Chapter 33

Patrick sloped off to the Piggery, saying he wanted to catch up with some mates on Skype, leaving Maisie no choice but to face Ray and Hazel. At any moment, Maisie expected them to confront her about Patrick but nothing was said. In fact, they acted as if nothing had happened, but Maisie spent the whole of Christmas evening on edge, waiting for the moment when one of them mentioned 'it'. She loved them dearly but for the first time since she'd come home, sitting in front of the festive edition of *Strictly*, *EastEnders* and the premiere of a Bond film, she wished she didn't live at the Driftwood with her parents.

When Patrick went home to Oz, she would have to think about renting a cottage elsewhere on the island, to give herself space. Yet she could hardly afford to do that; she was living rent free at the Driftwood. Maybe if she moved into Patrick's studio after he was gone, that would be better than nothing, though they would need the Piggery over the summer for the seasonal staff.

Boxing Day came and went and still no one said a word, but she had the feeling that the pressure was building hour by hour and Ray and Hazel were only waiting for her to tell them about Patrick before they broached the subject. As the hours ticked by, she wondered if her father hadn't actually seen them and wasn't even sure what he'd interrupted. He may have assumed that she and Patrick were just chatting, or more realistically, that they'd got together for a quick Christmas snog after Maisie had had too much to drink.

Days went by and the clock ran down towards 'The Birthday', and Maisie decided to leave well alone. If Jess, Patrick or her parents were planning any kind of 'celebration' during the day, she definitely hadn't got wind of it, and anyway, they knew she was working at the Driftwood so that ruled out a surprise party.

Work recommenced at Hell Cove while people were on holiday and glad of an excuse to escape the enforced jollity and socialising for a few hours. She and Patrick spent their days at the site and evenings when the Driftwood was closed visiting Jess and Will, Javid and Katya and the rugby crowd in various pubs around the islands while Hazel and Ray caught up with old friends and neighbours.

Then, before she knew it, Maisie found herself waking up on her fortieth birthday. More presents were exchanged and she joined Jess for lunch in their favourite restaurant on St Mary's. Jess had arranged for one of the boatmen to collect her in one of the few high-speed 'jet' boats that transported visitors between the islands and it was waiting to greet Maisie at the Gull Island jetty. 'Way to go,' said Jess, applauding as Maisie waved goodbye to the skipper at St Mary's harbour.

She hugged her friend. 'You are so naughty, arranging such a treat.'

'I was worried that if the weather had turned, you wouldn't have got here at all. Can't have you going home drunk in charge of the *Puffin*, can we?'

'It was a lovely surprise. Thank you.'

Jess linked arms with Maisie. 'Now we can celebrate properly. Come on, I've booked our favourite table.'

The favourite table turned out to be the best one in the house, in a bay window overlooking the whole of the Eastern Isles of Scilly. The sun had put in an appearance and although it was cool, the skies were clear. Cocktails were produced, along with a beautiful bouquet of flowers from Will and Anna Godrevy.

'Mum chose and hand tied them herself,' said Jess. 'Happy birthday, bestie.'

Maisie was already in an emotional state, and the flowers tipped her over the edge. Jess had gone to such an effort when Maisie knew she was still hurting over Adam.

'And lunch is on Will,' she said. 'So enjoy it!'

She laughed away her tears and they enjoyed the delicious meal, reminiscing about happy times, sharing gossip about Will and his latest 'fans', and just having a laugh. This wasn't the day to talk about her misgivings about Patrick or Jess's troubles with Adam. It was a cosy, girly lunch. At the end of the meal, the staff appeared with a beautiful chocolate cake topped with a sparkler and a glass of Champagne.

'Did you arrange this too?' Maisie asked Jess after the waiting staff had sung 'Happy Birthday'.

'No. It's as much of a surprise to me as you. By the way, you haven't asked where your present is.'

'I have a present too? The flowers and lunch are more than enough.'

'Rubbish. Here you go.'

Jess pulled a gift from her bag. It was an exquisite little silver trinket box from the Starfish Studio, with a silver cowrie shell embedded on the top. Inside the lid was engraved:

To my best mate, love, J xx

Maisie could hold it in no longer. She hugged Jess and let the tears flow.

'Has my mascara run?' she asked, dabbing at her wet cheeks.

Jess shook her head. 'No. You only look a little bit like a panda.'

After a trip to the ladies to redo her make-up, Maisie let the jet boat take her and Jess home again before it was dark. She was slightly squiffy and still in an emotional state as she stepped onto the quay with her arms full of flowers and gifts and the rest of the cake, but there was work to be done.

She started to prep the buffet ready for the New Year's Eve party and check that the empty staff studios were ready for the folk band who'd been hired in. Hazel's sister and brother-in-law were also supposed to be arriving that afternoon and were staying the night in the other one.

She flicked on the lights. She'd cleaned the studios a couple of days before but she switched on the heaters and took in some fresh towels and toiletries to the unit that her aunt and uncle were going to occupy. She looked around the little rooms. They were modest, like everything about the Driftwood, but they were part of her home and heritage. She might have passed a landmark birthday, but she had plenty to be happy

317

about. She might be fighting to keep her livelihood out of Hugo's hands but he couldn't touch the Driftwood if she and her parents refused. And she was with Patrick ... for now. Life definitely gave with one hand and took away with the other but she still felt happier than she had since the Christmas Day bombshell of the previous year.

It was dark outside and she folded the towels and laid them on the bed. The sound of the door opening made her jump then smile as Patrick said, 'Hello, gorgeous,' in his deep Aussie tones.

He stepped inside and closed the door.

'Thank God I've finally got you on your own,' he said hugging her. 'I never thought I'd have a chance to give you your birthday present.'

'A birthday present? I didn't expect one.'

Perhaps that wasn't quite true, she admitted to herself.

Patrick smiled. 'Can't have a milestone like this pass by without recognition. Here you are.'

He pulled another small parcel from inside his coat. It was similarly wrapped to her Christmas gift, and Maisie wondered if he'd ordered both at the same time.

She carefully unwrapped the tissue paper and took the lid off a small flat box. Nestled inside was a white gold bangle with an opal as its centrepiece. She gasped in delighted horror. 'Patrick. You are terrible. You can't give me this. It's gold, isn't it?'

'Plated maybe. I don't know. Does it matter? Do you like it?'

'I love it. It's just so delicate.'

'Put it on, then.'

Her fingers weren't quite steady as she slipped it over her wrist. 'It's gorgeous. Absolutely amazing. Thank you, even though you are a very bad person for spending so much.'

She grabbed him and gave him a long, deep kiss.

'Wear it tonight, then, and by the way, happy birthday,' he said when they pulled apart before dragging her back into his arms for another kiss.

She gave herself over to the moment with him, wishing it could go on forever but the sound of voices outside brought her back to reality. 'I should go. There's work to do and the band and guests will be here any minute.'

Patrick started to unbutton her top. 'They can wait.'

'Not really ...'

He stopped the protests by locking the door, picking her up and dumping her on the bed.

Half an hour later, Maisie hurried back to the pub, running her fingers through her tousled hair on the way. It was past six o'clock and she could hear a few familiar voices in the bar. The band members were walking around the side of the pub with instrument cases and sports bags. Ray must have already met them at the quay in the Land Rover but she'd no idea how they'd got across from the main island because the ferry wasn't running this late. Ray must have fetched them in the *Puffin*.

'Where d'you want us, love?' the leader asked.

'Um. In the studios, if you don't mind. This way.' Still feeling flushed, Maisie showed them into their quarters for the night while Patrick went back to the pub to stock the bar. There was no sign of her uncle and auntie yet.

After settling them in, she hurried back into the pub kitchen. It was deserted apart from Patrick who was filling a bucket with ice cubes from bags in the freezer. She heard familiar voices and giggles from the bar.

'Oh, Jess and Will are here early,' she told Patrick. 'They said they'd try to make it in time to help us set up. Have we been missed?'

Patrick put the lid on the ice bucket. 'I don't think so, but Jess's dying to see you again.'

'I'll pop into the bar and say hello before I get changed.'

Maisie pushed open the door to the bar and almost had a heart attack. Lights blinded her and a collective shout rang out.

'Surprise!'

The place was as packed as sardines in a tin. Jess, Will, her parents, Archie, Fen, Javid, Katya, the Bartons, the Jenkins, rugby club mates and helpers from the building work. A huge homemade banner with 'Happy 40th Birthday, Maisie' painted on it in Archie's hand had been hung on one wall, covering his pictures.

'Oh my God,' she squeaked, taking her hand from her mouth. 'I knew you were up to something, Jess Godrevy!'

Everyone laughed as Jess ran forward and hugged her. 'And you're not angry?'

'Angry? I'm bloody furious.' Then she burst out laughing and kissed Jess on the cheek. 'Of course not, but you are naughty! Was this all your idea?'

Jess heaved a sigh of relief. 'And Will's. Your mum and dad said you'd moan for about a minute then be secretly delighted.

We helped them decorate the bar while you were cleaning. After all you're not forty every day, are you? You have to make hay while the sun shines, now you're on the slippery slope to old age.'

'Oh, just you wait until it's your turn,' Maisie said, still reeling from the shock and yet secretly delighted to have all her friends around her to mark the occasion, now that it had finally come. After all, she thought, the alternative wouldn't have been much fun.

Jess laughed. 'Not yet.'

Adam was notable by his absence. He'd stayed away but Jess seemed happy enough. She was probably putting on a brave face for Maisie but Maisie wasn't going to probe. This was a happy occasion for everyone who'd organised it, even more than herself. And for once why not do as Jess suggested? Relax and have a few drinks. Be the customer. With the amount of people wanting to talk to her and buy her drinks, she didn't think she'd have a choice. Patrick grinned from behind the bar, where he and Will were rushed off their feet. Realising she was still in her scruffy jeans and cleaning top, she managed to slip upstairs and change into something a little more glamorous. Then it was back to the bar.

Someone handed her a glass of Prosecco, the band started up with 'Happy Birthday' and another cake covered in candles was brought out, made by Davina from the Fudge Pantry.

'No need for the lighthouse tonight, eh, Maisie? That cake will keep every ship within fifty miles away from those rocks,' Archie quipped as Maisie prepared to blow them out.

'Thank you, Archie. You're barred!' Maisie shouted back

then took a huge breath. It took three goes but she did it and the bar rang with cheers and applause.

The night was clear and cool as Patrick held Maisie in his arms on a quiet patch of beach in front of the Driftwood. Some early fireworks still flickered in the night sky above Petroc and St Mary's but the thunder and hiss of rockets was muted. Ray and Will were going to set off their own display after Big Ben's chimes. Bass thumped from the Driftwood along with chatter and singing. It had been a wonderful evening full of laughter, partying and dancing but she was glad to have Patrick to herself for a few minutes at least.

The stars pricked the skies above them and the rest of the world seemed miles away. Even with the muted sound of revelry and music drifting across the sand, she and Patrick might have been the only people on Gull. Huddled in his arms, her heart was soaring but breaking too.

She loved Patrick; no point in denying it to herself even though she could never tell him.

The voices grew louder and the music stopped to be replaced by the sound of the radio coming live from London and blaring out from the bar.

'We'd better not miss this, much as I'd love to stay here all night,' said Patrick.

People spilled out and he and Maisie walked back to the terrace. Voices hushed as the first chimes of Big Ben rang out. One, two … five, six … eleven, twelve. A huge cheer rang out and everyone started wishing each other a happy New Year and kissing loved ones, friends and neighbours.

The hiss of a rocket and deafening bangs made Maisie jump. She looked into the night sky to see starbursts of purple, dazzling white and red explode behind the Driftwood. 'Oohs' and 'ahs' echoed through the night air as rockets whizzed high into the sky. Some people began to sing 'Auld Lang Syne', but Maisie only had eyes for Patrick. The shaky, wobbly music and even the pop of the fireworks faded as Patrick took her into his arms and lifted her off her feet. He held her up by her bottom and she wrapped her legs around his waist as they kissed, long and deep while the cacophony carried on around them.

If people were watching, she no longer cared, she thought. They were out and proud. Patrick led her away from the terrace and onto the sand. They picked their way by the lights from the terrace and the fireworks illuminating the sky.

'Everyone knows about us now. There's no way to put the genie back in the bottle,' said Maisie.

Patrick lifted a strand of hair off her face. 'What if the genie didn't want to go back anyway?'

'What are you trying to say?'

'I'm not *trying* to say anything. I *am* saying it. I don't have to go back to Oz. I don't want to go back.'

Maisie's legs wobbled. 'You don't really mean that. You can't stay here on this little scrap of earth. You'd go mad, and within a week, you'd be longing for the big wide world.'

'I've seen it. I like this scrap of earth. I like sharing it with you.'

She pushed him away and laughed. 'Oh, Patrick. I'd love to believe you.'

He took her arm and spun her round. She half stumbled in the sand.

'Then believe me. I have fallen for you, and I want to stay here at the Driftwood with you.'

She groaned. The glimpse of a future with him was so tempting, it was agonising to contemplate. 'I'd braced myself for you leaving. I was ready for it. Don't lob a great big rock in the pool now.'

'Why not? I'm selfish. I have thrown the rock and you can tell me to piss off, and I will, but it won't be because I chose to go; it'll be because you made me leave.'

'I don't want you to leave!' she shouted to the velvet sky and dark sea. 'I want you to stay, but I'm scared.'

'I know. Me too. Both of us have had to lose too much in a short space of time. Both of us have every reason to protect ourselves and keep the world at bay, but I'm willing to risk it. Question is: are you?'

She didn't think she could live with herself if he let her down now. He might do that. One day in the future. Who could predict when or where or how?

She held on to him, laughing but wanting to cry at the same time. 'Damn you for doing this. For walking into my pub and my life and doing this to me. I hate you, McKinnon. I hate you and I know I'll regret this one day and I'm an even bigger fool than I thought I was but, yes. Yes, I'm willing to risk it.'

A huge bang made Maisie almost fall on top of Patrick.

'Jesus, are your dad and his brother-in-law trying to blow up the bloody pub?' he asked, laughing.

'I don't know but we'd better go and find out.' She held out her hand. 'Come on, then, let's get this over with, although after that snog I don't think anyone will be surprised.'

Patrick's arm was firm around her waist as they made their way into the pub. The pyrotechnics were over but the band was still playing and people were filtering back into the bar. For the first time, Maisie noticed Hugo was standing in the corner by Archie. Basil was poking around as usual, like a furry Hoover. Heads turned and people raised eyebrows, smiled knowing smiles or simply gawked. Javid raised a glass to them, but Maisie's attention was mostly for her parents.

Hazel didn't look happy. Ray smiled but Maisie felt his concern. Time would tell and maybe prove them wrong: prove her wrong too. Who knew? She and Patrick might grow old together on Gull Island and maybe even bring up a new generation of Samsons – or McKinnons – it wasn't too late. She smiled. Hugo looked like he'd swallowed the lemon in his gin and tonic. He really *had* fancied her, then. Tough.

He'd get over it. He had plenty of admirers, eager to further the Scorrier dynasty. The Driftwood's troubles would still be there tomorrow. She wouldn't think of that now, only of the joy she felt to have this man's arm around her and to have his big warm body in her bed. Why not enjoy that for the rest of tonight? In fact, they'd spend the night together in Patrick's quarters. A single bed between the two of them. Now, that was going to be fun and she was only forty once, so damn it ...

Chapter 34

Maisie, I have something to tell you …
Maisie, I don't know how to say this but …
Maisie, I've not been totally honest with you …

Maisie, I've lied to you and deceived you but I want to put things right because I love you and I want to stay with you.

After they'd gone inside, Patrick re-took his place behind the bar while Maisie laughed and chatted with her mates. He'd never felt so happy or so terrified in his life. There had been two things he'd been certain about before he'd walked into this pub on that October day. One was how much he was devastated when Greg died; two was that he was going back to Melbourne as soon as he possibly could.

Now there was a third. He loved Maisie Samson. And she felt the same way too, or at least she didn't want him to go. And that realisation had turned the second certainty upside-down. But now he had no choice; he had to finally face up to his responsibilities – whatever they were – and face up to Maisie's reaction.

Damn you, Paddy boy. Just tell her.

But not now, with dozens of people around. When the

music's stopped and the fiddler's gone, then he would. Within the hour, the moment they were alone, on the first day of a new year. A new start for him, a new life for them both.

'Oi! Crocodile Dundee. Where's my pint?' Patrick snapped out of his euphoric, terrified trance to see Archie glaring at him, holding up his empty glass.

'Coming.'

Maisie was across the pub, chatting to Jess and roaring with laughter. Her skin glowed, her eyes shone, he'd never seen her so happy or light-hearted. Would she be the same when he told her his confession? He hadn't done anything so very terrible yet, far from it. She surely wouldn't mind?

A few people drifted off. The fiddle player played the Irish Rover and announced their final tune would be the 'Black Velvet Band', old folk songs. He'd heard them in the Irish pubs in Melbourne a few times so Patrick joined in with everyone else.

'Her eyes they shone like diamonds. I thought her the queen of the land. And her hair it hung over her shoulder tied up with a black velvet band …'

Maisie pulled a face at him and mimed fingers in her ears at his awful singing, so Patrick sang even louder. She couldn't actually hear him, he knew, above the drunken carousing of the rest of the revellers. Archie was in full voice, even at his age his deep baritone was strong, not to mention Will with his beer-fuelled tenor and the rugby guys giving it all they'd got. Even Hugo Scorrier was singing along, smiling and waving his glass in time to the music. Patrick suspected he was pissed before he'd even arrived at the pub and wondered how he was going to pilot his boat home in the dark. At least it was a calm night.

The band reached the finale of the song. Patrick gave it all he had.

'*They'll feed you with strong drink, me lads, 'Til you are unable to stand, And the very first thing that you'll know is you've landed in Van Diemens Land …*'

The chorus raised the rafters and the band stopped with a flourish. The room erupted with applause and whistles. Plonking glasses on the bar, Maisie joined Patrick. 'Better call last orders,' she said. 'We've pushed it enough and, to be honest, I'm dying to get you to myself.'

'Me too,' said Patrick. 'You have no idea how much.'

Twenty minutes later, Maisie rang the bell. Otherwise the party would have gone all night and she wanted to be with Patrick. 'Time, gentlemen, ladies and pets, please. Finish your drinks. I'm sorry but the party's over …'

'Spoilsport!'

Groans from the bar, but there were also a few bleary-eyed resigned nods. People got to their feet while a few ignored Maisie's pleas.

'Come on, people,' said Patrick. 'It's been a great night but some of us want to get to bed.'

'Whose? Yours or Maisie's?' a bloke piped up.

Patrick shot him a friendly glare. 'Yours if you don't behave.'

Patrick saw Hugo put down his pint on the table. Basil had hidden under the table during the singing but stirred. Hugo stood up.

'I have an announcement to make. Or should I say,' he said,

328

stepping into the space that had now cleared in the middle of the bar. 'Patrick has an announcement to make.'

Patrick's hackles rose. What the hell was this? It couldn't be about him and Maisie getting together, could it? Was the guy that crass? Shit, it *had* to be, well no matter. They knew they'd have to put up with a bit of banter.

Hoping to stall Hugo, Patrick laughed. 'What's this now, Hugo?'

Maisie frowned and glanced at Patrick. She shrugged, smiling, but he felt her underlying anxiety. No matter how many folk knew about them, Hugo was seriously out of order.

'What announcement's this, then, Patrick?' Will piped up. He might be a friend but for once, Patrick wished he'd stay quiet.

'I've no idea. Hugo's winding us up,' Patrick said.

'Winding you up?' He laughed in a nasty way that made Patrick's skin crawl.

Maisie approached Hugo's table. 'I think you've had enough, Hugo.'

Hugo stopped her with a sneer. 'I haven't had anything. Patrick's had plenty though, judging from the way you two were down each other's throats during the fireworks.'

A ripple of disapproval went through the drinkers.

Hot anger flared in Patrick. 'Right. That's it. You've crossed the line. You're leaving, mate.' He made a grab for Hugo's arm but Hugo backed away into the corner, rocking the table. Beer sloshed onto the tiles.

With a whimper, Basil darted from under the table. Archie grabbed his collar and patted him. 'It's all right, boy. Just a bit of argy bargy.'

'Calm down, boys,' Hazel called but Patrick's touch paper had been lit and his anger blazed.

Maisie stepped between them like a referee. 'I'll deal with this,' she said. 'Hugo, I don't like seeing you in this state and you'll regret it in the morning. Would you please let someone take you home?'

Hugo glared at her but didn't move. Patrick braced himself, ready to haul the bastard off her if he made the slightest attempt to touch her. 'I will go home but I won't be the one regretting tonight. And seeing as my cousin is clearly too shy to make his important announcement himself, I'll tell you.'

'*Cousin?*'

Patrick wasn't sure who repeated the word amid the cat-calls and snorts of disbelief. 'What the hell are you on about, Scorrier?' Will asked.

'You've had too much of the Rat and Ferret, Hugo. Go home.'

'What did he say?' Fen demanded in a loud voice.

Hugo steadied himself on the table. 'Well, Cousin Patrick?'

Patrick darted a look at Maisie. She was staring, open-mouthed, not at Hugo, but at *him*. His stomach turned over and over.

'Hugo ...' he began.

'Hadn't he mentioned it? No, I didn't think so,' said Hugo, swaying slightly.

Maisie turned back to Hugo. 'You're tired and emotional, Hugo,' she said. 'I'll get someone to take you home.'

Panic, sheer molten panic flowed through Patrick's veins.

'Don't you want to hear the full story?' Hugo asked.

He lurched towards Maisie.

Maisie reached for Hugo's arm to steady him but Hugo flung her arm off him. She flinched and made to grab him before he fell over. Jess gasped and stared at Hugo in horror. She seemed about to jump into the fray herself but Patrick thrust himself between them.

'You're out of order, mate,' he said.

'I'll take the silly bugger home,' said one of the boatmen from Petroc.

'No. No one will take me anywhere until I've said what I have to say.'

Hugo's voice rose as he backed into the corner, his eyes darting about as if the people in the bar were a pack of hounds waiting to pounce on him.

'Or should you tell them, Patrick? Should I call you by your real name – Henry Patrick Aldous Scorrier McKinnon, my cousin, the heir to Petroc Island and the real owner of Scorrier Holdings.'

Chapter 35

Maisie could hear the old clock ticking in the few seconds following Hugo's announcement.

Then uproar. Chaos. The thumping of her own heart. The cries of derision. The howls of laughter.

But Maisie had eyes only for Patrick. Only for his ashen face and his hands hanging loosely by his sides.

'Is it true? Do you own Petroc?' she asked.

Patrick's words, loaded with quiet misery, cut through the mayhem. 'Yes, I do.'

She held on to the table for support. Murmurs started around her. Jess's hand was over her mouth. Her father was breathing heavily and her mother let out a gasp.

'I'm sorry,' Patrick said, looking at her.

Hugo sneered. 'Oh dear.'

'Get out,' said Maisie quietly, standing between them.

Patrick rounded on him. 'You heard,' he said.

Maisie turned to him. 'Not him. You.'

Patrick's face. She'd never forget it. The colour drained from it within seconds. Then, without a word, he nodded, turned away and walked through the open-mouthed throng of revellers, past her parents and through the back door.

'What a shame. I was looking forward to an emotional family reunion,' said Hugo as the door closed with a clink.

Maisie stared at him in disbelief. She felt light-headed. 'And you can fuck off too.'

'Now come on, I'm not the one at fault here. I haven't lied to you.'

'Get out,' Maisie shouted, not caring who heard her or if she caused a scene.

'Come on, love.' Amid the chorus of mutters and hubbub, an arm snaked around Maisie's back. It was her father's.

'I knew this would happen. I knew he was trouble,' Hazel said softly.

Maisie was in no state to argue. She felt physically sick.

Patrick owned Petroc. Patrick was part of Scorrier Holdings ... all this time, he'd been deceiving her and lying to her? But it didn't make sense. Why had Patrick been so shocked and angry with Hugo if he was working for him? Patrick looked like he'd seen a ghost when Hugo outed him. And Hugo had said Patrick was his *cousin*? How could that be? And why had he lied to her and come all this way to Gull and taken the job and slept with her and made her believe he cared about her?

'We'll sort this out, hun,' said Jess, touching Maisie's other arm. Something warm and wet rasped against her fingers. She glanced down. Basil gazed up at her out of his big brown eyes.

Will took Hugo's elbow. 'You'd better come with me, pal, you've caused enough damage for one night.'

Maisie forced herself to snap out of her catatonic state and flash a weary smile at her customers.

'OK, folks. The show's over and so is the party. I think we

can agree we've had enough entertainment for one night so I'd be grateful if you'd go back to your beds now.'

'You'll thank me for this in the morning, Maisie!' Hugo shouted while Will pulled his arm. Basil lingered next to him in the doorway and lifted up one paw and let out a whimper.

'Oh, go and boil yer 'ead, Hugo,' Archie shouted.

'The truth hurts!' Hugo shrieked as Will tried to bundle him out of the door.

Doesn't it just, thought Maisie as Hugo scuffled with Will and Javid. It cut you to the bone and brought your whole life tumbling down around your ears. And even worse, she didn't even know what the truth was any more.

Basil's barks filled the room and there was a crash of breaking glass as Hugo flailed around. He swung a punch at Will who ducked just in time. Expletives filled the air and people pressed against the walls while Hugo ranted about 'all he'd done for this effing community' and 'how beeping stupid they all were' and that they 'ought to be thankful to him and Graydon' and that Patrick was out 'to ruin them all'.

To Maisie's horror, Ray Samson joined the group trying to remove Hugo but he clung on to the doorframe for grim death. Any moment now Hugo was going to be dragged out by the hair and what if her dad had a heart attack? Maisie realised she was actually shaking. Hazel's arm snaked around Maisie's back. 'Come on, love. Let's get you out of here.'

'Wait!' Hugo screamed as a terrified Basil filled the bar with deafening barks. 'It's not just that bastard Patrick who's lied to you. Your parents have agreed to sell the Driftwood to me. I bet you didn't know that either!'

334

Chapter 36

In the first light of a gloomy New Year's Day, Maisie stood in the doorway to the bar and saw hell. The place looked like a drunken hurricane had blown through it. Streamers hung limply from the ceiling and the floor was littered with party poppers, silly string and bottles. The tables were still covered with dirty glassware and paper plates holding half-eaten sausage rolls and sandwiches. Cards and unopened presents were piled on a table in the corner. A balloon with 'Fabulous at 40' on it bobbed up and down in the draught from the front door.

And the place reeked. Of booze, sweat, stale food and sheer overwhelming misery.

Fighting back tears, Maisie picked her way over the sticky floorboards, stopping to gather up the pieces of a broken bottle. She carried it gingerly to the bin behind the bar and dropped it inside. The drip mats were soaked and the bar was coated in a residue of sticky alcohol. The whole place was a health and fire hazard and she had never hated anywhere more in her entire life.

Pushing half-empty glasses aside, Maisie put the black

coffee she'd just made on a table opposite the window and sank down onto one of the cleaner chairs. She felt like an empty shell on the beach: a nothing, tossed about at the mercy of the sea. She had no idea if Patrick had gone back to the Piggery. Her main focus had shifted yet again: to the news that her parents were planning to sell the pub.

They were still upstairs in bed, and probably too ashamed and upset to come down yet, after the mother of all rows that had taken place last night. Maisie had asked Jess to leave so she wouldn't have to witness it.

'Why?' she'd asked them. 'Why have you done this?'

'We only decided a few days ago. We were going to tell you after your party but we didn't want to spoil it,' her mother had said.

Her dad had wrung his hands in guilt. 'We knew you'd be upset, love, but we're too old for this. Hugo offered us a great price, more than we could hope for, and everyone else is selling up.'

'They're not. Not everyone, Una and Phyllis have changed their minds.'

'Have they? For how long? You're flogging a dead horse.'

'We're profitable. I can make the pub profitable.'

'Maybe, but it's such hard work. We're worn out with it. We want to move to the mainland. We've seen a nice bungalow in St Just. You can almost see Scilly ...' her dad said. 'You own a third of the Driftwood. You could buy us out if you really want to with the money from your flat in St Austell. It would go some of the way at least.' Ray Samson had tears in his eyes. 'Look, love, if selling upsets you this much, we'll stay.'

Hazel stayed tight-lipped.

'You have to do what you think is best,' Maisie had said finally, and left them to go to her room to sob her heart out.

Now she heard signs of life from the flat but she couldn't face them yet, and the fallout from the other bombshell of the night was beginning to hit her afresh. Abandoning the coffee, she hurried into the kitchen and grabbed an old coat from by the back door. She needed time and space to think of what to do next, though God knew what that would be.

Her phone beeped in her pocket.

Hun, r u OK? Stupid question. Phone me.

Jess's text was very early. She and Will wouldn't have got back to St Saviour's until well after two. Maisie ignored it: she didn't know how she'd hold it together if she did speak to Jess, or anyone who'd seen and heard what happened last night. She'd thought the Driftwood was the centre of the community and it was the centre of her world, yet it had crumbled.

Maisie sneaked around the side of the house. She couldn't resist a quick glance at the Piggery. The curtains were open but that didn't tell her whether Patrick was in there or not. She definitely didn't want to see him or anyone yet so she headed straight for the beach. It was a grey morning, with thick skies and no sign or sound of a human. The tide was out about as far as it ever could go and an oystercatcher pecked the shoreline with its long orange bill. A mottled grey seal bobbed up and down in the channel, watching her. Gulls wheeled around in the sky, crying. She zipped up her jacket and walked towards 'her' rock.

She'd gone over Hugo's revelation and Patrick's response time after time. She half wished she hadn't chucked Patrick out, although she'd been so shocked last night, throwing him out had probably been self-protection.

Now she wanted to know everything. No matter how angry she was with Patrick, she had to see him, if he was even still on the island. The future of the Driftwood and Gull was at stake, and that was bigger than her own shattered ego and heart.

Maisie began walking around the headland in the direction of Hell Cove, trying to clear her mind. The spring tide had uncovered expanses of sand and rocks that rarely saw daylight, which meant she could walk all the way to the cove on the beach. Head down against the wind, she shoved her hands in her pockets and forced herself to put one foot in front of the other.

She'd almost reached Hell Cove House when she saw Patrick on the beach in front of it, throwing a stick for a small dog she didn't recognise. He was wearing the same clothes as when she chucked him out of the pub the previous evening. So he hadn't slept in the Piggery then? He'd taken her order to get out of the pub as an order to leave the premises full stop. She felt a momentary pang of guilt. Had he been wandering the island all night?

Then she reminded herself that the little dog wasn't the only creature she didn't recognise. Patrick wasn't even Patrick any more. He was Henry Scorrier, and far more importantly, he was a serial liar.

He spotted her and stopped walking. The dog raced around

him, a young Jack Russell. Maisie quickened her step, her heart in her mouth. She wanted to run to him, hold him and kiss him as she would have before but knew she never could or would again.

He stuck his hands in his pockets and waited for her.

'Where have you been?' she asked, almost before he was within earshot.

'Staying at Hell Cove House. The Bartons spotted me outside the community hall when they walked home last night. They let me sleep in one of the cottages. Not in the main house, they have a friend from St Mary's staying. That's her dog.' The Jack Russell dropped a stick at Patrick's feet and he flung it towards the sea. The dog skittered over the sand in pursuit of it.

'So they know the whole story?'

'They know nothing more than they saw in the pub. They didn't ask and I certainly wasn't going to tell them.'

'Tell them what exactly?' Maisie's voice rose. She'd meant to be calm and cold when she finally confronted him but it was impossible.

'I owe you an explanation.'

'We owe each other nothing,' she said quietly. 'I've been a fool.'

'No. I'm the fool. I'm sorry. So sorry that this got so out of hand.'

'Who are you, Patrick? Who are you really?'

'Hugo's right. I am his cousin. His father and mine were brothers, though they never really got on. When my grandfather, Julian, died, he left Petroc to my dad, Hector, but Dad was only twenty-two and he'd just met my mum, Chloe.'

'I knew your parents' names,' Maisie said when she realised she'd heard her parents talk about them, 'and that they'd died in an accident in Australia. A car accident near Sydney, not a plane crash in the Outback as you claimed.'

'I tried to stick close to the truth. Not in the details, because that would have given the game away ...'

'The *game*?' Maisie could barely get the word out. 'Did Hugo recognise you?' she said, almost choking on the words.

'I doubt it as he's only ever seen photos of me as a baby. Maybe he had a private detective checking me out or he just put two and two together. It was only a matter of time and he told me himself he thought I was hiding something, but I swear, Maisie, I was going to come clean with you and everyone.'

'When?'

'After your party. When we were alone together. On my life, Maisie, you *must* believe me.'

'I don't have to believe another word you say, *Henry*.'

Patrick covered his face with his hands and let out a cry of agony. 'Don't call me that.'

Maisie didn't feel a shred of sympathy for him. 'All you had to do was tell me the first time we met. It's that simple.'

'No. It wasn't. It wasn't that simple for me. You don't understand.'

'Then try and help me understand. Help me understand why you would do this to me – to us all.'

340

A woman appeared at the gate to Hell Cove House and whistled to the dog, which ran back to her.

'Walk with me?' Patrick asked.

Maisie nodded.

'It's your ancestors who are from Scilly, isn't it? Not Greg's? I knew you were hiding something, I felt it, but I was too bloody infatuated to follow my instincts. Jesus, you must think I am such a fool.'

'No. I don't. I'm the bloody fool. I love you, Maisie.'

Maisie felt as if he'd dealt her another blow. They were empty words coming from a serial liar.

'Mum and Dad never wanted Petroc. They were young and bohemian – hippies – and they took off and instantly fell in love with Australia where no one gave a toss about their background. We were happy, we would have been ... if they hadn't been killed.'

'And I'm very sorry for that, Patrick. Truly I am, and I can understand that it was a horrific shock to you, but the fact is that you do own Petroc and the fortune that goes with it.'

'Yes, but Mum and Dad never drew on any of it and the fund built up. They left Graydon in charge and when Hugo grew up, he started to run the business. He knew I existed somewhere but I never had any direct contact with him. I changed my name to Patrick McKinnon when I was eighteen. The trust fund is still in the Scorrier name and administered by my team of lawyers and accountants and all the decisions and paperwork were signed off by them. But when Hugo made an offer to buy me out they had to contact me directly. Greg had been diagnosed by then and he said I should come here and see the place for myself before I made a decision I might regret forever.'

'I'm deeply sorry about Greg, but pretending you're some kind of impoverished barman when you have so much power over us was cruel.'

'I'm sorry. I never meant it to be. The only time I've ever touched the money was to arrange for some treatment for Greg ... and help the islanders here. Hugo has offered me a very generous settlement. I could rattle around the Fingle, never having to worry about money and being a barman as a hobby, but I don't want the money. Never did and never will.'

Maisie gasped. 'You wouldn't say that if you were in financial trouble or lived hand to mouth. We don't at the Driftwood, but some people here do.'

'That was tactless. I'm sorry, but like I said before: people treat you differently when you have money. There's no peace with it.'

'And even less without it,' said Maisie tartly. 'Why didn't your dad turn Petroc over to Hugo and take the money if he wanted it so much? Why haven't you?'

'I don't know. Maybe for the same reason you don't like Hugo. Maybe Dad didn't trust Graydon to own it completely, only to run it. Maybe he wanted to leave the door open for me to take it over one day, though he never said so. I was only thirteen when they died and I never thought about the place, I was too busy being a teenager, getting into trouble and playing Aussie Rules. It was only when they said it was mine but it was in trust that I realised it was going to be my responsibility.

'Since then, through my lawyers and trustees, Hugo and Graydon have been given carte blanche to run Petroc, and reap all the profits. They've spent years building up the business and, as you know, Hugo's now hell bent on getting Petroc transferred to him once and for all. I didn't know his plans for Gull and the Driftwood until I'd been here a while. I swear and I don't agree with them pressurising people like the Bartons and your parents.'

'What Mum and Dad do is their own decision. But why should you care? You've said yourself that you only wanted to take Hugo's offer and wash your hands of us all.'

'That was before I came here. Before Greg made me come.'

'Why did you stay on and ask for the job?'

'I wanted to see for myself what was really going on before I signed over my power to stop it. And I wanted to be close to you ... believe me.'

Maisie tried not to burst into tears at his admission. She *did* believe him but it was too little truth too late for her to take him back into her life.

'Why did you buy those supplies and encourage us all to fight Hugo?' she asked.

'Because I didn't want Hugo to buy Gull. I wanted you all to succeed on your own terms.'

'You mean you wanted to have your cake and eat it.'

'Yes. Yes, I did.'

'In fact, you wanted to get out of this mess without having to help us out of it.'

They'd stopped on a stretch of shingle, halfway back to the Driftwood. 'Wouldn't that have been the best solution?' Patrick said. 'I did want that until I decided to stay. I was about to come clean, Maisie, you have to believe me.'

She couldn't speak any more.

'But you never will, now, will you?'

'I can still stop Hugo,' he said. 'I *won't sell* and I'll stay and sort it out for as long as you want me to. I've nothing to lose now.'

Maisie bit back her frustration. Within a moment, she'd heard the Driftwood was safe and that Patrick would stay. She had everything she wanted, so why did she feel as if she'd lost everything?

'I genuinely don't mind you being wealthy. I'm not one of these people who think everyone with money is a bastard. I'm not envious – I don't care – but the important thing is, Patrick ...' She said his name as if it burned her mouth. 'Is that you *do* own the place, and more hurtfully, that you chose to lie about that.'

'I can't undo that. I wish I could but I can stop Hugo from buying anything on Gull. Save the Driftwood. Your parents don't have to sell.'

'They *want* to sell, Patrick. That's the point. They've given up on the pub and they own most of it so why would I stop them? I don't want you saving me or the Driftwood. I want you to get out of my home and out of my life. If that means I lose everything in the end, I don't care. I won't put my future

344

in the hands of someone I can't rely on to be honest with me, ever again.'

'Maisie, wait!'

She stumbled off over the loose shingle. 'Go home, Patrick, to your real home, and do what you want with your money. We don't need you.'

Chapter 37

Ray and Hazel were waiting on the terrace when Maisie arrived home.

Her mum ran forward to meet her and hugged her. Maisie patted her back briefly and then pulled away. 'Thank God. We were worried you might have ...'

'Done something stupid? I have. Trusted Patrick Scorrier.'

'I'm sorry about the way you found out. Hugo's a bastard – Patrick too. We had no idea,' said Ray. His face was grey with fatigue and Maisie felt terrible. They probably hadn't slept a wink either and her father didn't need extra stress.

'Why would you?' Maisie asked, patting her dad on the arm.

'Patrick's the one at fault. He stitched us up,' said Hazel sharply. 'He was probably only working here to size up this place's prospects for Hugo.'

'No. No, he wouldn't do that,' Maisie cried.

Her mother frowned. 'How do you know what he'd do?'

'I just do. I've seen him this morning and stitching us up wasn't why he took the job.'

Ray and Hazel exchanged glances. 'We've been talking. Now

we know what the Scorriers were really up to, we don't want to sell. Not after this, love. We can carry on for a good while yet. Hugo's offer was – is – so tempting but we won't take it now.'

Maisie felt tears coming. 'I don't mind,' she said. 'You have to do what's right for you and anyway, some battles aren't worth fighting.'

It took the Samsons most of the day to clear the Driftwood up. Maisie spoke to Jess on the phone for over an hour, telling her about Patrick – the parts she could bear to share, anyway. Later in the afternoon, Ray and Hazel went to see Javid and thank him for his help with Hugo but in reality Maisie guessed that they all wanted some space and time alone.

She was pottering around, tidying up the last of the mess because she couldn't face her room, when Patrick knocked at the back door.

'I've come to collect my stuff,' he said.

'It can wait. There are no flights out of here until tomorrow.'

'I want to be out of your hair. I can stay at Hell Cove overnight.'

'That place isn't finished,' she said.

'No. But it will be. I'll make sure of that ... Maisie, I can understand why you're angry.'

The hurt bubbled over again. 'No. No, you can't. You can't possibly understand how I feel. Please collect your stuff and leave.'

His face was agonised and she thought he was going to plead with her. If he had he would have destroyed the tiny fragment of feeling she had left for him. The respect had already vanished, she didn't even like him any more but she did, despite all the anger and disappointment boiling within her, still love him.

There was nothing she could do to remove that pain but she could remove the source of it.

Patrick nodded, turned away and quietly closed the door behind him.

Maisie watched him enter the Piggery and leave a short time later with a bag of stuff. He glanced at her and nodded but she turned away.

When she looked up again, he was gone. She ran into the bar to see if she could catch sight of him through the front window but it was too late. In the gathering dusk, she stood, her arms clasped around herself so tightly she was almost hurting herself. She was afraid that if she let herself go, she might quite literally fall apart. She stood in the same place until darkness fell. Finally, she lowered her aching arms, surprised to find that she was no longer crying. She switched on a lamp because a gentle light was all she could bear to shine upon her misery. She felt angry with herself for letting another man make her feel less than the strong woman she was.

She stooped to pick up a glass that had rolled behind a chair and threw out a hand to steady herself on the table top. An overwhelming feeling of exhaustion overcame her, rapidly followed by light-headedness. There was a strange metallic taste in her mouth, and a few seconds after that, her stomach turned over. She staggered across the hall to the bathroom

348

and flipped the loo seat up just in time. Even while she was throwing up, she knew exactly what was wrong with her because she'd had the exact same light-headedness and strange taste once in her life before.

Of course the nausea, faintness and exhaustion could be down to a hangover, lack of sleep or the shock, but Maisie knew it wasn't. She sat on the floor, leaning against the bath panel, trying to regain her breath after being sick. There was no doubt in her mind: she was pregnant with Patrick's child.

Chapter 38

Two weeks later
The Fingle Bar, Melbourne

'Patrick? Patrick McKinnon? What the bloody hell do you think you're doing? Are you determined to destroy yourself again?'

Patrick tried to open his eyes and failed. Evil elves had crept up on him in the night and superglued the lids together.

'Come on. Get out. Jesus. This place stinks like a turps factory. It's past noon and it's a lovely day. Look.'

Patrick prised his eyelids apart. The rattle of the blinds opening was like a load of barrels thundering past his head and the light blinded him like a nuclear flash.

'Jesus, Judy. Leave me alone.'

'No, I won't. You bloody idiot. I've put up with you hanging around the place making everyone miserable and carrying your own personal storm cloud with you. I've heard you whingeing about how sorry you are, and how bloody guilty, and I've held my tongue but I won't have you killing yourself.'

A red face framed with a shock of platinum blonde curls loomed inches from Patrick's.

'Get up!' she shouted, making Patrick's ear drums throb and his head pulse like his own personal metal band had set up inside his skull.

'What's the point?' he muttered, then immediately regretted it.

The sheet was whipped from his body and he looked down in horror.

'Fucking hell. I've no clothes on, Judy!'

'No. Because you stank and me and some of the bar team stripped you last night before we threw you on the bed. You were making a nuisance of yourself in every bar in the city. It's a wonder the coppers didn't throw you in the cells. Now, I've got a pot of black coffee on and there's plenty of hot water. Get yourself into that shower, Mr High and Mighty.'

Judy threw the sheet back on him, covering his dignity.

Patrick pushed himself up on his elbows while his stomach did a triple Salchow. His head felt like it had been used for kicking practice by the Wallabies.

'I'm not back in prison, you know!' he called as Judy bustled out of the door.

'No. This is worse. I'm your boss so present yourself in that bloody bar within twenty minutes or you're out on your arse, mate.'

Under the steam of the shower, with a couple of paracetamol swishing round his stomach, Patrick gradually came to something like life. The bender had obliterated his pain for a while but it came back to him now in all its horrible glory. He was lost. He'd been lost and alone before. After his parents died, at school, in prison, and again after Greg had gone. No one had died this time but this loneliness was worse.

Since he'd left Maisie, and all the way home on the plane, he'd asked himself the same questions time and again. What if he'd marched into the Driftwood and the moment he'd spotted Maisie, said: 'I'm your Prince Charming and can solve all your problems. Jump on my white horse and we'll live happily ever after.'

He could have done that, but he'd walked onto Gull swearing on his life that he didn't want the place, not a stone or grain of it and definitely not one of its residents.

Once he'd started lying – or rather, not telling the truth – it had become harder to unpick the web he'd woven and he was enjoying being Patrick McKinnon. For God's sake he *was* Patrick McKinnon. He'd never been Henry Scorrier. Just like his dad and mum had never truly been Scorriers. They'd wanted to escape the life set out for them and so had he, but they wouldn't have wanted him to do what he'd done to Maisie.

Judy was sitting under an umbrella on the terrace when he finally made it down. She was leafing through a newspaper but glanced up when she spotted him.

'You're two minutes late but I'll let it pass this time. Your coffee's here.'

He walked gingerly to the table, wincing at the bright sunlight bouncing off the Yarra despite his dark glasses and the heat pounding down, searing his skin.

'I'm sorry,' he began.

Judy shoved a mug at him. 'For the love of God, will you

stop saying that and do something to put things right with this woman?'

'I've tried. I've tried calling her, emailing her and she doesn't want to know.'

'And are you selling the bloody island?'

'I don't know. After I've sorted a few things, probably. How can I go back after what I've done?'

Patrick took a slurp of his coffee and almost gagged but Judy was as sympathetic as a croc about to swallow a fluffy duck.

'*Probably?* That's pathetic and, more importantly, it's not the Patrick I know.'

'Which one is that?'

'The one who lost his parents and turned his life around. Who stopped drinking and destroying himself. Who came here and made himself one of the family. Who loved Greg and me and supported us through the darkest, shittiest times of our lives. Who loves this Maisie and wants her more than I've ever seen him want anything. The poor little rich boy who knows it's time to grow a pair and do what's right, even if it means I lose him to some strange bunch of Poms on the other side of the world.'

Patrick couldn't speak or drink or move. There were tears in his eyes and he couldn't see the river any more. Judy patted his arm and spoke to him gently.

'What I want to know is – and what my Greg would want to know, Paddy boy, is – are you really going to give up that easily or are you going to fight?'

353

Chapter 39

'Good afternoon and thanks for coming out on this glorious sunny day. The Samsons have kindly passed on all the details of my proposal, which I hope you've all had the chance to read by now. Don't worry, I'm not about to play lord of the manor. I'll leave that to Hugo.'

No one in the Gull Island Community Hall laughed at Patrick. Maisie cringed. She'd only heard about Patrick's return a few days earlier, after she'd received a call from Judy Warner. She'd avoided taking any of Patrick's calls or emails but her mother had answered the house phone to Judy and Maisie didn't want to insult Judy by refusing to speak to her, even if she was trying to plead Patrick's case.

In the end, Judy didn't make any excuses for him at all. She had only phoned to make sure that Maisie was the first to know that Patrick would be back and wanted a meeting of all the Gull islanders affected by Hugo's proposals. Maisie had agreed to pass on the message and so here they were, assembled in the room on a dull January Sunday afternoon. She hadn't even seen Patrick before she'd entered the meeting room but she'd heard on the grapevine that he'd chartered a fast boat to bring him from St Mary's where he'd been staying in a rented cottage since arriving by plane the day before.

After his joke had fallen flat, he shuffled papers nervously, and Maisie felt a glimmer of sympathy for him. His idea had potential, in fact it was a good one, but whether people would trust him enough to go for it was another thing altogether.

Why did he have to look so amazing? He was very tired but also freshly gilded by the Australian sun. In comparison, Maisie was shattered and desperately trying to hide the fact she was throwing up every morning and feeling sick at the sight and smell of every pint.

Patrick cleared his throat again.

'As you'll have read, I'm proposing a compromise: a trust in which I have no say and which is run by a committee of islanders and an independent representative. I'll put in the initial investment required to bring the properties involved up to standard and it will run as a co-operative, with everyone sharing in the profits. I won't be breathing down your necks – in fact I'm going back to Melbourne – but I will take more responsibility for matters in the future.'

'What about Petroc? Will you sell it to Hugo?' someone demanded.

'Hugo will still be in charge of Petroc. He's made a success of it and I've no wish to interfere,' said Patrick. 'It's in all our interests that Petroc remains successful to help fund Gull, but

I'm still the owner. Hugo will have to consult me in any major matters and he'll have nothing to do with Gull at all.'

There were hmms and huffs, which Maisie took to be approval. She felt sorry for Hugo in one way, having made Petroc the success it was while never actually being its legal owner. Patrick was speaking again. 'I know you'll want to discuss this among yourselves so I'm going to answer any more questions you may have and then leave you to vote on it. If you agree, I'll get my lawyers to draw up detailed contracts and we'll set the plans in place.'

Patrick stayed an hour or so more to explain how the Gull Island Trust would work and answer more questions, then he left. Maisie and he hadn't exchanged a direct word although he'd looked at her with longing and pain. She'd looked at him with guilt; he had to be told about the baby while he was here but she was worried about his reaction. Would he be horrified and hot foot it out of Scilly, or would he feel it was his 'duty' to stay and help her? God knows it was his child and she could use the financial help, but did she want to be beholden to him in that way?

The atmosphere warmed once he'd put his offer on the table. Maisie and the other residents stayed for another hour to discuss it. They were getting the best of both worlds. Security and freedom. Only Maisie was the one who felt she was getting neither. She hated being forced to be grateful to Patrick. And yet what he said made sense and she gave him credit him for facing up to his responsibilities and putting things right.

But saying she agreed to being part of the scheme had hurt.

She went home after the meeting but there was no sign of Patrick. According to Javid, he'd been taken back to St Mary's and then to London to meet the UK branch of his lawyers and to give people time to consider the offer, but he was coming back to Gull again a few days later.

For the next two days, Maisie was at a loss. Then the day came when Patrick was due to return for the meeting: the final time he would ever set foot on the island and probably the last time she would ever see him. Gull seemed a strange land as she walked up the hill to the community hall on Wednesday afternoon. Towering dark clouds gathered to the far west as another storm marshalled its forces, ready to unleash rain and hail and gales on Scilly. Patrick was flying from London to Newquay according to Javid and then on to Scilly, all being well.

Maisie stared at the weather front. She hoped he made it or it could be another couple of days. She couldn't wait any longer to put an end to this. Everyone had agreed to meet with Patrick at the community hall and give their verdict.

Fifteen minutes after the start time, the door opened and Patrick strode in. His hair was wet and he was breathing heavily. 'Sorry I'm late. I almost didn't make it.'

'Lucky you did. We were going home,' said Una.

He nodded at Maisie. This was agony. She had to speak to him today.

The meeting started and the islanders delivered their verdicts. It was a 'yes' from the Fudge Pantry, the Hell Cove Cottages, from Javid and all the others. That left the Samsons and the Driftwood.

'Maisie? Hazel? Ray?' Patrick asked.

Ray stood up. 'Yes. We agree.'

Patrick's shoulders slumped visibly in relief. 'Thank you. I hope this will be the start of a long and happy relationship.'

'It had better be,' said Hazel.

Maisie winced. 'Mum ...' she murmured.

'How do we know we can trust you?' said Hazel.

'It's in writing. I can't back out,' he said. 'I swear I won't.'

Patrick continued to be interrogated by a group of islanders but the atmosphere had lifted, and there were smiles and excited chatter over the buffet lunch after the contracts were signed. Maisie was almost faint with the tension of wanting to speak to Patrick, but he was pinned down by locals and she realised she'd have to wait until everyone else had left to get him on his own. The room was stuffy as the heaters belted out warmth and she felt overwhelmed.

'I'm going for a breath of fresh air,' she told her father.

'Fresh air? You'll be blown away, love, and it's raining out there.' Her father put his arm around her. 'Are you OK?'

'Yes. I just need a few minutes on my own.'

'You'll come back in?'

'Yes. I need a word with Patrick. Don't let him go without seeing me, will you, but I'll only be ten minutes anyway.'

She escaped through the front door with a longing glance at Patrick and wrapped her scarf around her neck. The wind buffeted her and the cold rain was like needles against her face. That was it. Signed, sealed and delivered. When she'd enlightened Patrick and she'd heard what he wanted to do, she would tell her parents they were going to be grandparents.

She had enough light to see by for a little while yet so climbed onto the hillock behind the community hall. Streetlights twinkled on St Mary's behind her, and across the channel on Petroc, the windows of the tavern, hotel and even a few of the holiday cottages glowed. The Driftwood was in darkness, but its pale walls were just visible on the shoreline above the grey beach.

Maisie lowered her head and walked higher. She'd been feeling a little less fragile over the past few days. She was now around eleven weeks on, according to her GP. She knew exactly when she'd fallen pregnant. A condom had failed during one of their evenings at the Flower Farm but Maisie had told Patrick not to worry because she had virtually no chance of ever getting pregnant again. Her periods had always been all over the shop so she hadn't thought anything when she skipped one before Christmas.

A gust almost knocked her off her feet and the rain turned to sleet, soaking her woollen mittens. She had to go back inside the hall to see Patrick and seek some shelter. It dawned on her that she could no longer do what she wanted: there was her baby to consider now. Her precious baby. Instinctively she clutched at her stomach and smiled for the first time in days. What would Patrick think?

Should she tell him at all?

She turned to walk down the hill, pulling her hood together against the driving sleet. People were walking out of the community hall, hurrying back on foot to their homes. A powerful gust hit her, funnelled by the hillock and the hall. Maisie lost her footing and fell with an 'oof' onto the wet grass at the side of the path. She was winded but not hurt because the rough tussocky grass had broken her fall.

'Maisie. Are you all right? Let me help you.' A hand grabbed hers.

'Hugo!'

He pulled her to her feet, holding her arm.

'What are you doing here?' she asked.

He finally let go of her hand.

'What do you think? I'm not going to take this lying down, you know, no matter what bloody Patrick says. I've run Petroc on my own since Dad became ill. I've made a big success of it and he just turns up now and takes over.'

'He's not taking over Petroc. You have sole charge of it. He owns it, Hugo, whether you like it or not! And I thought he'd already spoken to you about his plans.'

'He has but I'm not giving in. You think the sun shines out of his arse, don't you? If you hadn't been so bloody-minded, I could have offered you a way to keep the Driftwood in your name with an injection of cash to bring it up to the standards of the Rose and Crab.'

'What do you mean?'

His voice softened from the bitter tone he'd adopted. 'Like I said I genuinely care about you ... I always have,' he said.

'You're offering us a loan?'

'An investment. You wouldn't have to worry too much about repaying it ... the terms would be very favourable and you and your parents would stay as owners.'

He cut a pathetic figure, Maisie thought, but was too angry to feel any sympathy with him. 'But what would be in it for you, Hugo?'

'We could come to an arrangement.'

'What kind of arrangement?'

'Now your eyes have been opened to the kind of man Patrick really is, perhaps – in time – we could get to know each other better. I'd like us to be a lot more than friends and business partners. I always have done.'

Maisie groaned inwardly. Was Hugo trying to say he was in love with her? That was a complication she couldn't handle. The wind howled and she shivered. She longed to be back in the warmth of the hall. 'I'm sorry. I want us to be friends too and for you to understand that I want the Driftwood to be independent. I can't forget you tried to persuade my parents to sell the pub.'

'I admit that was probably a misjudgement, but I was trying to do the right thing for you, too. I always have been.'

She sighed. 'Then you've gone about it in exactly the wrong way.'

'Is there a right way?'

'No. I'm not ready to talk to you about this now. It'll take time for me to get over it and I need to get back into the hall. Mum and Dad are waiting for me.'

'And Patrick?' Hugo added bitterly. 'Are you going to forgive him after all the lies he's told you? If you are, you really must be blinded by love for him ...'

Maisie didn't know how to reply. Although she was angry at Hugo's comments, she'd also been asking herself the same questions. Could she forgive Patrick? There was no easy answer.

'I'm leaving. You should too.' She hurried off, but Hugo caught her up and laid his hand on her arm.

His tone was almost pleading. 'Don't be fooled by him again!'

'I know my own mind. Leave me alone.'

He kept his hand on her arm for a second then let go. 'If that's what you want.'

Maisie escaped before he said anything else. He was a sad figure, infuriating and a bit pathetic at the same time. She didn't want to cause pain to any man, but she absolutely couldn't return Hugo's feelings. The thought of him having been in love with her all this time made her want to run away, even though she felt sorry for him. She rushed down the hill towards the warmth and lights. She thought she heard Hugo shout after her and that he was following her so she quickened her step, almost tripping over the tussocky grass.

'Maisie! Wait!'

Damn Hugo. She'd had enough of being told how she thought and felt. The past few weeks had been a turmoil of emotions, fuelled by her hormones and worries for the future. She stumbled again, threw out her hand to try and stay upright, thought she had ... then heard her own cry as she slipped in the damp grass and rolled down the grassy bank. Seconds passed when she didn't know which was way was up or down or whether she could stop.

There was a roaring in her ears then a jolt.

Finally she was still, with a hard wet surface under her

body. Her leg throbbed. There were lights a few metres ahead and people shouting. She'd ended up on the tarmac car park outside the hall.

She pushed herself up, scrambled to her feet, trying to ignore the sharp pain in her knee. She was out of breath but relieved to be in one piece and away from Hugo. As she limped to the porch of the hall, she looked round for him but he wasn't there.

'Maisie!'

Ray ran over. 'Are you OK, love? We were just going to send a search party for you, This wind has really got up.'

Patrick was behind him.

'I'm fine. Don't make a fuss,' she muttered.

'Maisie? Are you OK?' Patrick was by her side, holding her arm the way Hugo had, his face creased in concern. Maisie wanted to hold on to him and be held by him but things weren't like that any more … would probably never be now the trust was shattered.

'Yes. I just tripped. I'm fine.' But the baby … Panic flooded her veins. She didn't care about herself, but what if the fall had hurt the baby?

Hazel joined them, pointing to her feet. 'You're soaked, love, and what's that on your tights?'

'I fell over in the mud. I'm OK, *really*,' said Maisie, still light-headed with the shock, and desperate to get home and calm down in private.

Patrick cut her off. 'My God. You've cut yourself. Look.'

She stepped under the light of the porch and brushed at her tights. 'It's only mud. Hugo was up on the hill. We had a

363

bit of a chat.' Immediately she regretted mentioning Hugo.

Patrick stared at her, his eyes full of concern. 'Hugo? A "chat"? What's he done to you? Maisie?'

Whatever Maisie was going to reply, she'd probably never know because a crushing pain robbed her of words and breath. She clutched her lower belly and her tights were wet and warm. Feeling woozy, she doubled up and let out a howl.

'My God, what's wrong? She's bleeding,' Patrick said.

Her mum reached for her arm. 'Oh, love. You must have hurt yourself. Was it Hugo?'

Maisie tried to speak but couldn't. A thick veil had been pulled between Maisie and the world and her legs gave way. Patrick was holding her under her back as she crumpled onto the tiles. 'Fetch Javid and call an ambulance. Tell them Maisie's had a fall and she's bleeding,' she heard him saying.

Maisie stared at the floor. 'It's not me, it's not me ...' she mumbled.

'It is, my love. It is. But help's coming,' her mother said.

'I'll knock that bastard to kingdom come,' Ray shouted.

'No ... no ... he hasn't done anything. I fell over ... owwww.' She doubled up in agony.

Patrick was by her side on the floor. He looked like a ghost but so did everyone. 'You'll be all right, Maisie. We'll look after you.'

'But it's not me,' she said with a sob. 'It's not me, it's the baby. Our baby.'

364

Chapter 40

The trip from the community hall to the hospital was the longest of her life. The ambulance station was literally next door and two of the island's first responders were still inside the hall and rushed over, but she still had to wait for them to call the paramedics and then, eventually, load her very carefully into their Land Rover.

'Who's coming with her?' Javid asked.

'I am,' Hazel said.

'Mum ...'

'We're both coming, love.'

'I'll follow.' Patrick reached for her hand.

'Patrick ...' She tried to grasp but his fingers slipped through hers as she was loaded into the Land Rover.

The yellow ambulance boat was already waiting when they reached the quayside. Patrick arrived as the paramedics took charge and were helping her from the Land Rover. It wasn't easy, carrying her from the quayside to the cabin, and Maisie kept begging them to be careful for the baby's sake.

'C-can I c-come?' Patrick shouted as Maisie was settled in a chair on the deck. She could hardly hear him in the wind but she realised he must have run all the way from the hall.

Hazel glanced from Maisie to Patrick.

'We must go,' said the paramedic. 'Get on board if you're coming, mate.'

'Yes. Yes, let him,' Maisie said without thinking.

He climbed on board. 'Are you sure?'

'Yes.'

Ray intervened. 'You just think about yourself and this little one,' he said, squeezing her hand.'

Just the little one. Maisie didn't care about herself ... except the little one did depend on her, she supposed. What if rushing down the hill after her row with Hugo had caused the fall and made her lose the baby?

'Patrick ...' she cried, not knowing if he would hear her above the engine.

'I'm here.' He grasped her hand. With everyone aboard, the engine picked up. Maisie lay back on the stretcher. Patrick had to let her go as the paramedic sat next to her and spoke into to her ear.

'Might be a bit of a bumpy ride but don't you worry. You lie nice and still and let us take care of you.'

Then it was over the sea, the wind howling and the waves buffeting the boat. Hazel soothed her, stroked her hair and said she'd be all right. Patrick kept his eyes on her, dumbstruck. The doctor asked her how far along she was and who her GP was and a host of questions about her previous miscarriage.

An eternity passed before she was across the water on St Mary's, where she was carried off the boat and wheeled up the quay, the paramedic by her side and her mother holding her hand. Another ambulance waited to take her the short drive through the street to the hospital. Chilly air hit her face, then there was a rush of heat and she was blinking in the bright lights of the emergency department.

'You're in the best hands,' her mother whispered.

'Maisie. I'm sorry.' *Was that Patrick?*

In a second, everyone was gone and it was just her being hooked up to machines, tears falling down her cheeks. The consultant obstetrician had examined her as soon as she'd arrived at A&E and said that her cervix was still closed so they were going to scan her to see what was happening.

'Please, please be careful. If there's even a tiny chance you can save it, please help me,' she said as the consultant had taken her history and prepared to examine her.

She'd never been so vulnerable or felt so reliant on other people.

'We will. The bleeding has settled, which is a positive sign, so try not to worry, Miss Samson. I know it's a very anxious time for you but let's do some more tests and we can find out what's going on.'

Not again, she begged silently. Not again. Please not this little scrap too.

Chapter 41

Hazel stood opposite Patrick in the overheated waiting room outside the radiography suite. She'd barely exchanged a word with him since they'd left the community hall. Her focus had all been on Maisie, and Patrick didn't blame her. Now they were alone and all any of them could do was wait. When Ray nipped to the gents, Hazel took her chance.

'I knew you'd break her heart. From the moment you stepped into the pub, I knew. I saw her face. I saw yours. And I knew.'

This isn't helping, Patrick thought, not me, not Maisie, not the baby – Jesus, their baby, *his* child.

'I'm sorry,' he said. What else could he say?

'You should be.'

'I am. Believe me I am.'

Hazel curled her lip. 'Why would I believe you? You've lied so much already. This stress can't have been good for Maisie.'

'And I've tried to put it right. It hasn't been enough. It will never be enough, but I've tried.'

Hazel was out of her mind with worry like him, he told himself. This was her grandchild, her flesh and blood, and

Maisie had waited so long and endured such heartbreak before. What he needed was to be with Maisie, to hold her hand, kiss her lovely face and beg her to forgive him and let him stay but he'd give up all of that and never see her again if only the baby would be OK. He already knew how much the baby would mean to her.

Ray pushed open the door into the waiting room. He looked bloody awful.

'Any news?' he asked Hazel, ignoring Patrick.

'No. They're still doing tests.'

'Poor Maisie. Poor girl.'

Hazel's face crumpled and she let out a sob. Ray pulled her into his arms. 'I know. Try not to worry, she'll be OK. I hope the baby will be too. She's been through so much.'

Patrick closed his eyes as Hazel cried and Ray tried to soothe her. He knew they didn't want him there and yet nothing was going to stop him from being near Maisie. Sweat broke out on his forehead and he felt sick. This was what happened when you let yourself care about other people. When you let someone into your heart, you asked for pain and suffering and fear. It was the fear of caring too much that both protected him and had led him into dark places as he grew up. He'd let that guard down with Judy and Greg, and later with Tania, and taken the consequences.

He didn't think he could stand it again with Maisie, and yet he was – taking the punches again because he had to and he loved her.

Ray shot him a glance of despair over Hazel's shoulder. It was a plea, a 'what can we do?'

Chapter 42

The radiographer guided the ultrasound probe over Maisie's stomach, intent on the screen. Maisie had her fist up to her mouth, trying not to cry. The screen was turned away from her so her only clues as to whether her baby was still growing inside her or had ebbed away were from the radiographer's face, but she was too professional to betray any sign of emotion.

The radiographer frowned and peered at the screen then glanced back at Maisie. No smile, no flicker of sympathy, just a look as if she wanted to check that Maisie was still there and hadn't vanished miraculously.

'I'm just going to call my senior colleague in to have a look,' she said. 'I won't be a moment. Do you want us to call anyone in?'

Maisie felt as if she was ebbing away herself. What did that mean? Call in a senior colleague? And who should she call in to be with her when they broke the news? Her parents? Patrick? Both?

'Shall I ask your partner to come in? Or your parents? They're all outside,' the radiographer said, this time with a small but encouraging smile.

'Partner? Did Patrick tell you that?'

'Mr McKinnon didn't use that word. I apologise if I'm speaking out of turn. I should never have assumed, but you and he did say he was the father.'

'He is. He is ... but ...' Maisie herself didn't know what Patrick was or would be so she certainly couldn't explain to the consultant. Maisie nodded. No matter what she thought of him, this was his baby too. Had been his baby? Still was his baby?

'Yes, he can come in.'

She smiled. 'Are you sure? It might be a good idea because I've some rather mixed news to share, so Mr McKinnon may want to hear it too.'

Mixed news? What the hell did that mean? Positive or bad, or both? Whatever it was, Patrick deserved to hear the news about their baby. She owed him that much. 'Yes. Ask him to join us. And it's not Mr McKinnon,' she murmured to herself as the consultant exited the room to find Patrick. 'It's Scorrier. Henry Patrick Aldous Scorrier McKinnon, a regular one-man bloody cricket team.'

The next few moments were the longest of her life. On her own in the tiny room, her stomach smeared in sticky gel, utterly alone.

Patrick walked in first, followed by the radiographer and her older colleague, also a woman. Patrick's face was the colour of froth on a pint.

'Have a seat, please, Mr McKinnon,' the consultant said.

'I'm Mrs Dixon,' said the older woman, and smiled at Maisie then joined her younger colleague by the screen.

Patrick took the stool next to Maisie's bed, never taking his eyes off her. He was too big for it; he looked like an adult on a child's stool. That was the bizarre thought that struck her while the two radiologists examined the scan again. He covered her hand with his fingers. She didn't move it away or make any attempt to hold his hand. She was lost in a no-man's-land, too afraid of any kind of movement even to hold his hand. She didn't know if she wanted to, but she didn't want to push him away. Not now. They exchanged looks. He mouthed something; she didn't know what, because the consultant was talking to her. She turned the screen towards Maisie and Patrick.

'OK,' said Mrs Dixon. Maisie's heart thumped wildly. Patrick's hand tightened around hers. 'It looks like there might be a positive outcome.'

'Thank God for that.'

Patrick gave her hand a squeeze as the consultant continued. 'However, I'm afraid that it does seem as if you may have lost one of the embryos. See that tear in the side of the womb? I'm very sorry about that, but the other embryo is still in situ. See it here.'

'*One* of the babies? What do you mean?' Patrick asked. Maisie was still in shock, trying to take in what the consultant was saying.

'You were having twins, Miss Samson. It's not uncommon with Poly-cystic Ovary Syndrome but the other embryo is still intact. You're still pregnant. Looks like you won the lottery twice.'

Maisie burst into tears.

She looked up at Patrick. He was crying too.

The younger radiologist smiled at Maisie.

'The chances are that you'll be fine but we can't make any guarantees, of course. We'll need to keep a close eye on you and you can carry on your life pretty much as normal but you'll have to be extra careful, of course ...'

The tears wouldn't stop. Maisie tried to take in what the radiologist was saying but all she could focus on was that while she'd lost one baby, she still had a life growing inside her. Patrick held her tightly, shh-ing and soothing her and she clung to him and didn't care who saw.

'I n-need to tell Mum and Dad. Can you fetch them?' she asked.

'I'll ask your parents to come in,' the younger radiologist said.

'Do you have any more questions?' the consultant asked.

'I – I d-don't know. Lots but I can't think straight.'

'That's understandable. Have some time to take it all in and I'll come and see you again in a little while when you're on the ward. We'd like to keep you in overnight to keep an eye on you.'

'Thank you.'

'Thanks.' Patrick still held her hand.

The consultant left and the younger medic followed to fetch Ray and Hazel.

'Should I leave?' he asked.

'No. Stay for a while. No matter what's gone on between us, we need to face them together.'

'OK.' Patrick kissed her head and whispered, 'Will I need more body armour?'

Before Maisie could reply, the door opened and her mother rushed forward, tears pouring down her cheeks. 'Oh, Maisie, I'm so sorry about the twin but I'm so relieved to hear about the other one.'

Patrick stood aside and her father joined in the embrace. His eyes were bright. 'We're just glad you're OK, love,' he said as her mother stroked her hair.

Once Maisie was settled in a room, Patrick came to see her again.

'You're still here,' she said when he walked in. His colour was back again.

'Of course I am. I'm not going to leave you like he did. Can you not get that into your head?' he said gently.

'I don't want you staying out of pity or because you think it's your duty.'

'It's not my duty, I love you. Will you not believe me? Just because that idiot you were with ran away at the prospect of fatherhood. Look, there's something else I should tell you. Tania didn't only leave me because I had no ambition; she also left me because I *wanted* kids. I wanted responsibility, a family, to settle down. She wasn't ready, not then or maybe ever, and I can't blame her for that, but the demon was out of the box after we'd told each other.'

'I didn't know that.' There was a lot she didn't know about him, she'd realised, and perhaps it was time to give him a chance and find out more.

'I've never told anyone the real reason we split, not even Judy,' he said. 'I'd been honest with Tania about wanting a family. She was brutally honest in saying no and she was absolutely right to. I was angry and hurt at first. I blamed her; I said some things she didn't deserve, but we've spoken while I've been here. We're friends. I told her to be happy and I mean it because I've found something I can believe in. I want my future to be here with you, if you'll have me.'

'Don't just stay because you want to be a father and you lost your own family ...'

He groaned. 'That isn't fair.'

'I'm sorry, but nothing's fair ... and the craziest thing about this is that I want you to stay. I want to be with you and bring the baby up together. I want it to have a father, but a father that I can trust and be happy with and I don't know if I can trust you again. I don't know if I can trust any man again or if I'll be better bringing up this baby myself. If he or she makes it.'

'He – or she – will.' He squeezed her fingers.

'You don't know that.'

'No, I don't, but if I could do anything to make sure our baby does, I'll do it. I'll stay here at your side night and day or I'll leave and never come back. Whatever it takes to make you and the little one feel safe and calm. Say the word.'

'I don't know, Patrick. I need time.'

'I'll sit here for now then. I won't say anything but I'll be here. Or I'll go out for a while? Give you time to yourself. You must be tired?'

'Yes. I am.'

'I'll be outside getting a drink. If you need me, ask one of the nurses to bring me in.'

Maisie sank back against the pillows. Tears trickled down her cheeks for the new and fragile life inside her, for past and recent betrayals and for a future that she couldn't imagine without her baby and without Patrick – or with him.

She must have dozed because when she woke, the consultant was by her bed, checking her chart. Mrs Dixon was frowning at the notes and looking back at Maisie. Maisie glanced at her, waking in a sweat of terror.

'Is the baby OK?'

'It's fine, Maisie. It will be an anxious time for you and I can't tell you not to worry, though for both your sakes, I obviously advise it.' She smiled. 'You could talk to some parents who've been through miscarriage. There's a group we can put you in touch with who've been through similar experiences. You and your partner might find meeting them a help, and meanwhile, we'll keep a very close watch on you, I promise you that.'

Chapter 43

The following afternoon, Maisie was released with a list of dos and don'ts, and collected by her parents. She couldn't help her heart soaring when she saw Patrick waiting for her on the jetty at Gull. He, Ray and Hazel walked with her to the pub and, after a cuppa, her parents made their excuses and left.

The room was filled with the scent of flowers. Bright narcissi and spring blooms filled half a dozen vases and a pile of unopened cards waited on the bar. She felt wrung out and knackered but the sight of the bright blossoms and her own home gave her energy. She still had a new life inside her, and Patrick was by her side.

He pulled out a chair for her and then sat down next to her.

'The flowers are beautiful.'

'They're from Jess and your other friends and neighbours. You're well loved,' said Patrick.

Maisie gave a rueful smile, thinking of Hugo. 'Not by everyone. Like Hugo.'

'Everyone who matters, and actually I went to see Hugo this morning.'

She gasped. 'And you're both still alive?'

'We both needed to talk about a few things.'

'That's an understatement!'

'Yeah, well. There's wrong on both sides. I didn't tell him who I really was so no wonder he was narked. Now I need to build some bridges. It's been tough for him with my uncle's illness and, in future, I have to deal with him in a business sense.

'Did you argue with Hugo on the hill? Did he have anything to do with you falling over?' he asked.

'Nothing,' said Maisie, which wasn't strictly true but probably wise to gloss over the full story. 'And the doctor said the fall had nothing at all to do with losing the twin,' she added, feeling tears well up again at her loss. 'It would have probably happened anyway.'

'Good, because if it had ...' He sighed. 'Maisie, I'm sure Hugo's always wanted you personally, as well as wanting Gull Island. From his point of view, I can see why he's upset about me turning up here and taking over. His father's deteriorated over the past few months and I feel for him, even though I think the bloke's a prize prat. I'm going to see my uncle when I've made sure you're OK. I need to face up to what I've ignored for the past thirty-odd years – and to the future.'

There was a pause as if neither of them knew how to begin before Patrick broke the ice. 'Your mum and dad let me stay in the Piggery last night when we finally got home.'

She sucked in a breath. 'Wow. Frankly, I'm amazed.'

'Me too. They're willing to give me a second chance, I think, but said it's up to you what happens next. I hoped you wouldn't be too pissed off that I waited for you to come home.'

'I'm not pissed off. I'm just tired and I want my baby to be OK.'

'I want that more than anything in the world too. Look, I know you must still hate me right now.'

Maisie thought back to her confrontation with Hugo. Maisie loved Patrick, but was love enough to overcome everything else?

'I don't hate you. But what's happened between us has punched a hole in the trust we had. I appreciate you're trying to put things right ... and I admit I said some harsh things to you that I didn't really mean.'

He took her hand, stroking the veins gently. 'They were things that had to be said for both our sakes, even if they were painful for us. Can we call today a fresh start, a blank page? We could try to move forward if we wind back from me walking into the Driftwood that first day ...'

Maisie was inclined to believe him. She wanted to believe him so much. 'Do it then,' she said.

'What? *Now*?'

'Yes. Right now. Walk out of that door and come back in and start again as you should have done.'

'Will it make a difference?'

She lifted her chin. 'I don't know. Why don't you try me?'

He picked up his rucksack, and walked out of the front door into the dull January afternoon, leaving the door open as it had been on that sunny day in October. Maisie took her place behind the bar and picked up the menus, wiping the covers with a cloth. She glanced at the sign on the wall: The Landlady is Always Right.

Was she? Had she made a huge mistake in leaving the front door open and handing Patrick a second chance? Or the best decision of her life?

She closed her eyes and in the empty silence, imagined the buzz of chatter and laughter and clinking glasses. She imagined the distant ferry hoot and the sound of customers talking on the terrace.

The silence lengthened.

Her pulse raced. Perhaps it wasn't possible to turn the clock back after all, or maybe Patrick had decided not to do it. Was her big mistake to let him walk out?

Footsteps rang out on the quarry tiles. She opened her eyes.

A tall, lean blond stood in the porch, hesitating over whether to come in or not. He pushed his tousled hair out of his eyes nervously and said in a broad Aussie accent, 'Are you open?'

'Just,' said Maisie, her heart pounding.

He shrugged the heavy bag from his shoulders. 'Good, because this bag weighs a ton.'

'What are you having?'

'A Coke. A pint of full-fat, please.' He left his pack by a table and approached the bar. Uncertainty flickered in his eyes, the colour of the sea on a summer's day. He looked like the same man who'd strolled in all those months before, and yet he was very different. Less cocksure, less of a charmer – and even though she knew the worst of him now, she liked him all the better for it.

Maisie picked up the soft-drink gun and squirted Coke into a pint glass. 'You're not from round here, by the sounds of it,' she said.

'No. I'm not.'

She pushed the glass at him. It was barely half full but she couldn't play this game any more.

'Who are you?' she asked.

They exchanged looks over the untouched Coke. 'My name is Henry Patrick Scorrier McKinnon and I'm an alcoholic and a liar and the father of your child,' he said. 'I also happen to own Scorrier Holdings, the scumbags who wanted to take over your home and livelihood. I don't want to do that to you or anyone that lives here, but I can't run away from the inheritance or responsibility I've been given. I can't be someone else even though I've tried, so I've come up with a compromise that I hope you and your family and friends will accept. It may not be perfect but I think it could work, if we all come together. And I also love you more than I've ever loved anyone in my life.' He smiled. 'Can I have my drink now? I'm dry as a drover's dog.'

Shaking like a leaf, Maisie nodded. Patrick sipped his drink.

'And if you don't mind me asking, who you would be?' he asked, putting the Coke on the counter.

'I'm Maisie. That's my name over the door. I don't take crap from anyone and I don't like liars but I'm willing to give you a try. Because despite the fact I scare the living daylights out of half the men on these islands, inside I'm just human – like you. I make mistakes and I often feel like crying when people expect me to smile and laugh. I'm having a baby and I'd do anything to protect it but I want it to have a father too, a father who I love and who loves me. I'll have a drink with you now, if you want to stay a while.'

Patrick's mouth tilted at the corners and he leaned across the bar. His mouth was warm and sweet as he kissed her and when his lips left hers, he whispered. 'I do.'

Epilogue

Six weeks later

Patrick slipped his arm around Maisie's back as they walked out of the hospital and into the spring sunshine. It was a mild February day, and the palm trees along the seafront were rustling softly in the brisk breeze. Maisie patted her bump, hidden under her jumper but still visible as they walked down the road into the centre of Hugh Town. Patrick tightened his arm around her.

It was Patrick's thirty-eighth birthday and after her latest antenatal scan, the two of them were heading for lunch with Jess and Will at the restaurant overlooking Porthcressa beach. Across the deep water channel, the island of St Saviour's floated in the distance, its green fields bursting into life in the spring sunshine.

'Feeling better now we know the little sprog's doing well?' he asked.

Maisie smiled at his nickname for the baby. 'Yes, but I don't think I'll really relax until he or she's here safely.' She was sixteen weeks now. Less than five months to go. She wouldn't say she'd learned to *relax* but she no longer spent every moment terrified of something terrible happening.

'We'll soon be halfway there,' said Patrick.

Maisie laughed. '"*We*"? Remind me again who exactly is having this baby?'

'Sometimes I think I am,' said Patrick wryly. He was right. It had been a tense time for both of them but as the days lengthened and the weather improved, Maisie felt she was emerging into the sunshine too.

They strolled hand in hand along the seafront, nodding at familiar faces. Maisie was so relieved and happy that everything was finally out in the open. Patrick had rented the little cottage at the campsite for the foreseeable future, and Maisie had recently moved in with him. It was better for everyone to have some space, including Ray and Hazel. After some pretty frank discussions, they were starting to trust each other again.

Patrick had every right to live in one of Petroc's luxurious holiday homes, of course, but that was too close to comfort for either Maisie, Patrick or Hugo. He'd met with Hugo and their respective lawyers several times and assured his cousin that he could continue to run Petroc the way he wanted, which Hugo was slowly beginning to accept. He'd been to visit his uncle Graydon too and now understood, he said, some of the pressure that Hugo had been under even if that didn't excuse his harassment of Maisie and the Gull islanders. Patrick intended to offer to sell Scorrier House to Hugo at some point but that was for the future. Maisie's focus was on her baby and slowly finding her way forward with Patrick on Gull.

The first wave of investment in the Gull Island Trust – instantly known as GIT by everyone, of course – was underway and with the extra money and contractors from the mainland, Hell Cove was already ready for the new season. Work on the Fudge Pantry had also begun.

'I hope you've remembered my birthday present,' said Patrick.

'We're past that sort of thing, aren't we?' said Maisie, thinking of the card and bottle of non-alcoholic fizz waiting back at the campsite cottage, along with a painting of Patrick serving behind the bar at the Driftwood, which she'd commissioned from Archie. They really knew how to party these days, she thought with a smile, but hoped he'd love the picture.

'Besides, what could I possibly get for the man who has everything?' she added.

'You're never going to let me forget what I did, are you?'

'Nope. I'll keep reminding you until the day you die.'

He caught her in his arms. 'So you're planning on letting me stay for a while longer, then?'

Maisie was about to reply when she felt a fluttering sensation in her stomach. Patrick started to speak but she put her fingers on his lips.

He stared at her as she stood stock still, her hand on her bump. Could it have been? Had she imagined it? Was it too early? She hadn't had time to feel it the first time, but now ...

'Oh!' It was there again. A brief and gentle flutter like a butterfly stirring deep inside her.

Patrick's brow furrowed. 'What it is? Are you OK?'

She felt like crying. 'Yes ... I think I just felt the baby moving.'

'Really?' he said in wonder, laying his hand on her bump. Maisie stood a few moments longer knowing it was too soon for Patrick to feel those stirrings of life yet.

'You'll feel it too in a few weeks,' she said gently, taking his hand away and smiling at him.

'Clever little sprog must know it's my birthday,' he said, speaking to her bump. 'And by the way, I love you both.'

Maisie felt the gentle warmth of the spring sun on her face as she looked up at him. 'You too, Crocodile Dundee. You too.'

THE END

Acknowledgements

I can't tell you how wonderful it's been to work with the fabulous Avon team on this new series of Little Cornish Isles books. My editor, Rachel Faulkner-Willcocks, has done a fabulous job of editing *The Driftwood Inn* and seeing it through to publication – thank you, Rachel F-W. Along with Rachel, there are so many other people at Avon and HarperCollins who help to bring my stories to readers and I'd like to thank them too, including publishing director Helen Huthwaite, and ace publicist Sabah Khan. I am one of those authors who can't wait for their copy-editor to work their magic on a manuscript so thank you to Jo Gledhill once again for waving her wand over my work.

My agent, Broo, has made my publishing journey exciting and fun – and successful – over the past eleven years. She's always on hand with a soothing word or a glass of very nice wine and I hope we work together on many more books and share many more glasses.

Of all the people who have helped me with research on the Little Cornish Isles series, I'd like to mention Hilary Ely, whose photographs and posts about Scilly inspired my first visit in 2014. She's been holidaying on the isles for fifty years, I've just been for the third time and can't wait to be back. Special thanks also goes to my friend Nell Dixon – author, midwife, and a wonderful mum to three amazing daughters – for sharing her experience of multiple miscarriage. I'm so glad you now have your family, dear Nell.

This book has required research from around the globe. So thank you to:

In Melbourne – Judy Worrall, Joy Herring and Cassandra O'Leary.

On Scilly – Churchtown Farm and Scilly Flowers, St Martin's – https://www.scillyflowers.co.uk/ – and Seaways Farm and Juliet's Garden, St Mary's http://www.julietsgardenrestaurant.co.uk/

On the 'mainland' – Jadie at the Tame Otter, Hopwas, Stephen Mooney, Amy Owen and the bar team at the Spread Eagle, Cannock and Marie Deakin of Mim's Café, Bridgtown. What other job requires hanging around pubs at eleven o'clock on a Monday morning for 'research'?

Thanks too to my author friends Elizabeth Hanbury, Jules Wake, Claudia Carroll, Bella Osborne and Cressida McLaughlin, and to bookseller Janice Hume, plus all the fantastic book bloggers who have supported the Cornish Cafe series and my other books so enthusiastically.

To my wonderful family, I love you, especially Mum and Dad who listen to my endless highs and lows of publishing. Thank you for your support, the lifts to the station for my London trips and also for the bacon sandwiches on writing days.

To my father-in-law, Charles, thanks for answering my

Return to the little Cornish Isles . . .

Coming 2018